INFINITE PIECES VOLUME 3

A Good Day To Die and Other Thriller Stories

Infinite Pieces
Book 3

STERLING & STONE

STERLING & STONE

Layover

WADE PETERSON

Layover

WADE PETERSON

PEOPLE!

Saul Freedman hated them. His stomach rumbled in solidarity with the thundering jets passing over the terminal. He glanced at his phone out of reflex, confirming that the line had not moved in the five minutes since he last checked. Saul was only two body-widths from the coffee kiosk's counter, but the jackass ahead of him was refusing to budge.

"I specifically ordered turmeric, and this doesn't have it," Jackass said. "You don't smell turmeric, do you?" He pushed the cup forward and absently hitched his pants up by a belt loop. A wild-haired kid three spots back made another attempt at wheedling his mom into going to the baked pretzel place across the way instead. It was accompanied by a loud "pleeeeeeeeeeeeeeeeeeeeeeease."

A purple-haired girl in cat eyeglasses behind the counter sniffed at the cup and raised her eyebrows. "I smell spice?"

Jackass leaned in. "Whatever it is, it's not turmeric. You're not confusing it with pumpkin spice, are you?"

"I'll add more," said the barista.

Jackass doffed his glasses and rubbed at his forehead. "No, I want you to make it over. It'll taste like ass if you mix pumpkin spice and turmeric."

The girl turned and reached for a container. "I can make it again, but this is our turmeric." She held out the canister and turned the label towards him.

"Can I smell it?" he asked.

She recoiled. "It's not hygienic..."

But Jackass grabbed her wrist. For a moment, Saul thought she was going to punch the guy out, but her snarl faded as Jackass brought the canister under his nose. He took a mighty sniff. "Whatever is in there isn't turmeric."

"Jesus," Saul muttered. He knew Jackass heard him, saw his shoulders bunch beneath the high-end mountain climbing jacket that Saul had once fancied buying himself. But the man didn't turn around. The whining kid changed tactics.

"I need to go peeeeeeeeeeeeeeeeee."

The barista's lips pressed together, and she shrugged. "This is all we have. I can try adding more to your smoothie?"

Jackass dropped the cup. It splattered on the counter, and he walked off. "Forget it. And I better not be charged."

Saul stepped up. The barista grabbed a towel and mopped at the counter. He squinted at her name tag, but its ink was all smudged and dotted with red syrup, as was the upside-down cartoon character pin on her apron. "Sorry about that," she said. "I'll be right with you."

Saul sighed. "I got a plane to catch, and this will only take a second."

"So will this," she said, scrubbing up the spill.

He waited, watching her wipe up every last drop of turmeric coffee.

Then, finally, she let out a breath, tossed her rag to the side, and put on a wide smile.

"How may I help you?" Her eyes blinked rapidly behind her glasses, and Saul wondered if she were cursing him out in some kind of blinking Morse code.

"I want a pesto chicken on whole wheat bread — not the ciabatta — and double shot soy latte, no whip, under hot, with two pumps of sugar-free almond syrup, and I'm not kidding about no sugar. I'm diabetic."

"Dude," said someone behind him. Saul didn't bother turning around. With luck, he'd never see these people again. From the corner of his eye, he spotted the weary woman who had been behind him in line. She led her wild-haired son by the hand towards the bathrooms. He really hoped they weren't on his flight; the kid looked like a seat kicker.

SAUL MADE his way down the concourse, slaloming past tourists stopping to stare at departures screens, cutting through the economy travelers hoping their boarding group would be called next, and getting the stink-eye from a driver for not moving aside fast enough for his electric barge's geriatric passengers. He arrived at his own fortress of solitude: a pair of rent-by-the-hour work pods. One was already occupied with its privacy glass darkened and noise canceling engaged.

Rumor had it the cancelation was so good that a couple could have the loudest screaming sex ever, and those passing by would never know. Saul shook his head at the idea. Maybe the noise canceling was good, but only if the couple were serious contortionists. There was barely enough room for him in the pod with its tiny desk, his coffee, and his bag.

Saul punched through the options on the touchscreen mounted outside the pod's door, sloshing coffee over his hand as he paid for an hour's time. He cursed, set down his bag, and wiped his hand on a pant leg, then stepped inside and closed the door behind him.

Pressure built on his eardrums when the door sealed and the fresh air pump kicked on. Then, the active noise canceling engaged, centering Saul in an audio dead zone. The silence unnerved him; he fiddled with a knob built into the desk, cycling through various white noise, nature sounds, and instrumental options. He finally settled on a track called "Serenity."

Saul took a cleansing breath, then pulled his laptop from his bag and plugged it into the pod's private gigabit feed.

He clicked through a series of terms and conditions for pod use, wolfing down the sandwich. Then, once he had agreed, he engaged his own security measures and VPN. He saw himself reflected in the privacy glass divider between his pod and the one next door. He wondered what the chances were the person in the other pod was staring back at their own reflection.

How startling would it be if the privacy glass suddenly cleared, and for a split second, they each thought they were the other guy? He laughed, catching sight of his pesto-flecked teeth.

His computer finally connected, and he checked the time in Istanbul. The banks would be closing now, and while their systems never truly went to sleep, some things were better accomplished when the junior varsity cyberse-curity team was in charge. Or, for some of his accounts, was absent altogether.

Not that he was worried about their varsity squad, either. He couldn't imagine a life where one sat around collecting a paycheck, letting their skills go to waste while they waited for something bad to happen. Saul had honed his craft for years. He could route wire transfers in and out of accounts, leaving nothing behind but a faint vanilla aftertaste in the bank's logs.

The people who got caught doing what he did were the ones who didn't understand the game. Trying to leave no trace was like trying to spray Febreze on dog shit. It just didn't work. Sure, it may not stink so much, but it was still shit, easy to recognize and sticking to anything it touched.

Saul processed his dog shit through a series of shell companies in several time zones in countries with lax oversight until it came out the other end like vanilla ice cream. Shitty vanilla ice cream, to be sure, but Interpol didn't bother itself worrying about that when there was dog shit emanating from other numbered bank accounts around the world.

And for this service, Saul collected a pittance, a flea's bite off the dog, but what a dog! He would never be a rich man — that was for the bosses above him, those who had the connections and muscle to keep what they took. And Saul didn't begrudge them of it, mostly. He was a lone wolf, responsible for only himself, and being the boss was the opposite of that.

The way to get caught was wanting more than vanilla ice cream. People in his position often got greedy, thinking they could skim a little more here and there, do a few side projects for higher commissions, or just take the entire bankroll and disappear. But they almost always got caught. Even if there was a decent shot he could get away with it, Saul didn't see what more money would get him other than unwanted attention and a life on the run. He was happy with what he had, flying under everyone's radar.

Even if it meant flying from LA to Boston every other week and working remotely. Even if it meant showing respect and obedience by walking into the mobster's lair and putting his head in the lion's mouth to see if he would live another month. None of this passive-aggressive bullshit his corporate foes put up with. You do your job, you live. You fuck up, it'll be a bullet to the back of your head, professional-like. Unless he did something they took personally. Then he would be in a world of shit no amount of vanilla could cure. That kept him up some nights, not knowing when or how the end would come...

The sweet latte hit his system, and Saul's brain began his daily workflows, starting with the account in Istanbul, whittling away five million dirty euros into tiny chunks, little line items of widgets and bobbins ordered by one shell company and fulfilled by another, financed by a third under byzantine repayment terms and scheduling that would result in contaminated money getting that sweet vanilla scent of legitimacy through purchase invoices, interest payments, and 30-day penalties. All queued up and ready to process.

Then Saul hesitated. His neck itched, and the plush seating felt uncomfortably warm. He had the sense of being watched, so he glanced out through the pod's one-way privacy glass, seeing nothing but a mostly empty terminal with a few people hunched and slumped in rows of uncomfortable chairs and a pair of flight attendants power-walking to their next gate.

The line at the coffee kiosk was gone, and the purple-haired barista leaned against the counter, splitting her attention between the passing flight attendants and her phone.

Saul shook his head and returned to the Istanbul work-flow. Then, the laptop screen flickered. It went black for a moment.

That was odd.

Saul had made sure it was fully charged.

And then it turned back on, displaying a low-res interface straight out of the 90s.

Hello Saul.

Saul blinked. What the hell was going on? He reached for the power button to reboot.

Do not disconnect your computer. If you do so, outstanding warrants in your name will be sent to the US TREASURY SERVICE, INTERPOL, & a business interest in Cyprus.

Warrants?

To prevent this and release yourself from confinement, play the game. Shall we begin?

Hell, no.

A picture of Saul getting into the work pod, coffee in mid-slosh, face fully exposed, appeared on screen. Then another window showing the warrants and that lame mugshot from when he was 18 and stupid, looking half-stoned and sheepish, back before he knew the difference between dogshit and ice cream.

Saul's hand flew to the door latch. But it didn't budge, not even when he leveraged his weight against it. He stood as best he could and lowered his shoulder. But the inner door's spongy plastic surface absorbed the blow. He tried to get any momentum or leverage in the pod's confines but managed only to strain his legs and batter his shoulder.

He wasn't scared of the authorities. The worst they could do is throw him in prison. But he had a sinking feeling he knew who the business interest was in Cyprus and how personally they might take it if they believed the authorities were onto him.

You ARE COMPETING **against another player.**
   The first to finish wins.
   The other will be executed.

EXECUTED?

THE GAME IS SIMPLE. **Who is guilty?**

A 10-MINUTE TIMER appeared on his screen and began counting down.

COMPLETE **the tests before (1) the timer runs out or (2) your opponent completes their test.**

. . .

AT THE TOP of the screen, next to a flashing red ISOLATION MODE banner, a cartoon picture of himself appeared, labeled Player One. A second was labeled Player Two.

Saul tried the door again, but it was still locked. A man walked by, a suitcase rolling behind him. Saul pounded on the door, trying to get his attention, but the door's inner surface muffled the sound.

Saul screamed, and his ears felt pressure as the noise-canceling kicked in. And outside, the man walked on, oblivious.

Saul fell back onto the pod's padded chair and fished out his phone. Angry red exclamation points, barred circles, and a *No Service* filled the upper corner. He tried placing a call anyway, but his phone just pulsed twice in error before displaying the unhelpful suggestion of moving to a different location and reconnecting to the network or wifi.

Who would he call anyway? The police? He studied his old mugshot and the picture of him getting into the pod, wondering if this was some elaborate hoax or con job.

Could he afford to wait out the timer and see what happened? They knew who he was, yes, and seemed to have control over the pod, his computer, and at least one camera in the area. That pointed to hackers and blackmail. Saul relaxed. He knew how these cabals operated.

The execution angle had to be a bluff; hackers couldn't get money out of a dead mark.

"Amateurs," he muttered. The question was: would he play along? Depending on whose money they wanted to steal, it could go badly for all involved. Saul could get whacked just for being seen as a weak link. If he did nothing and got arrested, his chances of getting killed decreased, but they weren't zero. Especially where the client from Cyprus was concerned.

These damned amateurs were going to get him killed.

He would play their game for now.

STEP 1 OF 4: Identify all criminal actions in the following gallery.

THE FIRST PICTURE was of a man about to shoot another in the back of the head; the next picture showed a bag of white powder exchanging hands. Each frame held an unchecked box in its corner. Saul assumed he was supposed to take the implications at face value, but in his head, he wanted to argue about the lack of context. Maybe the man with the gun was an actor in a movie; maybe the powder in the baggie was just baking soda. There wasn't anything objectively criminal in the pictures. This wasn't like identifying stoplights, bicycles, or crosswalks from random street pictures. He clicked their checkboxes anyway.

The following series of photos were more obvious. Dead bodies packed in a shipping container. Passports and ID cards exchanged for wads of bills. He picked those, too.

The next pictures threw him. Two people holding hands and crossing the street, a man mowing the lawn, and a woman drinking coffee. How serious was this supposed to be? There wasn't anything obviously criminal unless you counted jaywalking or noise ordinances, but again, there was no context. The coffee drinker surely was okay unless he was supposed to believe there was something in the coffee, or it was one of those lefty political things, and the beans weren't fair-trade. In the end, he left those ones unchecked.

The last two frames made him lean back from the screen. Both showed Saul at the airport. One of him talking to the barista after Jackass left, and another taken as he was checking over his Istanbul workflow.

He didn't want to click either. His legs trembled with the urge to run, his knees knocking against the desk's underside. The unease grew the longer he stared at the images as the timer counted down.

He sensed another trap closing around him.

Saul pushed the laptop away and put his hands in the air. "Nope. No. Not playing."

The pod's air pressure increased, and "serenity" was replaced by a modulated computerized voice. "If you quit Player One, Player Two will win by default."

Saul looked around and found the partially concealed speaker grille. "You can hear me? Let me out!"

"I cannot let you out unless you win the game. You're already behind your opponent."

"I don't care, I'll..."

He had been about to say, "I'll take my chances with the cops," but considered that would sound like an admission of guilt, and he wasn't going to hand these amateurs any ammunition to use against him. "You know what? Forget it. This little extortion game has been cute, but it's all pixels and manipulated images." He shook his head. "You don't have the leverage you think you do. I'm not playing."

A whirr like a mechanical cicada came from the speaker, increasing in volume higher and higher, sending needles through Saul's ear drums. He clapped his hands over his ears, which blunted the pain somewhat, but that high-pitched keening made thought impossible.

Right when he thought his ears couldn't take it anymore, the noise ceased. Saul took several shallow breaths, the phantom echoes ringing in his ears.

"A little demonstration of your pod's capabilities, Player One," the voice said. "The game controls your environment. It controls the sound in your ears, the light in your eyes, the temperature for your body, even the air filling your lungs."

"What the fuck is this?"

"And let me be especially clear: this game isn't concerned with money."

They didn't want money? Then what did they want? "I don't understand. Who are you?"

"My identity is not important. I simply facilitate the game. Now, do I need to convince you how important it is for you to continue? If so, choose any one of the passengers outside the pod."

"Why?"

"The game will mark them as a player, and they will be killed. Perhaps then you'll see the importance of cooperating."

Saul blanched. He knew it was a bluff, but he couldn't risk it. "Fine, I'll play." He didn't attempt to argue about nuance and just assumed the pictures of him doing his job and being short with the barista were wrong.

"Good," the voice said. "From your responses, it's clear you know right from wrong."

"I know what's expected," Saul said. "That's not the same thing."

"The game continues."

The pictures on Saul's screen cleared and then were replaced with a new set.

• • •

STEP 2 OF 4: Identify all persons harmed or about to be harmed by your criminal actions.

IN THE GALLERY were pictures of a man checking his pockets, an airport cop, and an elderly person in a wheelchair. Other than that, there was no context. He left them unchecked, but the continue button remained grayed out. After a few seconds, Saul selected them all and was allowed to continue.

The next gallery confused him. It was the same scene with different angles: the barista, the wild-haired kid who Saul reckoned to be no older than ten, and the kid's mother, who was struggling with a tote bag and the child's backpack. Again, the game wouldn't let him continue until he selected all three images. He wondered what picking random strangers meant in this game, even if he'd been forced to choose them against his will. Dread settled in his chest.

The next gallery made him angry. Saul's best client, sitting at an outdoor cafe in Cyprus with his bodyguard and Saul himself.

"Everyone?" he said.

"We're all connected, Player One."

Saul shook his head. "You can't pin this all on me. I'm not that important! Not compared to him." He waved his hand at his client's photo.

"Exactly. You aren't important, Player One. You are merely a participant."

"I never shot anyone. I never stole from anyone. I just move money around."

"You're the grease that makes the engine possible," the voice said. "Without you, it would seize and destroy no more."

Saul rummaged through his bag, searching for something useful he could use to pry the door open. "Yeah, right. I'm responsible for all the evil in the world."

"You're one of thousands. You just happen to be playing the game today."

"What about you?" Saul asked. "Are you playing the game?"

"We all play the game, Player One, even game masters."

So, he did have a title.

"But your time is ticking away, and Player Two has already started their last task. It would be unfortunate if you were to die complaining about not having any power when you have every chance to avoid that fate by playing."

Saul's search of his bag came up empty. He chucked it back on the floor. "Why pick me? Why not go after the people at the top?"

"It's the little gray men like you that enable those at the top to build so large, Player One. If there are no gray men, then those who spread evil across the world would be nothing more than village idiots."

"They'll just find someone else to replace me."

"Will they? They would like you to believe so. Perhaps there are a limited number of cogs like you."

"Getting rid of me creates a supply shortage?"

A modulated laugh. "Now you're getting it."

"You're delusional."

"Win the game, and you'll never hear from me again."

A squeak against the glass made him yelp. He swiveled around. The wild-haired kid pressed his nostrils flat against the glass. Saul yelled and pounded on the door.

"Hey! Get outta here!"

The kid blinked and laughed. Probably couldn't hear a damn thing. Or see more than a shadow moving behind the privacy glass. Then the kid's mom came running. She grabbed his wrist and gave him a tug, nearly yanking him off his feet. Her knuckles were white from the power of her grip, and her son contorted his face in pain. She whispered something in his ear, then dragged him away.

"That was reckless, Player One," the voice said. "Those interacting with a player become a player themselves. By your actions, the child and his mother are now part of the game. One wonders why you would bring danger to them like this."

"How can I control what goes on out there? I mean, how could I? These are your rules, not mine."

The voice didn't respond. Saul watched the kid and his mom disappear from view. Outside his pod, those who had been watching turned back to their own little worlds.

Saul turned back as well.

He glanced at the glass where the kid's snot-streak remained. The countdown timer ticked past the five-minute mark and turned red. Saul wiped the sweat from his forehead and clicked on the remaining images. The game continued…

STEP 3 OF 4: Identify all persons guilty of criminal acts.

THE FIRST PICTURE in the gallery was his best client, shown on his boat in Cyprus. Saul hesitated but clicked the box. It was no secret the self-proclaimed "legitimate businessman" had evaded investigation and arrest by several agencies over the years.

The next pictures were of young men at a computer, faces partially obscured by hoodies, but Saul knew them. A hacker he occasionally worked with and an enforcer who once threatened to slice off Saul's eyelids. Saul left that one unchecked.

A cop in the airport. Unchecked.

The barista staring daggers at Saul as he left. Unchecked.

The wild-haired kid's mom. He hesitated. She was a player now, according to the game master. Unchecked.

A shadowed cartoon figure with a question mark over their face labeled game master. Checked.

A shadowed figure labeled PLAYER 2.

"Can I assume this other player is like me?" he asked.

"If you're asking if I pick civilians for players — why do you care?"

Saul paused for a moment. "It matters."

"You think you have a conscience, Player One? How interesting. You and Player 2 share employers. They broker legal services in the same way you provide financial services. But more importantly, why didn't you pick the mother, Player One?" the game master asked. "You're clearly able to accuse the others without hesitating. She injured that child, and here you are worrying about another player you've never met."

Saul paused, considering. "She's doing her best. Is the kid hurt? Yeah, but he'll get over it."

"Tick, tick, Player One."

The speaker went dead. The timer kept counting down, and for all Saul knew, the game master could be lying about Player 2, assuming they even existed. He checked their box anyway. Then he went back and hovered over the mother's checkbox. Was he making a mistake? What did it even mean to make a mistake at this point in the game?

"If you're trying to make a point, I get it," Saul said.

"But you're no better. Putting yourself in the lineup for selection means you know so, too. Does including yourself ease your guilty conscience?"

The speaker didn't respond. Saul confirmed his choices. Sweat tickled his scalp despite the cool air blowing on him from above.

STEP 4 OF 4: Please indicate you are not a robot.

MUSCLE MEMORY HAD him clicking the "I am not a robot" checkbox, but his cursor hovered over the CONFIRM button.

Then he clicked, "I am not a robot."

Thank God. He'd done it. The game was over.

But then more text popped up on screen.

CONGRATULATIONS. YOU HAVE COMPLETED THE TEST and unlocked the assassin. Would you like to kill player 2 now? Y/N

SAUL PUSHED THE COMPUTER AWAY. "Fuck. No. I don't want to kill anyone."

"Even if it means you're killed instead?" the voice said. "By your own logic, you wouldn't be killing anyone. An assassin will be the actual instrument of death. You'll just be the middleman. A minor cog. The CAPTCHA speed bump of irritation that's forgotten moments after it passes us along."

Saul sat back and pressed fists to his eyes. "Whatever this game is, I don't care. I'm not playing it anymore. Blind me, deafen me, suffocate me; I'm not player one anymore; I'm just Saul."

PLAYER TWO HAS COMPLETED their test and unlocked the assassin.

"GOODBYE, SAUL," the game master said.

"Hey!" Had they really gone?

He waited ten seconds, then wrapped both hands around the pod's handle and heaved, but the door didn't budge. People passed by, not glancing from their phones. He tried throwing himself at the glass, the walls, and the partition but couldn't get any leverage in the pod's confines.

A figure approached, and his stomach sank. Purple hair, cat eye glasses, and red-stained smock. He noted that the odd pin next to her name tag was a cartoon caricature of the barista done in the same style as Player One had been in the game.

"Fuck me," he whispered. Was she the assassin?

The barista smirked as if she could see through the one-way glass and knew exactly why he was trapped. She tossed a hexagon-shaped key in the air, catching it between thumb and forefinger.

She tapped the key on his door.

"I'm sorry," he said. His voice sounded weak even to his own ears.

The barista tapped the key on the glass. "You'll have to wait. I have another customer."

Then she turned and stepped to the next pod, inserting the key and giving it a turn. A mechanical noise whirred from within, and the glass window between the two pods cleared. The Jackass. He was the other Player.

A hazy mist filled his space. The Jackass pounded on the door with one palm, his other hand clutching at his throat. He turned and threw himself against the partition. His eyes bulged red, and his shouts were distant, muted things that barely reached Saul's ears.

Jackass reached out and pressed a mottled red and purple hand to the partition, and Saul found his own hand pressed the glass in return. The man's bloodshot eyes met Saul's.

Moments later, the fans pitched down and stopped. The haze cleared in the other pod. Then, the partition's glass darkened. Saul couldn't see Jackass anymore but still felt his sightless eyes on him.

New text flashed on his computer.

CONGRATULATIONS, you are human. A representative will be along shortly to release you from your pod.

"WHAT?" Saul asked. "Why?"

"Each test measured your capacity to tell right from wrong," the voice said. "You accepted that your actions affected others. Player Two did not and chose to assassinate you. And so the game ended for him. There is still humanity within you, Saul. Be sure to use it."

The door clicked, and Saul flinched. The pressure on his ears eased, and the door's seals broke with a faint hiss.

Saul reached out with a shaking hand and opened the door. The yeasty smell of baked pretzels hit him, and he stuck his head out, not trusting that the barista wasn't waiting to brain him.

But nothing happened. He stepped out and thought he saw a flash of purple hair disappearing through a side door by a set of water fountains. He glanced at the other pod. A scrolling "Out of Order. Service Requested" scrolled across the pod's payment screen. The game interface on his laptop faded to black, and then his laptop chimed as it rebooted.

A thought struck him.

He grabbed his computer and bag and strode away from the pod. Walking over to the wall, he pressed his back to it.

He was out.

He was free.

Or was he?

The game master had said Player Two's game ended but didn't say the same for Saul. He glanced up at a security camera. Were they still watching him?

Saul studied the people around him. But no one seemed to be paying him the slightest bit of attention. His laptop felt heavy. As though the weight of all his crime gave it added heft. He opened his computer and looked at the screen.

The Istanbul transaction still awaited him.

Then, he spotted a child's backpack lying next to a planter. He recognized it, put his laptop away, walked over, and picked it up. He began looking for its wild-haired owner.

Translation Game

SEAN PLATT

Translation Game

SEAN PLATT

AMI ZIPPED UP HER LEATHER JACKET.

She had it specifically made to disguise the Kevlar she wore beneath. She grabbed her helmet, eager to get out of the apartment, given it reeked of week-old takeout and oil paint. In the distance, sirens wailed their constant urban lullaby. She was almost out the door when Lucy appeared in the kitchen doorway.

Her sister's hands signed faster than Ami could talk: *can't believe you're going.*

Ami set the helmet down with a sigh, and she signed back: *I've got this. I know the risks.*

Lucy narrowed her eyes. *You always say that, but one day, your luck will run out.*

Ami's jaw clenched as Lucy continued: *One wrong word and you're dead. We're dead!*

"For fuck's sake, Lucy!" Ami snapped. Her voice sounded harsh in the silence. *Five years and not one slip-up. Despite what you think, I'm not some amateur.*

I never said that.

I know.

Lucy's eyes softened, and she pointed at the fresh scar on Ami's forearm, still pink and puckered. *I can't lose you too.*

Ami tugged her sleeve down. *That wasn't — you know, I fell off my bike.*

A sharp knock cut through the tension.

Ami yanked the door open, revealing Goblin's hulking frame holding a thin box. The smell of pizza hit Ami immediately. The smell of pepperoni and melted cheese filled the apartment.

"Dinner's up," he rumbled, chipped tooth catching the light as he grinned.

"Not for me," Ami said, squeezing past him. "But make sure Lucy eats, yeah?"

She clattered down the stairs, boots echoing in the stairwell. Goblin's voice faded into the silence behind her. "Sure thing, boss."

Ami's Ducati sat at the curb under the sickly orange streetlights. She straddled the bike, yanked on her helmet, then gunned the engine. A second later, she shot into traffic, weaving between cars with inches to spare.

Horns blared in her wake. A police cruiser flashed its lights behind her. She ignored them both.

Before long, the Bay Bridge stretched before her. A glittering spine connecting Oakland to San Francisco. City lights shrank in her mirror, swallowed by the encroaching darkness.

Eventually, the Port of Oakland hulked ahead. Labyrinths of steel containers and skeletal cranes silhouetted against the night sky. Ami slowed at the gate, flipping her visor.

The guard nodded with recognition, and the barrier rose with a rusty groan.

Ami rode through the maze down to the appointed warehouse, which seemed identical to a dozen others. She parked, turning the bike to face the exit. Then she pulled off her helmet and left it with her bike.

Inside the warehouse, three chairs waited in a pool of sickly fluorescent light. Rusted chains hung from the ceiling, swaying gently in the draft. Water dripped somewhere in the darkness, its rhythm steady, like a ticking clock.

Gregor loomed by the door, biceps straining against his tight black T-shirt. The stench of stale cigarettes and cheap cologne beat on her nostrils. Ami stopped and raised her hands. A second later, his meaty hands roamed her body, lingering a beat too long on her hips.

"Enjoying yourself?" Ami asked with obvious disdain. "'Cause I think you missed a spot."

His mouth curled into a sneer.

"That's quite enough, Gregor," said a smooth voice behind them.

Ilya materialized from the shadows in a crisp Armani suit. "Ms. Tan. Punctual as always."

Ami shrugged away from Gregor, then walked over and snagged a Coke from the nearby cooler, condensation slick on her palm. She plopped into one of the empty chairs while fishing out her phone. She pulled up Instagram and scrolled. Catching sight of one of Lucy's paintings. It was a self-portrait. Raw and vulnerable.

Heavy footsteps approached.

Ami locked the screen and looked up. A moment later, Ivan Volkov entered, flanked by his bodyguard, Mark. The latter scanned the room, his hand never straying far from the bulge in his jacket.

"Solnyshko," Ivan rumbled, walking over and squeezing her shoulder with a meaty hand. "Ready to work your magic?"

"Always, Ivan." A curt nod to maintain her professional distance. "Though I prefer *skills* to *magic*."

Ivan bared his teeth and laughed.

Within minutes, the Harmony Peace Association arrived with Jing Chen at the head of the pack, his face an impassive mask. If Ivan exuded barely contained violence, Jing radiated cold calculation, his eyes sliding over Ami like she was part of the furniture.

Soon, each man's men lined the walls, a living barrier of muscle and concealed weapons. Just far enough away from the conversation to maintain the illusion of privacy.

Ivan leaned back and lit his cigar. Then, in Russian: "Tell our friends we're ready to begin."

Ami turned to Jing, her posture subtly shifting. Work time. And in Mandarin: "Ivan's ready. You?"

Jing nodded.

Ami grinned. "Then let's begin."

For the next two hours, Ami translated a smooth volley of words from Russian to Mandarin and back again, turning Ivan's crude threats into diplomatic overtures while softening Jing's icy rebuttals into warm exchanges.

By the end of the evening, the two had ironed out the mishap of the missing inventory. Come to an uneasy peace. Jing and his men left first.

Then Ivan. "See you tomorrow night."

Ami waved. Then exited, taking a new route home. It wasn't that she didn't trust Ivan or Jing. Simply that she was devoted to protecting Lucy.

The night flew past.

It was just another night in Oakland's underworld.

What could possibly go wrong?

❧

* * *

Ami's Ducati purred to a stop outside of Ivan's

sprawling estate. It was as close to a castle as one could get in San Francisco. Security cameras swiveled to track her approach.

She parked next to the town car that sat in the driveway. She dismounted and removed her helmet before making her way up the marble steps. The front door opened before she could knock, revealing the always stunning Sofia.

Her crimson gown probably cost more than Ami made in a year (and Ami made a hell of a paycheck). Silk clung to her curves like liquid fire. "I'm ready."

Ami nodded.

Ivan appeared behind her. "Have a good time at the ballet, my love."

Sophia almost tripped on the stairs. "I will."

He watched her walk to the car. Ami held out a hand. A moment later, he tossed her the keys. "Get my prize home in one piece."

Ami saluted him. "You know I will."

Sophia wobbled on her too-high heels, and she grabbed Ami's arm for support, fingers digging deep. A moment later, Ami had the back door open, and Sophia was seated inside. Ami got in the driver's seat, started up the car, then pulled away down the driveway.

And then they were away. Sofia's perfume, filling the car.

Neither of them spoke.

Twenty minutes later, Ami pulled into the theater's parking garage, tires squealing slightly on the concrete. Ami opened the back door and helped Sofia out. Escorting her past the box office and into the lobby.

"Enjoy the show," Ami said, forcing a smile.

Sofia didn't respond, taking a program from the usher.

Ami watched until she disappeared into the crowd

before retreating outside. She checked her watch. Still plenty of time.

And then she walked to the Tulip Hotel, keeping watch. Was that car following her? Did that pedestrian look a little too interested? No. No one was interested. And she was just cautious.

Ami nodded to the doorman at the boutique hotel, then crossed the gleaming marble lobby to the front desk, where the clerk's smile never faltered.

She held out a keycard. "All ready for you, Ms. Tan."

"Thanks," Ami said, taking it.

Then she made for the elevator. Mirrored walls fractured her reflection into a kaleidoscope that went on for eternity. Or at least until the fourth floor, where Ami stepped off.

She walked down to room 412, swiping the keycard. Then she stepped inside. Making a quick sweep — habit, mostly — before moving to the window. Before her, Oakland sprawled in a patchwork quilt of neon and shadow. Dreams and nightmares dancing cheek-to-cheek under a light-polluted sky.

Five minutes later, there was a gentle tap on the door. She walked over and peered through the peephole. Smiled, then opened the door to Sofia.

A moment later, she slipped inside, and Ami locked the door behind her.

They stood for a moment in silence, the air charged with unspoken tension.

Then Sofia surged forward, capturing Ami's lips in a desperate kiss.

* * *

Much later, Ami turned her head to study Sophia. Her makeup was smeared, and without it, she looked much younger than her twenty-six years. "You need to leave him."

Sophia blinked back tears. "I can't. He'll hunt me down and kill me. You know that."

And she did. Ami had no idea what happened to Ivan's previous girlfriend, Katarina, but it hadn't been good. He'd caught her cheating with one of his bodyguards. Ami leaned over and kissed Sophia's cheek. "I'm sorry."

Sophia snuggled closer.

And then Ami's phone buzzed. She groaned and extracted herself. Rolling out of bed and finding her jeans. Fishing the device from her pocket.

A text from Ilya.

Emergency meeting. Docks. Now.

"Shit," Ami said.

"What is it?" Sofia bolted up.

Ami glanced at her. "I have to go. Ivan called a meeting."

"What about me?"

Ami reached for her bra and t-shirt. "Go back to the theatre."

Sofia grabbed her arm. "What if he knows?"

"He doesn't know. It's just a meeting." Ami gently disentangled herself. "I swear."

Sofia nodded. "All right."

Ami ran all the way back to the parking garage. And minutes later, she was headed for the docks. Each red light was an eternity, each green a fleeting mercy. They'd ironed everything out the previous evening. And shouldn't be meeting for at least six weeks. What the fuck had gone wrong? She weaved through the late night traffic, the familiar scents of the bay — salt, fish, and diesel — growing stronger. And then she arrived.

Was waved through the entrance.

It was quiet this time of night.

Her engine, one of the only sounds. Aside from the lapping of water against barnacle-crusted pilings and the distant roar of traffic.

She made her way into the warehouse, expecting to be last to arrive.

But she wasn't.

She was first. She paced, waiting. A minute later, Ilya arrived. "I thought I was late," she said in Russian.

He shook his head, closing the door behind him. "Right on time."

Ami glanced around. "Where's Ivan?"

"He's not coming."

"And Jing?"

"Nor him."

Ami felt a chill. Fuck. Had Sophia been right? Ivan knew about them? But how? They had been so cautious.

Ilya smiled. "There is no meeting."

"So what am I doing here?" Ami asked.

Ilya gestured to the back of the warehouse. To where his office was located. Ami glanced at the exit door. Then followed him.

There was no one in the office.

Simply a bottle of champagne and a couple of glasses. Ilya entered, reaching for the bottle, and began unwrapping the foil around the cork.

Ami was confused. "What is this?"

Ilya tossed the foil on the ground. "You and me, Ami … we could be good together."

Ami blinked. "What?"

He grinned, popping the cork. Poured out the champagne. "Don't you feel it when we're together?"

Ami almost rolled her eyes. Almost. "Yeah, no, Ilya. I work for your father."

"*Work!*" His snorted. "That's all you do. Ivan takes advantage."

Ivan takes advantage?

What the fuck did he think this was?

Ilya looked her in the eyes. "You deserve to have fun. You've earned it."

Ami licked her lips. The taste of Sofia's kisses still lingered on her mouth. "As much as I appreciate the offer, Ilya. You're not my type."

Ilya's hands tightened on the bottle. "What do you mean? Not your type."

Ami glared at him. "None of your damn business."

Ilya set the bottle on his metal desk and lunged, grabbing her arm, squeezing his fingers into her skin. "Everything in this family is my business."

Ami reacted on instinct, driving her knee into Ilya's groin.

He bellowed and lost his hold on her, crumpling to the ground. And Ami bolted. But he scrambled after her, hand clamping around her ankle, yanking. The concrete floor rushed up to meet her face.

Ami landed hard.

Ilya crawled on top of her, grain her left hand, reaching for her right. Ami gouged him in the cheeks with the car keys. He wrenched back, howling. Then punched her in the face.

Her head cracked against the edge of the desk, and for a moment, the world went fuzzy. The taste of metal flooded her mouth as color exploded behind her eyelids.

She blinked the stars away, aware of Ilya looming over her.

His hand went to his waistband. "You stupid bitch. You could have made this easy."

Ami's leg shot out, her boot finding Ilya's knee with

deadly precision. A hard CRUNCH echoed off the containers, followed by his agonized howl as he staggered back, his leg buckling unnaturally.

Then she scrambled up, realizing she had dropped the keys. Most likely when he punched her. But she wasn't going to stay and search.

She turned and ran.

She'd just about made it to the warehouse door when a gunshot cracked like thunder.

White-hot agony blossomed on her left arm, robbing Ami of breath. But she didn't let it stop her. She tore through the door. Running through the maze of shipping containers.

Where the hell was security? There had to be someone. *Unless Ilya had sent them away?*

Fuck.

She had no friends here.

The dock's edge beckoned, a black maw of churning water.

Another bullet pinged off the closest shipping container. Decision made. Ami ran for the water. And dove without hesitation.

The water was shockingly cold, driving the air from her lungs. It was like being stabbed by a thousand icy needles, every nerve ending screaming in protest. Her arm burned. She sank, wiggling out of her leather jacket, which was now like a second skin. And then she dropped the kevlar. Slowly surfacing, oily water streaming down her face.

More gunshots, muffled by the water.

Ami kicked out. She needed to get away and find help.

A muzzle flash erupted from the dock.

Ami plunged under the waves, the round slicing through the water inches from her head. She swam until burning lungs forced her up for air. This time, Ilya was ready.

The bullet grazed her temple. White hot agony exploded across her temple

But darkness was creeping in at the edges of her vision. Her limbs felt leaden, unresponsive. She broke the surface with a gasp, managing a desperate gulp of air before the water closed over her head once again.

Able her, Ilya was silhouetted against the night sky.

The darkness beckoned.

I'm sorry, Lucy. I should have listened to you.

Then, there was only the cold embrace of an unforgiving bay.

***

Ami woke to the gentle lapping of waves. The taste of salt and metal filled her mouth, mingling with an acrid stench of diesel fuel and rotting seaweed.

She lifted her head. She lay face-down on a narrow strip of rocky beach, grit, and small stones digging into her cheek. She spat out a mouthful of salt and sand. She sat, her body groaning. Felt like she'd been hit by a truck. No, not a vehicle. Ilya.

The sun broke the horizon. Morning. She had been out all night.

Ami staggered to her feet, head pounding and vision swimming. Blood matted her hair on one side, and her clothes were stiff with dried saltwater. Her vest and jacket were gone. Thank God for her boots. She limped away from the water's edge. Every step sent fresh waves of pain through her battered body.

A few early morning joggers gave her a wide berth when she made her way up to the street. But she ignored their stares. Down the street and around the corner was a small Chinese restaurant. Ami wasn't sure they'd be open, but she was willing to chance it.

The neon *OPEN* sign was the one thing that had gone right in the past twelve hours. Ami pushed through the glass door to the overwhelming aroma of frying oil and garlic.

She walked through the restaurant to the kitchen.

"*Telephone*," Ami said in Mandarin, her voice raw from the saltwater.

The elderly woman at the stove took one look at her bedraggled state and pointed to a stand next to the door. It held a cordless phone. Ami's fingers shook as she dialed.

"Yeah?" Goblin's gruff voice was like a shot of hot adrenaline to her battered system.

"Goblin. It's Ami. I need—"Her voice cracked, and she swallowed hard. "I need help."

There was a beat of silence, then: "Where are you?"

Ami stared. "Where am I?"

She'd forgotten.

The woman pointed to the wall. The restaurant's address was listed on a worn yellow book advertisement. She read it off.

The adrenaline was fading, leaving a bone-deep exhaustion in its wake. She swayed on her feet, fighting to remain conscious.

"Stay put," Goblin said. "I'm on my way."

Ami hung up and set the phone back on the stand. "Thank you."

Then she went and sat by the window.

Within seconds, the woman bustled back from the kitchen carrying a steaming cup and a damp cloth. The scent of jasmine tea cut through the haze of pain. Ami shook her head. "I don't have any money."

The woman brushed it off and set the cup down regardless.

"Thank you."

The woman hustled back to the kitchen. Ami dabbed at her face, the white cloth coming away stained with grime and blood. Then she drank the jasmine tea. By the time Goblin's hulking form filled the doorway fifteen minutes later, she was feeling better. "You got any cash?" she asked.

His eyes widened at her battered state. "Twenty bucks."

Ami gestured to the table. "I'll pay you back."

Goblin extracted the bill and laid it down. Then, the two of them exited the restaurant. Only when they were inside Goblin's car did he finally ask. "Jesus, Ami. What happened?"

"Bad date," she said as he pulled away from the curb.

Goblin gripped the steering wheel, but he didn't press her to talk, concentrating on the early morning traffic.

When he finally pulled up outside her apartment building, he turned to her. "You need a doctor?"

"Nope," Ami said, reaching for the door handle.

Goblin's hand on her arm stopped her. "You sure? You look like hell."

She forced a smile. "Nothing a hot shower and some sleep won't fix." In addition to her resignation. God, she hated to tell Lucy she was right. Hopefully, she could get that shower before Lucy saw the state of her.

"Okay," Goblin dropped his hand. "But give me a call if you need anything."

"Will do."

Ami got out of the vehicle and slammed the door, watching his taillights disappear around the corner before heading to the lobby. She took the stairs up. It hurt like hell, but it helped to stretch her sore muscles.

She exited the stairwell and turned left. Then stopped, staring at the apartment.

The front door hung slightly askew, splintered wood around the lock.

Ice flooded her veins. Ami sprinted toward it.

Inside, the living room looked like a war zone. Shattered glass lay on the floor. Furniture was overturned. Family photos lay face-down.

No use shouting for Lucy. Her sister wouldn't hear her.

Ami's gaze locked onto a crimson smear on the kitchen tile. A bloody handprint marred the wall. The metallic scent of spilled blood hung heavy in the air.

"*No, no, no,*" Ami said, following the grisly trail down the hallway toward Lucy's bedroom.

And when she arrived at the door, her world broke into pieces.

Lucy lay crumpled on the bedroom floor, glassy eyes staring at nothing. A pool of congealed blood spread out from beneath her still form. The stench of death filled Ami's nostrils.

Ami screamed, her legs giving out. She crawled to her sister's side, gathering Lucy's lifeless body in her arms, a keening wail tearing from her throat. Equal parts grief and rage.

Ilya.

Ilya had done this.

She held tight to Lucy for at least an hour. But finally, she had enough strength to release her hold and pull out her phone.

Through tears, she scrolled to Ivan's contact and hit the number.

"What is it, Ami?" Ivan asked. His voice was thick with sleep.

"*Your son,*" Ami said.

"What about him?" Ivan sounded much more awake now.

Ami took a breath. "Your fucking son killed my sister."

A beat of silence. Then: "Explain."

Ami's words tumbled out in a frenzied torrent, tripping over the language for the first time while she tried to detail everything that had happened to her since last night. Finally, she stopped. She'd run out of words. Run out of rage.

Now, she just felt grief.

"I'll take care of it," Ivan said, his tone grave. "Stay where you are. I'm sending help."

The line went dead.

Ami dropped her phone, continuing to cradle the husk of what used to be Lucy in her arms.

Time seemed to warp around her. She should move, breathe, do something. But grief and exhaustion had turned her limbs to lead and barred her from action.

Minutes, hours, days later — Ami had no idea — a knock at the door startled her. Ami lay Lucy gently down and stood on shaky legs, then made her way down the hall to the front door while using the walls for support.

Standing outside were Marco and Sergei. She had seen their faces a hundred times and shared drinks and jokes with these men. But now their expressions were solemn.

"Ami." Marco's thick accent cut through the silence. "We are so sorry."

She nodded, not trusting herself to speak.

They both entered, and Sergei closed the door behind them. Then he held out his arms and gave Ami a hug.

She leaned her head on his shoulder, trying not to cry.

"Is anyone else here?" Marco asked, scanning the room.

Ami shook her head. "Just ... just me and Lucy."

Marco, his face contorted in empathy, reached forward and squeezed her shoulder. Then — so quickly Ami almost missed it — his hand flew to his waistband. The glint of a silenced pistol.

Her blood ran cold. How could she have been so stupid?

Sergio's arms tightened around her, crushing her ribs. She groaned, thrashing. He pinned her tighter.

Instinct overrode thought. Ami dropped, her feet connecting with Marco's right knee, and a bone-jarring crunch echoed through the room.

He bellowed and stumbled, knocking into Sergio, who lost his grip on her. Ami bolted for the fire escape.

The whisper-cough of a silenced pistol preceded the bullet whizzing past her ear. The glass window shattered, spraying everywhere.

Ami dove through the opening, landing hard on the metal grating. She scrambled to her feet, running down the stairs. More gunshots peppered the stairs.

But the metal lattice provided cage-like protection.

She heard a loud clang. Sergio barreled out the window, following her. Ami made it to the second floor, then jumped.

Her feet hit the pavement, and she lost her balance, her knees slamming into the concrete, jarring her entire body. But she was up and running, pushing her battered body past its limits.

She glanced back and saw Sergei land and pursue.

Fuck.

Ami darted down an alley, scrambling a chain-link fence. Dropping to the other side. Her lungs burned, every muscle screamed, but she kept moving.

She emerged onto a busy street, nearly colliding with a group of tourists. *Perfect.*

Ami melded into the flow of bodies, letting the current of humanity sweep her along. Her heart pounded in her ears, and she risked a glance back. Sergio's face was carved with frustration while he scanned the crowd. Ami pointed to the guidebook one of the tourists held as though she were asking a question. Sergio's eyes glided right by her without recognition.

As soon as Sergio and Marco were out of sight, she ran. Going deeper into the maze of Chinatown streets. Left, right, doubling back — anything to be sure she wasn't being followed.

There was only one person she trusted.

And that's where she was going.

Goblin's apartment was a fourth-floor walk-up in a run-down building on the edge of Chinatown. The lobby door was busted, so she was able to go right in, taking the stairs two at a time, her legs threatening to give out with each step. She arrived at 403 and pounded on the door.

He answered almost immediately. "What the — Jesus, what happened, Ami?"

She shouldered past him into the apartment. Forced the door closed and locked it. Then she turned to him. "Lucy's dead. And Ivan's men tried to kill me."

Goblin's face hardened. "Dead?"

She nodded.

He went to his bedroom and returned a moment later with a gun. Then he made sure the door was locked before guiding Ami to sit on his threadbare couch. Then he said, "Start from the beginning."

Ami told him everything — far more than she had said to Ivan — she confessed it all: Sofia, Ilya, Lucy ...

Goblin reached for his phone. "I'm calling it in. I'll have Ivan picked up and—"

"And what?" She grabbed his wrist. "We don't have

enough to bring down Ivan's operation yet. At least, that's what you keep telling me. And if they find out I've been informing on them ..."

His jaw clenched. "Your sister is dead."

"And I will be, too, if the police get involved."

"Ami."

She jumped to her feet, cheeks flushed. "I've spent two years spilling Ivan's secret for you."

Goblin spread his hands. "So what is it you want?"

She curled her lips. "His head on a platter."

"You know I can't give you that." Goblin shook his head.

Ami brushed her hair back behind her ears, then fixed him with a look. "I wasn't asking permission."

And then she was out the door, slamming it behind her. And once again, she ran.

"Ami!"

She ignored Goblin, flying out onto the street.

The familiar chaos of Chinatown enveloped her at once in a haven of neon signs and chattering voices. She walked, her mind churning with half-formed plans, each more desperate than the last.

Ivan would pay for Lucy's death.

As would Ilya.

Lucy was gone.

Ami had nothing left to lose.

And Ivan Volkov was about to learn just how dangerous that made her.

* * *

Ami waited through a trio of heartbeats, her fingers hovering over Jing Chen's name before hitting dial. When he answered, his voice was cool and measured.

"Ms. Tan. I was wondering when you'd call."

"We need to talk, Jing. In person."

"Volkov tells an interesting story about you attempting to kill his son last night."

Ami stiffened. "Lies. But I can explain, but not over the phone." God knows if Goblin was listening in.

A heavy pause until Jing finally spoke. "The usual place, one hour."

The line went dead before Ami could respond.

She had one shot at this ... and failure meant certain death. By the time she arrived at the Beijing Palace, she felt sick.

But she stepped inside.

Waiting for her was Jing's men. He gestured for her to follow, leading her behind a curtain that separated the main dining area from a private back room. She was checked for weapons by a man whose breath reeked of stale cigarettes and alcohol.

When he was satisfied, he pushed her forward. "Go on."

Ami walked to the back of the room.

Jing sat motionless at a round table covered with a white tablecloth, his suit looking especially crisp in the warm glow of the lantern lamps. He tracked her movements, gesturing to the empty chair across from him.

"Speak," he said.

"Ivan lies," Ami said. Her voice caught. She cleared it. "That inventory that went missing? He stole it. He's trying to dismantle the agreement between the Bratva and the Harmony Peace Association."

"Why?"

"Why do you think?" She asked. "Power. He wants to control the port."

Jing sat in silence. "Bullshit."

Ami shook her head. "It's not. And your cousin, Guo?

43

He didn't go back to Shanghai. The Russians killed him. Butchered him."

Jing's fingers tightened around his teacup, a muscle twitching in his jaw. "More lies."

"I know where they dumped the body."

Her words hung between them.

Jing set his teacup down on the table. "Tell me."

She shook her head. "Nope. It's my only insurance."

Jing studied her, weighing his options for a painfully long moment until he finally nodded. "Very well. But if you're playing me, Ms. Tan, you'll wish Ivan had gotten to you first."

Ami felt a weight slide from her shoulders. She might not be able to point the weapon at Ivan herself. But she sure as hell was gonna get Jing to do it for her.

His man grabbed her arm and hoisted her out of the chair. She was led out of the restaurant via the back door to a black SUV. She was forced inside. Bodyguards on either side, Jing in the front next to his driver.

The SUV purred as it navigated the narrow alley, then headed out onto the broader city streets. "Go straight, then take the highway past the port." Ami sat rigid in the back. "There's something else you should know …"

Jing said nothing.

"I've lied as well."

Jing adjusted the rearview mirror and met her eyes. "Explain."

"I change what Ivan says. Inflammatory statements, mostly. Insults and threats — I always smooth them over. It's why the peace accord has lasted this long."

"And why should I believe you?" Jing asked.

"Because in about twenty minutes, you'll see for yourself that I'm telling the truth about Guo."

Jing nodded and readjusted the mirror. "I guess we will."

Ami kept giving directions until they arrived at a winding dirt road on the outskirts. "Stop!"

The driver did. And the occupants of the SUV got out. Ami's heart pounded as they walked to the spot where she had last seen Guo's body. She hadn't meant to see. It was when she'd first started working for Goblin. She'd followed them here. Watched them dump the body. But she'd had no evidence.

And Goblin hadn't yet learned to trust her.

They were almost there—

Ami stopped. Her skin prickled with a cold sweat. "No, no, no, no, no!" The earth was disturbed. A mound of freshly turned soil was all she needed to see to know that Ivan had been there. He was a step aside.

Cleaning up.

He knew she'd go to Jin.

Ami dropped to her knees and started digging. But she needn't have bothered. There was nobody here.

"Well?" Jing said.

"He was here, I swear." Her heart beat even harder. "Ivan is covering his tracks."

Jing's face darkened. He pulled out a gun. "You test my patience, Ms. Tan."

"Wait!" Ami raised her hands. "Let me make a call. I know who can tell us where Guo is now. Please."

Jing considered for a moment, then he gestured to her with his gun.

Ami got out her phone and dialed Sofia's number.

"*Ami?*" Sofia answered in a panicked whisper less than two rings later. "What's going on? Ivan is going crazy, he—
"

"Sofia, listen to me: I need to know if Ivan moved a

body recently. From the abandoned lot out by the port. It's important."

A sharp intake of breath. "Y-yes. I overheard him talking to Marco. They took it to the old meatpacking plant on the waterfront. But Ami, please, be careful. He's—"

The line went dead.

Ami looked up at Jing. "I know where Guo is."

* * *

The stench of decay was a nauseating cocktail of rotting meat, mold, and something unmistakably human. Ami's gorge rose with each step as the group walked deeper into the abandoned meatpacking plant. And then there it was in the corner. A dirty tarp.

Jing glanced at his man and nodded.

He walked over and unwrapped the tarp, revealing Guo's body in pieces. Almost unrecognizable except for that tattoo on the neck. It was most definitely Jing's cousin.

Jing's sharp intake of breath cut through the oppressive silence.

He whirled to look at Ami.

And then the air exploded with a deafening bray of gunfire. Ivan's men had found them.

Ami's world narrowed to the thunderous echo of bullets and the acrid sting of cordite. She dove behind a bank of renovated cupboards. Covering her ears as Jing's bodyguards returned fire.

Ami glanced across the warehouse. A corroded door hung askew from its hinges. She Army-crawled toward it, bullets whizzing close enough to ruffle her hair. Halfway there, she clambered to her feet and bolted.

Hurling herself through the opening into the crisp afternoon air.

Then she ran as if the hounds of hell were snapping at

her heels. She kept going until she became aware of her buzzing phone. She pulled it out.

Sofia's name flashed on the screen.

Ami accepted the call. "Sofia?"

"I'm afraid Sofia can't come to the phone right now." Ivan's voice was cold.

Ami froze in her tracks. "Ivan."

"You are a clever girl, Ami. But not quite clever enough. It was obvious you turned either my son or my girlfriend. They were the only two that knew what was in the tarp."

Ami said nothing.

"Now, if you'd like to save Sofia some pain—" He broke off, and Ami heard Sophia scream.

Ami clenched her phone. "Let her go. She has nothing to do with this."

"Oh, but she does," Ivan said. "You made Sofia a part of it the second you fucked her. And unless you want to hear her scream more — and I can promise she will wail like a cat being skinned alive — you'll bring yourself to me. The warehouse. One hour."

The line went dead.

"Fuck!"

Ami paced, her mind racing. Then, finally, she dialed Goblin's number.

"Ami?" He answered before the first ring finished. "Where are you?"

"You still got men watching the warehouse?"

"No, I pulled them when you flamed out. Why?"

"I might need them," Ami said. "I have a meeting with Ivan."

"You certainly do not."

"He's got Sophia."

"And then he'll have you. I can assemble a team. But you need to stay put."

"There's no time. I'm sorry, Goblin. But I have to do this."

Ami hung up before he could protest further. He called her back, but she ignored it, going in search of a cab.

Maybe Goblin would get there in time. Maybe he wouldn't. But Sophia was not about to pay for her mistake.

* * *

Ami made one stop on the way to the port, at a small store in Chinatown where she picked up a switchblade. No defense against a gun, but it made her feel more confident.

The cabbie had wanted to wait, but she insisted she'd be fine.

She probably wouldn't be returning. Her only hope was she'd spill some of Ivan's blood before he took hers.

Ami approached the warehouse with measured steps, her footfalls echoing throughout the empty port.

Ivan had pulled any workers.

The place was as silent as it had been the other night.

The concealed knife pressed against Ami's shin in her boot: cold comfort in the face of near-certain doom.

The door was already open.

A wide cavernous mouth, waiting to swallow her.

No point in hesitating. She stepped through.

Inside, standing against one wall, was the Harmony Peace Association. And before them, Jing. His impassive face was a mask of barely contained fury. The other wall was bordered by the Bratva. Ivan sat in one of the chairs. Ilya stood behind him, his face bruised from his assault.

And before them, on the floor was Sofia.

One of her eyes was swollen shut, and purple bruises blossomed across her cheekbone. Her lip had been split and oozed fresh blood. She kept her eyes on the floor. Ami could see her shaking from across the room.

Standing next to Ivan was a man she'd never seen before. He twisted his hands, looking entirely out of his element.

"Who's the fresh meat?" she asked.

"Ah," Ivan's voice dripped with artificial warmth. "Our new translator. So you see, your services will no longer be required."

"And Jing agrees?" she asked.

Ivan glanced over at him and nodded. "Our recent misunderstanding regarding his cousin's untimely death has been most satisfactorily resolved."

Ami glanced into the corner. Marco lay on the floor. A bullet hole in his forehead.

"What did he say?" Jing asked.

Ivan's translator did his job.

"No, no," Jing said. "I want Ami to translate."

She did.

Jing's jaw tightened further. "Tell him I am not satisfied."

Ami did.

Ivan stiffened.

"When exactly was Guo killed, Ivan?"

Ami translated.

Ivan met her eyes. "Before the accord."

Ami hesitated.

"What?" Jing asked.

"After the accord. Guo discovered that Ivan was trying to cheat you. So he had him killed."

The atmosphere shifted instantly.

"What did you say?" Ivan asked.

"The truth."

Ivan nudged his translator.

"She said you were lying," the man said, wincing.

Ivan's face contorted. He reached for his gun. "Shut your treacherous mouth, bitch."

One of Jing's men stepped in front of Ami, blocking her from view.

"Continue," Jing said. "Word for word, what else has Ivan told you?"

Ami weighed her options. This was it — her one chance to tear down the whole rotten edifice and find some measure of justice for Lucy. She drew a deep breath.

Her Mandarin was smooth, leaving her lips like a bullet. "Ivan said, and I quote: 'I'm sick to death of dealing with these fucking rice eaters. Time to end the accord once and for all.'"

"Now wait a minute—" the translator started before his skull exploded.

Ami didn't know who shot first.

She dove to the ground while everyone else seemed to run.

Gunsmoke stung her nostrils, bullets whizzing past close enough to ruffle her hair. She scrambled forward, grabbing Sofia's wrist and pulling her toward the exit.

"After them!" Ivan yelled.

Only a spray of crimson mist erupted from his chest. He looked down, surprised, and then Jing's bullet caught him in the head, blasting apart his skull into a million puzzle pieces. Then he toppled.

Ami and Sophia bolted outside.

But Ilya followed.

He tracked them toward the shipping containers, and Ami realized they were cornered. She yanked the blade from her boot. But it wasn't going to help. Not against Ilya's gun.

A vehicle flew towards him.

Ilya turned, firing. It was too late. It struck him, sending his body flying.

Ami grabbed Sophia, holding her close.

A moment later, Goblin emerged from the vehicle and gestured toward them. "Get in."

The wail of approaching sirens pierced the night.

"Now!"

Ami pushed Sophia over to the car and climbed into the back seat. Goblin reversed and sped away. While cruisers converged on the scene. Ami turned and watched through the cracked rear window, watching officers join in the firefight.

"I should be arresting you," Goblin said, but there was no real heat in his words.

Her eyes met his in the rearview. Then he reached into his jacket and pulled out a thick manila envelope. He tossed it into the back seat.

"New identities. For both of you. Birth certificates, social security cards, the works. You'll be ghosts if you want to disappear."

Sofia's hand found Ami's in the backseat, her fingers braiding and squeezing tight.

"Thank you, Goblin."

The big man grunted, his eyes turning back to the road. "Don't thank me yet. This won't be easy. You're both going to be looking over your shoulders for a very long time."

Ami looked over at Sophia.

She smiled, then rested her head on Ami's shoulder.

Ami looked out the window. The city lights blurred as the car left the port behind. Her old life was ash. Time to rise. Sometimes, survival was the sweetest revenge.

Vlog Her

EMME JACKSON

Vlog Her

EMME JACKSON

HAVE YOU EVER HAD A DREAM THAT JUST HAD TO COME true, or your heart would break? I'm not talking about winning the Powerball or meeting Zac Efron. I'm talking about the ones that live in your soul. The kind that launches you out of bed at 5 a.m. and stays on your brain long after your head hits the pillow at night. That dream.

For me, it was acting, and I was determined that someday I was going to be on the stage. It sounds vain and cheesy, looking back on it now. Yeah, I know what you're thinking, girl, grow up already. That's pie in the sky. You have to accept reality and move on. Only I can't, so here I am. Stuck. I'm getting ahead of myself, though. I need to go back to the beginning. Since I'm a theater nerd, I'll set the scene for you.

The year was 2013, and it was my birthday. I'm a May baby, so everything was green, and spring flowers were blooming. Yoga pants were just becoming mainstream. James Franco was in theaters in a weird *Wizard of Oz* reboot. The news was full of stories about some Snowden dude. I don't know what he did because I wasn't really paying attention, but you get the gist. Anyway, "Heart Attack" by Demi Lovato came on, so I started singing into my hairbrush. I had an audition for a big Broadway show, and I needed to practice.

I sent in the audition video on a whim. It's not like my mother, Becky, would ever let me go, but like I said, some dreams live in your soul. I was shocked when I got a call-back, and I admit, I started freaking out. Broadway was calling. I couldn't miss that audition, but Becky didn't support me doing anything outside of her YouTube channel. I always liked to use her first name when she upset me. The term "mom" often felt too endearing. Anyway, I got with my BFF Ellie, and we hatched a plan. I'd lie to my parents and say I was spending the weekend at her parents' cabin for my birthday. Ellie would then lie to her mom and say that mine had a scheduled surgery and couldn't take me to this life-changing opportunity. Her mom loved me, so naturally, she'd volunteer. I was a little nervous about intercepting Mom's phone for the inevitable "Is this okay?" mom-to-mom text, but Mom went to bed early with a headache that night. Everything was going according to plan. It was going to work.

You're probably wondering why all the scheming was necessary. Why not just ask your mom? Surely, she would have supported you if you'd given her the chance. Yada. Yada. Sorry, but no. My mom was, well ... different. Dad and I never thought she was dangerous, but life with her was never going to be pleasant. From constantly shaming Dad about his ten extra pounds to closing my channel the second I got close to passing her own, we were constantly surrounded by toxic energy. People who saw her on her vlog, "Mommy Time with Becky Ward," thought she was normal, but that was all fake.

The older I got, the worse things became. I'd wake up

with a camera in my face. Family dinners, dentist appointments, you name it; nothing was off limits if she thought it would grab people's attention. Imagine getting your first period, and before you've even processed it, the whole world knows what kind of tampons you use. If she had a few unsubscribes, it would send her into a spiral. Sometimes, she'd even send nasty messages, and that never ends well on social media. Haters gonna hate.

Mom started getting kind of twitchy and desperate after I hit my teens. How do you keep a mom channel going if your kid isn't a kid anymore? She kept buying me clothes with sparkly unicorns and saying things about me taking a gap year before college. She even started bugging Dad about having another kid. I'm pretty sure he snuck off on a business trip and had a secret vasectomy. So, my fourteenth birthday brought with it nothing but unease for Becky. I was turning another year older and closer to being free of her grip.

Ellie, always the rebellious spirit, bought me an early birthday present. A shirt that said, "Filmed Without Permission." She kept asking me if I'd worn it yet, but I hadn't dared. When you live on eggshells, you'll do anything for five minutes of peace. You don't do things to stir up trouble. Unless you've lived it, that can be hard to understand for people. Even your best friend.

Anyway, there I was, sitting at my dressing table, hairbrush mic in hand, pouring my heart into it with everything I had. There was this energizing sensation pulsing through my body. I'd never felt anything like it. I think it was happiness. I'd never been that freaking happy. I was pretending I was in my audition. I could picture it just like I was there. The stage was draped with red, crushed velvet curtains and smelled like Murphy's Oil Soap. The lights were shining on me just right. The directors were so impressed they turned to each other and nodded — "She's the one!" There's a crowd, and they're chanting my name: "Alex! Alex! Alex!"

"Alexia!" And then there she was, stepping into my room, as unwelcome as her mother at Thanksgiving. She was wearing fuzzy purple slippers and waving a garden spade. "Can you keep it down? I've got a headache." She always had "a headache" when someone else dared to be noticeable. I was supposed to behave like the houseplants she always forgot to water.

"Whatever." It just slipped out of my mouth. Mom's least favorite word. I bit my lip and prayed she hadn't noticed.

"Don't whatever me," she said. The vein on her forehead popped out. It matched her slippers in color. My happiness melted into the floor. This next part is cemented into my memory. She pointed the spade at me. "You will not disrespect me in my own home." She stomped her fluffy footwear down on each syllable for emphasis. I took a step back. Something was up with her. This wasn't a regular Becky tantrum. I was used to those. This was something new, so I pushed down the snarky comment, fighting my tongue for purchase. The one about how I got disrespected in my own home all the time.

"Yes, ma'am," I said. I couldn't afford to get grounded. It would ruin the plan. She was about to say something, but then my kitten, Floyd, ran out from under the bed and attacked her fluffy foot. Startled, she let out a scream and kicked her foot up in the air with Floyd still attached. He looked like a rodeo clown. It was funny, and I couldn't help but laugh, but Becky wasn't laughing. She swung at Floyd with the spade in her hand, barely missing him. He was smart enough to detach and run, but then she cornered him, and he hissed at her. I dove in like any good cat mom would and scooped him up, gripping him close to my body for protection. She glared at me, and for a brief moment, I thought she might hit me, but then she seemed to collect herself. She smoothed down her hair and walked back toward the door.

"Wash up and change clothes. Your father's bringing home cake." Cake? I wasn't going to be home. I was supposed to leave any minute to go to "Ellie's cabin for the weekend" aka New York. Had she forgotten? Floyd squirmed in my hands, but I didn't dare put him down.

"Chocolate, ripple, crunch?" I asked, embracing the change of subject.

"Angel food with strawberries," she said. *Hello, I'm allergic to strawberries. They give me hives.*

"Of course," I said. I carried Floyd back to the dressing table and gave him a treat. I could tell he was still freaked. He was just a baby, for Christ's sake. I heard the door shut, and I let out a deep breath. I put Floyd down, and he darted under my bed to hide. I walked over to my closet, and my hands were still kind of shaking. I spotted the shirt Ellie got me for my birthday. I knew she'd ask me about it, so I pulled it out and changed into it. Then, I put a button-down flannel over it to hide the wording. It seemed like such a small thing at the time.

I took a quick glance out of the window. Becky was outside planting flowers. Fake dahlias. Every year the same thing. At least she was occupied. It was the perfect time to slip out. My phone pinged.

ELLIE: U ready?
    Me: I guess.
    Ellie: U ok?
    Me: Yeah. Just mom being mom again.

Ellie: Want me to come beat her up?

Me: It would just make her crazier. Be there in a sec.

Ellie: Cool. We're stopping on the way out for choc ripp crunch.

I SNATCHED up my backpack and grabbed Floyd from his hiding spot. Taking him along hadn't been the plan, but I couldn't leave him there after that spectacle. I was so close to my dream. I could almost see the bright lights of Broadway, but as it would turn out, I would never make it to that audition.

∽

* * *

After I disappeared, the poop emojis hit the fan. One particular Twitter handle, Truthtlr14, was ruthless. She accused Becky of my murder almost daily. Accusing a high-profile mom influencer of murdering her own kid was media gold. It was like throwing chum into shark-infested waters, and boy, did the haters go into a frenzy. Soon, Becky's mug had been plastered everywhere, from the Huffington Post to an episode of *Dateline*. She wasn't smart enough to decline to comment. By the time the episode finished airing, everyone was convinced she had done it. There was also a lot of speculation as to who Truthtlr14 was, but they never came forward. People thought he was an insider because of his knowledge of the family, but our lives had been so public it was hard to tell. A few people even theorized that it was me. Those were your diehard Becky fans, though. The ones who wanted her to be innocent. Funny how people believe what they want, isn't it? For what it's worth, I always suspected it was Ellie. She took my disappearance hard. As for Mom, she finally made headlines, but they weren't the kind anyone would want.

Police Search Home of Famous Influencer Becky Ward

Did Becky Ward Murder Her Daughter?

Alexia Ward Scored Broadway Audition But Never Arrived

Becky Ward Questioned in Daughter's Disappearance

Case Grows Cold in Disappearance of Alexia Ward

No More Mommy Time: Becky Ward Shuts Down Popular Channel

Case of Alexia Ward Grows Cold: Police Claim Lack of Evidence

Since a body was never found, the police couldn't charge her, and the story eventually died, but the damage had been done. She may not have been arrested, but she'd been tried in the court of public opinion and found guilty.

Becky Ward's career as an influencer was over. At least, most people thought so, but ten years later, that was about to change. Mom was asked to do an interview for Celeste Martin. Celeste had the hottest YouTube channel in the parenting space. She also looked like a Kardashian, and she had a set of twins that looked like they belonged in *Baby Vogue* if that had been a thing. She was doing a segment called *Where Are They Now*, and she wanted to kick it off with Mom. Of course, Mom wanted to do it, but Dad always felt like Mom's channel had driven me away, and he was furious. So, they fought about it. But a little thing like an argument never stopped my mother from doing what she wanted to do.

Still, when the day came, she was nervous. Since they lived nearby, it was being filmed in Celeste's studio, which was unfamiliar turf. Plus, Celeste had declined to give her the interview questions ahead of time. Things could derail quickly, but she had to take the chance. The spotlight beckoned. So, it happened on the day of the interview that Mom pulled out of the driveway in her black Mercedes and headed to Celeste's studio. She told herself it didn't matter that she was out of practice and was feeling halfway positive until she arrived, and the half-moons of Celeste's still-perfect post-baby breasts highlighted her inadequacies.

Despite her appearance, Celeste was not one of those perky moms who smiled too much and just wanted everyone to like her. Underneath the perfectly plucked brows was a cunning intellect. Before her twins were born, Celeste had been a real journalist. Her interviews were known for having a serious edge. She was like the Barbara Walters of YouTube if Barbara Walters had worn Lululemon and drank almond milk macchiatos.

The interview began with the usual awkwardness of first interviews between strangers. Mom used to say a good interview was like a tennis match. They had a rhythm to them and a bit of competition. They soon settled into a comfortable pace. Celeste asked about Becky's career in real estate. It was the perfect opening. She had gone from being a disgraced public figure to one of the top agents in the area in the 10 years I'd been gone. She was quite proud of how she'd rebuilt herself, even if she had used her infamy to do it. People are often curious about the accused. They'll go to an open house with their husband just so they can say they've met you. They'll even buy the four-bedroom stunner with a fireplace in the master that you showed them. They just won't invite you to dinner parties or coffee. They won't let you enter the inner social circles that normal life depends upon on the off chance you'll go all Lizzie Borden on them. But she always left out that part. Mom chose to focus on her wins, not her losses.

There were a few more questions like that, a gentle volleying back and forth. But it was inevitable that I would invade the conversation. After all, viewers didn't really care about what Becky was doing. They wanted to know about me. They wanted an answer to the mystery.

"So, Becky, do you think Alexia is out there somewhere watching this interview?"

Mom had let herself be lulled into a false sense of security. She hadn't seen this coming, not yet, at least. If this was a tennis match, by now, she was realizing she was up against Serena Williams. The thought of losing to a player half her age stabbed her ego. She plastered the appropriate expression on her face, but the corners of her eyes belied malice. If you watch the interview, you will notice Celeste shiver ever so slightly. I wonder if she sensed then that she'd poked the wrong bear, as Mom used to say. "I'd like to think so," Mom replied. "Her father and I have never given up hope that she'll come home."

"You really believe she is still alive then??"

If you've made a career of touting parenting advice, then admitting your child ran away from you must taste like swallowing vinegar. "Yes, she left a note," Becky said.

Celeste's brows creased as she scanned her memory. This had never been revealed to the public. "And what did the note say?" Celeste asked.

"That she was going to make it in show business and wasn't coming home until she had." It sounded put on even to my ears.

"If that's the case, then why didn't she go to her audition? That was a huge opportunity to just miss."

"I don't know," Becky said with a shrug. "If I knew that, then we wouldn't be here today."

The note wasn't exactly a revelation at this point. For the most part, people had moved on. The interview wound down and ended with polite thank yous from each side. They were on camera, after all. The initial reception to the interview was lukewarm. Celeste moved on to bigger and better things and assumed that Becky would crawl back to her life of semi-anonymity, but my mother was never the predictable sort.

* * *

A week after the video dropped, Mom started getting emails from some of her old followers. They had tracked her down through the Realty company. She was surprised by the outpouring of love and support. Some of them had been through similar tragedies and lost children due to one circumstance or another. They wanted to know how she'd managed to stay so strong.

That day, Becky did two things that would seal her fate. She sent a scathing email to Celeste Martin, letting her know that her interview style lacked charisma. Next, she got on YouTube and rebooted her old life. Becky Ward still had things to say, and the world seemed ready to listen again.

Dad, on the other hand, wasn't being heard. He never had been, and it was getting old. I think he only stayed so he could be sure he'd be there if I ever came home. Mom, surprisingly, had never suggested moving either, despite her thriving real estate career. She must have seen better homes they could upgrade to all the time. Deep down, he assumed that she'd stayed for the same reasons he had. It was the tenuous thread that had held them together, but the thread was becoming taut.

It didn't take long for Becky to plow back into content creation. She answered questions from fans and explained her extensive journey through therapy. She even started talking about writing a book. I think she was as shocked as anyone by what happened next.

It was just an ordinary Tuesday, but I remember it like you always do the biggest moments in your life. I'd never had stage fright, but Alex Ward was about to sweep back into the world of the living. I couldn't help but wonder what my parents were going to think. The doorbell rang. Here goes. I summoned every ounce of courage that I possessed. Footsteps shuffled inside across the familiar polished wood floors. I considered running away. What I was about to do was crazy even for me, but then the door opened, and she was standing in front of me, hand on one hip. No turning back now. I smiled awkwardly.

"We don't need anything right now," she said. She thought I was selling something. The door started to close, and I panicked.

"Mom," I said, my voice weak and wavering "It's me."

The door swung back slowly. Her eyes studied me as if she was seeing me for the first time. Hair color, eye color, build. I looked for a hint of recognition in her steel blue eyes. I never noticed before how cold they were. Finally, I saw her eyes alight with understanding. The corners of her mouth turned up.

"Alexia," she said. She gripped me savagely and pulled me close.

"Dave," she called out. She was still gripping me tight. My lungs burned, and it was getting harder to breathe, but then Dave arrived, and her grip loosened. I gasped like I'd been underwater. Becky stepped away from me so Dave could steady me. I couldn't look at him. How could I? His eyes searched me, desperate and hopeful for a second, then crushed the next.

"No," he whispered. Not the response I'd hoped for. His eyes were wild, like an animal backed into a corner.

"It's Alexia," Becky says. "She's come back to us."

"No," Dave said, louder, surer this time. A lump rose in my throat, and I fought the urge to flee. "I know I've changed a lot," I said. My hands were shaking, so I held them down at my sides and tried to hide it, "But it really is me."

"How dare you," he hissed. The words slapped me like a physical blow, and I shrank away a little. *I shouldn't have come here.* Becky grabbed my hand and dragged me inside, closing the door behind her. No hope of escape now.

"He's in shock, is all," she said dismissively as if she was talking about something ordinary. Poor Dad. He was tight, like an over-filled balloon. Again, I felt like I shouldn't have come.

We moved into the kitchen, where Dad was pacing. Things had changed since I was here last. The walls had been painted an ugly pea green. The table looked new and expensive. Dad's hands gripped his sandy hair, tinged with gray. He recoiled a little at the sight of me in this place I no longer belonged. I gripped the table. I wanted so badly to sit down, to let my mind stop swirling.

"What the hell do you think you're doing?" he yelled. It wasn't directed at me; it was Becky he was blaming.

"I'm trying to welcome our daughter back home," she said. "Have you lost your mind? Isn't this what you've been praying for all these years?" He looked at her then with pure hate. I recognized it.

"That's not Alexia," he said. He pointed at me. A trickle of sweat ran down the bridge of my nose, but I didn't dare swipe it away. I didn't move. I wanted to be anywhere but there. The moment was a car crash in slow motion, a tumble into the Grand Canyon, and skydiving without a parachute all rolled into one. They started fighting right there. Then the balloon burst, and Dad let years of frustration tumble forth until it was all spent. I sat down and took a deep breath, just like my therapist had taught me.

Dad stormed off. I'd never seen him stand up to her like that before. Becky followed him and continued shouting. It was mostly obscenities, but Dad was undeterred. He packed his things quickly. I stayed at the kitchen table, and suddenly, I felt something at my feet. I looked down. It was Floyd. I pulled him up into my arms and snuggled him, and he let me. He rubbed his head on my chin and purred like I'd never left. At least someone was happy to see me. He smelled amazing. Familiar. Tears burned the corners of my eyes, and I let them fall. Floyd licked them away. I heard the front door close, followed by the sound of Dad's truck driving away. It hurt that he left, but it was for the best. Mom and I had a lot of unfinished business we needed to work out.

Becky was overjoyed by my return, if only because she couldn't wait to share her vindication with the world.

Suddenly, she was on top of the news again. If there's anything the media loves more than tearing someone down, it's a comeback story.

* * *

Mom and I soon settled into a routine. I took a job as a barista at a little coffee shop in the square on Main Street. I liked the people, and the work kept me busy. Some of my customers claimed to recognize me. Most were kind but curious. They told me they were glad I had returned. Occasionally, though, someone would come in to tear me down. They'd shout things like, "How could you do that to your mother!" or "You're a filthy fucking liar!" I was always shocked by their anger. One lady threw a latte at me. Fortunately, I have excellent reflexes. Roger, the owner of the shop, escorted her out. It had been nice of him to hire me. I think he knew my presence would bring in some much-needed business, but I wondered how long it would take him to tire of being a bouncer in a coffee bar. I often thought the entire experience felt like a study of human nature.

Becky, on the other hand, split her time between showing houses and creating content meant to show me off to the world. At night, after a long day, we'd sit down at the table together to eat dinner. We both had a lot to say to each other, but instead of speaking, the words hung in the air and waited for their moment in the spotlight. It was going to be a long summer.

I'd only been home a week when Celeste struck back for that email. It was the match that lit a media firestorm. Celeste, never one to miss an opportunity, had posted Becky's full email online to show just how deranged Becky was. Celeste even went so far as to accuse her of hiring an actress to play me. That took things too far. A war of sorts broke out between them, and their ratings soared.

It wasn't long before Becky was nearly back to her original Mommy Time numbers, and each move by the dueling Mommy vloggers was more intense than the last. They both began hurling veiled threats at each other. They may have both been milking the system, but there was no doubt that the mutual hatred was real. I kept waiting for a bit of peace, but I should have known better. Becky and peace were mutually exclusive concepts.

I was just finishing up my shift on a stormy Thursday afternoon when I received a call from the hospital. Becky had been in a pretty bad accident. Her injuries weren't life-threatening. She'd been very lucky, they said, but she was going to need a ride home. I told them I'd be right there. I assumed the wet road conditions were to blame, but a couple of uniformed police officers were there to greet me. They informed me the accident had been intentional. Becky's brakes had been tampered with. They wanted to know if anyone held a grudge against her. I could tell by the way they looked at me that I was a suspect, so I told them about Celeste. I left Dad out of it. He would never do such a thing, and he'd been through enough. I showed them Celeste's latest video. The one where she promised that Becky's ruin was coming. I don't know if it satisfied them. They just said they'd be in touch.

I went out and pulled into the circle as instructed by the hospital staff. A nurse stood waiting with Becky in a wheelchair. She looked broken, like an injured bird, crumpled and helpless. She slid gingerly into the car. A hiss of pain escaped through gritted teeth. I open my mouth to say something.

"I'd rather not talk about it," she said.

"Have you got any prescriptions?" I asked.

She pulled a form out of her purse. I nodded and took a right turn, heading towards the pharmacy. I had to ask for her birthdate, which was awkward. On the way home, I noticed the occasional sidelong glances. She was wondering if it was me who'd cut her brakes.

By the next day, though, she had acquired a neck brace and was filming a video accusing Celeste of attempted murder. She also claimed she'd been mugged at gunpoint earlier in the week, which was the first I'd heard of such an incident. Inwardly, I cringed. If her audience didn't think she was crazy before, they certainly would after this. People tuned in for the same reason they watched people getting hit in the balls or falling off skateboards. Human pain is the one form of entertainment most people can't resist.

After dinner on Saturday, I felt that familiar craving for normalcy. I poured myself a glass of wine and stared out of the window. The landscaping was full of freshly planted flowers. I went outside and took a closer look. They were all fake. It was considerable work for a woman in a neck brace. A few minutes later, she wandered out with a strange look on her face. I asked her how the rest of her day had gone. She eyed me warily and mumbled, "Fine," then left. I returned inside and saw her go upstairs, taking her pain pills with her. I finished my glass of wine and poured another.

* * *

That night, I dreamed I was trying to cross a gentle stream. It was shallow and tranquil at first. The way the sunlight glinted on the top of the water was beautiful. But as soon as I got to the middle, it got deeper, and the water began rushing around me. Suddenly, it was a raging river, and I was swept downstream. I tried to clutch for something to hold onto, but there was nothing. And the further I was carried, the more I began to struggle. It was as if an invisible force was pulling me under, and I knew I was about to die.

I awoke in a pile of sweat and twisted sheets. My stomach muscles were sore from dry heaving half of the night. I dragged myself up and into the bathroom to splash some cold water on my face. The nausea seemed to be over, but it left a trail of red dots around my eyes. True crime aficionados call it petechial hemorrhaging. They talk about it in strangulation cases. But for me, it was caused by the pressure in my head from vomiting. It could have been food poisoning from Becky's chicken. She never was much of a cook, but I wasn't sure. It was my turn to be paranoid and skeptical.

I blinked and tried to focus on the red digits on the clock. It was noon already. I needed to get cleaned up. I would have liked to spend the day in bed, but I had to run an errand. I took a shower and drank a little coffee. I felt better. Almost human.

My phone beeped.

ETHAN: Haven't had an update in a while. Let me know you're okay.

Me: I'm okay. Food poisoning last night. Over it now.

Ethan: Food poisoning?

Me: Think so. Don't worry. Almost there.

HE WAS GETTING WORRIED, I could tell. I wasn't sure how much longer he could keep this up. I deleted my text history. I had caught Becky eyeing my phone the other night. I wouldn't put it past her to try and sneak a peek at it. Not that she could get past my password.

I started out the door and was surprised to find Dave's mother on the doorstep.

"Is Dave here?" she asked.

71

"No," I said. "I haven't seen him since he left."

"He came here yesterday morning to get some of his things. I can't get him on his phone." Her face was flushed, and her panic was palpable. "I thought maybe..." Her voice trailed off. I wanted to hug her. To make all her fears go away. Becky might not care much about me, but Dorothy loved her son the way a mother should. She'd always been my favorite grandparent, the one I'd called Nana.

"I'm sorry," I said. "If I see him, I'll let you know."

She nodded and turned to leave. At the last minute, she spun around. "Be careful," she said, then trudged back to her car.

I watched her leave and then got into my car. I went to the library and pulled out my laptop. I had hour after hour of video footage to comb through. When I found what I was looking for, it flooded me with mixed emotions. I didn't know it was possible to feel so vindicated and so sick at the same time. I called and made the arrangements. It was time to end things.

After I arrived home, I waited. I sat in my room and watched Becky come home and check her email. It was a moment I had waited for a long time. She sat and stared at her computer screen. I watched her search her brain for an escape route and come up empty. I went downstairs, and our eyes met. She stood and glared. I pulled out a gun, and the defiance slid off her face. A rush of adrenaline surged up my spine. Justice would finally be done.

"Who are you? Really?" she asked. She crossed her arms and tried to act like she wasn't the least bit worried, but the twitch above her right eye said otherwise. She knew her time was up. She couldn't run anymore.

"Why don't you take a seat," I said. I motioned the gun

to indicate the couch. I didn't want her in the chair. Too close.

"Well," I began. I sat down on the couch opposite her with the gun trained at her chest. I felt Ethan enter the room with the video camera, but I didn't dare take my attention off her. Not for a second. "You know me as truthtllr14."

"I knew that when you showed up," she said. Her lips curled into a sneer. "Tell me something I don't know." She was trying to unsettle me. It wasn't going to work.

"I'm Ellie." Nothing. Not a single hint of recognition on my mother's face. I'm on the sidelines cheering, but no one can see me. I'm on another plane, watching the scene unfold. I'm excited but a little sad that the charade is over. Ellie had done an amazing job of pretending to be me, and she hadn't even been a theater nerd. She had wanted to be a lawyer so she could help. That was her purpose. I watched Becky sink into the couch like cotton quicksand.

"Did she hire you to do this? I guess you think this is ratings gold." She spat out the words like they left a bad taste in her mouth. Does she seriously not remember? Was she that ignorant of my life?

"Alex's best friend," Ellie says. That got her attention.

"You're that little bitch next door. The one Alexia was always abandoning us for," she said.

Ellie's hand was getting tired from holding the gun. She crossed her legs so she could prop it up on her knee without losing her position. From my place just beyond the veil, I could feel every feeling, sense every thought. I was the perfect spectator of life; I just didn't have one anymore. Ellie's hands were sweating, and it made the gun slippery, but I knew she'd win. She had to.

"That's right," Ellie said and smiled at her. I smiled, too.

"You're the one that killed her," Becky said. "With that stupid shirt." Ellie's finger longed to pull the trigger and blast her into next week. If I still had teeth, I'd have been clenching them like the Ethan who was operating the camera. He loved Ellie, and he was scared for her.

"I think we both know who killed her," Ellie said, but she was shaken by the remark. Becky eyed the camera and scoffed at her.

"You think I'm that stupid?" she said.

"It was worth a shot," Ellie said. She leaned back and relaxed on the other sofa. She was trying to look more comfortable than she was. "It doesn't matter. We've got you on video killing Dave." Becky's hand balled into a fist. Her fury was rising, but she didn't dare let it out. Not yet. She looked down and away from Ellie and studied the coffee table in front of her. There was nothing there but a useless crystal ashtray, but I could feel her intentions, and I didn't like it.

"And what exactly is your plan?" she asked. This was an obvious question. I could feel her stalling.

"To find Alex," Ellie said.

I started to feel nervous. Becky was coiling like a rattlesnake. Things aren't the same on this side. Mostly, you just experience the feelings of the living passing around you, like smells in the air. Their world is usually only of a passing interest. After all, you're not a part of it anymore. You're really not even supposed to be here. It must be a strong emotion, or maybe the memory of a strong emotion, for you to experience it on this level of existence. Those strong emotions are what tether you here and cause you to be stuck.

Becky didn't respond at first. She seemed to be turning this information around in her mind.

"You remind me of her," she said. "Impulsive. Foolish.

I bet you came here on a whim, didn't you?" Ellie just smiled. She thought Becky was grasping at straws.

"You sure think you know me for someone who never paid much attention." Now Ellie was the one stalling. I felt her wondering why the cops hadn't arrived. Ethan had sent them the footage of Dad's murder a while ago. They should be beating down the door.

Then Becky lunged. She grabbed the heavy ashtray and hurled it at Ellie, who shifted her head away on instinct. I watched as she dropped the gun. Ellie struggled to hold Becky's arms as Becky clawed the air. Everything was happening so fast. Becky tried to reach for something. The gun. Ellie grabbed Becky's hair, yanking her away. She screamed like an Amazonian giving a war whoop. Ethan intervened with a punch to her windpipe. Becky choked, red-faced. There were voices outside. They'd heard the struggle and tumbled in. Becky recovered slightly and made one last gurgling push for the gun, but one of the officers was too fast. There was a flurry of motion and the clicking of handcuffs. Ellie and Ethan both breathed a sigh of relief. I would have, too, if breathing was still something I did.

The police found Dad and me buried in the garden beneath the fake dahlias. Ellie cried when they told her. She already knew, of course. The second she saw Becky bury Dave on the security cameras she'd hidden, she'd known I'd be there too, but the confirmation still stung.

Becky is waiting for a mental evaluation to see if she's fit to stand trial. I went to watch her in her jail cell. She was telling one of the other inmates about the book she was going to write, but they didn't care. It was the last time I would ever see her.

I brushed Nana's cheek at Dad's funeral. I could feel her pain radiating outward, but she wouldn't be without him long. I could smell her cancer even if she didn't know yet. I wish Dad could have stayed to see it. He'd had been touched by the turnout, but he didn't linger here.

Now that my disappearance had been solved, Ellie could finally see Ethan and how he felt about her, and she realized that she loved him back. She was going to be okay.

As for me, I told you in the beginning that I had a dream and that I was stuck — and that was true. My soul needed to realize that dream so badly it kept me chained here. I needed just one last performance to let it all go. The narrator may not be an exciting part, but it is a part nonetheless, and I have played it. I can see the bright lights of the city now. It's not Broadway, but it will have to do.

Bedlam Beth

SEAN PLATT

Bedlam Beth

SEAN PLATT

THE BITTER TANG OF BLOOD MINGLED WITH THE PEATY aroma of whisky as Beth poured two fingers of Artemis Tull into a cut crystal glass. She took a swig.

Amber liquid burned a fiery path down her throat before settling like molten lead on the barren floor of her stomach. The whisky's warmth did little to thaw the icy rage that filled her bowels.

The soft glow of gas-lit chandeliers cast sinister shadows across the mahogany furniture and velvet draperies.

She set the glass down on the end table with a hard grimace and an unsteady hand while looking around at the opulent New York apartment. Soaring ceilings adorned by intricate plasterwork infuriated her further. She wanted to tear all the gilt-framed masterpieces from the walls with her bare hands, smash the crystal chandelier and stemware to dust, and set the lush Persian carpets ablaze. Watch it all turn to ash, like her former life.

It was just the two of them in the room. Beth walked

over and sat in the ornate wood chair next to the bed. She looked at Richard lying on his side.

Bound and helpless, his once-pristine suit was now rumpled and stained with sweat. His gaze was focused on the only door, a trapped animal seeking escape where none existed. Because nothing could stand in the way of her reckoning.

"There's no one out there to help you," she said.

His eyes flew to her. She saw hatred in them despite his trying to hide it.

"Drink?" Beth held the half-empty bottle toward the bed with a wry smile. It was hard not to snarl at the contemptible wretch. "Guess not, seeing as you're all tied up at the moment."

He strained against his bonds, rough hemp biting into the soft flesh of his wrists. Beads of sweat stood out on his pale brow despite the chill in the air. His grunting was loud in the otherwise quiet room, like a pig squealing for its life. The only other sounds came from the window. The clomping of horses on cobblestones on the street below.

"What the hell is going on here, Elizabeth? You better be careful, or I'll—"

"You'll *what*, Richard?" A harsh bark of laughter revealed the jagged gap of black where her front tooth used to be. "In case you haven't noticed, I'm the one calling the shots. Literally." And she pulled out a revolver and aimed it at his chest, her finger caressing the trigger. "And I've got a bullet in the chamber with your name on it."

Richard recoiled.

Beth leaned back in the armchair and dangled a long and lazy leg over the side. She took another swallow of Artemis. This time, eschewing the glass. Holding the bottle to her mouth and relishing the burn.

She caught a glimpse of her reflection in the mirror to the right of the bed. Her left eye was swollen nearly shut, and her lip split and caked with crusting blood. Her formerly fine silk dress hung in tattered ribbons from her thin frame, mottled splotches of crimson marring the darkened, delicate fabric.

She had a hundred and one opportunities to change into a less macabre dress before arriving in New York, but all the horrified looks from passengers on the train were worth it just to see the unbridled fear in Richard's eyes now.

"What happened to you?" His eyes darted to the massive stone fireplace on the far wall.

"Eyes on me!" All traces of humor vanished from her tone like smoke on a windy day. He bared his teeth but did as she requested. She smiled, then leaned forward and tapped the revolver against his forehead.

He winced.

"We've got a lot of ground to cover, and I'd hate for you to miss the important bits. You want to know what happened to your sweet, innocent fiancé, Richard?"

"'Course I do!" His quivering voice declared otherwise.

"Well, when do you think this story starts?" She sat back, studying his face. Strange, she once thought him handsome. Seemed like another lifetime ago. He stared at her. But she was genuinely interested in his answer.

"I don't know," he said.

"It was a cold December night ..."

Beth let her *Once upon a time* hang in the room like a noose around Richard's neck. He swallowed with effort. As though a rope were already at his throat.

"December?" He sounded confused.

"Yes ... did you think my story would start with you?"

He said nothing.

"Because it started the night you destroyed my life and left me for dead."

Richard swallowed again.

"The Wild Horses Saloon was my pride and joy — the most illustrious haven of high spirits and even higher standards west of the Mississippi. I had a loyal clientele and girls who'd walk through hellfire for me. Enough whisky to float a fleet full of schooners. It was a dream until you ripped it all away." She held out a bloody arm. "Like a rug yanked out from beneath my still dancing feet."

"You never—"

"YOU'LL GET YOUR TURN!" She was loud enough that Richard shrank back against the pillows.

Beth dropped her voice to a whisper, her gaze turning inward as the memories came thundering back like a herd of wild stallions. Kicking up dust. Kicking up emotions. "It was damn near three in the morning. I was dead asleep, curled up in my feather bed, blissfully unaware of the nightmare about to unfold. Then they came."

"*Who* came?"

But he knew.

She drew a breath, the sound like leaves skittering across a grave. "Masked men, a dozen at least. Busted down my doors like they were made of paper. Next thing I know, I got a gun barrel pressed to my temple and rough hands yanking me out of bed by my hair."

He turned his eyes toward the fireplace.

"Eyes on me," Beth said. Her voice hard like a gavel in a courtroom.

"They beat me, Richard. Beat me until I couldn't see straight until my blood painted the snow in crimson ribbons. I begged for help, screamed until my throat was bloody as the rest of me. The whole town heard. But do you know who came to help?"

Richard shook his head.

"No one. Nobody came. The mayor, Doc Harrington, even old Cecil. They all watched my bones break, and my body bleed. All three of them cowards just stood there, indifferent as the stars."

She closed her eyes and took a deep breath. She would not cry in front of this wretch of a man. He may have hurt her, but he did not break her. She opened her eyes and reached for the bottle, bruised fingers tightening around the neck of Tull.

"But it wasn't just me, dear Richard. They dragged my girls into the street like sacks of grain. Lined them up in front of the Wild Horses and put bullets in their heads." She spoke each name as though it were a bullet. "Lana, Kitty, Jade, Gwen … all of them gone in a merciless heartbeat."

"Elizabeth, what does any of this have to do with—"

"I told you to shut your fucking mouth!" Beth tossed the bottle aside, and poor Artemis shattered. The smell of whisky erupting from the broken glass. And she pressed the muzzle hard against Richard's sweat-slick forehead.

"Jesus Christ."

"You wanted to know what happened to your precious fiancé? Well, I'm telling you. So sit there like a good little boy and listen, or I'll take out your eyes so all you have left are your ears!"

He shrank back against the pillows, his horrified eyes wide enough now to nearly roll right out of their sockets without her help. She smelled urine. He'd pissed himself. The smell didn't bother her. If anything, it made her nostalgic for a Saturday night at the Wild Horses.

Beth gave him a frosty smile and settled back, gun still trained on his rotten heart.

"After my girls were executed like strays, they set fire to

the Wild Horses. Burned my life to cinders. Then they strung me up like a damn dog in front of the smoking ruins. Left me to die."

Beth pulled her dress away from her neck and leaned forward. The wound had healed, but the scars were forever. A necklace against her skin. She'd wear it with pride. She fought death. And fucking won.

She got up, kicked aside a splinter of glass, and walked around the bed to a table on the far side of the room. She stepped over the dead butler on the floor. His blood had soaked into the carpet, making it squishy. She pulled out a bottle of whisky. Freed it of its cork. Then walked back to her chair, leaving a trail of bloody footprints.

She sat and took a long pull from the bottle.

"Is that it?" Richard asked.

"I'm just getting started." She laughed. "By some miracle, I didn't die that night. Amos Flynn, the town drunk, stumbled across me on his way home from Rosie's."

She shrugged like the truth of it all meant nothing. "He cut me down and carried me to his place above the livery. Never thought I'd owe my life to that pickled old coot. But he tended my wounds, fed me broth, nursed me back from the brink of death like a guardian angel soaked in juniper fumes. It was spring by the time I could sit on a horse without screaming. But the pain was a small price to pay for—"

"For?"

She leaned forward, elbows on her knees, revolver dangling negligently from her fingers as she bored into him with her gaze, daring the soon-to-be dead man to flinch.

"For seeing spring arrive and, with it, a chance for revenge." She smiled. "Sheriff Hawkins hadn't been in town the night they strung me up. He was detained in Rivet's Gulch. No doubt a ploy to keep away because the bastard always carried a torch for me. Soon as he heard I still had air in these lungs, he did some digging on my behalf. Turns out, the mangy curs who attacked me and mine had ridden in from Broken Spur, led by the notorious Bender Brothers."

Beth sat back, a mirthless smile playing about her lips. She took another long swig, drawing the moment out as she swallowed, whisky burning like hellfire. Richard tried to keep his face still. But she saw the mask of guilt and fear.

"You've heard of the Bender Brothers, right Richard? Even all the way out here in New York City."

Beth didn't wait for him to answer. "The Benders were the meanest, most ruthless sons of bitches to ever spur a horse. They had a reputation for leaving a trail of blood and broken bodies wherever they rode. And they'd set their sights on the Wild Horses." She got up and walked to the window, looking out onto another world. Buildings pressed against one another like they were huddled there for warmth. Streets full of gentry. Horses and carriages. Starving dogs. All going about their day, completely oblivious to the justice unfolding in this room.

Beth turned back to Richard and narrowed her eyes. "So, have you?"

Richard swallowed. "Have I ever what?"

"Heard of the Bender Brothers?"

"'Course I've never heard of 'em. Why would I have heard of them?" Richard shifted uneasily, ropes creaking as he strained against them. "They're all the papers write about when they're telling stories of the West — but why would they target you?"

Beth's bitter laugh was a bone-seeping winter chill on bare skin. "You think men like that need a reason to destroy something beautiful? They did it because they could, Richard. Because they wanted to watch me suffer. And they thought they left me a broken shell of a woman. Know what clay is, Richard?"

He nodded.

"Yeah. That's me. I get harder when I go through the fire. Not softer."

Beth paced the room, revolver twirling in her hand. "So after a season of healing, I was strong enough to give the devil a run for his money. I packed my bag and, saddled a borrowed horse and set about attending to some unfinished business."

She paused by the window, staring out once again at the gas-lit street below. "First, I paid a visit to Mayor Harding and Doc Harrington. Two of the three men who stood by and watched as my world burned. They both begged for mercy when they saw me on their doorsteps. Just like I had begged for their help that night."

Beth turned back to Richard, a cruel smile playing about her lips. "I slit their throats, Richard. Their lifeblood spilled onto their wooden floorboards, and I watched them die. Just like they'd watched my girls bleed out in the snow. A fitting end for two spineless cowards."

Richard made a choking sound, his face gone milk-pale. "You ... you murdered them? In cold blood?"

"No, their blood was quite warm," Beth said, looking down at her hands. "Though I may have felt a chill from the air. As for old Cecil, I took my time with him. Carved him up like a Christmas ham, piece by piece, until he was begging for the mercy of death. But I didn't grant it until I'd paid him back tenfold for every ounce of suffering he'd caused me and mine."

She resumed her seat, crossing her legs with a sensuous rustling of silk. "And with that bit of housekeeping out of the way, I set off for Broken Spur. It was a long, hard ride, but I barely felt the miles. I kept picturing the look on Jeb's face when he realized the mistake he'd made in leaving me to die instead of filling me full of bullets.

"Who's Jeb?" Richard asked. "I thought the sheriff told you it was the Bender brothers who attacked your saloon?"

"Jeb Bender, the eldest brother. Meanest and most ruthless of the bunch by far. He's the one who put that gun to my head and brayed like a donkey while his men beat me senseless."

Beth leaned forward, inches from his face. "And he's the one I was determined to find. Didn't take me long. He was holed up at the Scarlet Dove with a pretty little thing named Cora."

A wistful look crossed her face, there and gone in a flash. "Cora reminded me of my Kitty. All big eyes and soft curves. Jeb didn't deserve a woman like that. But then, men like him don't deserve much of anything in this life. They're naught but rabid dogs, fit only for the bullet or the noose."

"Please ... Elizabeth, what does any of this—"

She punished Richard's interruption with a lingering look. He broke off, sighing.

"I bided my time, watching and waiting for when Jeb would leave the Dove. Planning to make him suffer in ways he couldn't even imagine. I'd start by cutting off his lying tongue, then work my way down and liberate him from his withered excuse for a manhood. By the time I was done, he would be begging *me* to end *his* miserable life."

Richard paled.

"But know what I don't have, Richard?"

He shook his head.

"Patience. Jeb took too long to show his face. So I walked into the Crimson Dove myself. Found him three sheets to the wind, one hand down Cora's bodice and the other groping for his shot glass, his piggy little eyes glassy with lust and liquor. I wanted to gut him right then and there."

"*And did you?*" The words seemed to leave him involuntarily.

She stood abruptly, the revolver clenched tight in her fist. "No. I walked up to him like a storm approaching the shoreline. Jeb didn't recognize me at first, not with my face all healed. But when he did, it was almost like the ghosts of his misdeeds had been expecting me."

Beth threw her head back and laughed without mirth. "He was expecting me, alright," Beth rested the revolver against her shoulder, pacing the room again, the weapon glinting in the firelight. She stopped to wipe her brow. It was warm in here. Not all that sweat on Richard's forehead was fear. She walked over to the window, slid the revolver into its holster, then cracked it open. Fresh air rolled in along with the noise. Even if Richard screamed, he wouldn't be heard. They were too far up.

"Fool that I was, I actually thought I could take him on my own. Walked right into his trap, bolder than a matador waltzing into the bullring. Jeb made me pay handsomely for my hubris. And that's when I learned you don't take vengeance with your heart. You take it with your mind."

"He had his boys work me over real good. Beat me until I was choking on my own blood." Her face twisted with remembered pain. "Then he handed me over to the Unholy Three."

"The what?" Richard asked.

"The Unholy Three. The meanest, most ruthless bitches I'd ever laid eyes on. I don't imagine you've ever heard of 'em?"

"No." The liar shook his head.

"Of course not. They're far too skilled to have their names spilled in the black ink of the press. Well, they loomed over me like vultures circling a dying mule, their eyes glinting with anticipation, their sneers promising pain beyond imagining. Like I hadn't already suffered enough."

"Did you kill them?"

Beth blinked. "Kill them?"

"Well, you're here."

Beth sat back. "You're getting ahead of the story. Don't you want to know about the Unholy Three?"

"Sure." She could tell by his tone that he didn't.

"Sadie was a former Union spy. She had a talent for disguise and an unrelenting thirst for blood. Ruby lived up to her name. A fiery-haired temptress who could charm the pants off a preacher while picking his pockets. And Belle, raised in the south with plantation money, nursing a bilious hatred of the aristocracy and anything that stunk of injustice." She paused. Remembering that night, the reason she went after Jeb sent Beth back into the dark embrace of her most hellish memories.

The crack of the gunshots, the screams of her girls as they fell. Kitty's face, her blue eyes wide with terror. Crying out when the bullet tore through her chest. Lana, her dark hair matted with blood, her lips moving in a silent prayer. But no prayer would help. Gwen, dead before she even hit the dirt. And gentle Jade, Beth's favorite. They didn't shoot her. Oh no. They slit her throat ear to ear, her blood staining the snow. And then, as she hung, spinning, ash falling on her bloody limbs, the acrid stench of smoke and burning flesh.

The world lost all its color, leaving only a monochrome of loss and vengeance.

Richard's eyes were darting around for an escape that wasn't there and would never be coming.

"Eyes on me," Beth said.

He jerked as though surprised to see she was not as lost in the past as he thought.

"You ask why a man like Jeb Bender would target a woman like me?" Beth sneered at Richard. "It was for the gold."

She took another sip of whisky. Silence stretched between them, filled with the sounds of the street below.

"Wild Horses was more than just a whorehouse and a gin joint. My saloon was a community. A place where folks came to forget their troubles, even if only for a spell. And like any good community, we looked after our own. The gold supposedly stashed in the saloon couldn't be found when the Bender Boys came to look for it. Know why?"

Richard shook his head."

"Because it was hidden somewhere they'd never think to look — and they tore the place apart. Because it was in the homes of the people who loved me. Gordy, the blacksmith, buried it deep beneath the coals of his forge; Angela, the seamstress, stitched it into the hems of her dresses; and Preacher Thomas sealed it up tight in the church's stone walls. They risked everything to keep it safe because they knew I'd do the same for them."

She swirled Artemis, watching the golden liquid, then set the bottle on the floor. "You asked what happened to the Unholy Three?"

Richard nodded.

"Well," she smiled. "I made them an offer they couldn't refuse. Promised if they helped me kill Jeb Bender, all that gold was theirs. Funny how loyalty shifts when there's money on the table." She chuckled. "He was trussed up like a hog for slaughter ten minutes later. And I was carving into his flesh with a rusted hunting knife, savoring each scream and plea for mercy like a fine wine.

He sputtered and cursed, spitting venom like a rattlesnake at me. Do you want to know what happened next, Richard?"

He didn't answer.

"I took my time with him. Each scream, each plea for mercy, was like a coin in my coffers. I used every trick learned from the men who hurt me. I took him apart like a doll. With precision and accuracy. His eyes, his nose, each finger, each toe, his cock. But not his tongue. I still needed that. And with Jeb falling to literal pieces, he finally told me the truth. The person who told him about the gold — that was you, Richard."

For a moment, his name hung between them like a horse thief from a rope.

"He's a liar!" Richard shouted. Then, like it would make any difference to his fate, he added, "And you can't prove it because that never happened. I don't even know this Jeb."

Beth listened for a moment to the clip-clop of the horses. If she closed her eyes, she might be able to imagine herself back home. But the air. It smelled different here in New York City.

"No. Although I did bring you this." She reached down into the satchel on the floor next to the window and pulled out a cloth packet.

"Sorry about the smell." It had been decomposing for some time.

She unwrapped it for Richard, given his hands were occupied with trying to loosen the bindings at his wrists. Held up a decomposing tongue, then tossed it at him.

He recoiled, gagging. "What the hell is that?"

"Jeb's tongue. You don't remember it? Because he was certainly able to describe you accurately. Telling me all about the man with a fancy New York City accent who promised him a fat stack of cash to put me in the ground and burn the Wild Horses to cinders."

"That's not true! I never wanted to hurt you, Elizabeth!" Richard shook his head frantically, his face ashen. "I loved you! Just because you left—"

"LIAR!" Beth backhanded him across the face, splitting his lip before using the other hand to wallop his skull with the butt of her gun. "You *never* loved me. I was just another possession to you — something to be bought and sold like cattle."

"After I put a bullet in Jeb Bender's brain, I rode east with the Unholy Three. They'd gotten a taste for blood and gold and were eager for more. We made for New York. Boarded a train and rode the rest of the way here. I'm sure you can imagine the looks people were giving us."

"I didn't do what you think I did—"

"It was so easy to find you." Her smile was cold and cruel. "Still a creature of habit, living in the same fancy townhouse, lording your wealth over everyone like a petty tyrant." She gestured toward the body on the opposite side of the bed. "You even had the same butler. Old Higgins. Always willing to cover up your crimes."

She leaned in close, her breath hot against his cheek. "I heard all about what you'd been up to while I was gone. How you'd gone through two wives already, both dead under mysterious circumstances. How you treated the rest of your staff like dogs, beating them for the slightest infraction. I even heard tell of the little girls you'd bring to your bed, barely old enough to bleed."

Richard squirmed beneath her.

"You're a coward, Richard, a man who hides behind money and power, using them to crush anyone who dares stand in your way. But now, do you know what you are?"

Beth traced the barrel of her gun along his jaw,

relishing the way he flinched at its touch. She'd dreamed of this moment for years.

"You're a sniveling worm, a pathetic excuse for a man. But there is nowhere left to hide. There are no more tricks up your sleeve. Your sins have finally caught up with you. I am the judgment you thought you could escape. I am the reckoning you've been running from. I am the devil who will send you to hell."

He screamed, tossing and turning on the bed. Trying to tear his bindings apart. But they only dug deeper into his skin, bloodying the sheets.

She let him have his tantrum.

A shadow moved behind the closed bedroom door.

Beth got up and cracked the door. "I'm good."

Then she closed it again and returned to her seat.

He watched her. "Who is out there?"

"Did you really think you could run forever, Richard? That you could destroy my life and walk away unscathed?" Her smile was cold. "Well, I'm here to collect what's owed."

"I don't owe you anything!" Richard protested. "You're the one who walked out on our marriage."

"Leaving here was the smartest thing I ever did. I'd rather die a hundred times than be shackled to a monster like you."

She was known as Elizabeth back then. Boarding a train with only the clothes on her back and the gold she had stolen from Richard's safe.

She'd shed her past like a serpent shedding its skin, the trappings of her old life falling away as the iron wheels rolled west. She buried Elizabeth Hollingsworth in an unmarked grave deep within the recesses of her mind, a ghost of a girl she no longer recognized.

And in her place rose Beth Sawyer. Quick with her wit

and quicker with her gun, she'd carved out a new life for herself in the wild, untamed West.

"I rode the first train west, all the way to Barren Flats. Walked right into the Wild Horses and made the owner an offer he couldn't refuse. By evening, I was running the saloon dealing cards and pouring whisky like I'd been born into the work."

A shadow crossed her face. "I should have known it was too good to last. Should have been ready for you to come looking for me. I let my guard down, and it cost me everything."

"Elizabeth, listen."

"That's not my name." She stood, looking at Richard. "One word from you earns three bullets from me. Understand?"

He nodded.

She turned to the door. "You can come in now."

Richard's eyes flew to the door as it opened. A trio of feminine figures were silhouetted against the hallway's flickering light. They stepped into the room, their footsteps silent on the plush carpet. They took their places beside the roaring fireplace.

A tall, willowy woman with raven hair and eyes like chips of obsidian, wearing a dress the color of spilled blood, her lips painted to match. She held a long and wicked-looking knife, blade gleaming in the firelight.

A stout, muscular woman with close-cropped blonde hair and a face lined with scars like old luggage. Dressed in men's clothing, a pair of black trousers and a white shirt rolled up to her forearms. A pair of stained brass knuckles glinted on her fingers.

And a slender, almost delicate-looking woman with fiery red hair and a dusting of freckles across her nose. Her green dress was simple, but there was nothing simple about the way she moved.

"You already know my friends," Beth said.

Richard's eyes widened in horror, his mouth opening and closing like a fish gasping for air, straining harder than ever against his bonds.

Beth smiled as he squirmed, sinking into his fear like a warm bath. She walked over and closed the window, sealing them inside the room. There was no one left in the house to hear his last words.

The staff had scattered as soon as they entered.

The Unholy Three remained silent, their faces impassive. There was a pot on the flames already. The raven-haired woman stirred contents with her knife, the metal clanging against the sides in a discordant rhythm. The blonde woman cracked her knuckles, the sound like the snapping of bones. And the redhead uncoiled her rope, running it through her fingers in a lover's caress.

Richard's face was ashen and slick with sweat. He looked at Beth with pleading eyes, but there was no mercy in her gaze.

The scent of molten metal filled the air, acrid and choking. The pot bubbled and hissed, the gold within glowing like the fires of hell.

Beth gave the trio a nod. Sadie put her knife away, donned thick leather gloves, and grabbed the fireplace tongs. Carrying the pot over to the bed, molten gold sloshing and bubbling with an eerie glow.

Richard thrashed against his bonds. "What is that? What is that?"

Ruby climbed up on the bed behind him, looped her nose around his neck, and pulled, keeping his head in place.

"It's your gold, Richard. You're so desperate to have it back. So here it is."

Sadie punched him in the guts.

He bellowed. Loud. Beth grabbed his jaw in an iron grip and kept his mouth open.

Then Sadie tipped the pot, watching dispassionately as liquid gold sluiced down his gurgling throat. His screams deflating into a symphony of agony.

He convulsed, his body spasming grotesquely as the molten metal burned through his insides.

And then it was over. Richard slumped back against the pillows, his eyes wide and glassy. Tendrils of hardened gold spilled from his mouth and nose, glinting obscenely in the firelight.

"It's done." Beth was breathing hard.

The four women looked down at him.

"What now?" Ruby asked, unwinding her rope from Richard's neck.

"Home?" Sadie asked, stepping off the bed and tossing the pot into the fire.

Ruby held out a hand, and Beth passed her the Artemis. Then she shrugged and gestured to the open safe. The man was so predictable he hadn't even changed the combination. "We have a new stash. We can start fresh. Rebuild from the ashes."

Bedlam Beth, born in blood. Hardened by justice. Free.

For now.

Dead Men Don't Sell

KIM M. WATT

Dead Men Don't Sell

KIM M. WATT

GLORIA STONE LOOKED AT THE THREE MEN — HER publisher, her editor, and her agent — seated across the table from her, took a sip of sparkling water, then said, "No."

"Gloria," Art started, his voice all soft edges, as if he were dealing with a three-year-old refusing to eat her vegetables, and for one moment, she considered throwing her drink across the table at him, imagining the splash of fizzy liquid swiftly followed by the smack of solid glass meeting his supercilious bloody nose.

"I said no," she repeated, keeping her voice level, even if one part of her was still wondering what sort of sound the tumbler would make. Would it be more of a crunch or a splat? But she could neither throw the glass nor raise her voice because no matter how much these men needed her, needed her work, they'd still all think, *women's problems. Hysterical. Irrational. Must be that time of the month.* As if rage wasn't a perfectly proportionate reaction to being treated like an infant.

"Gloria, be reasonable," Cameron said. At least he just

sounded annoyed rather than placating, his perfectly groomed eyebrows fighting valiantly against the Botox to knit together. "We've had this conversation before." He frowned at her over his Caesar salad (hold the dressing, hold the Parmesan, hold the bacon, only five croutons, and what was the point of that? It was a plate of insipid leaves with a couple of strips of grilled chicken trying desperately to liven things up).

"We have," Gloria agreed, winding pasta onto her fork. "But that was before my books were the top earners in your catalog." She raised her eyebrows at Art, who sighed.

"Yes," he admitted, lacing his hands together over his formidable belly. "But we want to keep it that way. Don't you?"

"Of course I do. But do my readers *really* want yet another book about murdered women? Aren't there enough out there already? Aren't there enough out there in *real life?*"

"No one wants to read about murdered men," Brice said, barely looking up from his tuna carpaccio. He was a small, slight man, his glasses pushed up on his forehead. She'd thought he might be her ally in this. Editing book after book about women getting killed in inventive ways must get wearying. "Murdered men aren't sexy."

Then again, maybe she'd misjudged him. "*Sexy?* You think murdered women are *sexy?*"

"Not like that," he said around a mouthful of fish, then glanced at Art.

The publisher cleared his throat, smoothing his waist-coat — seriously, who wore a *waistcoat?* — and gave Gloria an indulgent smile. "Sexy as in they sell," he explained. "Murdered men don't sell."

Gloria had the brief thought that she'd find it quite sexy to stick a fork in the big man's eye, then she gave her agent an appealing look. "Cameron. I can't write about more women being killed. I *can't*. Let me at least try. One book with a serial killer hunting men instead of women. *One.*"

"You're only as good as your last book," Art said, nodding sagely as he swirled his wine in his glass.

"Well, my last book was very bloody good," Gloria snapped. "Especially for your bank account."

No one spoke for a moment, the only sound Brice scraping his plate carefully with his fork. Cameron and Art looked at each other, and Gloria took a sip of her water, the pasta suddenly rough in her throat. It was so unfair the way they could dictate to her. Dictate to her *creativity*, like it was a shopping list rather than an art form. It shouldn't work like this, but it always did.

Finally, Cameron said, "Look, why don't we try it? One book, and we see what the response is. You've got a good enough readership now that they'll forgive a bit of a slip."

Gloria didn't answer, looking at Art. Her heart was going too fast. She *needed* this. She needed to not be thinking constantly about inventive ways to kill off women. It was getting so just the thought of sitting down at her computer made her stomach tight with anxiety.

Art set his glass down and leaned back, pursing his lips, which were damp with red wine.

Gloria put her fork down. She wasn't hungry anymore.

Art nodded slowly. "It's a risk."

"It'll work," Gloria promised. "Plenty of people are sick of the women-as-victims trope."

"As long as they're the same people who read your books," he said, picking up his glass again and raising it. "Here's to some sexy male murders, then."

Gloria raised her own glass, her smile stretched with disbelief. "To some sexy male murders."

They clinked glasses, the sound crisp and dangerous amid the low murmur of the restaurant, full of the promise of breakage.

#

Gloria lay in the middle of the thick wool rug that took up half the floor of her study, arms and legs starfished as she stared at the ceiling. There were cobwebs in one corner, and the window was wearing wintery smears. She'd have to get Eva to clean in here next time she was in. Gloria usually didn't let anyone into the study unless she was in between books, and she was very much not in between books right now. Or maybe she was if one considered that the five false starts in her drafts file were all as dead as the characters in them.

"Sexy male murders," she told the cobweb. "*Sexy male murders.* Male murder sexy. Murder sexy males? Someone targeting male escorts? Dancers? Models? Young farmer of the damn year calendar boys?" She groaned and pressed her hands over her eyes. This was not working. It was not working in the most spectacular way. She wasn't sleeping. She was living on coffee. She'd never been so blocked in her *life.* And Cameron was expecting an outline by the end of next week.

She'd tried all her usual tricks. Long walks, bundled up against the chill bite of the wind and the icy winter rain, people-watching and *what-if*-ing. Meditation. Kickboxing classes. Stream-of-consciousness journaling. She'd even tried a damn sensory deprivation tank, which had worked once before, but this time it had made her so anxious she'd banged on the lid and screamed to be let out ten minutes in.

"Ice cream," she said, sitting up. "I need brain food." If nothing else, there'd be some comfort to be had in shoveling fat spoonfuls of mint chocolate chip into her face, and she definitely needed comfort right now.

It was later than she'd realized, getting on for midnight. She'd lost another entire evening staring at a blank screen and poking her subconscious, waiting for something to happen. But the 24-hour store that sold everything from paint sample tins to Spam to fake flowers would be open, and she'd probably be able to find some form of mint chocolate chip ice cream. Or at least chocolate, which would do in a pinch.

The roads were slick with steady, drenching rain and quieter than during the day, but still filled with steady city traffic, taxis, Ubers, and delivery drivers weaving across lanes and shooting through amber lights. Gloria took her time getting to the shop. The sooner she had her ice cream and went home, the sooner she'd have to confront the empty screen again, and she did *not* fancy it. But it was only a few blocks to the store, and before long, she was digging through the freezer, pushing aside the endless cookie dough and cookies-and-cream variations (seriously, soggy cookie crumbs in ice cream? *Abomination*) in search of creative elixir. She finally found one tub of mint chocolate chip wedged at the very back, wearing a crown of ice crystals that made her think it had been in there since the store first opened, but she took it anyway. Even freezer-burned mint chocolate chip was better than the freshest cookies-and-cream monstrosity.

There were no parking spaces available outside the shop, so Gloria had parked in the alley around the corner. The rain-smeared streetlights didn't quite reach her car, rendering the shadows murky as she scurried toward it, clutching her prize, the wind off the river sharp-toothed enough to claw through every gap in her clothing. She threw the ice cream onto the passenger seat as she clambered in and tried to pull her door shut.

But it didn't close. She looked up, startled. Low light glimmered on a blade held to the window, and she saw gloved fingers hooked around the door. She didn't think, just reacted, slamming the door closed as hard as she could, crushing the fingers into the gap as the figure outside yelped.

"You *bitch!*" He — of course, it was a he — tried to jerk his hand away, and this time Gloria threw the door open, putting all her weight behind it. It caught the man in the chest, sending him stumbling back. Then she wrenched the door closed again as he recovered and rushed back. She fumbled the ignition, hearing a faint, panicked whimpering over the surge of blood in her ears. As the man lunged back to the car, she gave up on starting it and threw all her weight on the door again, sending it flying open to meet him. There was a sickening *thud,* understated yet somehow setting up shivers in her belly. The man vanished out of her sight as the door rebounded toward Gloria, slamming shut neatly. She fumbled for the lock, hearing the satisfying *clunk* as she was secured inside, then just sat there, listening to that awful whimpering while she panted, her hands shaking no matter how hard she pushed them against the wheel.

Finally, she swallowed hard, and the whimpering stopped. *Oh,* she thought, with a vague sort of surprise. *That was me.*

She peeked out of the window. There was a crumpled form on the ground outside, a pool of deeper shadow swelling around one end. She closed her eyes, pushed her hands even harder against the wheel, and willed herself to stop shaking. She didn't, but when she opened her eyes, she felt a little steadier. She took a couple of deep breaths and peered out the window again. The form — no, the *body* — was still there, unmoving, and that extra shadow was blood. A lot of it. She looked back at the steering wheel. She could just leave. Drive away. No one would've seen her here. But no, she needed to call the police, and before that, she supposed she should see if he was alive. They'd want to know. She didn't move for a moment, then looked around the car hopefully. Presumably, she had a tire iron of some sort in the back, but she'd never had to use it, so who knew? Besides, it was hardly any help in the boot.

Finally, she picked up the ice cream tub in one hand and eased the door open, keeping her eyes on the body, waiting for the slightest twitch to send her scrambling back to safety. It didn't move, and a moment later, she was standing over her attacker, ice cream tub raised defensively. It took a little longer before she was able to make herself crouch down and check for a pulse, but she hardly thought she needed to. That pool of blood was spreading by the moment, the rain already stealing it off into the gutter, and there was a sizable dent in the man's forehead. He was young, his pale skin vaguely fake-looking in the dim light, as if she were looking at a mannequin or an actor. She almost checked for cameras as if it might be some elaborate set-up. *The Murder Queen Murders Man!*

But there were no cameras, and mannequins don't bleed.

"I'm sorry," she whispered to him as she straightened up, then immediately scowled. *Sorry?* She was *sorry?* He'd attacked her!

"Police," she said to the alley in general and dug in her pockets, but her phone wasn't there. Of course, it wasn't. She'd left it in the living room when she was working in the hope of minimizing distractions, and she hadn't thought to pick it up when she'd rushed out for her ice cream. She looked around the alley, all low gray shadows and smudged angles, softened by rain. She should go back into the shop and get them to call the police. And tell Cameron. The papers were going to love this. *The Murder Queen Strikes Back!* Or, more likely, they'd take another angle. *Writer of Femicides Tastes Own Medicine.* The only thing that would've made it better for them was if she'd been inventively killed by the poor kid on the ground. It didn't work with him being the victim.

It would for her new book, though.

Gloria stood there in the deep shadows of the alley as the rain slowly soaked through her hair to her scalp and ran in chilled little rivulets down her neck and thought, *What if…*

\#

Later, sitting on the ground in the abandoned, dilapidated warehouse and eating ice cream out of the tub with her fingers, she wondered what she'd been thinking. The boy's body was spreadeagled on the ground, arms and legs akimbo (rather as she'd been lying earlier herself), with a pentagram drawn around it in his own blood, and *All Hail Satan* on the wall above. She wasn't sure she could even quite remember doing any of it, although it had seemed very logical at the time. And it *was* logical, right? No point in his death going to waste. This way, he'd end up in the news, capture the attention of the public, and prove that male murders *were* interesting. She was just a bit worried that the warehouse was letting a lot of rain in, as the writing was already running. She took another mouthful of ice cream and noticed that she'd gotten blood on the sleeve of her coat. She'd have to wash that. And check the trunk, although she'd gone back to the shop to buy bags to line it before she put the body in.

She put the lid back on the ice cream and got up,

looking around. She'd found this place when she'd been scouting location ideas for murders in her second book, and it had only grown more decrepit since. Large sections of the roof had fallen in, and the walls were crumbling. The whole thing made quite a striking tableau, lit by the headlights of her car, the body stark and the blood raw and vivid. This was sexy, wasn't it?

She'd soon know.

Gloria turned back to her car, stretching out the kinks in her spine. She'd have to book a massage for the next day. Lugging bodies was hell on the lower back.

\#

Gloria couldn't stop checking the news. It *had* to turn up soon. But all the next day, when she should have been working but instead was hitting refresh on the local news sites and listening to the crappy local talkback station, there was nothing. *Nothing.* In the afternoon, she finally went out in the car, driving past the warehouse. No police tape, no cars, nothing. He hadn't been found yet.

The next morning, she fielded a call from Cameron in which she told him she was *absolutely* almost done with the outline and would have it to him in just a few days, then went for another drive. Her route took her past the warehouse again, even as she told herself that this was how murderers got caught, returning to the scene of the crime. But the place was as still and lifeless as it had been when she'd driven in the other night. Apparently, the old warehouse wasn't much of a haunt for anyone but desperate writers.

On her way home, she googled pay phones and, after some driving around, determined that there didn't seem to be a single one in the city that hadn't been peed on (or worse), smashed to pieces, or was currently in use as a bedroom. So she went and bought a cheap phone at the dodgiest shop she could find, called the police, and immediately threw the phone away. Anonymous tips were more expensive than they used to be, but that was inflation, she supposed.

Then she went back to haunting the news channels.

#

The article was so small she almost missed it, just a few short paragraphs right at the bottom of the news section of a local site, wedged in between a piece on a hamster that had befriended a Rottweiler and another on a woman who had won three raffles in a row at the local rest home and was now banned from entering any other contests. The woman was most distressed by this, apparently.

Gloria was most distressed by the article on the boy's death. The journalist didn't even call it murder, just mentioned that the warehouse was dangerous but known to be used by local youths practicing parkour. The implication seemed to be that it had been an accidental death, and Gloria leaned her elbows on her desk, shoving her fingers into her hair. The rain. The rain must've washed the blood away to such an extent that there hadn't been anything for the police to find. It was just some poor kid abandoned on the floor of a crumbling building without so much as a story to mark his passing.

Or to capture the public's imagination.

"Dammit," Gloria whispered. If it had been a woman, it would've been different. There would've been speculative pieces about what she was doing in the warehouse, what she was wearing, who she might've been there with, how many of them, and how she'd been asking for it by being there in the first place. It wasn't that anyone cared more, just that it was *juicier*. Sexier.

Ugh.

Gloria got up and went to fetch the ice cream from the

freezer, wrinkling her nose at the smudges of blood on the lid. What a waste that had been. All that effort over nothing. She dug a spoon into the ice cream and popped some in her mouth, letting it melt on her tongue. What now? She needed a *story*. She needed to know what sort of death people cared about when it came to men. There had to be *something*, but how did she find out? There was no point in trawling through old cases. She'd already done enough of that, and anyway, people moved on. What excited the public ten years ago was done to death now. It needed to be fresh. New. She looked at the lid again. She needed a different sort of research.

Taking the ice cream with her, she went back up to her study, ignoring her phone ringing in the living room. It'd only be Cameron, *just checking in*. And while she finally thought she had a way forward, he should know better than to think she'd share her process. That was private.

\#

Two days and a lot of research time later, Gloria sat in an old white Toyota that smelled of cigarette smoke, parked across the road from a rundown apartment block. The car had been hired with cash from Craigslist, and she was wearing both a wig and leather gloves. In the apartment block was a man who had just been released on bail, having been arrested for beating his wife so badly she was still in hospital. His son, who had witnessed the whole thing (and presumably all the beatings that had undoubtedly gone before), was with his grandparents. Gloria knew all this because she had read every article and social media post she could find about him, making sure that he wasn't going to be much missed. It had been research, really. How would a female serial killer choose her victims? She felt that was the hook needed, the female killer and her personal, woman-specific method of hunting. How would she cover her tracks? What values would guide her, however twisted?

And now here she was, and of course, she wasn't *really* going to do anything, but on the other hand — she still didn't know how the public would react. Didn't know what sort of calling card would be needed to capture their imagination. Thinking that, she got out of the car and crossed the road, teetering on the unaccustomed high heels of her boots. The wind was cold on her bare thighs, and she hugged her short jacket closer to her. A female serial killer might start with seduction, right? Or at least temptation, using themselves as bait in a trap. She let herself into the lobby, the door hanging loose on the latch, and knocked on the door of the apartment to the left, adjusting the wig carefully.

Heavy footsteps behind the door, and then it was pulled open. She found herself looking up at a giant of a man, his hulking form filling the frame.

"Yeah?"

"Hi," she said, making her voice breathy. "My car broke down. Can I use your phone?"

He stared at her. "You don't have a cell?"

"Battery's dead."

He grunted, then stepped back, giving her a small space to edge past him into the apartment. She could smell him, musk and sweat and rage, and her chest gave a sudden squeeze of panic. She stopped and started to take a step back, but he'd already closed the door behind her.

"Go on," he said to her. "Down the hall."

She went, painfully aware of the shortness of her skirt and her back exposed to him, her eyes drawn to cracks in the walls and dents the shape of fists. The ghosts of one-sided battles lurked in every corner, taped picture frames and faded brown stains on the wallpaper and the suffocating scent of disinfectant. She couldn't breathe for it, her head swimming, and what was she *doing* here? What was she thinking? She had to get out. *Now.*

Gloria spun, meaning to push past the big man and run for the door, but his bulk blocked the whole hall, and when she tried to squeeze past, muttering something about calling her boyfriend, he pushed her back roughly, sending her staggering into the wall.

"Who are you?" he demanded. "Some bloody friend of Fiona's, trying to get me in trouble? That what you're doing? You a reporter?"

"No," Gloria managed, the word a squawk. "No, I just … I just…" She couldn't think of an excuse, a reason, and she wasn't even sure why she *was* here. He pushed her again, this time keeping his hand on her throat as he pressed her into the wall.

"I'm not going to prison," he snarled at her, his breath rank with old meat. "Fiona's going to take it *all* back. All of it. Or it'll be her fault what happens next. You tell her that."

There were black spots in Gloria's vision, and her knees were losing all will to keep her standing in the terrible boots, and she knew he was telling the truth. Knew that Fiona and her son would pay for her being here and that Fiona would somehow believe it *was* her fault for speaking out against a man who was going to kill her one day, and no one would protect her because no one ever did, they'd just say later, *why didn't she leave?* and cluck like reproving chickens over Fiona's foolishness, not this man's violence, because that was how these things worked.

Somehow, the knife was in her hand, and then it was in the man's belly, and he was staggering away, roaring, leaving the blade in her hand and fresh blood scattering the carpet, but at least it was *his* this time. Gloria lunged after him, waving the knife wildly, and the man gave her such a blow to the side of the head that she went tumbling into the little living room, rolling twice when she hit the floor and fetching up against a rickety table. She lay there, struggling for breath and looking at the knife lying on the carpet across the room while the man shouted something at her. He strode over, delivering a sharp kick to her back that sent her into a curled ball of agony. Then she heard him saying, presumably into the phone, "Police? Yeah, I've been *attacked* in my own home! It's—"

Gloria didn't hear the rest. Sickness washed over her in waves, but she wasn't really listening to that either. Because the man had kicked the knife when he charged toward her, spinning it closer, and if she could just uncurl herself, she'd be able to grab it, but her body didn't seem to want to listen. Everything was white, throbbing agony, and all she could do was lie there, trying not to throw up while the man shouted something at her. He stomped away, and she heard water running. Dealing with his wound, perhaps. She'd evidently missed everything vital with the knife. It had been so *easy* with the boy, but she'd got this wrong.

She took a deeper breath, forcing some air into her lungs. It was the size. She hadn't realized how big he was. A misjudgment. Two deep breaths. Uncurl. Reach. Her fingers curled around the handle of the knife.

He was sitting on the toilet, a bloody towel pressed to his abdomen, when Gloria came through the door and buried the blade in his throat. He didn't even have time to raise his hands, and by the time he clutched at her, she'd already stepped back out of reach, watching with wide eyes as blood spurted out of the gaping wound, drenching his bare chest and sagging jogging bottoms. He heaved, launching himself up and toward her, but his legs gave way beneath him, and he thudded to the floor like a felled tree.

Gloria retreated into the hall, looking from him to the knife and back again. When he didn't get up, she turned and fled out of the apartment into the frost-edged night, her back throbbing and the side of her face feeling like it was already swelling.

It didn't stop a small smile from curling her lips, though. This one. *This one* was sexy.

#

Apparently, this one was not sexy. Gloria scowled at her computer, eating mint chocolate chip ice cream that Cameron had delivered that morning after she'd sent him photos of the aftermath of what she told him was a mugging. It was much tastier and fancier than the one from the 24-hour shop, but she was hardly enjoying it, not with the article open in front of her.

"Home invasion," she read. "*Home invasion?* Seriously?"

Apparently so. That was the verdict of the police, despite the fact that the apartment had absolutely nothing to steal in it. Maybe they thought they were covering for Fiona somehow as if she'd hired someone to do her hubby in. Or they just didn't care. Gloria sighed and took another spoonful of ice cream. No one was going to care about a home invasion when it involved one big lump of an abuser. His death didn't even have the little frisson of *schadenfreude* that came with some rich guy being done over. She closed the browser and looked glumly at her blank outline, waiting patiently. At least the mugging story had bought her a month's grace with Cameron. Although what she was going to do with it was a whole other question.

She'd messed up, not thinking about the size discrepancy. Even with a more average-sized man, he'd still be able to overpower her. She needed an advantage. She frowned at the ceiling, noting that the cobweb had grown.

She was going to have to name the spider at this rate. An advantage. Like...

She opened the browser again, going back to the news, searching for the article she'd skipped over earlier. There. Like the smug-faced finance worker who'd been accused of spiking his colleagues' drinks with Rohypnol multiple times over Friday drinks. No one had come forward soon enough to be tested for the drug, so nothing had been proven. It was a he-said, multiple she-said situation, and he was more senior, better protected by lawyers and money, and effortlessly charming in interviews. *See?* that smooth-skinned face seemed to say. *Why would I need to drug women? Who wouldn't want a piece of this?*

Gloria tapped his face on the screen, smearing it with ice cream, then went back to Craigslist.

#

She had considered going the classic route of dropping a tablet in Brett's (of course, he was called Brett) drink, but given the fact that her face was still sporting numerous interesting colors and a split lip, she wasn't sure she'd be able to tempt even a drugged financier to leave the bar with her. So she'd dissolved it in water and decanted it into a syringe, and now she sat on the floor of the car park next to his car, hoping he was going to be at least taking a break from his body count while there was still a fuss in the papers. She couldn't do anything if he came back with company.

Her feet were frozen, and her fingers were stiff with the cold by the time he emerged around the corner from the direction of the main street, swaggering down the car park ramp, thankfully alone, and for one moment, she wondered if she should've just rammed him with a hired car. But no, that wasn't sexy. It'd just be called a hit-and-run. So she just got up, not even having to pretend she was a little shaky, and leaned against the wall, clutching her coat around her.

"Hey," he called as he saw her. "Are you alright?"

"No," she said, slurring her words. "I think … I can't find my car."

He laughed a warm sound that made her skin crawl. "I don't think you should be driving."

"I have to … I have to get home." She pushed off the wall, looking around. "I know I parked here somewhere."

"Let me help you," he said, coming close enough to take her arm. Gloria hoped the worst of the bruising was covered by her makeup and the flat light. If he noticed, he didn't say anything. "I'll give you a lift."

"It'll cost a fortune if I leave my car here."

"You're not driving," he said firmly, and she let herself be maneuvered into a low-slung Audi, sinking into the deep seat. He closed the door on her gently, then went around to the driver's side and climbed in. "What's your add — *hey!*"

The *hey* was because Gloria had just buried the syringe in his neck, then scrambled out of the car before he could add to her collection of bruises. She peered in at him as he pulled the thing out of his neck, not that it was going to help. The contents were already in him, and all she could hope was that they'd act fast enough. She'd made sure it was a pretty hefty dose because she didn't know how long it might take, and she wasn't making the same mistake as last time.

Brett clambered out of the car, keeping one hand on the roof as he rounded the back, heading toward her. "What did you do, you *bitch?*"

"Taste of your own medicine," she managed, trying to keep her voice even. She couldn't, though, because suddenly, this was far too real. He'd seen her face. She couldn't go back. He'd seen her face, and she'd *drugged* him, so she had to carry this through, and now she wasn't sure if she could. She shrank against the wall as he reached the passenger side, one hand on the open door and the other outstretched toward her.

"You," he started, then stopped, swaying slightly. "You…"

Gloria forced herself to straighten up and said, "You should sit down."

"No," he started, not sounding very sure of himself. "Police. *Police!*"

He shouted the last word, and Gloria shoved him, folding him through the door into the passenger seat. He almost slipped off onto the ground, but some instinct made him grab the glove box and steady himself.

"Police?" he said again, blinking at her.

"We'll go to them now," she said. "Get in."

And, miraculously, he did. Gloria shut the door carefully, then stood there for a moment, making sure she still had her back to the security camera (although she had a new wig to go with her heavy makeup, which had added different contours to her face). Her heart was going wildly. She had to finish this. *Had* to. He'd seen her. She had to remember that. Bile rose in the back of her throat, and she swallowed it down with difficulty. The last two … *deaths,* they'd been *deaths*, not murders, had been self-defense. This … if she did this, she really was a killer. She stood there for a moment longer, then got in the driver's side. There was no point overthinking it. She needed to get out of here before someone came along and saw her. That was the important bit right now.

The park was still and silent, empty of even dedicated joggers. Gloria wound her way through the less-used roads, the car's low-profile tires slipping on the dirt tracks. Brett sprawled in the passenger seat, held in place by the seatbelt, his mouth gaping and leaving him looking rather less smug than usual. Gloria had the fleeting wish that she could take a photo of him so undone and keep it, but that would be foolish. She should, though. She could post it all over social media as a form of punishment. Because on the way over, she'd decided she couldn't kill him, even if he had seen her face. She wasn't a *murderer,* and if that ruined her book, so be it.

The guy was a predator, and he was going to keep getting away with things, but maybe this would serve as a bit of a lesson to him. With any luck, he might be so humiliated at a woman getting the better of him that he might not even mention her to the police. She'd just dump him by the little lake that was at the end of the track and leave him to be mugged or get hypothermia or whatever, then drop the car on one of the dodgier streets with the keys in it. Hopefully, all that might get him to rethink things a bit, and she could go home and drown her sorrows in more ice cream.

She was still thinking that when she pulled into the little parking space at the end of the track and switched the engine off. Brett didn't so much as twitch. That stuff was *strong.* Gloria let herself out, went around to the passenger side, and opened the door, leaning in to undo the seatbelt. Brett slumped onto her as soon as she released it, and she shivered, trying to push him back into place, but all he wanted to do was spill out onto the ground. She fought gravity for a moment, then let him go. A few bruises wouldn't hurt.

He collapsed onto the ground soundlessly, and Gloria shivered again. She nudged him with the toe of her trainer as if he might respond to that when he hadn't responded to anything else. He didn't, of course, and her stomach flopped slowly over. She crouched down and prodded his neck warily, looking for a pulse. Nothing. His skin was still warm, but maybe not warm enough.

"Oh," she whispered to the night and heaved him onto his back. His eyes were open, staring up at the sky. "*Oh.*"

That made three.

\#

Death with a Smile! the headline blared, and Gloria clicked on the link, blinking at the article as if she couldn't quite focus on it.

The body of accused date rape financier Brett McNicolls was found in the remote reaches of Keegan's Woods by an early morning jogger. McNicolls' body had been arranged to create the mouth of a smiley face, the rest depicted in spray paint. McNicolls was recently forced to strenuously deny—

Gloria clicked over to X, then Facebook, and half an hour later, she leaned back in her chair, touching her fingers to her mouth to discover that she had quite the smiley face going on herself. People *loved* it. There were think pieces popping up everywhere, interviews with the date rape survivors, and even photos of Brett with smiley faces pasted over his own face. He'd become a meme. She'd *made* him a meme.

It was sexy. It was a sexy male murder, and she opened her outline doc and started typing, still smiling. Half an hour later, she stopped, though, and went back to the news sites. Something was niggling at her.

Revenge killing?

Serves him right!

I'll alibi anyone who needs it!

Police are questioning—

"Oh, no," she muttered. "They think it's about the date rapes." Which it was, of course, because it made him someone she could target without troubling her conscience too much (even though she hadn't entirely meant to kill him), but it also *wasn't* because it was meant to be about serial killers. Then again, if no one knew about the other two, how could they realize it was a serial killer? Not that *she* was a serial killer, of course, as the first two had been accidents, but people were meant to *think* it was a serial killer.

She went to get the ice cream, then came back to sit down again. Three murders made a serial killer, with cooling down periods in between. Technically, they needed to take place over more than a month to count as serial killing rather than mass murder. She scooped up a spoonful of mint chocolate chip ice cream and sucked on it as she opened her messaging app. *Hey Cameron,* she typed. *I need an extension on my extension! This Smiley face thing has given me an idea to go in a different direction. Extend it by a few weeks?* She added prayer hands, then flicked back to the news pages. By the time Cameron told her she had six weeks total, she was deep into a news story about a romance scammer whom no one seemed to want to press charges against. He had the same sort of smug smile as Brett, she thought. She didn't much like it.

\#

"Gloria, we need to talk," Cameron's voice was flat and tired-sounding over the speakerphone. "I've been trying to get you on the phone for three days."

Gloria pressed the ice pack to her jaw. The swelling was going down, but she was going to have to put some makeup on it if she went out. The photographer had punched her pretty hard before the Rohypnol had done its job. Never mind — a smirking man who persuaded young girls he'd turn them into supermodels if they just let him take these *super-special*shots had been a good addition to the Smiley Killer's collection. And he'd made four, which put the Smiley Killer firmly in the serial killer category.

"I've been busy," she said. "I started drafting."

"Ah. Well. That's what we need to talk about."

"Is it a short deadline?" she asked. "I thought it might be to capitalize on the Smiley Killer. That's why I started before you got back to me about the outline. I figured I could make any tweaks as I went along."

"There's the problem," Cameron said with a sigh. "*Capitalizing* It's lazy, Gloria. You're never lazy, but this is *lazy.* You're pretty much lifting it straight from the papers."

Gloria lowered the ice pack, staring at her phone. "What?"

"You're not writing true crime, you know? These are meant to be works of imagination. I feel like you're not really putting in your best work here."

Gloria pressed a hand to her chest. *Not putting in her best work?* The whole *country* was buzzing over the Smiley Killer, never mind the city. Every true crime podcaster and armchair detective was frothing with excitement, and the city police were piling more and more actual detectives onto the case, desperate to solve it before some rabid theorist on Spotify did. *Not her best work?* She'd captivated *everyone!*

Not that she could say that, of course, so she just said, "Oh?"

"Yeah, I'm sorry, Gloria. I know you really wanted to change things up, but I think we need to revisit the idea of sticking to what you're good at. Why don't you come over tonight? I'll order Thai, and we can thrash out some ideas for a new outline."

"I don't want to do that," Gloria said, setting the ice pack down and clutching the table in both hands, her knuckles creaking with the force.

"I've already talked to Art. It's not negotiable."

Bloody men, making decisions for her. *About* her, like she didn't know her own mind, didn't know what she was doing. *Not her best work.* "Cameron—"

"Just come over tonight, alright? Seven o'clock. We'll talk it all through. I'll get ice cream. Mint choc chip."

Gloria looked up at the ceiling. There were no cobwebs in the living room, and she felt oddly bereft. "Seven o'clock," she said and hung up.

#

Cameron opened the door at six-thirty and grinned at Gloria. "Just couldn't wait for the ice cream?"

"You buy the best stuff," she said, walking past him into the apartment. It was bachelor-chic, all big windows overlooking the river and black leather sofas, although the stuffed bookcases gave it some character.

"Wine?" he asked.

"Sure. I think I'm going to need it."

"Aw, it's not that bad." He set two glasses on the kitchen bar and went to fetch wine from the little glass-fronted fridge in the corner. "You're really good at what you do, Gloria. You need to accept that."

"I can be really good at other things, too," she said. "You just need to give me a chance."

"We did," he said, his voice serious.

Gloria sighed. "Do you have some peanuts or something? I'm going to have to comfort eat my way through this."

He patted her hand, and she barely managed not to jerk away. Comforting the little woman as if it wasn't *her* books, *her* talent that paid for his clichéd bloody monochrome prints and slowly dying designer succulents. "Gloria. It's going to be fine."

"It will be once I have some peanuts."

He snorted and went to get them, tipping some into a cereal bowl, then picking his glass up. "To doing what you do best."

"To doing what I do best," she agreed, taking a sip of the wine. It was pleasant enough, light and a little oaky.

Cameron took a hefty mouthful, then wrinkled his nose. "Tastes a bit odd. Is it corked, d'you think?"

"Tastes fine to me." She took another sip to demonstrate, and Cameron did the same, then shrugged.

"You're probably right. Endless variation even in the same batch, right?"

"Something like that," she agreed.

#

The doorbell startled her, and she froze, the can of spray paint still in one hand. The purple had been a good choice. It showed up nicely on the pale wooden flooring, and Cameron's black-clad body, arched into a smile, was a ghoulish sweep of contrast. Very goth, she felt, although her choice of an ice pick through the ear meant the blood wasn't as liberal as might've been ideal.

The door went again, this time accompanied by a knock, and she looked at the time. Just after seven. It'd be the Thai delivery. They'd go away. She waited, crouched on her haunches with her hands hanging idly between her knees.

Knock knock knock. More insistent this time, and then Cameron's phone went on the counter, ringing out clearly across the silent apartment. She sighed. They'd be able to hear it through the door. "Just leave it outside," she shouted. "We're busy."

There was a pause, then a familiar voice, muffled by the door, said, "Gloria?"

She blinked. "Art?"

"Yes. Open up!"

There was no pretending it wasn't her. She got up and went stiffly to the door, leaving it on the chain as she opened it. "We're kind of busy, Art."

Art grinned at her, that oily, self-satisfied smile. "Of course you are! That's why we're here."

"We?"

"Hi," Brice said, peering around the publisher's bulk and waving a bottle of champagne at her. "We got held up in traffic. We were meant to be here early to surprise you."

"Surprise me?" Spots drifted into her vision from somewhere, and she forced herself to lock her abruptly unstable knees.

"For your genius new outline," Art said. "Cameron *loves* it. We all do. But he's probably told you already, hasn't he?"

"Um, no." She tightened her grip on the door. It seemed to be the only thing keeping her upright. "He said it was lazy. That he hated it."

"That was just a way to get you here. He knew you'd just keep working and refuse to come out otherwise. It was going to be a bit of an impromptu celebration." Art tried to peer past her into the room, and Gloria pushed the door partly to. "Let us in, then."

"Can't. Cameron isn't here."

Art frowned. "Where is he?"

"Out. Gone for the takeout."

"Can't have," Brice said, leaning forward to check the label on a bag resting on the doormat. "Delivery guy was just dropping it off as we arr—" He stopped, looking into the room through the tiny gap, the angle allowing him a narrow view past Gloria's legs to the tall windows and the pale, stripped floor, and the body mired in purple spray paint. "Gloria?" His voice was a whisper.

Gloria slammed the door and put her back to it, even

as the men started hammering on the other side, and she heard someone shouting into a phone, demanding the police, an ambulance, and probably an armed response unit.

Her genius outline.

She looked at Cameron, curved into an endless smile. "You had to bloody lie, didn't you?" she whispered. "You couldn't just let me be right. Couldn't just let me have my story. You had to bloody *lie*."

#

Gloria hit play on the tablet again, pressing her fingers to her mouth to feel the smile as she watched the improbably beautiful actor tackling a man twice her size, engaging in a wild car chase, scaling the side of a building to let herself in a window, all the action of a full movie — a full *book* — crammed into a thirty-second trailer. She looked up at the woman across the table. "I didn't do half of this stuff. They've added it."

The woman shrugged, her smile mirroring Gloria's. "That's movies for you. It's going to be huge, though. The almost-true story of the Smiley Killer, coming to a big screen near you."

"Not near me," Gloria said, nodding at the bland walls of the visiting room. "Too racy for here."

The woman nodded. Her name was Andrea, and she'd been only one of a dozen agents vying for Gloria's true crime book, the one she'd written in the first few months of being imprisoned. It had been hailed as either a feminist manifesto or a gratuitous slash-fest vomited out by a sick mind, depending on who was reading it.

"You've got the money for as many appeals as you want," Andrea said now. "You'll be out of here and able to watch whatever you want in a few months."

Gloria pushed the tablet across the table and leaned back in her chair. "I hope so."

"Have you done any new work? I know it's not the most conducive environment, but it'd be good to capitalize on the movie coming out. Have another book in the pipeline."

Gloria nodded, folding her hands together primly in her lap. "I have," she said. "I'm just in the research stage at the moment."

Andrea didn't say anything for a long moment, not quite meeting Gloria's eyes, then she nodded and got up. "Alright. Well, anything you need, just tell me."

"I'm fine," Gloria said. "It's going really well."

It turned out there were a lot of things you could research in prison. And a lot of people to blame them on.

She was still smiling when she went back to her cell. No one smiled back.

It wasn't worth the risk.

U Up

CAMERON STONE

U Up

CAMERON STONE

I SOMETIMES WISH I HAD A MIRROR ON MY CEILING. NOT for that reason, though that could be fun, too.

It's because when you lay back, looking up, all of your extra skin just falls backward. Gravity does its thing, and your skeleton gets wrapped in tighter skin. That loose skin that hangs just under your chin, the bags under your eyes? It all disappears.

Or so I'm told.

But I'm a normal person, so my mirror is in the bathroom, vertical like a moron. And because gravity is doing its thing, I pull back on my cheeks with both hands. I don't try to smile, or else I look like Krysten Ritter without makeup. I blame college and the excessive overnighters I've had to pull for the dark circles around my dark brown eyes. I'm only twenty-two, but my eyebrows are already starting to get those hairs that grow in every direction except where they're supposed to.

The bathroom lights are a yellow-orange hue that makes me look jaundiced. The only cool thing about them is the way they light up my eyes with a bright white speck in the middle of the deep brown circles of my irises.

When I go out to the bar to meet people, old school style, I see why I go home alone. I was considered a twink maybe two years ago. No chest hair, young baby cheeks, still looking like a teenager.

Today, I'm — well, I don't know. Not thin enough or hairy enough to be an otter. Definitely not fat enough to be a cub.

I pull on the base of my chin, sliding my hand back to meet my Adam's apple. Instantly, I have a jawline of the broccoli-haired TikTok gods with squared-off shoulders.

I know I'm ugly, maybe. I know I'm not my type. And judging by how all of the pubic hair in my bed is mine, I'm not anyone else's type either.

But you can't get anyone if you don't try.

So I throw on a shimmery purple shirt. The heaviest thing on it are the buttons down the middle. It swings with every motion. I bought it years ago but was too scared to wear it.

Honestly, I didn't need it to get attention. But tonight? I think maybe I need the help.

Black slacks — thin to show off what little ass I inherited from my mother. Black shoes just comfortable enough to walk in, not enough to dance in. I'm not a cologne person, but why the fuck not? Something's gotta happen, right?

* * *

The bartender's name is Benny. He shaves every part of his body, and I only know that because he also dances on the boxes Friday and Saturday nights with translucent underwear. Most of the time, it's flawless. Today, thin black marks peek out of his chest, looking like ink-stained staples across each of his pecs. Today, he's wearing pea soup green undies with a white waistband. And that's it. That's all of it. The music has been female pop voices for the past six songs, and there are no signs that anything is going to let up. The inside is not what you would consider a typical gay bar. The walls are the kind of solid stone that makes you think about castles in Game of Thrones. We're talking head-sized stones that are always cold, even in the summer. The bartender hides behind a dark wood bar that's been chipped ever since I started coming here with a fake ID years and years ago.

I pull up to the stool and actually sit down at the end of the bar. Men come in and mingle. Lots of older men with white mustaches and flabby triceps. They smile like they're on something, but I couldn't tell you what. There's no weed smell, so I have to think it's some kind of pill.

It's a Thursday, so it's not packed wall-to-wall. But the college crowd is usually out on Thursdays because they're the smart ones who don't pack a lot of classes onto a Friday. They get a three-day weekend and an extra day to drink before boring school shit. To prove my point, there are maybe twelve people in this neighborhood gay bar. More than half of the seats are empty, with white painted wood panels making it look even more spacious. It's me, an old guy, and a few others, but no one seems interested in anyone else. The only person that I would give my phone number to is a young guy with a thick jawline and curly black hair. In the light, he looks light-skinned, maybe Latinx and Black. The muscles of his shoulders shift with every flick of his finger across his phone's touch screen. He looks up at me and smiles, then goes back to his table.

There's a thing you do when you're cruising or looking for others in a public space. You do the eye-meet thing. The length of the meet matters. You see if they're interested, then you turn away. It's not playing coy, but it's your way of saying: *I see you seeing me.*

Then, you look back to see if they're still interested. The more aggressive types will bring their drink over and ask your name by this point. The passive folks will keep looking or turn away from you, but usually just to push out their ass and show themselves.

I didn't invent the game, but I'm a highly ranked amateur. And tonight, there's no startup game here. The cute guy in the booth is more interested in his phone than in me. And I'm not into uphill battles today.

The clean napkin in front of me argues otherwise. The square white napkin, in place of an actual coaster, is dry. Bone dry. Tucson Sonoran Desert dry. No round circles. Not even a dark spot, black ink dark, because it touched a droplet of water or spilled vodka on the bar. I press out the edges with my fingertips and tap my foot as Lady Gaga reminds us all that she wants our stupid love.

I catch Benny's eye when he's wiping down some glasses and putting them back on the shelves under the counter.

"If you have a sec," I say.

Benny says nothing. Does nothing.

I wave the white flag of my clean napkin in the air. Still no response.

Any self-respecting man would have stood up and walked over. The key word is self-respecting. This is a moment in which I feel like I have to subject myself to this. I'm part of a buffet that no one stops at. In the sidewalk sale of life, I'm on the far end of the rack, shoved underneath the jackets that will come back into style in another twenty years but, by then, will be given out to the unhoused as a donation. Does it serve a purpose? Yes. Arguably a good one. Does it serve my needs?

Hell naw.

My ego and my efforts deflate. The napkin spins in front of me when I blow at the counter, pushing a thin layer of my breath underneath it to make it lift and spin around. It's a neat trick I wish I could show someone. If anyone cared.

When I look up, there's a man coming my way. He's pretending we don't notice the thick layer of makeup under his eyes because maybe he wants us to notice the rosy reds of his lips. He'll argue that it's a tinted lip gloss, but it's really lipstick. Even in the queer world, masculinity matters. Fem-shaming is a thing.

When he approaches, he waves. I don't wave back because I don't know him. But I do start to crack a smile. I turn my body toward him and open up my shoulders. Everything I know I'm supposed to do if I want to show him I'm interested. Then, he walks past me. I feel like an ass watching him, head turning to keep up with his pace. He ignores my smile and approaches the bartender, reaching an arm across the bar. He grabs Benny's head and leans in with a hug and a kiss on the cheek. Benny opens their conversation by singing, "How are you?"

I'm fine. Really. Thanks for asking.

It's a short walk back to my apartment, then my room. It's a million humid degrees outside, and the air conditioner refuses to do its one fucking job. I lay in bed, kicking off my covers until they're bunched up around the foot of my bed. I lay there shirtless, and my phone glows blue and white against the baby blue wall behind me. Shorts and pants on the ground, nothing but tighty whiteys and body stretched across the entire path of the slow rotation of the standing fan.

I could take the L and go to sleep. But it's a long weekend for me. No classes in grad school, no time on the schedule at work. I'm a free man for the next two-ish days.

I'm done with YouTube and IG and TikTok. Then I get that familiar ring. My stomach goes cold. This could go two ways. I could check out the message and see if I'm being called a troll again, or it could be something more — shall we say — fun.

My friends say I never know when to stop. By switching over to Grindr and checking the messages only proves their point. A new message from "Dickmatized01". I click, and it's a simple message. Two words.

U Up?

I respond: *Maybe.*

I go over his account. One picture for the profile: a thin swimmer's chest with wide shoulders and cute lips curled in a playful smile at the top. The rules are that you're not supposed to show genitals or anything obscene, so this is the most I can see.

When I see that he's interested, I'm met with a purple devil icon. He's interested in a brief hookup.

He sends me an address and says: *If you're interested.*

Oh. I'm interested.

The location is a fancy hotel about ten minutes away. If you want to stay at a chain hotel and feel bougie, this is where you stay. Tall white building with narrow windows in each room. The parking lot where the Uber drops me off is mostly empty, but when I walk to the front door, the brightness of the entryway has me frozen like a deer.

I send a message: *Here.*

He replies: *Pool.*

I'm not much of an actor, but when I walk past the main desk, I smile and wave. Stupid. Nothing says suspicious like smiling and waving. But the woman behind the counter didn't even notice.

There's a split in the hallway. Left goes to the rooms, right to the pool and hot tub.

My phone buzzes. *Soon?*

Here.

I walk into the pool area. It reeks of chlorine. The walls are a faded shade of yellow that might be intentional. Or it's just bad design. The only person in the entire room has dark and mocha-colored skin that is so ethnically ambiguous that I can't get a read on him. He stretches his arms across the lip of the pool and smiles big. He says, "You made it. I'm Neal."

He turns around and pulls himself up onto the pool edge. Water cascades off his back, down his ass, and back into the pool. He's in a red and orange speedo that helps me know that he's circumcised. His smile doesn't stop. He gets closer to me, and I can see he's about the same height. He takes a minute and stands with his hands on his hips, dark green eyes looking right at me, he says, "Look familiar?"

I raise an eyebrow. "What?"

"This is my profile picture. You should always make sure you verify who you're talking to." His voice is soft and soothing, even airy in some places. His gentle spirit takes my hand and leads me into the changing room. The soles of my shoes squeak as we cross the tiled floor into a changing room with a vague mint-green feeling to it. I reach for my shirt, and he says, "Actually, I'm going to change into clothes." He pauses, opening a red bag and pulls out underwear. "I didn't catch your name. You hungry?"

"Will," I say.

I tell myself: *Don't go.*

And alarm bells go off in my brain. But then I say: "And yes, maybe food is good."

All because I saw him naked for a moment when he changed out of his Speedo. He stands tall with a tight green shirt that barely hangs onto his shoulders. The word "wander" is stretched across his chest, with faded pine trees visible across his pecs. The end of his shirt barely covers the top of his dark blue jeans. White Nikes go over his black ankle socks.

Then we leave the pool, heading back through the hotel. He flags down an Uber in his app and says, "I know this is weird, but thanks. Y'know. For coming with me."

"This is definitely different."

He smiles. I smile. When we get outside, the Uber is there. We get in, and then we're on our way to a 24-hour breakfast place. It's a terrible idea. I could smash some pancakes loaded with syrup any time of day. But the thought of me, sticky and loaded with spongy sweet goodness, is not a flattering look. If he didn't already have reservations, then that would definitely do it. We sit in the back of the car and watch streetlights go past us. Blue-tinted, yellow-tinted.

I peek over at Neal, and the lights do wonders against his skin. There are some acne scars along his cheek, but they add character to his wide cheekbones and caramel-brown eyes. White and yellow and blues flash in his eyes, and each time, I feel like I'm looking at him for the first time.

The reason he didn't want to fuck right away is he saw what I look like. My profile picture is a backpack and some books. I'm actually reflected in the mirror in the back, but it's not the focal point. And maybe that's the perfect explanation of who I am. I want to be seen, but not directly. Kind of like an eclipse, I suppose.

When we get to the spot, Neal rests a gentle hand on my shoulder. "I got the tip, no worries. Don't sweat it."

But his gentle words actually make me sweat.

At the table, we get coffee. I grab my cup in both hands, holding it close to my chest. I'm not cold, but when I get nervous, I shiver. Neal seems as comfortable as ever. He keeps staring at the bare skin V of my chest.

I look down. "Did I spill something?"

He laughs and looks away. "I'm sorry." His mouth wide, he tries to hide his smile with his hand. "I just got caught looking."

My face runs red from blushing. "Oh. I mean."

"No, no. It's fine." He extends out the word "fine" like he's singing that, too. "You are cute, you know."

I smile and maybe stretch my shoulders a little to give him a better view.

He taps the table with his left fingertips and says, "You did that on purpose."

"I did."

He smiles. "Can I ask you a question?"

I nod, then say: "I was ready to fuck you a moment ago, but is it weird that I'm nervous about a question?"

Neal sips his coffee. "Are you seeing anyone?"

"Me? No. I guess I'm looking." I watch his eyes to see if there's hope or disappointment in them. I sense nothing. Let's just say he would be an excellent poker player. "Are you?"

Neal takes in a deep breath. "It's complicated."

"Oh."

"He didn't think I'd notice that he was cheating. We fought. We argued. I was going to leave, but I can't. I'm sort of trapped right now."

"So, while he's out seeing someone."

"I'm out seeing someone."

"I see."

"Is that weird?" he asks.

"It's understandable."

He smiles. "How did you come out?"

My stomach flips inside. He just jumps right into the trauma. But the response is automatic. "I came home crying. Same story about the cheating boyfriend. Except no one knew we were dating. My parents knew him and loved him. Called him a son they never had."

He makes a face like he stubbed his toe. "Oh, that's rough."

"Not the worst part of it. He tried to give me flowers when I confronted him."

"He had flowers?"

"They were for the other guy," I say with my eyes closed. The moment plays out like a shadow play against the inside of my eyelids.

"You killed him, right? And buried his body? Because that's all he deserves."

I laugh and open my eyes." He's happily dating some guy he met across the country."

"Fuck him." Neal holds out his mug, and we clink them together in a very caffeinated celebration.

"Fuck. Him." I drink. He drinks. Our eyes lock for a moment, and he's hiding a smile.

* * *

The evening ends with me sharing a recipe for my favorite waffles. His dark hair catches the light and reflects a shade of light caramel brown halo, which shifts when he peeks up after he realizes he's been looking for too long.

We share the bill, and when we stand outside, his breath blows out into thin wisps of steam. "Are you sure you don't want to share a car?

I nod, hands in my pockets to keep from grabbing him right there. We could be in his bed right now. He could be telling me to get out. He could be tying me up and leaving me for dead in a ditch somewhere. Everything is possible.

I was prepared for almost anything. Anything but this.

"I'm fine," I tell him. "But thank you. Really. This was." What were the words? "Nice. This was nice."

"Good. I'm glad you had fun." A white Prius rolls up, and Neal gets in. He waves through the glass, and he disappears down the road.

While riding in the back of a boxy light blue Kia Soul, I finger the screen of my phone. I can't not smile as I switch to messages and send: *I had a great night. Thanks!*

My thumbs shake as soon as I realize it's sent. Then I put my phone away and watch the blue-yellow-orange pattern of lights flicker over me as I'm driven to my own apartment. And wonder: *is he thinking of me, too?*

Where did I mess up that I go back to sleeping alone? Again.

The message.

I had a great night. Thanks!

That's where I messed up.

No. Not just messed up.

Fucked up. It's fucked up.

I get out of the Kia, climbing the steps to my second-floor apartment. I again can't not smile. And that's how I apparently fall asleep.

It's a good thing I get the smiling out of the way the night before. The next day — at work — I'm helping an older woman in her sixties find the perfect laptop. She's wearing a green dress and a thick black belt with a gold buckle that's about the size of my fist. She won't look me in the eyes unless she's scolding me about how she felt ripped off by some computer brand. I don't bother keeping track because her story changes every time she tells it. Her purse hangs off her arm like a forgotten battle axe. I wonder just how hard it would hurt if I ripped it off her arm and swung her over the head with it. Maybe knock some sense into her?

She finally points at an expensive laptop in the gaming area. She insists she doesn't know anything about gaming but drops the term "noob" one too many times when looking over the placard with the specifications. She adjusts her thin-frame glasses and winces, adjusting so she can read through the lower half of her bifocals. "This isn't a machine for noobs, is it?"

I laugh, but she's not impressed. "No, definitely not," I tell her after coughing into my fist. "Let me see if we have any in the back." I know we already do. No one buys that laptop because it's overpriced. You can go online and customize one for less than this. But a customer is a customer, and it gives me the opportunity to check my messages in the back.

Yes, I check Grindr at work.

But not for that, even though I never realized before that the nerdy-looking guy who works at the Chinese restaurant on the corner is into "water sports." I set myself to not available and check messages.

The number of new messages I have is between "fuck all" and "jack shit."

I want to cry but come out with a laptop instead. I sniff real hard, swallowing all of my disappointment deep into my stomach like Mom taught me, and I march out into the bright lights, white shelving, and blue signs hanging haphazardly from the ceiling. "You're in luck! We have one."

"You look like you're crying," she says.

I shake my head. "Allergies. It's really dusty back there."

She rubs her hand over her chin, which happens to have more peach fuzz than I have. "Oh?"

"It's a great laptop. I promise."

We walk up to the counter. I put the laptop on the counter and walk away. The whole time, my hand touches my phone. Not once does it shake, vibrate, or notify me of a message. No pings or chimes. Nothing.

I'm dead in the water. I'm gone. I'm a memory.

On my way home in traffic, I daydream about the outfit I'll wear back out to the bar. As much as I want to say, "Fuck the world" and blame everyone else, I have to remove myself from the problem. I can't say, "No one talks to me," if I don't get out there myself.

So, I decide to get out there.

I lay out maroon pants and a dark blue sweater vest. Nothing underneath. It's a risky move, but my arms aren't too skinny to pull it off. My stomach rumbles as the sun sets, throwing a shade of orange and pink through my bedroom window. Just as I unbutton my pants and decide to change, my phone rings.

Remember that feeling when you're ten, and you decide to tell everyone that Christmas presents aren't a big deal, but you're more than a little giddy about what's in the biggest box under the tree? That's how I feel now approaching my phone. Even though it's probably just a text from my dad.

It's not. It's a paragraph from Neal.

Now, I'm shirtless and sitting on my bed. I start to sweat from the anticipation. Just how much did I fuck up? Is he ready to call me a troll, too?

"That's so sweet!" he sends back. The rest of his paragraph is a homemade comedy of errors. "I left my phone in the Uber, then I tried to find it, but the company

141

wouldn't answer, and I actually called a few Ubers and canceled when they weren't the same ones."

Not a single bit of punctuation in sight, bless his heart. But his forest green eyes more than make up for the long-winded explanation.

As soon as the messages are marked "read", he sends back to me. "Same diner tonight?"

I typed: *Um.*

He sends me a frown emoji.

Sure. Why not. Winky face emoji.

He sends me a clapping hands emoji.

* * *

He's already seated at the diner, a steaming cup of coffee in his hands, an empty cup waiting for me. He stands as I arrive, and this time, he wears a button-down shirt that reveals most of his collarbone. This is what I would consider revenge for showing off my chest the other night.

Neal looks at me with open eyes and a big smile: "How was your day?"

My heart flutters inside my chest, and I try like hell to tame it with steady breaths and a smooth, slow inhale-exhale combination. "It was good. Well, actually, kind of slow and annoying."

He pouts, his thick lower lip jutting out just enough to almost look like he's sticking out the tip of his tongue.

"I work retail," I say. "Trust. It's expected."

Then I laugh, and he laughs. A bald man comes over to the table, thin with a striped shirt and an apron over the lower half of his body. His gay voice and overall tone reveal that he knows this is a date, and he thinks we're adorable.

"I really am sorry," Neal says when the waiter leaves. His soft voice is like butter on a sizzling steak. It cools everything off. Makes it easier to take in. "Honestly, if you want to be mad at me, I deserve it."

"For what?" I rip off two packets of sugar but only pour in the first one. "You didn't do anything wrong."

He leans forward slightly, a three-quarter turn of his face, and he says, "I would have messaged back." He smiles and brings up his shoulders while pretending to push some hair back over his ear. A TikTok-wide sign that you're being coy but serious.

"I appreciate that." The coffee scorches my tongue. And I'm thankful. Keeps me from wanting to say anything stupid.

His foot reaches out under the table and kicks the tip of my leather boots. "How hungry are you?"

I swear his eyes dilate.

"I don't know."

"Want to go back to my place?"

It's a no-brainer. "Yes. Yes, I do."

We wait outside for the car, and he holds my hand. We both exchange a glance, and in the moonlight's silver glow, his eyes seem almost blue. His lips shine, curled into a gentle smile. Subtle, yet friendly. If I wasn't sweating before the summer night's heat, I'm sure as hell sweating now. As we wait, Neal peeks at me through the corner of his eye. Then he looks down at my hand.

"Are you okay?"

"Yeah, my hands are sweaty. That's all. It's hot."

He squeezes me even tighter.

And I'm a sucker, so I let him.

It's an unassuming white KIA that takes us to the downtown artsy district. High-rises everywhere. And if the buildings aren't completely made of glass, they have red brick corners and wide windows and are more posh than posh. This is the young professional's district where there's a coffee house on every corner and green electric bikes leaning against every metal signpost.

We pull up to a gray building. The outside reflects so much moonlight I get the impression of a pearl, freshly shucked and polished.

He takes me inside, and we get in the elevator, going up to the twelfth floor in silence. We lean against the back. And I let Neal's hand touch the small of my back.

The door opens to a brightly lit hallway with a red carpet that has orange diamond designs down the middle. It's opulent, and I feel like I'm walking the red carpet to a Hollywood premiere.

Neal's apartment doesn't help me keep me in reality. Every wall has these thick white and black rectangles. Some are mesh fabric in one room, and some look like slat paneling. Everything is gray except for a dark wood coffee table and end tables. These are an espresso color, popular in Japanese-style design. I know because I almost picked it out for my own apartment until I saw the price tags.

"What are the panels?" I ask.

Neal ignores me, leading me through a short walk-in hallway, past the living room, and down another hallway to one of maybe two bedrooms. His bed is against the wall with more dark wood end tables on both sides. One of the closet doors is open and appears to be empty.

Because all of his clothes are in a pile just outside of his hamper.

Neal smiles at me, the front of his teeth showing. He grips the front of my shirt and pulls himself closer. Then we walk slower, slower, backward to the bed. The back of my knees hit the edge of the bed, and Neal kisses me gently. Then, without warning, he shoves me backward with a playful push.

Bending at the knees, my arms out to the side, I hit a

Jesus Christ pose and bounce onto the king-sized bed. He climbs up, knees straddling my hips. He reaches for the bottom of his shirt and, pulls it off in one smooth motion and tosses it at the hamper. He misses.

Neal leans forward, one hand right next to my left shoulder. His other hand presses against my chin to face him then guides it upwards. We're eye-to-eye. His pupils dilate. I close my eyes, expecting another kiss, but he somehow slides his hands under my shirt and guides it upwards. His lips touch every part of my stomach, then my chest. My hands get wrapped up in my shirt when he pulls it off my head. Then he spins the shirt around, twisting my wrists together.

This — this is new. And I don't hate it.

I look down at the shadows along Neal's body, and I see the rough outlines of scars along his side. I didn't remember them from his photo. Something about the limited light, the texture of his skin just makes them more visible. Neal sees me peek at them and pulls back. His shoulders drop. He's still straddling me, but he sits back so his ass is on my lap. "Long story," he says. "Do they bother you?"

My hands grab his thighs, and I squeeze. "No. It's okay. Really." My hands move up to the edge of his pants. Some fingertips slip into the waistband of his underwear, the others caress just beneath the scars. "I'm good if you are."

With the silver moon lighting up the room, Neal is a Greek god when undressed. He slides up next to me and is just as gentle with my nerves as I am with his scars. But the more we entangle, the more scars I uncover along his back, along his thighs. When he's ready, he spreads my legs. "Ready?" he asks.

And I nod.

After, we're both lying on the bed, nearly exhausted,

and I feel the warmth along my skin start to cool. I slip out from under his arm and into the bathroom that's attached to the bedroom. I keep the light off, though I keep the door cracked, and I can see myself.

Like, really see myself.

And I catch a glimpse of Neal's hand in the mirror. Maybe it's the lighting, maybe it's the endorphins. Maybe it's none of that, but when I smile — honestly smile — for once, I'm not disgusted. I turn the sink on and wipe away all evidence of our night together. That's the thing about guys: we're messy almost every time.

A door opens and closes in the distance, but Neal's hand is still in the mirror. Then it shifts slightly, and Neal wakes up.

A light flicks on, and it sounds like a backpack has just dropped to the floor.

"What in the actual fuck?" a voice says. I freeze, then try to take a peek through the crack in the door, but all I see is Neal pulling the sheets up over his feet.

The man's hand, thin and white, snatches the covers off the bed and tosses them to the side. Neal tries to get up, but the hand shoves him back down.

"I can explain," Neal says.

"I'm sure you can," the man says. "Explain this."

And then underwear gets tossed into Neal's face. I pretend that he's not smelling me when he makes a face and tosses them onto the bed.

"So, it's okay if you fuck around, but I'm not allowed?"

"Fuck you, Neal."

"No, fuck you, Raymond." Neal gets up and points a strong finger at the man named Raymond. I presume this is the boyfriend.

And then there is a loud slam that shakes the walls. Did he hit Neal?

I step out of the bathroom — a towel wrapped around my waist. It tangles between my knees, my poor shaking knees, but I try to keep my chest out and shoulders back. "What are you doing?"

Raymond pulls back a hand from the wall. White dust trickles off his knuckles. The gray insides of the wall are exposed through a fist-sized hole. Even what we think are the strongest things are secretly so fragile. I'm almost hypnotized by a piece of what looks like string or dried paint swinging back and forth in the hole.

The young man who approaches me has dark hair and bright blue eyes. A round plastic earring plugs up his left ear. He's attractive in a boy-next-door kind of way. If the boy next door enjoyed My Chemical Romance.

"Who the hell are you?"

Neal stands from the bed and pulls Raymond away from me and over to the dresser. It slams against the wall, the mirror and cologne bottles rattling. The hard glass-against-wood sound is enough to echo in my ears. I don't catch all the words that are being tossed between the two screaming red faces. Spittle explodes from Neal's lips. Raymond grabs Neal's elbows, and his knees buckle. He tries to pull away, his hips swinging as far back as they can go.

"Stop," Neal says. "You're hurting me." And then he gives up and collapses onto the bed.

I grab my shirt and pull it on, keeping the towel. My dick and balls swing underneath, and it's the most uncomfortable feeling when you're trying to escape.

Then Raymond turns his angry gaze on me. His jaw just quivers. Red patches grow, stretching out from his cheeks. Raymond grabs my hair. His nails dig into my head, scraping my skin. I hear a grunt, then hot, hot heat growing from the side of my head.

And the room spins. Somehow, my legs are underneath me now. My body is against the wall. The heat on my head grows cold, and the room won't stop spinning. I can see what I think is the bed, and there's a blurry, dark, human-sized shape on it.

"Neal," I say just under my breath. Or maybe I yell it.

Raymond grabs my head again, pulls me back, and my ear hits my left shoulder. Then, another grunt and the cold on the side of my head goes numb.

The room is still spinning, and the towel falls away. My bare ass scrapes and scratches against the carpet. It's not as comforting as you'd think. My head radiates heat and cold — back and forth — pressure building behind my eyes. I could be bleeding, but I have no way of knowing. Everything hurts and feels numb at the same time.

The bed comes into my view, then disappears. I only see the wall, then the ceiling. Pictures of flowers and Neal and Raymond on a beach come into view. They seem so happy, though I can't see their eyes. Neal wears thick black sunglasses — starlet-style sunglasses — over his eyes. His smile isn't as strong, not as pronounced as Raymond's.

I'd like to think that I saw Neal's true smile. And these pictures don't have it.

Raymond pulls my arms up over my head, and I feel the wood of the headboard against the back of my wrist. I hear Raymond shout at Neal, telling him to get the fuck out or else. I look for Neal, but he's not there. He's not here. He's not anywhere.

Something tight goes around my wrist. I want to pull up and away, but the room won't stop spinning. Any movement of my head or shoulders makes me want to vomit. I'm not altogether here, but if I were to vomit, lying on my back, would I ... what's the word? Aspire? Amputate?

Drown.

In my own stomach acid and old coffee.

My other hand is seized. I try to resist, but Raymond punches my shoulder, and my forearms go numb. He yanks my hand up, slams it against the wooden bedpost twice, and then ties it with something soft. Something silky.

It's enough to distract me from him spreading my legs and kneeling between them. He pulls off his shirt, a khaki one that professional golfers would wear, and I see the beginnings of a happy trail. He keeps one strong hand on my right knee while his other pulls down his pants. And then he's in his midnight blue underwear. He shouts at me to be quiet. He's already hard, and I know what's going to come next.

Each time I try to move, he punches my thigh just between some muscles. My legs tingle, and I'm not sure I can feel my toes. Raymond pulls my knees up as far as I'll let him. He punches my chest with one hand, then rubs himself just beneath the testicles. I cry out to hide the laughter that it all tickles.

But the laughter and the smiling, it's not real. Not real laughter. Not real feelings.

None of this is real. None of this is real.

Neal is just waiting for me. That's all.

He's right there.

Isn't he?

But he's not. He's gone. The door to the room is closed.

I shut my eyes and keep kicking, keep moving. Yanking on my wrists until my shoulders are too exhausted to move.

The door slams open, bouncing off the wall. My eyes fly open, and it's my beautiful boy, his face red and in tears, holding a knife that glimmers in the overhead light. He launches at Raymond and starts stabbing.

Something wet and warm slaps my chest. From the

way my head is positioned, I can't see what it is. But I don't have to know.

And then Raymond falls onto my chest. His blood leaks into the spaces between us. A second later, he grunts and falls over to the side of the bed. His right arm and leg stay on my body. The rest of him is soaking into the sheets and mattress.

"Please," I say. "Get me out of here. Please." The words erupt into crying. No, not crying. Sobbing. I'm pleading for my life.

Neal's face is bruised, but even through the yellows, blues, and black of his cheek, he smiles and holds up a finger. He says, "I need a minute."

"For what?"

Neal takes a step back.

"Please!" I'm screaming, kicking.

"I need to clean up." Neal disappears behind the door. "I'll be back soon with supplies."

My cries are now lost on a dead guy and an empty apartment. Panic sets in. My chest sinks down, and I feel like I'm covered in wet towels and breathing through a straw. I can't get enough breath to even scream, so I sound like a tired diva at the end of her tour. I'm scratchy and hoarse; screams for help are lost in the apartment.

Because no one will hear me. I now realize the panels on the walls in this room. In the living room. On the halls. They're soundproofing. Everything is designed so that what happens in this apartment can't be heard. My shoulders twitch, and there's a feeling like a fly crawling up my right side, just above my waist. Of course, I can't do anything about it. To distract myself, I breathe slowly.

Neal is coming back. He said he's coming back, so he has to come back. And he said it. He's coming back because he's getting supplies. To clean up. Then he'll help me. Clean first. Then help. Me. Help me. That's what he's doing. It makes sense. Or at least it starts to make sense until something moves in the corner of my eye.

Raymond.

He's still alive.

He hisses in pain when he pushes himself up. The blood has already started to crust in the crevices of his back. He shifts his legs to the side, sitting with his back against me.

It's a bold move, but I can't reach him. I can't do anything to him.

But Neal. He'll be back. He'll be back. He said so himself. He just needs supplies to clean up. To clean up — Raymond?

I'm yanking so hard on both wrists that my hands feel like they're burning. The silk ties tighten the more I pull on them. It's a tricky knot, so I twist my body. Maybe I can pull my arms out somehow. But everything I do doesn't work. The headboard posts squeeze against my hands. The ties start to rub my skin raw. I don't see blood, but it feels warm. Even hot. Maybe wet. I don't know. I feel everything and nothing at the same time. Fear and numbness. Hate and calm.

This is how I die. This is my end.

There's some comfort in knowing this, I guess.

Raymond grunts and feels the wound in his right shoulder. Where's the knife? Not with Neal. He didn't have the knife when he left, did he? I don't remember. If he didn't, where is it?

I just know that Raymond is here.

"Please," I say. "Please let me go."

My left shoulder pops out of its socket from pulling so hard. My chest can't expand. I feel like I'm spread open like an eagle, each of my wing-like arms pulled back. The more I twist, the more pain that strikes like lightning through my chest and down into my hips. My left arm is numb and weak. I can't move it, but that doesn't stop me from thrashing around.

Then, a sudden bolt of pain fires through my shoulder to my brain. I scream so hard I taste blood in my throat. It gurgles. My shoulder slid back into the socket, but with this much pain, I wish it hadn't.

"Fuck!" I'm screaming. "Fuck." Tears fill my eyes so much the world blurs again. "Please let me go. Please." My legs kick, but I don't know that I have the energy anymore. I can't fight this, and I don't know where Neal is. I want to say he'll be here. I want to say he'll help me. I want to die.

And then a feeling of calm comes over me.

And maybe that's it. Knowing how you die is a tempting feeling. And right now, it makes me feel like a superhuman. No one knows how they will die.

But I do.

This is it.

Raymond pulls his hand from the wound on his back and smells the blood on his fingertips. Then he tastes it and licks it off his lower lip.

"You're not getting help," Raymond says. He shifts his body again, this time one leg bent on the bed. The other on the floor. He faces me, shirt off, midnight blue underwear digging into his love handles. But when he twists his body, a scar pops out on his side. The shape, the scar, it's familiar.

It's Neal's scar, too.

"Neal?" I say. The words gurgle, so I swallow blood and try again. "Neal has that scar."

Raymond shifts his body, and his bulge pops. Then, he moves his body and strikes a pose like a supermodel. "This?"Raymond says. "This is what was supposed to happen." Raymond smiles when he sees the confusion on my face. Then he reaches back to his shoulder, and his hand comes away bloody. He smears it onto my chest with a bloody X shape and then punches it with the bottom of his fist. "This isn't."

I cough.

"He cut too deep this time." Raymond stands up and grunts. "Fucking asshole." His breath is shallow when he speaks, and his right shoulder drops further than his left. He's wounded, deep. Muscles cut, and the way he's speaking and breathing, his lung may have been punctured. But he's braving it all. Raymond's eyes look as if they're lit up by fire. The anger translates to closed fists.

Then, once again, he straddles me. My knees bend and kick, but I can't shake him off. Raymond leans forward, pressing his hands against my shoulder. I can't help but scream. I don't know what he's saying because my body is on fire. Lightning and fire and lava flow through my body and blood, everything in pain.

I do catch some of his words.

"Can't let you go." "This is a game we play." "Pray and play."

Neal went to clean up. He went to clean up —

Me.

I'm the thing to be cleaned up when they're done.

"No," I scream. "No, please don't." My chest aches when I scream, and I don't even know if I'm making words anymore or just sounds. Pathetic mewing sounds. I turn my head away, trying to not look at him, but Raymond's hands are stronger than they look. He twists my chin toward him. His hand slowly goes down my jaw to my throat. He holds me still. I can still breathe, but I can't swallow.

Fear or something else has robbed me of the spit in my mouth. I'm screaming with sandpaper lungs.

"Shut up," Raymond says. He squeezes my throat harder until I cough. Then he lets go and slides down me. All of me is exposed as he smoothly caresses his knuckles against my skin. He keeps his eyes locked on mine, so I happen to notice a brief flash of something. Then they widen for just a moment. A second later, he reaches back.

A second later, I see it.

He has the knife.

He smiles, lowering his head.

I bring my knee up between his legs and hit hard. He roars at me in pain, trying to hold my thighs down. But I'm too fast for him. My knee goes into his nose. He yells, collapsing on top of me. Then he grunts.

And stops moving. Blood pours from his throat. Somehow, he cut himself open when I hit him in the face.

His open eyes stare at me.

And I realize he's watching me watch the life drift out of his body.

My legs start to shake, and Raymond falls to the side. I see the knife again. It's between his legs and mine. From where I'm sitting, I might be able to twist it up. I make quick jerking movements with my legs, trying to slide my left leg out from under his. But my toes were never the most agile. I could never do that thing that all boys will deny they do — pick their underwear up with their toes and try to catch it in midair. I'm just not built that way.

But my life depends on this. This is the part where I break free. I have to. I don't want to be cleaned up.

If I can shift my body up just enough to use my toes to inch it up, but the tip of the blade gets caught against the lower edge of Raymond's midnight blue underwear, making any movement incredibly hard. My foot slides along the silk sheets. My ass slides up and down as my toes and heel try to pull and push down. Get some friction — any friction — with the knife.

But it doesn't work. Maybe I need to give it what it wants.

"I'm so sorry. I'm sorry." I pull my left leg off the bed. I close my eyes and swing my foot to the right. My heel just slides along the edge of the handle. It wobbles, but nothing else happens.

If you're going to do this, Will, you need to keep your goddamn eyes open.

Again, I pull my foot off the bed, swinging all the way to the left. My eyes close.

No. Damnit. Open. Keep them open.

So I do.

Keeping my eye on the fucked up prize. The edge of the knife. Then, swinging my foot hard to the right. My ankle slams against the handle, pushing the blade deep into Raymond's thigh.

And then I wrap my legs around his waist and pull up toward my shoulders. His head folds against his shoulder, but I pull him up by a few inches. Then, slide my leg down underneath his stomach with a quick push, then slide back up. His corpse hasn't started to go rigid yet, so for now, I'm moving a warm bag of flesh up my body. When his body is half on the bed, half off, I hear something slam. Something heavy.

I start to think that Neal is home. I have to move fast.

With another scoot of my knees, I hear something scrape along the floor.

Raymond's knuckles. His arm has fallen off the bed.

When the knife handle is at the same height as my nipple, I stop. Then, I yank as hard as I can on the ties that are wrapped around the bedpost.

My hands are small enough to cup my thumb into my

palm. I breathe in, hold it, and pull as hard as I can. I have to bite into my lower lip to keep the pain from becoming too much. I hear and feel a snap somewhere around my thumb. It goes limp, but my hand slides out from the smooth silk fabric. The other hand is too tight to go anywhere. The more I pull, the tighter it gets.

But I did it.

I reach down and pull the knife from the side of Raymond's thigh. A thin drip of blood flows into the edge of the puncture wound, but it doesn't gush. Imagine the sight of chocolate sauce just casually dripping down the side of the bottle. It's that slow, that thin, that patient.

I take the knife, flip it around, and slice at the silk tie that binds my other hand. There are sharp, cold feelings that start to burn along my fingertips. Feelings of something — loose skin? I cut. And seconds later, I'm free.

My shoulders pulse when I bring my hands together. And then I start to cry, holding my raw, wounded wrists to my chest. The only thing louder than my sobs is the sound of the front door. The apartment rattles as it slams shut. I hear keys being dropped onto a table and bags rustling.

I roll off the bed, grab my pants, and put them on. To hell with underwear. I scoop up a shirt — any shirt — and tuck it under my arm. I can get dressed when I'm outside when I have time to think.

I get the knife, then open the door, and prepare to run.

But Neal's already there, his forest green eyes and coy, dimpled smile. He has a couple of shopping bags. I hold the knife against Neal's stomach. He takes a step back, but the smile doesn't disappear.

His voice is calmer than you'd expect. "Good," he says. He sets his purchases down. Garbage bags, duct tape. And there, on a table behind him, an electric saw.

"You survived," he says with a smile. "I was hoping you

would, but it wasn't my turn to interfere. It was Raymond's turn."

"What?" I say.

Neal walks into the bedroom and peeks at Raymond's wound. "I got him good, hey?" Then he sees the bruise along Raymond's face. "I'm sure that felt good."

I make the mistake of letting the corner of my lips curl into a brief smile.

"He was afraid that I wasn't into it anymore," Neal says. "That I found someone else." Neal's forest green eyes seem lighter in the overhead light. His blue and white striped shirt barely contains his broad shoulders.

My jaw rattles, but I'm too tired to say anything. Anxiety and fear courses through my body, and it's hard to move.

Wake the fuck up, I tell myself.

But I was never the type of person to listen to anyone. Neal comes up to me, standing inches from me.

I hold the knife out again, but he doesn't move. Doesn't even flinch. Not even when I slash at his shirt. Instead, his eyes look into me, deep into me. He sees me. He sees me like I saw me earlier that evening. His smile is my smile.

He studies my expression. But other than that, he's calm. Whatever I do, he'll accept it. I could kill him right now.

Or...

I drop the knife to my side, and it slides out of my fingers. The handle bounces against the wooden molding of the wall and rests on the carpet. I step in closer to Neal and take his shredded shirt into my hands. Our lips touch, and he takes me into his arms.

* * *

The orange glow of the app lights up both of our faces. Me as the big spoon, him the little. And we lay on the bed, our legs intertwined. Neal points at the screen with his middle finger, almost tapping the screen. "What about him?"

It's a ginger-headed kid with a thick beard who claims to be nineteen. The freckles along his eyes are adorable. "He doesn't quite feel right."

"Fine," Neal says, his face as warm as a baby's blankie. "What about him?"

The man's hair hides all of his forehead. He's smiling, one dimple along the side, thin red lips. He wears a black cap that says "Dude" in white stitched letters. He's shirtless. His profile says: *Alone and ready for anything.*

"I don't think he's ready for us," I say.

Neal slaps my thigh with a gentle, soft, open hand. "Stop."

I laugh and open up the messenger and type out a text: *U Up?*

Dirty Girls: A Love Story

KATHRYN COTTAM

Dirty Girls: A Love Story

KATHRYN COTTAM

HIM

Pits.

It's always been his nickname. At first, because they said he smelled bad. Like that skunk Fergus ran over on the old gravel road by the Whittaker farm. Even though the place was ten miles from town, you could smell the animal's sickly sweet stench baking all day in the sun.

They said he needed deodorant. But his mother wouldn't buy him none. To her, he smelled just fine.

In grade six, he got acne.

His mother said not to scratch, or he'd spread his grease. But he couldn't help hisself. So, the acne settled in along his jawline. It was there when he dropped out of school to work for Uncle Pete at the chicken factory. A place where the air was so thick with white feathers they mixed with your saliva and stuck in your teeth.

It was there when Sarah Green let him feel her eighteen-year-old breasts behind the local Dairy Queen one summer night when her boyfriend Daryl was laid up in bed with the laryngitis. Or in jail for fighting. He couldn't right remember.

And even now.

In this bar tonight.

Even though the Friday Night Girls, with their low-cut tops, tell him he's handsome and squeeze his big shoulders and make jokes about the size of his feet. He knows them girls ain't laughing at his size fourteens. They are laughing at his pits.

He thought this town would be different.

But it's the same as the one before and the one before that. With the dirty girls already here and waiting for him. He doesn't know why they choose him, these dirty girls. But he knows one is waiting because the pain in his side has returned.

It's been there for nearly two weeks now, a thick band of steel that cuts into his ribs. It's there when he wakes in a tangle of damp morning sheets. At work, when he pours cup after cup of black liquid oil, trying to keep hisself awake.

And it's there when he crawls into his still-unmade bed at the end of the day. And by now, he can hardly breathe. But it's because — somewhere — there is a dirty girl trying to get his attention.

That pain is what drives him from his cracked leather stool at the bar.

Outside, the air is cool from days of uninterrupted rain. The puddles in the black pavement reflect the lights, wrapping him in neon when he steps through them. So bright it hurts his eyes. So he walks home through the park, a dark shortcut to his apartment.

A three-piece suit tosses a newspaper into the garbage bin. The man's aim falls short, and the newspaper lands on the ground, its pages flapping in the wind like a bird with broken wings. He watches the man ignore the fallen paper and walk away, and his fingers curl into fists. He likes things to be clean. He learned that from his mother.

His mother.

She washed dishes at the diner off the highway, a cracked linoleum of a place called Hermann's (with two n's, thank you very much). She didn't wear rubber gloves. Said if she did, she couldn't feel the grease. And then how would she know the dishes were clean? That's why her hands were always red and raw and felt like sandpaper to the touch.

When he came home from school — and later the chicken factory — she'd put one of their hands down the front of his pants, into his drawers, and check his privates. Made sure he was clean down there, always worried that some dirty girl might leave her stain on him.

Didn't matter that he stayed away from girls and boys. His mother still checked him, just in case.

Now he reaches down and grabs the newspaper, his big hands stopping its pathetic attempt at flight. He takes it and walks to the wooden bench beneath the park's single light. He turns the pages until he finds the classifieds. He needs to get rid of this pain in his side, this pain that feels like a thousand angry paper cuts. He scans the columns. His dirty girl is in here somewhere. Calling out to him. He just has to find her. And, of course, it doesn't take him long.

There she is. It's a small ad, but she's asked the newspaper to put a thick black border around it so he can find her: *For Sale. 1975 Buick Skylark. Good Condition. $1800.* He knows the ad doesn't really say that at all. It's an invitation. And it's meant especially for him.

He stares for a long while at her name: Rose, and a telephone number. Thinks about not calling for a couple of days. Make her suffer like she's making him. He can see her sitting on her white mattress in her dirty bedroom, staring at the phone. Her soft, bare thighs trembling in anticipation of his call. But he won't ring. Not tonight. Maybe not even tomorrow. And then when she thinks he's abandoned her, why he'll —

A shadow falls across him. A woman walks down the path with a small black poodle connected to her wrist by a thin red leash. For a moment, he thinks she is his mother. Gray hair cut in a severe pageboy, lips pressed firmly together, that look in her eyes.

"Filth," she says.

Then he sees his hand. It's down the front of his pants, and he's pulling on hisself. Making hisself dirty. His cheeks flame. He yanks out his hand and zips his pants. He'll go home, clean hisself up, call her. Then he'll call Rose and make her pay for being a dirty girl ...

Her

The girl who calls herself Rose moved to this town three weeks ago. She's never before lived anywhere with so much rain. But she likes the way the water washes away smells and memories. Makes even a fall day taste like spring.

She likes her cozy apartment. Even though there are still boxes to unpack, books to shelve, electronics to hook up, and curtains to hang. Already, she's said hello to the woman across the hall. And let the man from the second floor — call me Jim — help her with groceries. He has a nice face and crow's feet at the edge of his eyes that crinkle when he smiles. But she's not looking for company from him.

She smiles, lifting the sheet she has hung over the front

164

window for privacy. She looks out at the Buick parked under a canopy of cherry trees. Jim tells her in spring, the petals are tracked through the lobby like stray pieces of pink wedding confetti.

The Buick is a painful reminder of her father. When she looks at it, she doesn't remember the man who taught her how to catch and clean a fish. Or read her bedtime stories on the front porch despite the lazy buzz of mosquitos. Or hold her hand as he walked her to school. Instead, there is simply gray skin and stinking flesh and rasping breath while the cancer ate through his bones.

When the phone rings, the girl who calls herself Rose hopes it will be a response to her advertisement. She's nervous about the price on the Buick. Worried she's asking too much. The voice on the other end of the line is friendly and asks the appropriate questions. She tells the man it's a four-door sedan in good condition, Almond Mist in color. And then, for some reason -- maybe it's the kindness in his voice — she says it was her father's, and he's dead now, and she needs the money because she's just moved. There is a moment of awkward silence as though she has spoken out of turn, so she asks him if the price is reasonable. He says he won't know until he can have a look and asks to come tonight. But Rose is alone and knows to be careful, so they set up an appointment for the next afternoon instead.

And then she gives him her address.

HIM

He hangs up the phone and smiles. He knows he shouldn't be surprised by the girl who calls herself Rose, but he is. They make it so easy for him - these dirty girls. All alone, and she still gives him her address.

And then a cool chill slides down his spine. Sometimes, the dirty girls lie. They say they are alone. But when he arrives, a father or a brother or a friend is there as well. And so he has to leave them to their dirty world. And the pain in his side throbs on.

He climbs into his own blue four-door sedan. It's a good temporary friend because it looks like a thousand other cars. He cuts across the eastern part of town, through the area with the warehouses, the factories, the kitty walk.

Through his window, he studies the girls that stroll the street. They stand on the corner, their skin lit by rose-colored neon. Their breasts push against cloth too small to hold them. And they wear skirts too short to cover their private spaces. He stops at the light, and a girl with silver shorts, brasier, and boots approaches.

Even her skin is silver, covered in a confetti gel. She walks to his window and presses her breasts against the glass, asks if he wants to party. The fake eyelash on her right eye has come unglued. It flutters against her skin like an angry centipede caught in a spider web.

He wants to tell her about it, but his throat is dry. For a moment, the pain in his side abates. But he knows it's a trick. This girl doesn't want cleaning. She's far too bright and shiny. So he slams his foot against the gas pedal, the car jumps sideways, and the bumper hits the silver girl, knocking her to the ground.

But then she jumps back up and chases him down the street, screaming, the foul pit of her mouth the gateway to hell.

He stops at the third service station he passes and parks. Then he gets out and takes the window wiper from its home in a bin of oily water. He scrubs the glittery makeup from where the silver girl pressed her breasts against the glass. She tried to trick him. Make him think she could shine. But she lied.

For a moment, he thinks of driving back to her. A quick apology, a crinkle of bills, and she would be in his car. He could take her someplace dark, peel back her skin, show her — like he's shown others — that she'll always be dirty.

But then he remembers. The girl who calls herself Rose is waiting. He climbs back into the car. His hands on the wheel no longer tremble.

It only takes him ten minutes to find her apartment. He parks the sedan two blocks away from her building and walks. She is in the first unit on the ground floor. There is a light on in her suite. But there is a sheet across the window. For a moment, his hands curl into fists. Maybe she is just a tease, like so many of the others.

But then he slips past the thick hedges that border the apartment and around to the back of the building. There are no lights back here. Just darkness.

She has left this window uncovered for him. And now they can begin the dance.

He waits for her to start.

And within minutes, the girl who calls herself Rose walks into the bedroom and switches on the light. Her blonde hair is tied back in a ponytail with a pink ribbon to hold it in place. She is slender, possibly even skinny. He will be sure to tell her she could have worn more weight and still been pretty. She's not athletic, and he's glad of this. The athletic ones are strong, and they fight. And the situation gets very messy before it gets clean. And he likes things to be clean. Very, very clean.

The girl who calls herself Rose wears long-legged jeans and a T-shirt but no socks. She looks tired. She pulls the shirt up over her head to reveal a plain white cotton brasier. But unlike other girls, she doesn't toss her shirt to the floor. Instead, she folds it neatly, pulls open a dresser drawer, and places it inside.

The jeans she hangs in the closet. On one of those funny hangers with the two clips. His hand reaches into his pants. He grabs hold of his privates and strokes hisself.

Rose's panties are also white. When she removes them, she tosses them into the wicker laundry basket in the corner of the room. Her brasier she hangs on the metal hook on the back of the bedroom door. Her skin is smooth and pale. And he watches her pull back the sheets of her bed and climb in.

He imagines the feel of those sheets.

Tonight, they will be cool against her skin, but tomorrow — when he starts to clean — they will be warm from the afternoon sun.

She'll try to stop him, of course. They always do, but only because they don't understand.

He'll say the name of the girl who calls herself — Rose, Rose, ROSE! — and the cool metal of his knife will calm her heated flesh. And when he cuts his way through skin and bone and muscle, she'll tremble. But when he's done, she'll shine so bright she'll hurt his eyes.

And then he'll cut a piece of her hair to take with him. So he can remember her not as a dirty girl but as one that sparkled and shone. And that ache in his side will be gone, too. At least for a little while.

He glances up at the window. Her room is now dark, and even though he still pulls at hisself, he is limp. He tastes bitterness in his mouth. How dare she hide from him in the dark? For a moment, he considers throwing a pebble against her window. The noise would wake her, bring back the light.

But then he remembers. She doesn't yet understand how important she is.

But tomorrow, she will know. Tomorrow, she will understand everything. Tomorrow, she will shine.

HER

It's three o'clock in the afternoon, and the man who inquired about the Buick is punctual. He buzzes her door, and the girl who calls herself Rose goes down the hallway to let him in.

He's tall, at least six three. And he has a kind and pleasant face. Even his eyes smile. He says his name is John, and he shakes her hand, his grip dry and strong. He looks interested in the car. Before he came to the door, she watched him from her front window while he examined it in the street.

He asks to take the Buick for a test drive. Rose nods and holds out the car keys. He offers to leave his driver's license for collateral. But Rose thinks he shouldn't drive without it.

He points to a green Taurus parked down the block. Says it's his, and she should write down the license plate just in case; today, you can never be too safe.

Rose does as he suggests and feels silly that she didn't think of it first. John says he'll be gone twenty minutes at the most and wants to stop by his garage and have his mechanic give the car a once over. She tells him to take his time and ring her buzzer when he returns.

He smiles and unlocks the Buick door. And climbs in.

A few seconds later, he is gone.

HIM

He turns the keys in the ignition and is rewarded with the sweet purr of the motor. The car is exceptional, almost in mint condition. Worth much more than the eighteen hundred she is asking. He puts the Buick in gear and slides away from the curb.

For a moment, he thinks he might keep on driving. Go back home to his mother. Won't she be surprised to see him all cleaned up? Why she might not even recognize him. Then his face hardens, and he scratches his jaw and remembers why he can't go home.

His mother won't be there.

He cleaned her up long ago.

Besides, there is the pain in his side. Like the feel of a ripe tomato on a split lip. It reminds him of his purpose. Of the girl who calls herself Rose.

No, he can't drive away.

He has an appointment. He slips his fingers inside his coat pocket. Touches the short blade that is waiting for her.

When he returns, he wipes the car down with a handkerchief. The kind old men carry in their pockets.

Any place he touched is now clean.

Then he walks up to her door and uses the same white handkerchief to press her number on the call board. When she buzzes him through, he uses it again to open the outer apartment door.

A man walks towards him from the elevator. Wrinkles at the corner of his eyes, a smile on his face. Despite the pain in his side, he waits, holding the door open for the man. He's not worried about being seen. He will be long gone by the time anyone finds his dirty girl. Different city, different car, different name.

And besides, no one ever remembers him.

He seemed like an average sort of a guy.

It's been said about him before.

The girl who calls herself Rose stands in the door to her apartment. He sees the quiet panic in her eyes. And he says the one word that will bring her peace: *sold.*

She gives a little laugh of relief. Puts her hand on his arm and says she was worried his mechanic might find problems. After all, the car is so old. She holds the door wide for him to enter.

Come on in, and we'll sort out the paperwork.

And by that, she means money.

Her apartment is still in labeled boxes, ready for unpacking. He appreciates the order. His fingers slip into his pocket, and he pulls out eighteen one-hundred-dollar bills.

His fingers touch hers when he passes it over.

Her touch is cold, her skin is smooth; it sings to him. Demands to be cleaned. She sets the money on the counter in a pile. He tells her to count it and make sure it's correct.

And so she does.

She turns her back to him, and her long fingers count the bills: *one, two, three.* For a moment, he thinks maybe he'll just buy the car and leave. Maybe he was wrong about the girl who calls herself Rose.

But as she continues to count, she no longer uses numbers, and instead, she says: *pits, pits, pits, pits.*

The red stain is back across his face. And his hand is in his pocket. His fingers close over the blade, and he draws it out. The metal shines in his hand. He's so very close to her now. He breathes in the scent of the girl who calls herself Rose, and his thighs brush hers.

She turns toward him, surprised by his touch.

And then she says: *I'm sorry.*

He doesn't understand. What is she sorry about?

But he's more confused about the fact that her eyes are calm. This is the moment the dirty girls see the knife and always panic. And the pain is still in his side when it should be gone. He touches his ribs, and they feel wet. He looks down. The white shirt he ironed this morning is stained with red.

Why is his blood on the outside when it should be on the inside?

He stumbles back, dropping his knife.

And she dances with him, her fingers locked around the wooden hilt of a very large blade which is lodged deep inside of him, hurting him.

The girl who calls herself Rose twists the knife in his side. Again. Again. And yet again. Pain rips along his nerves, tearing through his skin, his flesh, his meat.

And all the while, she looks at him with large brown eyes, and her pink lips say: *I'm sorry, I'm sorry, I'm sorry.*

He tries to flee, but she continues to move with him. This way and that, they spin and pirouette across the room. And when he can no longer stand, he doesn't.

He falls, lying on the cool tile floor, watching his blood pool like a carton of spilled strawberry milk.

The pain in his side is gone now, and the girl who calls herself Rose has a smile on her lips. He wants to tell her he made a mistake. That his mother was wrong. That she's not a dirty girl after all.

But he's forgotten how to speak.

So, instead, he shines.

Just for her.

HER

The police say she's lucky.

Girl her size, up against a brute like that. It could have ended so differently. They ask questions, but she doesn't talk much. A specialist says she's in shock.

172

Her neighbors try to convince her to stay at the apartment. Mrs. Pointer — the woman across the hall — bakes her a tuna casserole with a cornflake crust. Jim offers to install brand new deadbolts, two of them, on her door. But thirteen days later, she moves.

She stands in her brand-new living room in a brand-new town with a brand-new name. Boxes are everywhere. There are books to shelve, electronics to hook up, and curtains to hang. The one thing she has done is put a sign in the back window of the 1975 Buick Skylark, four-door sedan, color: Almond Mist. It says: For Sale. $1800.

Then she drives to the outskirts of town, to the store named "Rod & Rifle." She picks out a Bowie hunting knife, seven inches of hard-pressed steel. She misses her old knife, the one the police took and think was his.

They tell her it's evidence, so they keep it. They always do.

Anyway, that knife was covered in his blood. And the girl who called herself Rose likes things clean. Very, very clean indeed.

Because if there's one thing she can't stand, it's a dirty boy.

Getting Lucky

SEAN PLATT

Getting Lucky

SEAN PLATT

PINK'S OFFICE SMELLED LIKE PISS AND STALE CIGARETTES.

Piss because the ongoing road construction set up a port-a-potty right next to his front window. And when he wasn't listening to the sound of a pile driver — the vibrations of which rattled his teeth every 3 seconds — he was coughing from the stench of smoke. His entryway had the only awning on the street. And when you lived in London where it rained — a lot — his little entrance became the gathering spot for the local chimneys.

Really, his office was the kind of place where dreams came to die, or at least take an embarrassingly long nap. But Pinky didn't mind (at least most of the time). He could live anywhere in the world without a lock on his door. Because everything would go his way. It always did.

He didn't even mind the smells and sounds outside his door.

The construction work had rattled loose a wall in his bathroom, and he'd found a small hoard of bills from the 1940s. And one of the cigarette smokers had turned out to be Ella. An old flame who phoenixed from the ashes.

There were no bones about it.

Pink was lucky. In fact, *lucky* was his bread and butter.

Need a promotion at work? A last-minute ticket to see The Stones? All green lights on your morning commute? Pink could make that shit happen and did. For a fee, of course. He dealt strictly in serendipity, those little everyday miracles that made life worth living. Some folks could only afford partial luck — 51% was Pink's most popular package. Couldn't swing a sunny wedding day? How about overcast skies where the rain stays away for just long enough to trade the *I do's*?

He specialized in repeat clients like Mrs. Higgins, whose arthritis he could ease for all thirteen of her grandkids' weddings. Old Tom, who always found a quid in his pocket for one last pint. And Sarah, the nervous student who aced every pop quiz her uni professor tried — and failed — to surprise her with.

Pink left the big scores— lotto jackpots, high-stakes poker wins, Silicon Valley unicorns — to the heavy hitters. He was fully content with his smaller yet perfectly satisfying slice of the pie. A typical day involved providing small miracles to make life a little sweeter for those who knew where to find them.

Pink's office was a cramped affair, barely bigger than a broom closet. A rickety desk dominated the space. It contained one thing: a register. His register contained every client's name alongside their desired stroke of fortune. The walls of his office, however, were covered in faded posters of four-leaf clovers and horseshoes. There was a stack of good luck keychains hanging from a peg. Seven horseshoes were nailed above the door. A jar of lucky pennies was on the floor. And in the grimy window was a whole collection of Maneki Neko cats brought back from Japan and gifted to him by a grateful client. It was all cheesy décor (that did nothing to provide luck), but he found it secretly comforting. Which is why he also carried a rabbit's foot (fake, of course, because the real ones were notoriously unlucky). For the comfort.

Today, Pink leaned back in his creaky chair, feet propped on his desk. Business had been steady lately. Far from earth-shattering, but still enough to keep him in ample tea (which was always piping hot) and biscuits (which never went stale). He was considering a trip to the corner shop for a cheese and pickle sandwich when the office door creaked open to a gust of London drizzle. In walked Harvie Bench, his oldest friend and most persistent pain in the ass.

"Pinkie!" Harvie's grin was as wide and empty as his wallet. "How's tricks?"

"Same old, same old," Pink said, dropping his feet to the floor and getting up to stretch. "What brings you 'round?"

Pinkie, of course, already knew, but it never hurt to ask.

Harvie's smile faltered. "Well, funny you should ask. I was hoping … maybe … a little boost for the ponies?"

Pink sighed. They had been down this road before. Many times. "Harv, we talked about this. You're tapped out, mate. Used up all the luck you're ever gonna see in this lifetime. And borrowing fortune from someone else is off the table. That's real bad luck. And you don't want that."

"Come on, Pink. For old times—?"

"Sorry, pal. I'm cutting you off. For your own good."

"Yeah, yeah. I get it." Harv's shoulders slumped. "Can't blame a bloke for trying, right?"

Pink walked over to him and clapped him on the back. "Tell you what. I'll meet you at the Flatulent Friar after closing. First round's on me. But no talk of horses, yeah?"

"Deal." Harvie brightened a bit and hit the door. "See you then, 'ya lucky bastard.'"

Pink's stomach grumbled. Time for lunch.

He grabbed his worn leather jacket from the back of his chair and headed out, locking up out of habit rather than necessity.

The alley was empty, which should have been his first warning. The usual throng of delivery boys, bin men, and shady characters conducting even shadier business was conspicuously absent. But, on the other hand, he didn't have anyone trying to wheedle a bit of luck for free. When he hit the road, he spotted a van at the curb. The engine was rumbling. Then, someone approached him from behind and grabbed him.

A second later, a bag descended over his head.

Pink didn't bother to fight. His luck would kick in sooner or later. "What is this?" he asked.

"Quiet," a gravelly voice said. And then whoever it was took his phone.

Pink felt the cold bite of handcuffs on his wrists. Normally, he would slip out of them EZPZ, but he was willing to find out what this was all about.

He was shoved into the van, and seconds later, it was off. He cataloged every turn and bump in the road, trying to keep his breathing steady.

After what felt like hours (maybe twenty minutes), the van screeched to a halt.

Rough hands hauled him out and marched him … somewhere.

When they arrived, the bag came off, and Pink blinked in the sudden light.

He was in some sort of cavernous warehouse. The kind of place you saw in the movies where drug deals took place (or where bodies disappeared). Dusty sunlight filtered through the grimy skylights, illuminating stacks of crates and piles of rusting machinery. And there, lounging on an honest-to-god throne, was Angelo "Lucky Legs" Lombardi. *The most dangerous man in London's underworld* (At least according to the man's business card. Pink had found one once).

Lombardi's eyes were cold and gray, like chips of slate. His fingers were overdressed with stacks of gold rings, and they were drumming an impatient rhythm on the arm of his wooden throne. "Mr. Phillips," Lombardi said. "So good of you to join us."

"Didn't really have a choice," he said, raising his bound hands.

Lombardi pursed his lips. "No, I suppose you didn't."

Pink was confused. Lombardi was way out of his league. The mob boss dealt exclusively with the premium fortune peddlers. What the hell did he want with a small timer like Pink?

He glanced around the warehouse. "So, why am I here?"

"You really don't know?" Lombardi asked.

Pink shook his head.

"Try and get out of those cuffs," Lombardi said.

Pink blinked.

Then shrugged. Reached into his pocket. Froze. His paperclip was gone. He always carried one. It had a multitude of purposes, including the ability to reset electronics, work as an impromptu zipper pull, organize papers … and, of course, Jimmy open a lock.

He tugged on the chain. It held. Which was odd because it should break due to weak metal or a manufacturer's defect. Pink looked around. Maybe there was an abandoned file somewhere? Nope.

Huh.

Pink had never been this —

"Unlucky?" Lombardo said.

"It's possible there's just a delay," Pink said. "Sometimes the shift to Daylight Savings Time —"

Lombardo snorted. "That was months ago."

Pink cleared his throat. "Are you meaning to tell me —"

"— that luck has up and vanished? Yep. Poof! Gone!" Lombardi's face darkened. "Do you have any idea what that means for a man in my position?"

Pink shook his head.

"It means," Lombardi said, his voice rising, "that three of my best men got pinched this morning by the blue bottles. My most profitable casino lost more in an hour than it has all year. And to top it all off, Duchess ran off when I got home from work last night. I spent the whole night putting up missing posters."

"Sorry about your dog," Pink said.

Lombardi turned red.

Shit. Wrong animal. "Cat?"

"Duchess is my girl — a woman who has endured more shit than a public toilet at Glastonbury. And I can't live without her."

"I ... I'm sorry to hear that," Pink said. "But what does any of this have to do with me?"

Lombardi gestured to the man standing at Pink's shoulder. "Free the bird."

The man produced a key, dropped it. Picked it up again and fumbled it. Finally, Pink snatched it and unlocked the cuffs. Tossing them to the floor.

Lombardi produced a coin from his pocket and tossed it to Pink. 50p. "What am I supposed to do with this?"

"Ask me heads or tails, then flip it."

Okay. "Heads or tails?"

"Heads," Lombardi said.

Pink flipped the coin. It spun through the air, then landed on his palm with a soft *smack*. He slapped it onto the back of his other hand, then lifted his palm to reveal ...

"Tails."

"Again," Lombardi said. "Tails."

It came up heads.

"Again."

Pink flipped the coin a dozen more times. Lombardi still never guessed right.

"You see what I mean?" Lombardi asked.

Pink nodded. "Yeah. The odds of that happening are astronomical. It should have landed heads at least once."

Lombardi gestured with his fingers, and Pink handed him the coin.

"You see my problem," Lombardi said, pocketing 50p.

"I do," Pink said. "But again — what does this have to do with me?"

"I need someone to sort this mess out."

"Don't you have contacts?"

Lombardi tapped his fingers again on the arm of his throne. "Yes, but my usual sources have suffered some ... unfortunate accidents."

"Accidents?"

"I was bowled over when my primary dealer drowned in a cup of French onion soup. Then, hit a really low note when a piano falls on the next one. And when the last got eaten by a peacock, I started to suspect foul play ... until I realized this all had to do with luck. Or the lack of it."

Pink blinked. "I'm sorry, did you say eaten by a peacock?"

"I did."

"Right," Pink said faintly.

Lombardi leaned forward, his eyes glittering. "So, Mr. Phillips, I want you to figure out why luck has abandoned me. And everyone else. I'm signing a contract in 24 hours, and I need every molecule of good fortune I can muster. You have until then to set things right."

"And if I can't?"

Lombardi smiled, showing his teeth. "Well, let's just say I might have to introduce myself to Ella."

Pink turned cold. "Ella?"

"24 hours," Lombardi said. "The clock is already ticking."

The man at Pink's shoulder grabbed his arm, dragging him toward the warehouse door, escorting him to the van, and shoving him into the back again. At least this time, they left the hood off his face. Small mercies. While they drove through London's winding streets, Pink worked to assemble the pieces of what little he knew.

What the hell was happening?

Luck couldn't just disappear, could it?

That shouldn't be possible. Even the unluckiest sod in the world occasionally caught a break. The law of averages demanded that shit.

But Lombardi couldn't even guess a coin flip right.

And Pink couldn't even get out of handcuffs.

He chewed on his cheek, then reached for the van door. They were at a red light. He should be able to open it and hop out. But nope. The door refused to budge.

Something was definitely up.

Ten minutes later, the van screeched to a halt. Lombardi's man got out, opened the door, and gestured for him to exit. When Pink got out, the man tossed him his phone and got back in the van.

"Hey, Pink said, looking around. "This isn't my office. It's a random alley."

The man glared at him. "What do you think this is? Taxi service?"

"Kind of."

The man snorted. A second later, the van roared away.

When they were gone, Pink pulled out his phone and dialed Ella's number. One ring. Two. Three.

"Come on, pick up …"

The call went to voicemail. He tried again. And again. Still nothing.

So he left a message.

"Hey, Ella, call me as soon as you get this. And if a man named Lombardi wants to talk to you, leg it."

Pink walked out to the street. He was a good twenty-five-minute walk from his office. So he started hoofing it.

But ultimately came to a stop.

The world had gone mad.

A man stepped out of a tailor's shop. Bespoke suit, all sharp corners, and pressed luxury. Only for it to be Jackson Pollocked by a flock of pigeons seconds later.

A woman fumbled with her umbrella, getting it open a heartbeat before the rain let loose. And then, a freak gust of wind blew and turned her into Mary Poppins. She disappeared into the sky, leaving a pair of hot pink trainers behind on the sidewalk.

A mime made their way across the road next to the construction. A large piece of cement fell, almost hitting them. They darted to the right, pausing for a dramatic sigh of relief. Then kept walking and fell down an open manhole.

"Bloody hell," Pink said, taking in the chaos.

It wasn't just Lombardi's luck and his own. It seemed as though all of London's had vanished as well.

But he needed more evidence.

So he ducked into the Scone Zone. The aroma of

freshly brewed tea, cookies, and — of course — scones should have tickled his nose. But today, he smelled nothing. And the place was unusually empty.

Pink walked up to the purple-haired barista at the counter. "The usual, please, Clare," Pink said.

"Don't know what to tell you, Pink," she said. "But we're all out."

"Of English Breakfast tea?"

Clare shrugged. "All the tea. Supplier completely dried up. Said something about it falling into the harbor."

"Alright. How about a scone?"

"Weevils in the flour. We had to chuck it all and reorder."

"What if I just order the clotted cream?"

Clare pursed her lips. "How clotted do you want it?"

Pink sniffed. Something in the air definitely smelled sour. "Never mind. I'll try again tomorrow."

Clare waved.

Pink made his way back to his office.

And stopped cold outside his door.

The lock was broken, and the door was open.

His hand went to the rabbit's foot in his pocket. But it was gone. Shit. He must have dropped it back at the warehouse. Or in the van.

"Hello?" he said, pushing the door with his foot.

Harvie sat at his desk, slumped in apparent misery. "Oh, hey, Pink."

Pink stepped inside. "You broke in?"

Harvie shook his head. "No. I found it like this."

Pink looked around. All the horseshoes were gone from above the door. But otherwise, his office seemed untouched.

"Sorry for barging in," Harvie said. "I … I didn't know where else to go."

"What's wrong?" Pink asked.

"Absolutely bloody everything." Harvie ran a hand through his disheveled hair. "I've never had such a run of bad luck in my life. Lost my job at the chip shop, tore a hole in my underwear, and I'm pretty sure I have hemorrhoids." His voice cracked. "It's like a bunch of grapes down there."

Pink winced. "We all get holes in our underwear."

"Both socks and the underpants? All at the same time?"

Pink walked over and shooed Harvey out of his chair. Once he'd gotten up, Pink sank into the worn leather. Only to have one of the wheels pop off. He tumbled onto the floor, landing hard.

"You okay, Pink?"

Pink sighed and got to his feet. "I'm fine. Why don't you tell me when this started happening."

"It's been a few days." Harvie's brow furrowed in concentration. "It started Tuesday when all the potatoes went moldy and hasn't stopped…"

His phone rang.

Ella.

He held up a finger, silencing Harvie. Then, he fished his phone out of his pocket. But it wasn't Ella. It was a completely different name.

And it couldn't be.

She'd sworn never to speak to him again.

Maybe his luck was turning?

He answered the call. "Fran?"

"Well, it's about fucking time you answered the phone," she said.

He resisted the urge to snort. It had rung twice. "Nice to hear from you."

"No, it's not," she said. "Right now, you're trembling in your boots and hoping I won't yell at you."

Pink looked down at his feet. They were shaking a little. But that was only because he fell out of his chair. "Nonsense,"he said. "But I would appreciate it if you wouldn't yell. I'm getting a bit of a migraine."

She laughed.

Fran — Francesca Hart — was known in certain circles as the Queen of Hearts. She was the daughter of legendary card shark Elvis Hart — Pink's mentor in the ways of luck manipulation — and after her father's death (and one broken engagement to Pinkie Phillips), Fran carved out quite a reputation for herself on the Vegas poker scene.

"How are the cards treating you?" Pink asked.

"Terrible. I'm a disaster. My luck has gone to absolute shit. I can't win a hand to save my life."

Pink frowned. Bad luck had hit Vegas, too?

"I'm trying to buy Dad's lucky chip back from that bastard Jack Porter, but at this rate, I'm gonna owe more than the damn thing is worth."

"And it's worth a lot." They said it at the same time.

"Yeah," Fran sounded sad. "And Pink, I hate to ask because we agreed not to speak again —"

"I don't remember agreeing to that," Pink said. "It was more of an order."

She ignored him. "— but … is there any chance you could spot me some luck? Just enough to get back in the game?"

Pink pinched the bridge of his nose, the migraine blooming behind his eyes. If Fran was experiencing issues with luck, then this situation was far more problematic than Lombardi even knew.

"Tell you what," said Pink, an idea forming. "I think I

can do you one better. Give me an hour, and I'll arrange for a little luck to come your way. I have a few tricks up my sleeve for emergency boosts."

"You're a lifesaver." Fran's relief was audible. "I owe you one."

He smiled, then hung up. He took his seat (on a slant) and cracked his knuckles, firing off a series of text at dizzying speed.

"It's a joy to watch you work," Harvie said.

Pink grunted but didn't let himself get distracted. And by the time he finished, he'd begged, borrowed, and bartered for the last bit of luck available that day.

And he sent it all to Fran.

"There," he said, slumping back in his broken chair. "That should do it."

He texted Fran: *All done.*

Ten minutes later, his phone rang.

Fran.

"That was fast," Pink said, answering the phone. "How'd it go?"

"What the fuck did you do?"

"What —"

"I lost everything, Pink. *Everything*! And now I owe that fucking snake Porter even more than before."

"How—"

"Whatever you did backfired spectacularly. I've never seen anything like it. It's a fucking shitstorm of a shitstorm."

"Why —"

"I'm gonna be fucking broke and —"she burst into tears.

Pink froze. He'd never heard her cry before. "Fran?"

She sniffed. "Pink ... what the hell is going on?"

He looked at Harvie.

The ceiling fell in.

Bits of tile struck his head, and the whole of the office filled with a cloud of drywall dust. Pink coughed. "I don't know. But I intend to find out. Sit tight. I'm coming to Vegas."

* * *

Pink ran through the sliding glass doors at Heathrow Airport, Harvie trailing behind him.

The terminal buzzed with usual chaos — announcements, harried travelers, luggage — but to Pink's trained eye, there was an undercurrent of … *something*. A wrongness that set his teeth on edge.

Flights were late. Some were canceled. The escalators were painfully slow. The elevators weren't working.

And for some reason, a zebra was standing in the middle of the concourse eating a potted plant.

Pink made his way to English Air (which sounded more like smog than an airplane company) and approached the ticket counter. He slapped his credit card on the counter like a gambler, tossing his last chip onto the table. "Two tickets to Las Vegas. Fastest flight you've got."

The agent — a middle-aged woman with exhausted eyes and a performative smile — stared at him. "They all fly at the same speed, Sir."

Pink forced a smile of his own. "I'll take whatever you've got."

She didn't respond; simply turned back to her keyboard and moved at the speed of molasses. Pink hoped the English Air planes were a mite faster.

"There are no flights. Not today."

"It doesn't have to be coach. I'll do first class." It's where he usually wound up anyway. By luck.

"No," she said. "There's no flights at all out of Heathrow today."

"How about Gatwick?" he said. "I can buy my ticket here and —"

"No flights out of the UK."

Pinky blinked. "How is that possible?"

"No tea," she said.

"You don't know?"

"No, I mean, there is literally no tea available."

"Let me guess," Pink said. "It wound up in the harbor."

"I wouldn't know," she said.

Pink leaned on the counter. "Are you telling me there is no way any plane is leaving the UK because there is no tea on board?"

"Do you want to fly without caffeine?"

"Fair enough," Pink said. "Give me two tickets for first thing tomorrow morning."

Pink walked over to one of the hard plastic chairs and took a seat.

"We're staying the night?" Harvie asked.

Pink glanced at him. "I'm not gonna risk missing the flight. Who knows. Maybe sheep will take over the expressway. Or the train tracks will freeze up."

He pulled out his phone and dialed Ella.

Once more, it rang through to voicemail. "Please call me Ella. It's urgent."

He hung up, and a second later, his phone buzzed.

Thank God.

Only it was Lombardi's number. A chill rippled down his spine, and it had nothing to do with the airport's overzealous air conditioning. "Hey, Mr. Lombardi, I was just about to call you."

"And why is that?"

"I need more time. 24 more hours."

"Really?" Lombardi's voice oozed with menace.

"Yeah."

"Because I hear you're fleeing the country."

Pink tightened his grip on the phone. He could almost feel Lombardi's hot breath on his neck. "I'm not running. I'm following a lead. This problem is bigger than London. It's hit Vegas as well."

"So —"

So? Lombardi was right. Why was he going to help Fran when Ella needed him just as much?

"I've got a contact in Vegas," He fibbed. "She's got some intel for me on what's going on."

For a moment, there was just silence. "You telling me the truth, Phillips?"

"You think I'd lie when luck has taken a vacation?"

"Very well. You have 48 hours, Phillips. Not a minute more. If you're not back with answers by then, well, me and Ella are gonna have that little chat."

The line went dead, leaving Pink staring at his phone. Then he tried dialing again. *Where the hell was she?*

He could only hope the flight tomorrow would actually get him to Vegas. And then he could start figuring out where Lady Luck had gone.

* * *

Pink huddled against the plane window, trying to disappear into his seat. A baby's wail pierced the air, joined a breath later by what sounded like an orchestrated chorus of infants. The drink cart careened down the aisle before hitting Harvie's seat and spilling orange soda all over him. The flight attendant handed him a meal. When Pink removed the cover, he couldn't actually figure out what he was supposed to be eating.

"Excuse me," Pink said, gesturing to the meal. "What is this?"

"Food," the flight attendant said.

"Are you sure?" Pink asked, shaking his fork out of a paper packet of utensils. He poked at the gray lump on his tray, half-expecting it to poke back.

Harvie glanced at him. "You gonna eat that?"

Pink shook his head. "Go ahead."

Harvie took the meal and added it to his own. "D'you think we'll see Gigi Fiddle?"

Pink stared at him. "Who?"

"Gigi Fiddle," he said, shoveling gray mush into his mouth. "Did you know she can escape from a steel safe while suspended upside down over a pit of ravenous sharks? And does it all in under three minutes!"

"We're not here for entertainment, Harv. We're here to help Fran. And save Ella."

"Right. Of course. Absolutely." Harvie said. "But if we happen to walk past one of her shows or attend one of her book signings…"

"She has a book?"

"She has three. Magical Tricks. Magical Illusions. Magical Escapes."

"Magical," Pink said.

Then he turned back to the window.

And despite the persistent soundtrack of teething babies, he somehow managed to nod off. Only to be woken half an hour later to find they were descending.

They touched down hard, and several passengers' belongings tumbled from the overhead bins. They then had to wait almost an hour until the gate was free (apparently, US planes weren't flying due to a shortage of soda).

But eventually, they made their way through the airport and out to the taxi cabs. The software that ran the meters was kaput. But Pink offered cash, and seconds later, he and Harvie were being driven to the Royal Flush.

It wasn't one of the sleeker, more modern casinos.

This one had crawled up out of the dirt when Vegas was built in the late forties. And it had been hanging on by its fingernails ever since.

Its facade used to be painted bright red, but now it was a faded pink. And the neon sign which stood at the entrance was on the blink. Now it just said: FLUSH.

Pink and Harvie got out of the cab and made their way through the front doors. The inside was just as worn as the outside. Lights pulsed in seizure-inducing patterns. But it wasn't on purpose. More than half the fluorescent lights were on the blink.

The slot machines chimed and whirred as usual, but there weren't any victorious cries. Simply the sound of money being eaten by machines.

Pink surveyed the floor, searching for Fran. He spotted her by the blackjack table. She sat slumped over an empty table, staring at her phone.

Pink made his way over, Harvie following at his heels.

Fran stiffened when she saw Pink. And then her crooked smile turned into a scowl when she eyed Harvie. "What the fuck is he doing here?"

"He's here to help," said Pink. Although, he was actually wondering himself why Harvie came along.

"Well you're too late. I've lost everything. I'll never get Dad's chip back now."

"Let me try." Pink walked to the nearest cashier's cage and bought a stack of chips. Then he made his way to the nearest slot machine and sat, ignoring the *OUT OF ORDER* sign hanging askew from the screen.

Then he fed it a twenty and pulled the lever. The reels spun in a blur of cherries, bars, and lucky sevens. He focused, calling on the well of luck that had never failed him before. For Pink, it shouldn't matter that the machine said Out of Order.

The reels slowed.

Clunk. Clunk. Clunk.

Nothing. Not even a single cherry lined up.

"Let me try something else," Pink said.

He moved to the roulette table. Placed a chip on black, his eyes never leaving the tiny white ball as it skittered and bounced around the wheel. Round and round it went, slowing, teetering …

And landed on red.

Pink tried game after game. Blackjack. Poker. Penny Slots. He lost them all.

Every. Single. Time.

"What's going on, Pink?" Fran asked. "I've never known you to lose a game. Ever."

He opened his mouth to respond —

"YOU!"

They turned towards the voice. Jack Porter walked towards them. His suit was tailored to perfection. His salt-and-pepper hair was slicked back, not a strand out of place. A gaudy signet ring glinted on his right hand and caught the casino lights.

He came with a matching set of men — both built like brick walls.

"Where the fuck is my lucky chip?"

Fran stared at him. "What?"

"Elvis' chip is missing."

Fran's eyes widened. "You lost my chip?"

"No, I lost my chip. Or perhaps 'stolen' is the more appropriate word?"

"I didn't take anything," Fran said. "I've been trying to buy it back. *You know that.*"

Porter turned to his team. "Search them. Get my chip. And if it's not on them, light them up. One of them will eventually talk."

Pink grabbed Fran's hand and ran towards the exit. "Harvie, come on!"

A second later, they were melting in the Vegas heat.

"This way," Fran said, directing them around back to the parking lot. They piled into her tiny red mini and hit the strip.

Behind them, Porter's men seemed to have run into an issue where their shoelaces spontaneously got tied together.

The three of them were about a block from the Royal Flush (which in Vegas is saying something) when a loud POP sounded, and the car bumped up against the curb.

"You gotta be fucking kidding me," Fran said. "These are new tires."

They all got out to inspect the vehicle. But it wasn't one tire that popped. It was three. Fran planted her hands on her hips and glared at Pink as though it was his fault. "What the fuck is going on?"

"It's not just contained to London," Pink said.

"What's not just London?"

"This … whatever it is … it's infected Vegas too. The whole bloody world's lost its luck."

Fran's jaw fell open. "There's no more luck?"

Pink shook his head. "I don't think so."

"That's not possible," Fran said. "There's a backroom baccarat game still pulling in winners."

"Let's go there," Pink said. "Maybe we can figure out why their luck hasn't dried up, but everyone else's has."

Fran nodded, pointing towards an old church. "That way."

But when they arrived, the building was emptying out. And no one looked very happy about it.

"The game's over?" Fran asked.

A man nodded. "Back room flooded. But everyone was losing anyway. Gonna try our luck at the Flush."

Pink was about to tell him not to bother when Fran tugged on his hand.

"Oh no." She pointed to his left.

Two mountains of muscle scanned the crowd of gamblers. Then, one spotted Fran. He growled, walking towards them. "Hand over the chip, Hart."

"RUN!" Pink shouted.

They ran toward the closest alley (which in Vegas is saying something) before they finally ducked behind a large dumpster.

"Now what?" Harvie asked.

"Let me think," Pink said, rubbing the sweat from his brow. And then an idea came to him. "Spyder."

Harvie spun around. "Where?"

"No. Spyder. He used to be one of the biggest luck dealers in town before he hit it big and retired. If anyone knows what's going on, it'll be him."

Fran shook her head. "Spyder's a myth."

"I can assure you he is not," Pink said. "Come on, we need to get to the bus station."

They wound up catching a cab. And though the air conditioning was busted, the radio was not. And the news that blared out at a hundred decibels confirmed that luck had appeared to run out the world over.

A blimp had been punctured by the Eiffel Tower.

An infestation of kangaroos had taken over the Sydney Opera House.

A sandstorm in Cairo had reburied the pyramids.

The bus station was crowded with the usual suspects.

"Where are we going?" Harvie asked.

Pink pointed to the door labeled: Janitor.

A man in overalls was leaning on a mop, looking bored. "Help you?" he asked when they approached.

"Need to see Spyder," Pink said. "There's no more bleach."

The Janitor eyes him for a moment. Then, he jerked his head towards the door. "Go on in."

Pink grabbed the handle and entered a narrow hallway.

Fran raised her brows. "There's no more bleach?"

"Code," Pink said. "For ASAP."

"You have code words for luck emergencies?" Harvie asked. "How often does this happen?"

"Quite a lot. Especially in the 70s."

Pink made his way towards a door at the end of the hall. He opened it up, and a second later, the pulsing beat of electronic music filled his ears.

The room was a fever dream come to life. Purple and red velvet drapes hung on all the walls. The air held a cloying mixture of incense and something sweeter. The floor shook in time to the DJ's beat. Pink's eyes struggled to adjust to the dim light. But finally, he saw Spyder.

He was sprawled across a chaise lounge at the back of the room like a debauched Roman emperor. His skin was a canvas of intricate designs, ink covering him from neck to fingertips. And his eyes gleamed with unnatural brightness when he spotted Pink.

Pink led the parade over to him.

"Look what the cat dragged in." Spyder's grin was wide. "Still chasing Dame Fortune's skirts?"

"Not so much chasing as appreciating."

"So what brings you to my neck of the desert? You retiring?" He gestured to the room. "Although that ain't really urgent."

"Not yet." Pink pulled up a chair and sat next to him. "The luck, Spyder. It's gone. Not just here, but everywhere."

Spyder's smile faded. "So you've noticed too, eh?"

Pink nodded.

"Yeah, something's rotten in the state of Vegas, alright. And word on the street is it all leads back to Maximilian Bump."

Fran blinked. "The tech billionaire?"

"The very same," nodded Spyder. "Last week, dude threw the party of the century. Every high roller and luck magnet in town was there. They even flew in from all over the globe. And now? They've all disappeared. Vanished right alongside every shred of good fortune in this godforsaken city."

"You think Bump is behind this?" Pink asked.

"I'd bet my last chip on it," Spyder said. "But no one's talking. People are scared of him. He makes his enemies disappear faster than an audience member at a Gigi Fiddle magic show."

"Don't suppose you know where I can find this Bump?" Pink asked.

Spyder gestured to his arm. Pink rolled up his sleeve. A second later, Spyder wrote an address on his skin in day-glo paint. "This is his desert compound. But be careful. Whatever Bump is up to, it's big. And dangerous."

Pink nodded. "Thanks."

"Good luck," Spyder said. "If you can find it."

* * *

Thankfully, Spyder lent them the Luckmobile (it said so on the side). Whenever Fran hit the brakes, a jackpot sound chimed throughout the vehicle.

But the further they drove into the vast emptiness of the desert, the more it began to shake and groan. Fran kept her hands on the wheel, and her jaw clenched so tight Pink could almost hear her teeth grinding.

Harvie shifted in the back seat. "Shouldn't we call the police?"

"And tell them what?" Fran said, glancing in the rearview mirror. "That some rich asshole stole all the luck in the world? They'd lock us up faster than a gambler gets on a losing streak."

"It's better than driving into the mouth of the monster," Harvie said.

"You don't have to come," Fran said. Then she turned to Pink. "Why is he here again? He's the reason we broke up. You can never tell him no."

"I tell him no all the time," Pink said.

"When it comes to luck. Not when it comes to us." She cleared her throat. "Came. Not when it came to us."

Pink sighed. "He's my friend."

"Yeah, and I was your fucking —"

BAM!

The car jerked to a stop. Fire and smoke poured out from beneath the hood. The three of them scrambled out of the vehicle.

Harvie watched it go up in flames. "Poor Luckmobile."

Pink glanced around the desert. They were in the middle of nowhere. It wasn't even a highway they had been on. It was more like someone had scribbled a line in the dirt and decided to call it a road.

"We'll have to walk," he said.

A chorus of howls echoed across the desert.

Harvie stiffened. "Are those…?"

"Coyotes," Fran said. "We need to move. Now."

And they did. Running in the direction that Fran's GPS assured them was Bump's locale. From behind them came the sound of hungry yips. Pink's lungs burned, and his legs felt like leaden weights.

"How fond of Harvie are you?" Fran asked. "We could use him as bait."

Right when Pink was about to suggest that Harvie might not need both of his arms, a glimmer of light caught his eye.

Civilization. Salvation.

Bump's compound sprawled like a mirage before them.

They ran towards the "house," and then floodlights blazed to life, momentarily blinding them.

When Pink's vision finally cleared, they were surrounded by armed guards. He glanced at Fran.

She gestured to a drainage ditch.

But it was too late to seek cover.

"Well, well," said a smooth voice. And a moment later, Maximilian Bump emerged out of the darkness. He was — tall, broad-shouldered, and exuded an aura of Jeff Goldblumness effortless control (he even looked like him). His perfectly tailored suit looked pristine despite the hour and the desert air. He was all teeth when he smiled.

"Pink and Company," Bump said. "Welcome to my humble abode. Spyder told me you were coming."

Pink grimaced.

Fran glared at him.

"You didn't know he worked for me?" Bump laughed.

Pink shook his head.

"Forced him into retirement," Bump said, flicking a nonexistent speck of dust from his suit.

"But why?" Pink asked.

"Why don't you come inside?" Bump said, gesturing to his compound. "I would love to show you."

"Don't suppose we have any choice," Pink said.

Bump rubbed his jaw. "Don't suppose you do." And then he led the way into the concrete bunker. Pink took

Fran's hand (just so she wouldn't be scared), and Harvie took his. The guards followed behind them.

Minutes later, Pink, Fran, and Harvie found themselves in a cavernous room humming with barely contained energy. At its center loomed a massive machine, its sleek metallic surface alive with pulsing tendrils of light. The air crackled with an otherworldly charge, raising the hair on Pink's arms.

"Beautiful, isn't she?" Bump walked over and placed his palm against the machine.

"What is it?" Pink asked.

"The Luck Extractor."

"The what?" Fran said?

"Luck Extractor. By midnight tonight, it will have drained every last drop of luck from the world."

"But why?" Pink asked.

"Because luck is chaos! It's disorder! A man forgets his umbrella and stays dry, while the woman with a raincoat gets soaked by a passing bus." Bump laughed, but it sounded bitter. "A man wins a raffle for a free car on one ticket, while the guy who bought 50 walks away empty-handed. A woman is late for her train, so she stops and buys a lottery ticket and wins millions. *That* is the world of luck. I'm going to level the playing field. No more random chance. Just cold, hard reality from now on."

"You're wrong," Pink said. "Luck isn't just chaos. It's hope. It's the belief that things can get better against all odds. Without a little luck in our lives, we might as well all give up now."

"That's what I've been saying all along." Harvie said.

"Bullshit," Fran said.

Bump's face hardened. "What?"

"You just don't want anyone to get as lucky as you.

That's why you're taking all the luck. You want to hoard it for yourself."

Bump turned to his guards. "Take them to the basement. Then kill them."

Pink's hand tightened on Fran's. They were out of time, options, and — apparently — luck.

The guards marched them through a door and down a concrete set of stairs.

As they made their way down, the air grew thicker until it felt like he was trying to breathe underwater. The acrid scent of ozone mixed with the metallic tang of machinery.

They reached the bottom, and the stairwell opened into another cavernous chamber. Down here were the bones of the Luck Extractor's massive form. A bone-deep hum emanated from the machine, vibrating through Pink's body.

Bump's head of security ushered them into a cement corner and pulled his gun. "End of the line."

Pink looked at Fran. "I'm sorry."

"Me too," she said.

He ran through ideas, searching for a solution that didn't end with the three of them full of lead. But nothing came to him.

The head of security raised his weapon.

Pink watched the man's finger tighten on the trigger.

He closed his eyes, bracing for the impact.

CRACK!

The gunshot echoed like thunder.

Pink braced for the searing pain of a bullet but instead heard a strangled grunt followed by the THUD of a body hitting concrete. Pink opened his eyes. The security guard was sprawled on the ground, limbs akimbo. A dark pool of blood spread beneath him.

The other guards looked at one another, seemingly equally confused.

Who had shot him?

No one else had a weapon out.

And then it hit him.

"*Bloody hell,*" Pink breathed. "It's still here!"

"What is?" Fran asked.

"Luck!" Pink said. "It's not gone, it's just ... inverted. Everything is backward! This is bad luck."

"So how do we fight it?" Fran asked.

The other guards pulled their weapons.

"We don't!" Pink said. "We need to save them!"

"Huh?" Harvie asked.

But Fran got it. "Save them like our lives depend on it."

Pink nodded.

A guard pulled the trigger. Pink leapt in front of the bullet. Which somehow instead hit the Luck Extractor, ricocheted about on the inside, then flew out and hit the guard in centre mass.

Another guard slipped on a wet patch of floor, but when Fran tried to break his fall, he wound up breaking his neck. One tried to strangle Harvie with his hands but wound up with his necktie, cutting off his own oxygen source. A third tried to bean Pink over the head with a metal rod, only to trip over his own shoelaces and impale himself.

"The machine!" Fran pointed at the Luck Extractor.

Sparks flew from its base, the beginnings of a fire.

"We have to protect it!" Pink said, grabbing a nearby fire extinguisher.

A door by the stairs flew open, and Bump burst into the room. "What's going on?"

Pink applied the extinguisher to the flames, but they were spreading too quick.

"My machine!" Bump said.

More guards entered, "Mr Bump. We need to evacuate."

He shook his head. "No! I need to save my machine."

Pink chucked aside the empty extinguisher and turned to Harvie and Fran. "Get out. But pretend like you want to stay."

"Huh?" Harvie asked.

"What about you?" Fran asked.

"I'll be right behind you," Pink said.

Guards grabbed each of them, and they tried to resist. But to no avail. They were led out of the facility. Such bad luck.

"What have you done?" Bump asked, running over to him.

The fire was increasing. The heat was so intense that Pink's skin tightened while the machine groaned and buckled.

"We need to save it," Pink said.

Bump nodded, lunging for the control panel, his fingers flying over the keys. But every keystroke only brought another error message. The coolant systems failed, and the backup protocols locked him out.

"What the hell did you do?" Bump said.

"Dumped the tea in the harbor," Pink said.

Bump looked confused.

"It's emitting bad luck."

And in that second, Bump got it. "Fuck."

But it was too late. The lights flickered and died, plunging the room into an absolute darkness. And then the Luck Extractor exploded. And took Pink with it.

* * *

"Pink!"

He blinked.

Opening his eyes to see Fran and Harvie standing above him.

"What happened?"

There was another loud explosion.

Debris rained down around them. A chair, a sleek leather briefcase, and something that looked suspiciously like Maximillian Bump's head.

The briefcase had sprung open on impact, spilling its contents across the desert floor — stacks upon stacks of crisp hundred-dollar bills.

"Let's get you up," Fran said.

Pink looked around. How had he wound up out here?

She dusted the dirt from his shirt. "The blast must have blown you free."

"Yeah, I guess so."

Harvie gathered up the bills, closed the briefcase, and tucked it under his arm. "Don't suppose either of you want some of this?"

Pink shook his head.

"Take it, it's yours," Fran said.

The three of them walked down to the dirt road. They arrived to find a vehicle driving towards them. A cherry red convertible. It stopped. Behind the wheel sat a woman who looked vaguely familiar.

"Need a ride?" she asked, her voice smooth as honey.

Harvie stared at her. "G-Gigi Fiddle?"

Fran bent to pick up an object at her feet. She straightened, holding it out. Elvis Hart's lucky chip.

"I think our luck might be changing," Fran said.

"I think it's more than that," Pink said. "We're bloody drenched in the stuff!"

His phone rang.

Lombardi.

Hopefully, it was good news.

But it wasn't Lombardi on the phone. It was…

"Ella?"

"Pink! Oh my god, you'll never believe it!" Her voice bubbled through the speaker. "It's like something out of a fairy tale. I was walking to work and this man named Angelo fell at my feet. He's charming and kind, and … we're in love, Pink!" Her words hit him like a splash of cold water. "We're getting married. Can you believe it?"

He blinked, looking at Fran, eyeing him with a mixture of interest and something else. Whatever it was made his heart skip.

He smiled. "I'm happy for you, Ella."

She disconnected.

Pink tucked his phone away and met Fran's eyes. "Don't suppose you'd be interested in a long vacation?"

Fran's phone rang. She answered. "Yeah. Really? Okay, thanks." She hung up. "Apparently I just won a trip for two to Vegas."

"I take it that's a yes, then?" Pink asked.

She leaned forward and kissed him. "Let's just say the house isn't the only thing winning tonight."

Then, they all climbed into Gigi's car and drove back to Vegas.

Blistered

KIM M. WATT

Blistered

KIM M. WATT

EMILY LAY IN THE HOSPITAL, HER ARMS ENCASED IN THICK bandages from her elbows all the way down to her wrists and hands. Her fingers stuck out of the wrapping, uncomfortable and as swollen as sausages. It was as though her hands belonged to someone else entirely. She swallowed, her throat feeling raw. She felt unsteady and displaced as if surfacing from an epically bad hangover.

"Emily? How're you feeling?"

Emily looked over at the dark-eyed woman sitting by the bed. Her hair was scraped tightly back into a bun, and she hadn't introduced herself. A disproportionately tall, skinny man had trailed in behind her. He now stood by the door, watching silently.

Emily swallowed, wincing at the pain in her throat, "No one will tell me what happened."

"Don't you remember?" the woman asked.

Emily shook her head.

"Okay, then. I'm Detective Alina Murillo. The string bean by the door is my partner, Detective Jake Byrne."

The skinny man nodded slightly. He was younger than

Murillo, with an unformed look about him, whereas Murillo was all sharp edges. The detective crossed her legs. "What's the last thing you remember?"

Emily licked her lips.

Murillo offered her a glass of water from the side table. Emily took it awkwardly in her bandaged hands and took a sip. "Thursday night. I remember studying."

"And where was that?" Murillo asked.

"Milton Community College."

"In?"

"Milton," Emily said, hearing the *obviously* in her voice even though she didn't say it.

Murillo either didn't notice or ignored it. "So you don't remember coming back to Ironfield?"

"*Ironfield?*" How could she be in Ironfield? She'd been at school two hundred miles away. And not only that. She'd left two years ago, left *forever*. Panic bubbled in her chest, tightening her throat further. "I'm in *Ironfield?*"

"Does that surprise you?"

"Yes, it surprises me," Emily said, her voice terse. Was this some elaborate prank? It had to be; she tried to say so but broke into racking painful coughs.

Emily gulped down some more water. "Why am I here?"

"In the hospital?"

"Ironfield."

Murillo raised her eyebrows. "You don't know?"

"I know I never wanted to be back here. I would never have willingly come here."

"Oh?"

Emily didn't elaborate. Nobody needed to know the details. Nobody but her.

Murillo tapped her fingers together. Thumb to thumb, index finger to index finger, and for one absurd moment,

Emily thought the detective was going to do itsy-bitsy spider. Instead, she said, "Why do you think you're here?"

"Someone's pranking me?"

"Who?"

Emily shrugged. It would help if she could remember. But she couldn't.

The silence stretched between them, broken only by Byrne shifting his weight and the distant sounds of the hospital outside the room. Eventually, Murillo said. "You had a bit of trouble when you were in school."

Emily didn't answer. Everyone got in trouble at school, and if she'd *acted out*, smoked more than cigarettes, or stolen some beer – well, who the fuck cared? Especially considering — nope. She wasn't gonna go down that road.

"Do you know where your injuries came from, Emily?"

Emily looked at her bandaged hands and shook her head.

"You were found at your family's hotel," Murillo's voice was calm.

Emily's head jerked up. "The hotel?" Ironfield was bad enough, but *there?*

Murillo nodded. "The restaurant and bar were burned down. Six people died."

Emily flinched. "Why?"

"That's what we'd like you to tell us."

"How would I know what happened?"

"You were the only person who got out. You were found in the parking lot."

"But I don't even know how I got here," Emily said in a low voice. "I should be at a media lecture right now."

Murillo reached out for the glass of water, and Emily let her take it. She sat it back on the bedside table. "What do you know about the fire?"

Emily's stomach rolled, bringing back the slick, greasy

taste of the smoothie they'd fed her for lunch. She swallowed hard. "I don't know *anything about it,* I don't even know why I'm here."

Murillo waited a moment, but when Emily didn't add any more, she got up, straightening the sleeves of her jacket. "You're going to be discharged from hospital soon, but you'll remain in town, understood?"

"I've got classes," Emily said. "And I can't... I don't want to be here."

"It doesn't matter what you want," Murillo said. "Six people are dead. You were found at the scene. You *will* stay in town. I'll put a police watch on you if need be." Then she turned and walked out, Byrne slouching after her.

Emily wanted to say. "Wait. Who died?"

But a part of her also didn't want to know.

Her face felt too hot and her hands too cold, and that damn milkshake was refusing to digest. Only once she was sure she wasn't going to vomit did she push the blanket off and sit up, swinging her legs over the side of the bed. She had abrasions on her knees, and her ribs hurt. She lifted the hospital gown up and peered down, discovering a blossoming, deep purple bruise on her right side. She investigated her head gingerly with her sausage fingers, finding a chunky dressing taped to her temple. That likely explained why she couldn't remember anything. She stood up, waited for her head to stop spinning, then took a deep breath and tottered to the door, pushing her I.V. along the floor, using it for balance.

She pressed her cheek against the glass pane and peered out, glimpsing a police officer sitting with his back to the wall, his legs stretched out in front of him. He was scrolling through his phone. What the hell had *happened?*

Her memory gave a mental shrug, and she retreated to the bed, head throbbing and stomach churning. She crawled back under the blanket and curled up as small as she could, arms around her knees. Ironfield, and confinement, and blooming bruises. If this was a prank, it was the worst one ever. She pressed her forehead to her knees.

She was back in Ironfield.

Her family's hotel had just burned down.

The police thought it was her.

Welcome fucking home.

#

She was discharged two hours later.

They'd given her some painkillers and some clothes from lost property. The police had kept hers and her phone. The oversized T-shirt, which read *I'd rather be fishing* flapped around her legs while she stood in the heat of the afternoon. Maybe she should go back inside where it was air-conditioned.

Because she had no idea what to do next. She had no phone, no money, nothing except someone else's T-shirt, flip-flops, and a badly-fitting pair of running shorts. Tears pricked her eyes. She tried to pinch the bridge of her nose, grunting in disgust when she bumped it with her bandaged hand.

She couldn't even stop herself from crying.

"Ems."

She jerked around, her movement unsteady.

Her brother stood a few paces away in the shade of the hospital's entrance. He was pale, skinnier than she remembered, a couple of days worth of stubble straggling across his jaw.

They stared at each other in silence.

Emily broke first. "What're you doing here?"

He shrugged. "I figured you wouldn't have anywhere to go."

"I wouldn't have thought that mattered."

He started to say something, stopped, then said, "Do you want a lift or not?"

She hugged her arms over her chest. "I'm supposed to stay in town."

"Obviously."

"*Obviously?*"

"You were at the fire, Ems. They're going to want to talk to you some more." He fished his keys out of his pocket. "You can stay with me."

"Where?"

"At the hotel."

"I thought it burned down."

'Mainly the main building. As you know."

She shook her head. "I don't know anything. Not about the fire, or what I'm doing here, or how I got here. I have *no fucking idea* what happened." Her voice spiraled as she spoke, and she broke off, swallowing hard and wincing. She licked her lips. "What about Mom and Dad?"

He grimaced. "They're away. Good thing, too. It'll destroy them to see it in its current state. So you wanna come or not?"

She nodded.

He turned and led the way to the parking lot with a long, easy stride. Emily hurried after him, flip-flops slapping against the pavement. She didn't really want to go. But it wasn't like she had a choice.

They drove to the hotel in silence, the road winding through the dusty outskirts of town to where the hotel crouched, low and dingy, on a couple of acres. The sign above the parking lot was faded and worn.

Emily could smell smoke well before they pulled in. There was a wing of rooms stretching out on either side of the hotel's main lobby, which stood slightly higher, its red roof rising to a peak. The peak was gone now, though, and what remained was charred and blackened. In a strange way, it looked as though something had been taking bites out of it.

Emily stared at it, her mouth sticky. Stuart switched the engine off, and they sat in silence.

Finally, he said, "I'm fucked."

Emily turned her head to look at him, her neck creaking. "Why you?"

"I took it on last year."

That surprised her. "You did?"

He nodded, examining the car key. "Mom and Dad signed it over to me. Tax thing, basically. And now, what do I do? God knows if the insurance is even going to pay out."

She rubbed her mouth with a shaky hand, the bandages rough on her lips. "I didn't know it was yours."

He smiled faintly, his gaze still on the ruined facade. "Would that have made a difference?"

And there it was. The accusation she had been waiting for. "I didn't do this."

"No?"

She shook her head.

"You know I was the one who dragged you out of the fucking foyer the other night. I couldn't even reach the others."His voice broke, and he swallowed. "Why were you here anyway? I was shocked when I saw you."

"You really think I'd come all the way back here just to set fire to this shit hole? Why?"

He didn't answer.

"Because I *never* wanted to come back!"

Stuart still didn't look at her, just swung the driver's side door open. "Come on. I need a drink."

"No," she said, "I'm not going in there."

"Stay here, then," he said. "Your choice." He slammed

the door and walked off, skirting the main building and heading for the far end of the left wing. There was an office there and four small rooms where they'd grown up, the walls stained with memories.

Emily watched him go with one hand pressed to her wounded forehead, applying just enough pressure that it hurt. The pain made things sharper and brought the world into focus. She took a shaky breath.

Okay, so she didn't know what had happened. But she wasn't going to work it out by staying out here. Plus, she was pretty sure she could still smell fish scales on her newly acquired T-shirt. And that wasn't helping her mood. So she got out and followed her brother.

He'd left the front door open behind him, the room inside dim after the bright day. Emily hesitated on the threshold, bracing herself for the pervasive stink of reheated soup and spilled beer. Preparing herself to see the stained oil paintings that had always hung on the walls, the clutter of forgotten dinner plates, and the humming undertone of the fridge laboring to stay alive.

But when she stepped inside, she was surprised to see how different it looked. The blinds had been replaced by pale curtains, and light now spilled in through the windows. The walls were bare and had been painted a soft white. A breakfast bar had replaced the rickety Formica table, and a grey couch stood straight-backed in the center of the floor. It was the same shape it had always been, but some of the old truths had been papered over.

"You changed it."

Stuart held a beer out to her. "Can't make things any worse, can it?"

That got a half smile from her. She walked over and took the bottle awkwardly in her bandaged hands.

"Besides, it needed doing."

She nodded, wondering if he just meant it had been old and dull or if it had been full of ghosts for him, too. It had never been a joyful place for anyone. But she'd had it worse. She sipped the beer, savoring the coldness in her burnt throat. "Did people really die in the fire?"

He examined her. "You don't remember anything?"

"Nothing between school and hospital. I don't even know what day it is."

"Monday."

She rubbed her forehead. "Jesus. I need to contact the school. I've missed so many classes."

"I think that's the least of your worries."

"What d'you mean?"

"Arson, arrest, dead people?"

"It's—"

"Nothing to do with you. You said that already." He swigged his beer, looking at her curiously. "I almost believe you."

"You should."

He pointed towards the bathroom. "Have a shower. I'll find you some clothes. And some plastic bags for your arms."

Emily went. She didn't know why it mattered that her brother believed her, not after all this time, but it did. It really did.

\#

The day passed strangely.

It was disconcerting being back here. A bit of paint and some new furniture couldn't hide the weight of history. It seemed almost impossible to relax. She was constantly waiting for someone to start shouting, for glass to break, for doors to slam. But other than her brother's shitty music, it was silent.

Whoever had been staying here had left, so they were

219

the only two occupants. She and Stuart didn't talk much, just drank their way steadily through the contents of the fridge, then moved onto the bottles of cheap spirits Stuart had saved from the fire. As he said, he wouldn't be serving them anytime soon.

At some point, caught between painkillers, alcohol, and exhaustion, Emily passed out on the couch. She woke in the thin hours of the morning, a blanket draped over her. Her head and side throbbed. But she didn't move. She had no intention of sleeping in her old bedroom. Too many things needed forgetting in that room.

Eventually, she fell asleep again, and the next time she woke, it was to someone banging on the door. She pushed herself onto her elbows, watching Stuart head to the door clad in just a pair of jeans. He pulled the door open.

"Mr. Bryant, is your sister here?" Emily recognized that voice. Murillo.

Stuart pulled the door open wordlessly. Emily sat.

"We need to ask you a few more questions," Murillo said.

"I've told you everything I can."

"Then you can tell us again. Get dressed."

Emily did. Swapping the fishy T-shirt for an old band shirt of her brother's. She needed some clothes that actually fit, but that didn't seem to be happening any time soon.

Neither Murillo nor Byrne spoke on the way into town, and Emily wasn't about to start a conversation. When they arrived at the station, they guided her into an interview room and left her there. They didn't come back until she'd been waiting long enough to start worrying at the bandages with her teeth. The skin underneath was almost unbearably itchy.

When they reentered the room, Emily met Murillo's eyes. "Do I need a lawyer?"

She detected a flash of hostility in the detective's eyes. "Do you want one?"

"Thinking about it," She said.

"It's just a few questions," Byrne said.

Emily shrugged.

They both sat opposite her. "This interview is being recorded," Murillo said, then reeled off their names and the date and time. She looked at Emily and said, "Can you take us through the events of Friday night?"

Emily shook her head. "Nope. Because I don't remember anything after Thursday. I've told you that."

"You have," Murillo said. "But I find it very hard to believe you traveled two hundred miles all the way back to your family's hotel, and you don't remember any of it."

"I find it very hard to believe that I traveled here at all," Emily said.

Murillo leaned back in her chair. "We'll find your route, Emily. There's no shortage of cameras. But cooperating is really advisable."

"I *am* cooperating. In fact, this is me cooperating. I just don't know anything."

Murillo pursed her lips. "A shame, that. Since this is now officially an arson investigation. Which means whoever set that fire is looking at six charges of manslaughter. Or murder."

Emily's throat was closing up again. "And you think I did it?"

"You were there. The only one who survived."

"Aside from my brother ..." Emily trailed off, swallowing hard.

A smile twitched on Murillo's face. "Are you suggesting he did it?"

"No! No. I don't know. But it wasn't me.."

"What's your relationship with your brother like?" Murillo asked, fingering her notebook.

Emily shook her head. "Haven't seen him since I left."

"You're not close then?"

"What do you think?"

"And your parents?"

"Again, obviously not," Emily said. "Can I have some water?"

Murillo nodded at Byrne. He got up and headed for the door. "Must've stung when they gave him the hotel."

Emily snorted. "Hell no. I would never have wanted it."

"Really? I'd be pissed. You're working to get a decent education while your big brother drops out and slacks around, not even trying to make anything of himself. And he gets handed the family business. All the assets. That didn't hurt?"

Emily looked him in the eyes. "Nope."

Byrne exited the room and was back within seconds with the bottle of water. He opened it for her, and she drank.

"Why don't we start again."

"Why don't we not," Emily said, getting to her feet.

"Where are you going?" Byrne asked.

"Am I under arrest?"

The two detectives looked at each other.

"Take a seat, Emily," Murillo said.

"Answer my question," She said. "Am I under arrest?"

"You are not."

"Great. Interview terminated." She limped to the door.

"You'd get your life back a lot quicker if you cooperated," Murillo said.

"Uh huh." Emily pushed the door open and entered the hallway. Only she had no idea which way to go.

Byrne appeared a moment later. "I'll walk you out."

#

Five minutes later, Emily found herself standing outside the police station, once again phone-less and money-less. She looked up and down the street, the sun already baking her head and shoulders. A horrible shaking started somewhere deep down in her chest. She stumbled down the steps to the curb, sidewalk hot under her feet, and sat just before her legs gave out. She pulled her knees up to her chest and pressed her face against them, breath coming in quick little gasps.

How could this be happening? *How?* She fought the tears, waiting for the trembling to stop. How was she going to get back to the hotel or, better yet, out of town? She had no money. She wasn't about to hitchhike. And she didn't want to call Stuart for help.

"Emily?"

She turned, spotting a woman who looked familiar. She was too skinny. And the frames of her glasses were different from the ones Emily remembered, smaller and bolder. Her hair was cut into something spiky and layered, but it was still the same pale blonde color it always was.

Emily forced a smile. "Jenna?"

"Hey. I heard you were in town. Welcome back."

"Thanks."

Jenna gestured to the curb. "Okay if I join you?"

Emily gestured with her bandaged hands. "Free country."

"Looks painful," Jenna said, nodding toward the bandages. "But then you always could make an entrance."

Emily snorted.

Jenna sat next to her. "I was in the station getting some details for a story."

"A story?"

"I work at the paper."

"Oh. *Oh.* Let me guess, your story is about *Emily the arsonist?*"

Jenna laughed. "No, that's not my assignment. Someone is leaving hotdogs in mailboxes around town."

Emily stared at her for a moment, then laughed. "You're kidding."

Jenna grinned. "No, wish I was. I figure in five years or so, maybe I'll graduate up to subterfuge at the vegetable competition. Until then, hotdogs."

"Thrilling."

"Well, it's Ironfield." Jenna rested her forearms on her knees, then turned to look at her. "I didn't think you'd ever come back."

"I didn't mean to. I didn't intend to. In fact, I don't even know how I got here."

"Drugged?"

Emily shrugged. "Maybe. Or this." She gestured to the gauze on her forehead.

"You want a lift back to the hotel?"

"You meant it?"

"Sure, why not?"

Emily couldn't think how to answer, how to explain the gulf between them. "Because I left."

Jenna shrugged. "It was kinda shitty how you never replied to any of my messages, but I guess I kind of understood. Life was shitty."

Emily nodded. "Yeah. It was."

"Come on." Jenna got up. "If I leave you here, you're bound to get picked up by the pound or something."

Emily laughed.

God, she'd missed Jeanna.

#

They detoured to Jenna's apartment first and outfitted Emily with shoes and clothes that actually fit, along with a few extras.

"I swear all my underwear is clean," she said.

Then they stopped by the pharmacy, and Jenna bought her a toothbrush and some toiletries.

Emily was bewildered by the ease of being here, the simple familiarity of the way Jenna talked, her gestures, even the scent of her. She felt lighter than she had any right to feel, especially considering she had arson and murder charges hanging over her head. Maybe she should call a lawyer.

But she didn't want to think about it now. She was enjoying being with Jenna, and Emily wondered why she'd cut off contact so completely. Everyone else, sure, but why Jenna? Although sometimes when one gouged out memories, it had to be all of them. Holding onto the good ones kept the bad ones close, too.

When they pulled up in front of the hotel, Jenna leaned on the steering wheel, looking out at the devastated facade. "Did a hell of a job, didn't it?"

"Yeah," Emily said. "You know who died?"

Jenna nodded, and for a moment, Emily thought she wasn't going to answer, then she said each name slowly. "Jordan, Shannon, Elise, Maddie, Kylee, and Tegan."

Emily stared at her blankly. "As in the squad?"

"Yeah," Jenna said. "The very same."

And *fuck*, hadn't they been the worst of school? Cruising in a pack down the halls, all impeccable hair and brilliant smiles, either in their cheerleading uniforms or looking like they should have been in them. And they'd been so stereotypically cruel that even now, looking back, Emily couldn't quite believe she'd survived them. That sort of bully felt like it belonged in teen movies, not in life. But it had happened, and some small, mean part of her wanted to say the fire couldn't have happened to a better group. But she bit down on the words.

And Jenna said them instead.

Emily gave a little hiccough of horrified laughter.

Jenna grimaced. "Sorry. Shit. That was an awful thing to say."

"Hey, I had the same thought," Emily said. "They were the worst. Weren't they?"

Jenna pushed her sleeve up, exposing a trio of round, glossy scars on the inside of her elbow. Old cigarette burns. "They were."

Emily stared at the burn circles. She remembered that day, the bite and hiss of heat. She pulled the bandage on her arm low enough to uncover a matching set of marks. Mirrored scars.

"They didn't deserve this, though," Emily said, not quite looking at the hotel.

"No," Jenna agreed.

Although neither of them sounded as though they meant it.

Emily reached for the door handle, hating the thought of returning to the hotel, fresh paint or not.

"Call me anytime," Jenna said.

"Thanks." She gestured to the building. "I better check on Stuart. Make sure he's not drinking through the entire hotel."

Jenna laughed, then handed her a cheap card with *Jenna Burgess, journalist*, on it. "You know where to find me."

Emily clambered out and watched Jenna pull onto the road, the old car backfiring twice. Then she turned to the hotel and its looming facade full of ghosts. Had she made the right choice in coming back here now?

She somehow doubted it.

#

Stuart was passed out on the couch, a bottle of cheap whisky open on the coffee table before him. Emily wondered how much was habit and how much was the aftermath of the fire. She almost wished she could feel guilty as if that was the only acceptable emotion, but she hadn't set the fire, and honestly, she wasn't sad that it was gone. She'd burned it down long ago in her mind.

Stuart's phone lay on the floor, so she picked it up, held it over his face to unlock it, and then went outside. She logged into her college messaging account, sent a suitably tearful missive about a family emergency to explain her absence, and then checked her inbox. There were a dozen or more messages, all from Cale, each of them increasingly anxious in tone. She frowned at them. Cale wasn't her boyfriend. He was barely a friend, just someone from her creative writing course. The rush of messages seemed excessive, even if she had missed class on Friday. She hit reply and said, *Had to go home, back soon*. It was all she could manage at the moment.

The messenger rang instantly. It was Cale. She hit answer.

"Hey, Cale.."

"What do you mean you've gone home?" he asked. "You said you'd never go back."

"When did I say that?" she frowned. She never talked about Ironfield. Not with him. Not with anyone.

"In your essays," he said, impatience clipping his tone. "What's happened?"

The essays.

Of course.

227

All those essays that their teaching assistant *(call me Ellis, I can't stand these formalities, this is a community college, what's everyone doing tonight?)* insisted would be *so good* if she could only dig deeper into her hurt, expose her trauma, sink into that well of endless pain. It had her vomiting up her fury and hatred, crying over her laptop in the dark corner of the apartment while her roommates slept. She'd more than mentioned Ironfield. She'd *eviscerated* it.

"Right," she said. "Well, something came up." *Like burning down the family home,* She swallowed a snort of laughter.

"Are you alright? Your voice sounds weird."

"Just a cold."

Cale was silent for a moment, then said, "I don't understand why you're back there, Emily. Not after what you wrote about it."

I don't understand either. "Writer's license and all that. I've got to go."

"Sure. Can I call you later to make sure you're alright?"

"I don't have my phone. I'll message you, okay?" She hung up before he could say anything else and then logged out of her account. She went back inside the hotel and laid the phone next to the whisky bottle.

He didn't stir, so she went and got herself a water, then sat at the breakfast bar, listening to him snore and thinking about the fire. She didn't *want* to think about it, but the mention of the essays had shaken her. If anyone was looking for a scapegoat, her motive was written in Times New Roman and available on the college submissions page. Plus, like Murillo had said, she hadn't exactly been a model citizen as a young teen. But between the bullying at school and the simmering, ever-present rage at home, who could blame her?

Emily finished her water and investigated the fridge, finding some yogurt that had just expired. It wasn't much of a breakfast – or lunch – but it was all she could stomach. She sat down again. There was evidence of arson, she'd been found at the site, and now the essays. It was all too *perfect*. Was she being set up? The idea seemed fantastical but, at the same time, sickeningly believable. But by who? Her brother? After the insurance money? She looked at him, still snoring steadily on the couch. He didn't look like he could mastermind a potluck, let alone kidnap her and plant her at a crime scene. And he'd have no idea about the essays.

She finished the yogurt while her mind rambled in painful circles, bumping up against the impossibilities of the past and the present in equal measure. Then she got Stuart's phone again, changed a couple of settings, and called Jenna.

She answered almost immediately.

"Alright, I *hate* it here. Can I stay with you?"

She could almost hear Jenna grin. "For as long as you like. I'm on the way."

Rumors were apparently flying all around, not only in the newspaper office, that Emily was back, she was injured, the hotel had burnt down, and *connect the dots*.

But by evening, Emily was the closest to happy she had been in a painfully long time. She and Jenna drank too much wine, ate some truly terrible noodle soup, and swapped stories of life since school. The years apart ceased to exist, and for the first time, Emily felt guilty for leaving. She shouldn't have walked out on Jenna. On everything else, maybe, but not Jenna. She was the one good thing about this place, about Emily's *life*, even. She wasn't going to make the same mistake again.

At some point around the second bottle of wine, they

settled on a plan. In the throes of giggles, they decided they would find the real culprit, clear Emily's name, Jenna would receive a nationwide award for investigative journalism, and they'd live happily ever after in some undefined location that was not here. It was perfect. *They* were perfect. And everything was going to be okay as long as they were together.

#

In the morning, faced with a notebook full of questions and no answers, Emily felt they'd been a *little* ambitious the previous evening. But it wasn't like she had anything else to do. So when Jenna went to work, Emily sat down with Stuart's phone. She'd taken off both the lock and location services yesterday. He'd called it twice. She'd let it ring through both times. Then she started snooping. She couldn't get into his banking apps, but the emails and bookings told her plenty.

The hotel was pretty much bankrupt. The dinner booking on the night of the fire was the first one they'd had in weeks. A flurry of emails showed Stuart trying to find a caterer who wouldn't swallow all the profit. There were virtually no room bookings, and sure, the odd person would pass through, but the business had always relied on regulars. Every other email was a demand for payment from either the bank or a supplier. Stuart's replies became ever more desperate, and she thought about how their parents handed the keys over. Dumping their problems onto Stuart. Probably didn't even tell him they were in financial difficulties. Just handed the hotel over like some gracious bequeathment. Fuck them.

But it made sense as to why they had given it to him. And why he might want to burn it down for the insurance money. The only thing she couldn't work out was why that night? Why when people were there, rather than all the nights when it was empty? And why frame *her?* Did Stuart hate her that much?

Jenna had left her car in case Emily wanted to use it. And when she drove out of town, hands clumsy on the wheel, she felt the town's eyes on her.

Stuart was sitting at the breakfast bar drinking coffee when she came in. He got up, took another mug from the cupboard, filled it, and placed it on the bar. "You see my phone?"

She shook her head. "Nope."

"Damn it."

She walked over and took the seat next to him. Grabbed the mug and took a sip. Hot, bitter.

"Thought you'd skipped town," he said.

"Thought about it. I stayed at Jenna's."

"Didn't take you two long to hook up again, then." His tone was noncommittal.

"I missed her." And she *had,* once she'd seen her, but also, she hadn't thought of her since she left, so it felt a little like a lie, uncomfortable and itchy.

"Yeah, you two were pretty much inseparable. Till the end anyway."

"What do you mean, till the end?"

He gave her a curious look. "You don't remember?"

Emily hesitated. "Well, I left. I didn't say goodbye or anything if that's what you mean." But now that she was thinking of it, she couldn't even remember leaving; she just felt the panicked rush of it, the scramble for escape, the shedding of the town like an old, constricting skin.

"The prom?" Stuart asked, still watching her with that same evaluating look.

"I didn't…" *Did* she go? She couldn't remember it. The whole idea seemed absurd, dressed up in finery like some fairy-tale heroine hoping for a happy ending.

"Do you remember me picking you up? Driving you straight to Milton?"

"From the *prom?*"

"From the prom."

"No. No, I took a bus. Didn't I?"

He laughed softly, got up, and retrieved the whisky bottle from the table. When he returned, he slopped some into his mug. He offered it to her, and she shook her head. He settled himself back on the stool. "How much *do* you remember?"

"I told you—"

"No. From before you left."

Emily shrugged a stiff little movement. "I've tried to forget. It wasn't much fun being here."

"No?"

"Well, Mom and Dad were always fighting." She looked around the room, eyes searching out the gouges in the walls from thrown glasses, plates, and whatever else was at hand. But the new paint hid a myriad of sins.

"What else?"

"School." She grimaced. "Getting bullied."

Stuart made a disbelieving noise. "You didn't get bullied."

"How would you know?' Emily said. "You dropped out. You don't know what I went through."

"I know plenty. You were *not* bullied."

Her hands balled into fists at her sides. "Of course I was. Those bitches—" She stopped. "I mean, I'm sorry they're dead, but they made our lives hell."

"Ours?"

"Me and Jenna."

Stuart smiled, an oddly sad expression. Then he got up and walked over to a magazine rack. He pulled out a photo album from amongst a patchy collection of old books and magazines. Then he returned and set it on the bar. "Do you look like you were bullied?"

Emily flipped through it. In her memory, she'd always been anxious and drawn to the outskirts of every room, with Jenna small and pale next to her. That wasn't what she saw here. A bright, explosive energy bled off the pages, every photo holding the both of them as if one simply didn't exist without the other. They pouted and posed for the camera while others moved in and out of their orbit, pale specters always outshone by their entwined luminosity.

"This doesn't mean anything," she said. "Anyone can look happy for a photo."

He tapped one of the pictures. "That's the truth there."

"It's not! You weren't *there!* And Mom and Dad *sucked*, it was so shit—"

Stuart held his hands up. "Yeah, they were shitty. No argument. But *you weren't bullied*, and—"

Emily got up and walked out.

"Emily!"

She sprinted for Jenna's car, fumbling at the door, expecting his hand on her shoulder at any moment and … and what? She didn't know, but she threw herself into the car, jamming the key into the ignition. She didn't look up until she had the car in reverse, pulling away from the empty parking lot.

She was back in Ironfield before she knew it, her head swirling with half-drowned memories.

Had Stuart been right?

Because there had been a prom, and she had left. But why didn't she remember? She should remember. She *should*.

\#

Emily called Jenna on the way back into town. "Can we talk?"

"Yeah, for sure. Meet me at Has-Bean. It's a block north of the police station."

Emily found the place and parked. Spotting Jenna by the clutter of wooden tables — all occupied — spilling onto the sidewalk.

"I'll get takeaway," Jenna said. "Hollie runs that place. Fucking gossip central."

She headed inside, and Emily retreated across the street to stand in the shade of the bank. She felt exposed, and the people at the tables seemed to be studiously not looking in her direction. She peered fixedly into a thrift shop window and willed Jenna to hurry up.

"What happened?" Jenna asked, handing Emily a take-away cup.

Emily took it awkwardly. She couldn't wait for the bandages to come off. "Stuart says we weren't bullied."

"What does he know? He dropped out before we even got there."

"I know. But he keeps saying I should remember more than I do."

"It's really common to block out traumatic childhood experiences," Jenna said firmly. "Come on."

They strolled down the sidewalk, seeking out patches of shade, until they found an empty bench in the shadow of an oak tree. Jenna sat down, and Emily perched next to her, wishing she'd asked for a cold drink instead of some-thing hot.

"What do you remember?" Jenna asked.

"That I left right after prom," Emily said.

"Same night. You didn't even say goodbye."

There was no reproach in her voice, but Emily winced. "I'm sorry."

"It's fine. I don't blame you for wanting to get out. Between your parents and school, life was shit."

Emily sipped her coffee and wondered if she'd have been so forgiving if their places had been reversed. She wasn't sure. But then, maybe it had been worse for her than Jenna. "You didn't want to leave?"

Jenna shrugged. "Not on my own. I'm not as brave as you."

"I should've waited."

"You shouldn't've done anything." Jenna tapped her cup against Emily's, a gentle toast. "We got through school. We can get through this. But you're in shit."

"What?"

"Apparently that detective's got you on CCTV at a gas station on the way en route from Milton, filling jerry cans."

Emily stared at her, ears ringing with a high, distant sound. "But *how?* I don't even have a car! How was I at a gas station?"

"A rental, maybe?"

"But I didn't! You know I didn't, right!"

Jenna grabbed Emily's cup before it slipped out of her hands. "I believe you. We'll figure this out."

Emily squeezed her eyes shut against tears. She'd turned her back on the one person who trusted and believed her for what? To go and write morose essays for a voyeuristic teacher's assistant in a shitty community college. "How?"

"Who had the most to gain from this?"

"Not me," Emily said. "I gain nothing."

Jenna set her coffee cup down on the bench. "The hotel's been going downhill the last few years. Used to be an okay place for dinner, but the kitchen's never open now."

"Then what was the squad doing there?" Emily asked.

Jenna looked around, then leaned in close to Emily. "Apparently, they were all a part of some WhatsApp group for fast-moving young professionals or some such shit. The police don't know who's behind it yet, but it invited them to a networking evening at the hotel, and they all fell for it."

Emily leaned back, recoiling from the faint trace of glee in Jenna's voice. The squad had been awful, but they'd *died*. That was horrifying. "But *why?*"

"To set you up. No one would believe you'd come back just to burn the hotel down. But if your bullies died in the fire ..."

"After all this time?"

Jenna shrugged.

"Stuart wouldn't."

"That place is broke, and so's he."

"But he wouldn't *kill* anyone."

"Maybe he didn't mean to. Maybe he got the dosage wrong."

"Dosage?"

Jenna's gaze flicked to the street. "Police report said they found Rohypnol in the squad's bloodwork. He must've dosed you all up with something. But he needed you to be alive to take the fall."

"Stuart doesn't even think I *had* bullies. How would he know about the squad?"

"Maybe he read your essays?"

Emily blinked. "How do you know about the essays?"

Jenna eyed her. "How much of last night do you remember?"

Emily laughed. Right. She'd been drunker than she thought. She set the cup down on the bench and rubbed her face, growling at the bandages. "I want these fucking things off."

Jenna squeezed her shoulder. "I have to get back to work. Keep the car and lie low, alright? You don't want to attract too much attention."

#

Back at Jenna's apartment, Emily logged into her college account, pulling up her *Submitted Assignments*. Who could've seen them? They'd have had to have access to her account or been in her classes. Cale was the only one who'd read all of them, other than Ellis. And he was such a dick, demanding she put less fact and more *truth* into her work. Parents are *trivial*, he'd insisted. Missing cheerleading is *trivial*. Facts are pliable. Tell your truth. Tell your *pain*.

So then maybe she'd embellished her life. That's what writers do. It's not like she was going to publish these. She scrolled through the assignments, skimming the titles. The time the squad held her down and poured so much vodka down her throat, she'd almost ended up in the hospital. The time she'd had her head shoved into an unflushed toilet. The stolen clothes in the locker room. The cigarette butts in her lunch. The prom she'd missed because her dad had beaten her so badly that—

She pressed her hand to her mouth.

She hadn't submitted that one. Hadn't been able to because she couldn't plaster a new truth over it like she had done with the others. Couldn't, because she'd almost killed someone. She'd been drinking, and had stolen her dad's car, and almost run an old woman off the road. He hadn't beaten her that time, but he'd locked her in her room like so many nights before. Keeping her there until Jenna had snuck in and released her.

Emily sniffed. She couldn't quite tell how much was invention. She'd been a victim; she *had*. Her parents had been neglectful and endlessly furious, and school had been a treacherous swamp of allegiances and hatred, but nothing here was as it had happened. That much she knew. Not that they were lies, more like exaggerated truths.

And then there was prom and the flight from Ironfield, and *why couldn't she remember?*

She called Jenna. "Are you okay?"

"No," Emily said. "What happened at prom?"

"At *prom?*"

"I can't remember. Stuart says he picked me up and took me to Milton, but why?"

Jenna flattened her voice. "Your brother's an alcoholic, an arsonist, and probably a murderer. I wouldn't listen to him."

"That's why I'm asking you."

Jenna sighed. "I can't right now. I'm working. But we'll talk tonight, okay? I put a jug of smoothie in the fridge. It'll be good for your throat."

"Jenna—"

"Rest. I'm sure the doctor told you something along those lines." And then the line went dead. Emily pressed her fingertips to her mouth. She was certain she had almost run over the woman the night of the prom. And that's why she hadn't gone. She was locked in her room. Had she been so drunk she simply didn't remember what happened after that? What about her essays? How many were lies, a misremembering, a reinvention of the past? *All* of them?

She got up and went to the fridge, finding the smoothie. She took a few sips, but she wasn't hungry. So she put it back to finish later. Then she got in the car and drove back to the coffee shop, to Hollie's Gossip Central. She couldn't ask the squad what school had really been like, but she could ask Hollie. She'd been one of the ones on the edges, like Emily herself, so maybe she'd know.

Hollie was not friendly.

Emily had barely walked in the door when Hollie emerged from behind the counter, pointing at her like she was a stray dog. "You're not welcome here."

Every head in the coffee shop turned toward them. Emily held her bandaged hands up as though in peace. "I just want to ask you something."

"Murderer," A slim, well-dressed man sat at a nearby table.

"I haven't killed anyone," she said. "I'm trying to find out what happened."

"You finished the job you started at prom," Hollie said.

"*What?*"

"Don't play stupid, Emily. What're you doing, coming in here to *gloat?* I should call the cops." Hollie already had her phone out.

"Please, Hollie. I don't even remember prom! Or the hotel."

"Or terrorizing half the school?" the man at the table asked. "That's some selective amnesia you've got going on, Emily."

Emily stared at him. "Do I know you?"

He snorted, meeting her eyes. "Of course not. I was in the computer club. Didn't even cross your radar. Which was lucky, I supposed, considering what you did to everyone else."

Emily touched her head. It was throbbing, and she was thinking of the essays again and Ellis saying, *find the truth, not the facts*. Her stomach rolled. Had she looked so hard for a truth that she'd stolen someone else's instead?

"I didn't hurt anyone," she said.

"No. You hurt *everyone*," Hollie said, blinking back tears. "I wish you'd stayed gone. Or burned up in the fire with the others."

"I was the *victim*."

The man at the table laughed. "So your family was a bit shit? Pretty normal around here. But you took it out on *everyone*."

Emily felt her knees going, a tide of memories igniting with the explosiveness of a smoke bomb. She grabbed a chair for support.

"Emily?" Hollie said.

But it was the last thing Emily heard.

When she came around, she was sitting on the floor with her back against the wall. The cafe was empty. Hollie crouched in front of her, eyeing her warily. She was softer and more rounded than she'd been in high school but with the same pretty face.

Emily felt a sudden, visceral stab of jealousy, followed by a wave of nausea. "I'm so sorry. I really was awful to you."

"Yeah, you were," Hollie replied, handing her a glass of water. "But it was high school, and it's over. Drink up and get out. You're still not welcome."

"I didn't burn down the hotel," Emily said. "I didn't kill them."

"Uh-huh." Hollie started to get up, and Emily grabbed her arm. She flinched, recoiling, and Emily let go immediately.

"Oh fuck, I'm so sorry. Really."

Hollie stared, her face pinched, then said, "You really don't remember?"

Emily shook her head. "Nothing."

Hollie looked around the shop, then back at her. "I don't know about the hotel, but the prom ...you and Jenna were banned from attending because you'd been caught kicking the shit out of a sophomore. I mean, the school was *finally* catching on, but it was your final year, so a bit late, you know? And then the hall burned down, and we only just got out. Everyone knew it was the two of you because Jenna always had a thing for fire. She almost burned the science lab down once. D'you remember that?"

Emily shook her head, her whole body trembling. She still couldn't quite touch the memories, and she thought they might drown her when she did.

Hollie sighed. "If it helps, I remember you from middle school before Jenna moved here. You were okay then. So maybe you didn't set the fire at prom or at the hotel. But you were still *such* a bitch in high school."

"I'm sorry," Emily said. "Really."

"You already said that. Now fuck off, I'm about to lock up."

Emily got up slowly, holding onto the wall. *Jenna always had a thing for fire.* She pushed her bandage down, looking at the shiny discs of the cigarette burns, the images spooling around her. Jenna pinning Emily's arm to the bed, grinding the cigarette into her skin while Emily smothered her scream. It'd make them best friends, Jenna had promised, best friends forever. They'd never be apart.

And then Emily had left Ironfield. No, not left. Her brother had ripped her out of Jenna's orbit and flung her loose, and now his hotel was burned down, and he was drinking himself to death alone. *Alone.*

Emily lurched for the door, bouncing off a table and a chair, her vision slightly blurred. What the fuck was wrong with her—

The smoothie.

Jenna had done something to it. But she couldn't let it stop her.

#

If anyone had seen Emily driving to the hotel, they'd have already called the police on her. Whatever Jenna had put in the smoothie was taking its toll. But so far,

241

she'd managed to keep going. When she arrived in the parking lot, she spotted black smoke roiling from the left wing.

Thank God she'd taken Stuart's phone.

She dialed 911 and reported the fire. Confirming it was a new one. Then she ran to the front door and yanked it open. Smoke and heat belched out. Stuart lay motionless on the floor.

Emily stumbled in, her throat already burning, her head swimming with the heat. Thank God the fire was centered in the kitchen area, so she had some tiny margin of time. She grabbed Stuart's arms, dragging him towards the door. Then, a form loomed out of the smoke. Someone wearing a firefighting apparatus.

Oh, thank God.

But she hadn't heard sirens. And why were they wearing a T-shirt and a pair of jeans? She peered in through the mask.

Jenna.

Jenna lifted the mask, grinning. "There you are. I thought you'd come."

"What the fuck are you *doing here?*"

"What do you think?" Jenna asked.

"Get his feet," Emily said.

"I don't think so," Jenna said. "We were meant to be best friends forever. Stuart might have sent you away. But then you never came back, and that's on you. Do you know how long I waited?"

Emily coughed, covering her mouth with her bandaged hand. "You set all of this up."

"Sure. I found your silly little college and read all your essays. It wasn't hard to hack your account. And you've always used the same password. Your writing is good, but you didn't even mention me! Not once!"

"I didn't remember," Emily said. "I still don't. Not really."

"Doesn't matter now. This time you'll be caught on the scene, red-handed."

"This time? You mean like Friday?"

Something exploded in the kitchen. Emily swallowed a scream. "So you thought you'd *frame* me?"

"You just love pretending you're so innocent, don't you? Love to be the victim, like you never hurt anyone. You were into it, though. You just needed a little nudge."

A shelf crashed to the floor, and Emily flinched at the sudden rush of heat. "We need to get out!"

"You don't," Jenna said, lifting her hand.

She held a taser.

Emily threw up her arm. The darts embedded themselves in the thick bandage of her forearm. Jenna snarled and pulled out a fresh cartridge. Reloaded. Then she pulled the mask back into place, lunging at Emily, trying to press the barrel into Emily's side. Emily tackled her, driving her across the smoke-filled room, trying to grip her wrist. It was impossible with her bandaged hands, so she just kept pushing her towards the kitchen.

It was getting harder to breathe. She got lost in the smoke.

Slammed Jenna into the wall. She cried out, dropping the taser. Emily clawed the mask off Jenna's face and chucked it, spinning around to run back to Stuart. But she wasn't quick enough. Jenna grabbed her shirt. Emily fell back on purpose, jamming an elbow into Jenna's belly. They tumbled to the floor, kicking and clawing at each other.

Emily pressed her arm against Jenna's windpipe, trying to pin her down. Jenna punched Emily's forehead. She cried out, the shock jarring her previous injury. Her vision blurred for a moment. But it was more than enough time for Jenna to reverse their positions.

Emily twisted and bucked, trying to push Jenna off, but she wasn't strong enough. She searched for a weapon, anything she could use against Jenna. Her hand knocked against something on the floor. The taser. She fumbled for it, her clumsy sausage fingers refusing to do her bidding. Tears trickled from her eyes; she couldn't breathe. And Stuart was about to die because of her.

Nope.

She was not gonna let that happen. She got the taser. It was a tenuous grip, but she had it, jamming it into Jenna's side. And then Emily forced the trigger down. Jenna's body bucked and convulsed, and then she collapsed.

Emily could breathe again.

Emily pushed Jenna off and crawled back to Stuart. She grabbed him by the arms again and dragged him towards the door. Snot ran from her nose. Tears from her eyes. She couldn't even open them anymore. The smoke was too intense.

She stumbled, falling to her knees. She lost her bearings again. She couldn't tell where the door was, or the window, or *anything*. She pulled herself up and started again, inch by painful inch. This time, she tripped over Jenna's outstretched body.

Jenna grabbed her ankle. Emily screamed and kicked her way. But it didn't matter.

They weren't going to make it.

So she crawled to Stuart and curled up beside him. "I'm so sorry, Stuart."

And then a massive, misshapen form swelled out of the smoke. And she was scooped up and carried out. She tried to point, tried to tell them to watch out for Jenna that she was poison, but her throat wouldn't work.

And then they were outside, and she had an oxygen mask. She spotted Stuart on a stretcher.

"Stu." Her voice was even worse than before.

Even so, he opened his eyes a crack and smiled. It was barely anything, but it was enough.

#

"This is disgusting," Stuart croaked, peering at the smoothie. He sounded like he smoked five packs a day, but otherwise, he'd escaped mostly unscathed.

"I know." Emily's bandages had been removed from her arms, but she had new ones on her shoulders and neck. "The catering sucks."

"Thought you were used to an all-liquid diet," Emily said.

Stuart gave her the finger. They were still wheezing with laughter two minutes later when the door opened. Detective Murillo came in alone for once. She looked at the two of them propped up in their respective beds. "How're my kids doing?"

"Depends on you," Emily said.

Murillo pursed her lips. "Then I've got good news. Jenna's been arrested. Arson. Murder. Attempted murder."

"Thank God," Emily said. "Wait a minute. She said you had me on camera."

"No," Murillo shook her head. "We had her on camera. Wearing your clothes, using your credit cards. She was careful, but she didn't avoid all the cameras. We got her on some traffic ones between here and Milton as well. Even caught her on campus."

"How did she get Em here?" Stuart asked.

"Rohypnol. There were traces of it in the smoothie in her apartment. It's what she used on the squad as well."

Emily wondered how Jenna had dosed her with it first. Sarah had said something about finding the door open.

Had she come in and been hiding. Watching while she slept, stealing clothes, her credit card, dosing her food? It made her skin crawl.

"So it's done?" Stuart asked.

"You'll both have to give evidence, but yes. A lot of old stories coming out now, too. Boyfriends' cars catching fire and so on."

"Great choice of bestie," Stuart said.

Emily grimaced. "Sorry."

"Listen to your big brother next time."

Murillo smiled. "Jake will take your statements when you've recovered. Until then, take it easy."

And then she left.

Emily leaned back against her pillow. She had never felt more relieved in her life.

"Em?"

"I really am sorry."

"It's fine. The hotel was dying anyway."

"Not about the hotel. About you. You almost died."

He laughed. "You do owe me for that. You can help me sort out all the shit with the insurance."

Emily glanced out the window next to the bed. The hospital stood on a hill at the top of the town. But Ironfield no longer felt so scary.

Her past was still blurry, swallowed by her eagerness to rewrite history. But now she got to start again, and however ugly the truth might be, she'd take it as it came.

Make amends.

And she'd start with Stuart. She turned back to meet his eyes. "Whatever you need."

Gina, Is That You?

SEAN PLATT

Gina, Is That You?

SEAN PLATT

"*THAT'S* WHAT YOU'RE WEARING TO THE INTERVIEW?"

An ugly, belittling, familiar smirk accompanied the words.

She said nothing.

"It's The Fly Girl Fashion House. Not The Fat Chick Whorehouse." Sputtering laughter, followed by the snort. *Always* the snort.

Her fingers flew to her face, tapping lightly at her foundation. She'd gone heavy with the makeup. She knew that. She'd *had* to. The pencil skirt was hers, and she spent hours getting the fit just right. It skimmed her curves but in all the right ways. And no matter what he said, she looked ... professional.

She forced a smile. "I'm going to take the car to the station if that's okay? It's supposed to rain."

"So?"

She patted her hair. A French twist, but a little loose — perfect with the skirt. It had taken nearly two hours to pin it up. "My hair."

His gaze drifted upward, and his expression soured. "Does it matter?"

Again, she offered no response, jingling her keys and waiting for the self-satisfied sniggering to ebb. "I should be back by dinner."

The fridge door made a sucking sound as it opened. Then, a rattle and thud as it slammed back shut, followed by the pop-fizz-cracking of a freshly opened beer. "*Should* be?"

"The train schedule's always a mess. You know that."

"I *know that*? What the fuck is that supposed to mean?"

She busied herself, pretending to look in her purse for something but really just avoiding eye contact. She could *not* be late for this. "You want D'Agostino? It's Wednesday. Egg parm."

"*I know* it's Wednesday, egg parm. I *remember*."

The stench of beer breath turned her stomach. "I can stop in after. It's just a few blocks from the interview."

The scrape of a kitchen chair filled her with cool relief.

Seated was *so* much safer than standing.

She edged toward the door. "Ziti or fettuccine?"

"It'll be cold by the time you get your fat ass back here."

Pouty now, but that was manageable.

"We can reheat it." Her words were too bright, but it was too late to do anything about it.

"Aren't *you* just the gourmet? How about actually cooking something for a goddamn change?"

"Ground chuck is on sale. I'll do meatloaf this weekend, 'kay?" She slid her portfolio case over one shoulder and opened the garage door. The scent of oil and freesias filled the kitchen. She breathed it in.

"Got your little cartoons?"

Cartoons? Anger rippled through her.

Five years of shitty tips and sixty-hour work weeks, scraping together every nickel she could to pay for her classes — her *dream*. It had been nearly impossible, even when they were *both* working. And would have been out of the question if it weren't for Ma's generosity. She'd let them move in after they were married. Ma never asked for rent so long as they chipped in for food and utilities whenever they could.

She'd finally earned her design degree *and* at the top of her class. Her drawings — her *cartoons* — had even won the Fashion Next award for new talent. The prize included a five-thousand-dollar check and a trophy presented by the assistant editor of *Turn-Out* magazine.

The memory of her name reverberating from the speakers when they announced the winner was everything — because she'd never won *anything*. The walk across the stage to the podium to receive her pretty little statue: a golden dress form inscribed with *her* name. Her chest bursting with enough pride and joy to make her faint. The vivid details were engraved on her mind.

She'd relived that moment often. She'd *needed* it.

The five grand went fast, especially after he lost his job. The statue, before it was shattered — deliberately, of course — held pride of place in the living room. Turned out it was only plaster — it had taken hours to pick all of the dusty, white shards out of her hair. But it had looked nice up there on the mantle for the short time it stood.

She wished Ma had still been alive to see it.

The hard lump in her throat softened after two hard swallows. She checked the time on her phone. "Okay, well. Wish me luck?"

"Right." Another snort. "I'm sure today's yer lucky day."

She sighed and turned away, stepping carefully down onto the rickety, wooden step. It shuddered beneath her.

"Get me ziti. And look for a meter on the street. The station parking lot is fucking robbery."

"Yup." Her foot found the second step lightly, carefully.

"And hey ..."

She paused and turned back to him. Hopeful. "Yeah?"

"Might want to lose the fucking bitch face before you get there."

Crack. She *actually heard* a crack.

At first, she thought it was the stairs — a generous word for the five slapped-together, splintery planks beneath her pumps. They were so old and rotted, it was a wonder they had held out this long.

But no. The cracking sound had come from her chest. Her *heart.* It had finally broken. She stared at him as though he was a stranger. Why now? There had been so many others — so *many* opportunities — for the full fracture. It was a wonder *it* had held out this long.

The kitchen door slammed shut at the top of the stairs.

She waited for tears. They always came. But this time, none did. It was strange.

She picked her way carefully down the last couple of steps, lingering at the stack of boxes lining the wall.

Ma's stuff. It still smelled of freesias, her favorite scent.

It had felt wrong, stuffing what was left of her into moldy cardboard boxes in this dank garage. Shameful. *Ungrateful.* But *he* complained that the house stunk of "old lady." Even now, she'd come home to wide open windows, the house chilled to near freezing, the incessant drone of sports, while he snored from the comfort of Dad's old recliner in front of their slightly newer TV.

She had never told him that her father had died in that chair.

Ma had walked her home from school — she always did, even after a ten-hour shift. Dad was asleep, drink in hand, his highball half-full. Ma was afraid it might spill on the living room carpet. She tried to slip the glass out of his hand without waking him, but his fingers were locked around it. And stone cold.

It took three EMTs to pry him out.

"Did he suffer?" Ma had asked them, her eyes shiny with tears.

One of them, a heavy-set woman with a soft manner, laid a hand on Ma's shoulder. "Not one bit. Massive stroke. He didn't feel a thing."

Ma's customary brightness dimmed. "Figures."

"Excuse me?"

"That man got away with everything."

Years later, when Ma learned she was sick, she'd laid all her papers out on the kitchen table. Everything was in order, including the planning and payments for her funeral. She had only two final requests. She wanted to pass on at home. She'd seen her own mother die in a state hospital, and she was having none of that.

"It's a hell hole, where they dump the mentally ill in with the criminally insane," Ma had said before making her second request, this one about the house. "Honey, promise me that when I'm gone, you'll sell this dump and get the heck out of this neighborhood."

She had promised, desperate to change the subject, unable to bear the thought of losing Ma, even after the disease had cruelly taken nearly all her mind, one tiny piece at a time.

She remembered the day she realized that something was seriously wrong. Ma had been heading out to work back when she still could. She punched her clock as a piecemeal seamstress for Rowe's on the Wharf — one of the best they ever had, according to everyone on staff. Ma had caught her boot heel on the garage steps and toppled sideways, slamming into the banister. The entire staircase had wobbled so violently that she'd nearly fallen on the cement floor.

She ran at the sound of Ma crying, then found her looking up from the middle step, her expression dark and furious.

"These steps are fucked," she spat.

The shock of her mother using any profanity, never mind *fucked*, was staggering. She dragged her straight to Doctor Cardinal. He put her through all the tests, but they both knew the results before they saw them. Alzheimer's ran in the family.

She was heartbroken, terrified. But Ma just accepted it without a lick of fuss. That's how Ma was ... about *everything*.

The disease accelerated fast. Consumed her. An onslaught of names and memories gobbled up on the daily. It claimed her strength, humor, intelligence, and then, finally, the last of her reason. By the end, Ma would wander the house day and night, babbling like a newborn.

It drove him *nuts*. But they couldn't afford to put her in a home. Even if they could, she would *never* abandon Ma and cast her off to one of those places. Not only had she made the promise, she wanted her mother around for as long as she could possibly have her.

There were still the occasional moments. A brief flicker, a flashlight beam of clarity through the thickness of her fog. Ma would make her promise on repeat, swear that she would sell the house and move to the city or somewhere — *anywhere* — fresh. A place where she could make new memories.

But he wasn't having it. "If you think we're walking away from a *free* house, then you're nuttier than your fucking mother."

It had hurt the first time he'd talked to her that way. But once it was just the two of them, she longed for the days when it was only *talk* that hurt her.

She was at work when Ma had died. He was alone in the house with her. Apparently, he'd fallen asleep watching the game. He woke up to find her face-down in the bathtub, fully dressed and "blue as fuck."

She rushed home, already out the door without saying goodbye.

They said Ma had been dead for a couple hours when he found her. But the kitchen garbage was full of empties that weren't there when she'd left for work that morning. She counted *nine* beer cans — an impressive number for a guy who'd been sleeping through the day.

He didn't want to discuss the situation and said it was bad enough that *he* had to be the one to find her like that. She'd pressed him, unable to let it go. That was the first time he'd hurt her with more than words.

Like Alzheimer's disease, *that* ran in the family, too.

It was also the first time she noticed the smell.

Alone in the locked bathroom, an icy washcloth pressed to her swollen jaw, it had wafted over her like a gentle summer breeze. Fresh strawberries dipped in honey-mint. The scent of freesias.

She'd whispered ever so softly in case *he* was listening. "Ma?"

It came again. A warm rush of freesia-scented air. The aroma was a blanket of comfort. She had curled up like a puppy on the tiled floor and fallen asleep. When she woke, someone had covered her with a towel. She checked the bathroom door but found it locked.

She liked to think — part of her was *sure* — that it was more than Ma's perfume lingering in the house.

She felt along the wall for the door opener, then pressed the button. The door rumbled open, filling the garage with a steely gray light from the overcast sky. Misty tentacles of cold, dank air drifted in, smelling of rain.

"*Damn*," she whispered.

She rummaged through the boxes until she found what she was looking for. Ma's flowered, collapsible umbrella. The flea-bitten handle was slightly bent and spotted with rust. But it would have to do. No *way* was she heading back into the house for her own umbrella, not when she was already so late.

She slid into the driver's seat, blew out a long stream of air through her nose, then lowered the visor flap. The dull glow of a scarred mirror washed her face in sallow light. The yellow-blue patch of bruising was easier to cover now that the purple had faded, but still in dire need of a touch-up.

She couldn't interview for her dream job looking like *that*.

Keeping an eye on the kitchen door, just in case, she fished the makeup bag out of her purse and went to work on her face.

* * *

One block from the train station, the gray clouds finally gathered and overlapped. The day went dark, and the heavens opened. Raindrops pelted the hood like machine gun fire as she slowed to a crawl. She flipped the switch for the wipers. They managed a trio of sweeps before the right-hand blade snapped like a bread stick. The remaining wiper skittered across the glass, squeaking out a narrow swipe of visibility through the gloom.

"Oh *great*! Perfect!"

Traffic crawled, block by block, as potholes filled with rain and gutters turned into muddy, trash-strewn rivers.

She checked the time. Nine minutes until her train.

"Come on ... *Please*."

She rounded the last corner to the station and looked downhill to the parking lot. There were a few spaces available, and they were *so* much closer to the kiosk than the street meters. The thought of walking into the office of the director of Fly Girl, looking like a bedraggled sewer rat, made her want to weep all over again.

Look for a meter on the street. The station parking lot is fucking robbery.

She touched her fingers lightly to her bruise. It was better but still tender to the touch. He'd never know.

Unless the rain cleared, and he took a stroll down here just to check.

Her mind filled with his snarling face, crimson and blotchy with fury, spittle flicking as he raged close enough for her to see the plaque on his teeth.

She forced the image away, stuffing it way down with all the others, then peered through the misty window for an empty meter.

Three times around the block before she finally passed a metered spot just as it opened, spying the prior car pulling out from its space in her rearview.

Damn! She hit the brakes, and the driver blared a horn behind her.

"Sorry, sorry!" She flapped her hands and waved her forward. The driver pulled around and then gave her the bird as she passed. "Yeah, yeah, just go."

She checked the time. Four minutes. She could make it if she ran.

Each of her four failed attempts to parallel park elicited a fresh round of blaring horns. Her heart pounded as she dug the coin purse out of her bag and tipped it upside down.

Four dimes and a nickel.

"No, no, no, no ..." She always had plenty of quarters. He must have stolen her tips. *Again.* A pile of quarters could purchase a six-pack and had plenty of times before. She slid four dollars from her purse and lowered the window, frantically searching the street for an open corner shop, a liquor store — *anything!*

She spotted one. A Laundromat.

"Yes!" She flung open the car door and grabbed Ma's umbrella. She pressed the button, and it popped open like a tiny flowered firework. A wonky shape, but at least it would keep her hair dry.

She snatched her handbag and portfolio, then stepped out of the car and plunged her left foot into a pothole filled to the brim with oily, muddy rainfall. Her shoe was saturated. But so was her stocking, halfway up her leg, all the way to the edge of her cream-colored skirt.

"NO!"

She managed to keep her right foot dry while angling her way out of the car. Then she sprinted for the laundromat as best she could in heels.

Her sodden leather pump squeaked as she ran, the wet friction rubbing her heel raw into an instant blister.

She reached her destination soaked from the knees down, her hair still surprisingly dry — a minor victory in what was turning out to be one of the worst mornings of her life.

A single occupant stood in the laundromat, tying the

string shut on a small pink sack. An elderly woman, silver-haired, thin, fine-boned, dressed in a wax jacket covered in little pink cherries. She was adorable.

She looked up and smiled. "Hello dear. Nice morning for ducks!"

"It's not a nice morning for anything! I need change!" She shook her head and reset herself. "I'm sorry. Hello ..."

She scanned the room and spotted the machine. Her heart sank at the sight of a piece of paper taped to the top.

Please, please, please, don't say out of order.

"I'm afraid it's out of order, dear. Bad luck."

"Is there any other kind?" It was hard not to cry.

The woman laughed. "You could just risk a ticket."

"That's a pretty big risk, at least in my life ..." Why had she said that?

She never told anyone ... any of it.

The woman walked toward her, the laundry bag slung over one arm. Her hair was spun silver, combed back from her powdered face in a gentle swoop. She looked her dead in the eye, blue eyes sparkling with soft concern. "I'm very sorry to hear that."

"It's ... I'm ... okay." The woman's expression made her want to cry. "I've got a job interview. In the city. I have about," she checked the time, "*three* minutes to make my train."

"I guess you'll have to take your chances." The woman held her gaze with a radiant smile and walked towards the door.

She nodded. "Your hair is lovely."

"As is yours," said the woman.

They stood at the doorway, watching a fresh sheet of

rain pelting the street. She raised the umbrella and looked at the woman. "Here. Take this."

"Oh no, dear. I couldn't!"

"Please."

"You'll be soaked through. Your interview."

She gently took the woman's hand. It was soft and delicate like a freshly bloomed rose. "Hold on tight now."

Her eyes glistened with a sweet bit of sadness, then she raised the umbrella and pressed the button. It popped open, and she giggled.

"Oh, not in here!" She opened the door and held it for the woman. "That's bad luck!"

The woman reached up and ran a soft fingertip across her cheek, tracing the yellowed bruise hiding beneath two coats of concealer. She tapped her lightly, just between the brows. "Luck lives right here. *Be* lucky, honey."

She held the umbrella aloft and stepped out into the storm.

And there it was. The sweet, honey-mint scent of freesias.

Her breath hitched. Holding her portfolio overhead, she left the laundromat and looked up and down the street.

But the woman was gone.

She checked the time, glanced at her car, and groaned at the blinking red light.

I guess you'll have to take your chances.

She reached down, yanked off her pumps, and raced to the train.

* * *

The train smelled like a soaking woolen mitten. It was packed with passengers — the train before it had never arrived. She didn't know how that was even possible. Did it just fall off the track somewhere?

She was sopping by the time she reached the crowded platform. Soggy tendrils of her lost French twist trailed cold rivulets into the collar of her blouse and down her back. There were no seats left in her carriage and barely any standing room. She was squished tight against a plexiglass panel with two fingers gripping a stabilizing pole.

But she'd made it. She was on her way to the city.

The train chugged along an elevated track through the misty, melancholy gloom. They passed a clutch of police cars and emergency vehicles, their flashing blue and red lights reflecting off the rain-slick blacktop of a residential home. She counted nine officers, four EMTs, and a fire truck.

"Oh my god!" a young girl exclaimed. "They're wheeling out stretchers — two, no three!"

The standing passengers crouched low, and the others shifted in their seats, craning their necks to peer out the windows at the unsettling drama unfolding on a street that could have been their own.

"Can you see who? Are they hurt?"

"Their faces are covered over. Those are friggin' bodies."

The track sloped downward, and they were suddenly at street level. A collective gasp rippled through the carriage as they passed the grisly sight of three gurneys draped in blood-drenched sheets.

She pressed her nose to the glass.

At the top of the gurney, in the place where a head should have been, the sheet lay flat and soaked in crimson. Was she the only one who saw it?

"What the fuck!"

"Jesus! So much blood!"

"How awful!"

"What the hell is going on?"

261

She shuddered and turned away from the window.

A twenty-something man in a leather jacket held up his phone and waved it at the crowd. "Check the news! They're saying it's that psycho again."

"The one with the hatchet?"

"That's the fourth one in three weeks!"

"It's official. We got our own serial killer."

In a flurry of rustling bags and bumping elbows, the crowd dug for their phones. The carriage went quiet as they scrolled through the latest local news, absorbing the horrific but spotty details of the monster stalking their streets.

"They don't got much. A few descriptions, suspicious characters."

"This says they think it might be a priest or something."

"Bullshit!"

"Says they spotted a heavy-set guy, long greasy hair."

"Girl says she saw a sailor in the alley, staring up at her window."

"A sailor? You mean, like, the navy?"

"I don't know. Says a sailor coat and hat."

"Says he chops hands first, feet, then the head. Clean off."

"Fuck. Lock your shit, everyone."

"And get your ass home before dark."

She'd heard all she could stand. So she hugged her portfolio close against her chest and focused on the metallic clack-clacking percussion of the train wheels rumbling beneath her.

The even rhythm vibrated up through her legs, spread through her body. It was saying something — and right then, it was all she needed, or *wanted*, to hear.

Over and over. Relentless, insistent, urgent.

Be lucky. Be lucky. Be lucky.

* * *

She walked into the reception area of Fly Girl, cold

and wet. Twin ladder runs stretched across both legs of her stockings and her heels, rubbed raw. But her punctuality was not in question.

The receptionist, a ghostly girl with long, shiny black hair, gave her the once over, from grubby pumps to the wet, tangled mess of her hair. Her gaze moved at lightning speed.

But she saw it — *felt* it.

She smoothed back a stray, wet lock from her forehead and cleared her throat. "I'm here to see Ms. Ginger, please."

The girl pecked at the keys of her shiny laptop, squinted at the screen, then offered her a professional smile. "You must be her two o'clock. Right on time. I'll let her know you're here."

She sat in a sleek leather chair, shivering.

After a few moments, the girl spoke to her again. "Chamberlain will be right down to fetch you."

"Chamberlain?"

"Ms. Ginger's assistant." She flashed another robotic smile, then tapped her own eyes and turned back to her screen.

She froze. Then dug into her purse and pulled out her compact. The bruise was on full display. She patted it with powder, but it wasn't enough.

A shadow moved in front of her. It was the receptionist. She held out a small bottle of concealer. "I find this works."

She flashed her a grateful smile. Smeared some concealer on her pinky, tapping it over her skin with a much lighter hand than the one that caused the bruise in the first place. When she finished, she patted it with powder. Much better.

She returned the jar to the receptionist.

"Thank you."

Then she returned to her seat. Her stomach squirming with bat-sized butterflies as she waited for *Chamberlain* to *fetch* her. The urge to scan her portfolio bubbled up inside her. A craving compulsion to check, rearrange, purge — for the thousandth time — anything that might make her work more appealing or improve her chances.

But it remained zipped shut and balanced on her lap.

And her mind echoed the old woman's mantra.

Be lucky, be lucky, be lucky.

* * *

Ms. Ginger, dressed head-to-toe in butterscotch cashmere, stood over the glossy white conference table. With excruciating slowness, she flipped through the portfolio, scrutinizing each page, her face a vacant mask, a Siamese cat in a picture window.

Finally, she looked up with a flicker of a half-smile. "You're very good. Instinctive. Unique."

An electric charge shot through her veins. "Thank you." With effort, she managed not to stutter.

"I'd like to offer you the position."

"Really?"

"Yes, really."

"My God." She was breathless and lightheaded, her heart beating dangerously fast!

"Is that a *yes*?"

"My God, yes! I mean, yes, that's a *yes*!"

Ms. Ginger smiled fully. "Wonderful. Congratulations."

"I just can't ... I can't believe it!" This was actually happening. She'd gotten the job!

"It's only entry-level, mind you, but I've had dozens of applicants. You're a lucky girl."

"I am. I really am."

Be lucky, be lucky, be lucky.

"But you're also very talented," Ms. Ginger beamed. "I think you've got quite the career ahead of you." She walked around to a steel chair and took her seat. "Now, what part of the city do you live in?"

"Oh, I don't live in the city. I'll be commuting."

The warm smile faded from Ms. Ginger's face.

"I don't mind." She flapped her hand. "Just ninety minutes on the train and a few blocks. It's nothing."

"Commuting?" Her nose twitched.

"Is that a problem?"

"Only if you're serious about a career in fashion. This job involves long hours, late nights, research, fittings, meetings ... we'll need you *here*."

"I will *be* here. I promise. You have no idea how much this means—"

"You're willing to relocate?"

"I ... that would be ..." Her ribs tightened. She swallowed hard. "I have a house. It was my mother's."

"I see. Well ..."

"My husband ..."

You think we're going to walk away from a free house?

"Oh, married?"

"He won't want to move just yet ..."

Nuttier than your fucking mother.

"Lots of girls share an apartment at first."

"Oh, that ... that would be ... but my husband ..."

Said he'd kill me if I ever tried to leave.

"Perhaps you should go home and discuss. We can circle back to where you live another time. In the meantime— she held out a hand — "welcome aboard."

And she shook.

* * *

Tracks of drizzle zigzagged across the train windows as familiar rooftops came into view. Smoke streamed from the textile mill, smudging a thick gray bank of clouds with filthy brown streaks. Misty tendrils of fog mixed with steam billowing from the sewer grates. They curled around the street lamps and porch lights and hovered in jaundiced patches over the scrubby backyards.

The sack full of takeout in her lap had gone stone cold an hour ago. She pictured the gelatinous mass of fettuccine in its Styrofoam box, imagined it landing, with a wet thud, on the plate, ready for nuking.

She could hear him, smell him, *feel* him, deep in the jagged cracks of her heart, in the empty hollows of her chest.

"I said fucking *ziti*."

"They were out."

"*Out?* What time did you get there? What the hell were you doing? Where the fuck were you?"

"At my inter—"

"WHERE THE FUCK WERE YOU?"

Crack!

It could go that way. Easily. Or, if she were lucky, he'd be passed out in front of the damn TV. Then she could slip upstairs, lock the bedroom door, and be safe until morning … maybe.

But who was she kidding?

She wasn't lucky.

And never would be.

The train wheels rumbled beneath her, but had nothing interesting to say.

* * *

She angled the nose of the car toward the side of the road and idled, just for a moment, outside the house. The living room window glowed with the TV's azure light. Ma's beautiful, homemade, white lace curtains billowed like twin ghosts dancing in the dirty rain.

It was a bad sign.

She waited for the nerves, the tight chest, the fear, any of the old emotions to rise inside her. But they did not. She had nothing left. Not even common sense, life-preserving fear.

He'd taken it all.

She'd been gobbled up.

Just like Ma.

She missed her *so* much.

Better not linger too long. He'd hear the car and wonder where she was.

So she turned into the driveway.

AND THERE, in the glow of the headlights, a man stood in sideview next to the garage. He froze, then slowly turned and looked *right at her*.

The man was dressed in mostly black — pants, sneakers, and a black knit cap pulled low over long, straggly hair. Over a white collared shirt, he wore a dark woolen jacket with large shiny buttons engraved with the image of a ship's anchor. It was covered in white linty specks that glowed in the headlights' glare.

Some might mistake the white shirt, buttoned right up to his chin, as a priest's collar. *Some* might call the woolen jacket a "sailor's coat." But she knew its proper name. A vintage peacoat that surely smelled of thrift store and vape.

He turned, facing her dead on. That's when she saw the glint of metal poking out of his right sleeve.

His eyes flashed with fear, a dark, erotic violence she could barely stand to look at.

But his expression held something else. Something immediate. A question. Choices. An impending decision.

She could sense his thoughts.

As clear to her as a fresh drop of rain.

Too late to hide. Do her first? Time to run?

He drew his brows together. He bared his teeth. He lifted his right hand and showed her his toy: the axe blade sharpened to a gleaming edge.

She just ... laughed. What were the chances? Of all the houses in the whole town to choose from. It was funny. It was *hilarious*.

She smiled at him, enjoying the bleak confusion overshadowing his animal expression.

Then she rolled down her window and caught the scent of freesia.

She gestured to him with a hooked finger. *Come here.*

His face darkened with suspicion.

But he came closer, trailing the fingers of his left hand along the hood of her car as he inched toward her window. In his right hand, the axe flashed in the light of the bare bulb hanging over the garage.

She gestured again, impatient now. *Come. On.*

He was at her door now. She smelled the acrid reek of his flop sweat and the mothball stench of his woolen coat.

He bent down and rested an elbow on the driver's side mirror. His blade made a metallic *tick-tick* as he tapped it rhythmically against the edge of her open window.

Then she looked up at him.

"Careful on the steps. They're fucked."

Then she aimed the door opener at the garage. After three clicks, it rumbled open. His eyes stayed on hers. Then he turned and looked at the open garage.

He pointed the axe. "Those steps?"

She nodded. "Yeah. Wouldn't want you to fall."

When he smiled, it was so broad, so childishly *merry*, he was almost ... handsome.

. . .

HE TURNED TOWARD THE STAIRS. And right before he placed his foot on the lowest one, he nodded at her. A final thanks. Then he climbed them carefully, catlike, with the lithe grace of a trained dancer. He looked back at her once. She crossed her fingers: *Good luck.*

He laughed.

She watched as he held the axe high, twisted the knob, pushed the door wide, and stepped inside.

She leaned one ear out the open car window and held her breath, waiting ... until it came. His voice hard and nasty.

"Gina, is that you?"

And then she hit the garage remote once again. Watching the door close, allowing the smell of freesia to swallow up whatever sounds were about to happen ...

The Final Rose

LINDA BLESER

The Final Rose

LINDA BLESER

EMMA HELD THE PHONE AWAY FROM HER EAR AS HER BEST friend Laura screamed, "Oh my God! I can't believe you made it!"

Emma couldn't believe it either. She'd auditioned for *The Resort to Romance* reality show months ago, surprised when she made it to each round of auditions. Now, here she was, one of the nineteen final contestants to appear on the show.

Laura's high-pitched scream brought her back to earth. "I can't believe it, girl. When do you leave? Should we go shopping? Can I tell everyone? Do you know who the guy is?"

Emma laughed. "One question at a time. I leave in the morning. I don't have to go shopping. I've been preparing for this for weeks. And no, you can't say a word. I'm not even supposed to tell anyone, so it's our secret."

"My lips are sealed."

"Good, and they must remain sealed. I'm not supposed to contact anyone while I'm on the island, so this is the last time you'll hear from me until the finale."

"But..."

"I know." They'd talked on the phone or in person every day since becoming best friends in elementary school. Emma couldn't remember a time they'd gone more than a week without touching base. This was going to be the hardest part of living on an isolated island with a dozen other women and one handsome bachelor.

"Any idea who the bachelor is?"

Emma shrugged. "It's a super secret. But *RealityRules* threw out the names of a few eligible bachelors—Cody English, David McGregor, and Grant Simmons."

Another squeal pierced her ear. "Oh my God! Grant Simmons is the hunkiest, most eligible bachelor in New York."

"I know."

"And he's rich."

"I know."

"And gorgeous!"

"You already said that."

Laura let out a soft sigh. "I'd give anything to meet him."

"Well, we don't know whether it's Grant Simmons or not. I thought I heard rumors he was engaged." Emma let out a bitter laugh. "Not like that would stop some men."

She didn't have to spell it out for Laura. Emma had cried on her shoulder for months when Carsen, her ex-fiancé, cheated on her.

"You have to call and tell me all about it. And send pictures. Lots of pictures. I can at least live vicariously through you."

"I told you. I can't. I signed a non-disclosure thingie. Besides, they take our phones away the minute we step foot on the island."

274

"Laura tapped her chin. "Hey, didn't Carsen give you a Polaroid camera last Christmas?"

"Don't remind me. He tried to talk me into taking some *boudoir* photos." She made air quotes around the word. "Only he wanted me to pose like a men's magazine centerfold."

"So ... did you?"

Emma laughed. "I'll never tell. But it's not a bad idea. I might just sneak it in and take some photos to document my experience. It'll be like you're right there with me."

Laura seemed content with the promise. "What are you wearing to meet Mr. Gorgeous?"

Emma almost didn't reply. This was one of the areas where she and Laura were different. Laura loved to shop. She followed every fashion show and read every fashion magazine, where Emma preferred comfort over glamour. "I'm going casual," she said.

"What? Every other woman will be glammed up with sequins and sky-high heels."

"Yep, and we'll be taking a boat to the island. I plan on being comfortable."

"But..."

Emma didn't let her friend finish. "You know me. I've never been one for sequins and lace. That's fine for other girls. It's just not me."

"Suit yourself," Laura said. "But at least bring something pretty to wear for the cameras."

"Tell you what," Emma said. "We'll go shopping, and I'll let you pick a few things out for me. But I'm absolutely not wearing heels on the boat."

* * *

As it turned out, she'd made the right decision. While the other women struggled in high heels on the slippery decks, Emma stayed upright in boat shoes. While the other women complained about the sea spray turning their hair to frizz, her messy bun was contained under a NY Yankees cap. And while they shivered in the sea breeze, Emma was warm and dry in a yellow wind-breaker.

"You were smart to dress for the boat ride."

Emma turned to the woman beside her. She was gorgeous, with high cheekbones and full lips. Her hair was pulled back in a makeshift ponytail, and a pair of high heels dangled from her fingers. She held out her other hand. "I'm Tamara."

"Emma," she said, taking the woman's hand. "Are you as nervous as I am?"

"At least, if not more." She tried to hold back a grin. "Is it too late to turn around?"

"Definitely. We've already signed our lives away."

"More like sold our souls to the devil," Tamara replied.

Emma hoped she was joking. She glanced over as some of the other women struggled to get off the boat, slipping or hobbling on broken heels. She jerked her head in their direction. "Should we help them?"

Tamara smiled and looped her arm inside Emma's. "Let's go."

One by one, they made their way to the dock, laughing and giggling all the way. Emma knew at some point they'd be forced to compete against each other, but for now, they were all enjoying the adventure. They were met at the dock by the production crew and the host of the show, who was shorter than he looked on television.

Mack, the executive producer, called for attention. "There's been a change of plans," he informed them. "I know I said we'd go back to the house to refresh after the boat ride, but we've decided to change it up a little. He gestured to a black limo parked in the distance. "We thought it would be fun if our bachelor welcomed you right off the boat."

His announcement was met with a series of moans and groans.

Tamara leaned close and whispered in Emma's ear. "I bet they planned this all along."

Emma hoped the microphones hadn't picked that up. She glanced up as the limo door opened and watched as he stepped out of the car, wearing high-gloss polished dress shoes that probably cost more than her entire outfit.

RealityRules was right.

It was Grant Simmons, the most eligible bachelor in New York. And yes, he was absolutely gorgeous. But as handsome as he was from a distance, he was even more so face to face when it came to Emma's turn to introduce herself. Eyes the color of caramel drizzle, a smile that curled up on one side, and dimples that didn't quit.

She held out her hand. "Emma," she said. "Emma Glade." She thought it would be hard to ignore the cameras and production crew, but when Grant looked into her eyes, it was as if just the two of them existed.

He glanced at her clothes. "I see you came prepared for the boat ride." The look on his face said he approved of her choice. He gestured to her cap. "Yankees fan?"

"Season tickets."

"Who's your favorite player?"

"Aaron Judge."

Grant nodded. "I look forward to talking more inside."

And just like that, she was dismissed. It had taken all of maybe three minutes that went by in a blur. But she'd felt a spark. And they had a common interest. Baseball. She felt good about it.

She joined the other women inside. Most of them had kicked off their shoes and were rubbing swollen feet. The rest were in front of mirrors, trying to rescue their wind-blown hair.

One of the women nudged her. "You were smart. The rest of us look like drowned rats."

Emma smiled. "I'm Emma."

"Kacee," the other woman said.

Emma felt an immediate connection. Kacee reminded her of Laura, and she felt a twinge of homesickness but covered it with a smile. "Nice to meet you."

Tamara came over and joined them. "So it looks like the producers are going to let us get cleaned up before the first rose ceremony."

"Thank God," Kacee said with a grin.

Tamara looped an arm through Emma's. "And we're sharing a room."

Emma was delighted. She liked Tamara already and looked forward to having someone to talk to.

Once upstairs, Emma looked around their suite, which featured a small kitchenette with a café-style dining table and chairs. Each of the beds was covered in cream-colored duvets and plush, lace-trimmed pillows. There were two dressing tables, and they each did their hair and make-up before going back downstairs for the cocktail party.

Emma wasn't surprised to see that the ballroom, which looked so impressive on the television, was a stage set with plenty of room for the cameras and crew. It felt strange at first, but eventually, Emma became accustomed to the microphones and production assistants giving stage direc-tions. What would eventually be about twenty minutes on the show took hours to film.

The highlight of the session was when Grant offered the "Love at First Sight Rose" to Tamara. Emma was glad, although not everyone seemed to share her appreciation. It wasn't surprising since they were all competing for the attention of the same man.

After filming wrapped, Emma was pulled aside by one of the production assistants for a private interview.

The PA gestured to a chair. "Have a seat, I'm Carly, I'll be your…"

"Handler?"

Carly shrugged. "And confidante, I hope." She sat across from Emma. "So, let's get started. I'll ask some questions, and I'm looking for your honest reactions. Okay?"

"I'll do my best."

Carly nodded to the camera operator, and Emma tried to act normal, which wasn't so easy with a camera and microphone in her face.

"So tell me," Carly said. "What was your first reaction when you saw Grant?"

"I thought, wow, he's even more handsome than I imagined," Emma said. "And maybe a little shorter." She caught herself and raised a hand, palm out. "Oh, don't use that. I didn't mean it the way it came out."

"No problem," Carly said with a grin.

The rest of the interview went well, with only a little prodding from Carly here and there. But Carly's next question caught Emma by surprise.

"So, tell me about your last relationship."

"My last relationship?"

"Yes, before coming on the show."

"We were together two years. We broke up six months ago."

"And why did you break up?"

Emma blinked back tears that always seemed to lurk below the surface when she thought about Carsen. "There was another woman. I guess I wasn't enough."

"Does he know you're here?"

Emma shook her head. "No."

Carly motioned to the camera operator, then slapped her hands on her thighs and stood. "Guess we're done here. For now, anyway. You're free to wander. Craft services are set up in the lobby if you want something to eat or drink."

Emma had something else in mind. She went back to her room and unpacked her Polaroid camera. While everyone else was occupied, she took a handful of candid pictures. Laura would be thrilled to see all the behind-the-scenes pictures.

Once she ran out of film, Emma grabbed a protein bar from Craft Services and then made her way back to her room to find Tamara there.

"So, what did you think?" Emma asked.

Tamara brought the rose to her nose and smiled. "I think he's dreamy." She placed her rose in a crystal bud vase on the nightstand. Emma noticed there was an empty vase on her side as well. Most likely, one for each contestant. The longer you stayed, the more roses you'd acquire.

Emma kicked off her shoes. "Hey, when you had your interview, did they ask a lot of questions about your ex?"

"A few," Tamara said. "Just background information, I guess." She walked over to the nightstand. "Oooh, what do we have here?"

"Just some pictures I took around the set to show my friend. We had to turn in our phones, but no one said we couldn't take Polaroids."

Tamara made a humming sound as she shuffled through the photos. She stopped and stared at one in particular.

Emma was just about to ask if there was a problem when Tamara turned with a bright smile.

"I'm heading for the hot tub," she said. "Want to join me?"

"Not tonight," Emma replied. She planned on taking a long, hot bath and then writing everything about today's events in her journal. If she couldn't talk to Laura, she could at least share a day-by-day account of her time on the island.

Tamara changed into a barely-there black bikini and waved on her way out. "Toodles."

Emma smiled. Who said *toodles* these days? She grabbed a pair of pajamas, then headed to the bathroom. The cabinet was equipped with fragrant soaps, lotions, and moisturizers. Emma sprinkled lavender bath crystals into the tub and ran hot water. Leaning back, she sighed and relaxed for the first time all day. She'd always assumed what she saw on television was exactly what happened on reality shows. In truth, there were stops and starts, long hours of boredom between filming, and more petty bickering than she'd seen since high school.

The conversation with Carlie kept coming back, bringing with it memories of Carsen. He'd been the perfect lover, her best friend. She'd thought he was the one. But apparently, she wasn't enough for him. Betrayal burned like acid in her belly, and a familiar refrain echoed in her mind—*you're not good enough.*

Pushing thoughts of Carsen aside, she let the warm water soothe her muscles, closed her eyes, and drifted off.

A scream jerked her awake. She flailed in the cooled water. Another scream had her surging up out of the tub and throwing on her clothes before she even knew where she was going. The bedroom was empty. Tamara was still gone ... and so was her rose.

Emma ran outside and followed the sound of screaming, stopping in her tracks when she reached the crowd gathered around the hot tub. Tamara was in the water, floating face up. Her eyes stared blankly at the sky, and her first rose floated next to her. Odd, she hadn't remembered Tamara bringing it with her. But then again, she'd been very tired.

Mack stepped forward, turning to Emma. "When did you last see her? You might have been the last person to —" he broke off.

"I…" She shook her head. "I went to take a bath. She said she was going to the hot tub." Emma knew she was babbling but couldn't stop. "I fell asleep in the tub and woke when I heard the scream."

Mack turned to one of the other women whose name Emma couldn't remember. "You're the one who found her?"

The woman nodded. "I came out to have a smoke and …" her voice caught on a sob. "How could this happen?"

Mack knelt down at the side of the hot tub and lifted an empty syringe. "This might explain what happened."

Emma stared at it. Granted, she didn't know Tamara that well, but there were no signs she had a drug habit. But what other explanation was there?

"Cameras," Emma said. "There are cameras everywhere. Can't you check them?"

Mack shook his head while the crew pulled Tamara's body from the hot tub. "We already checked. The cameras were …" he stopped as if searching for the correct word. "Vandalized."

"Vandalized? Who would do that?"

Mark shook his head. "Dunno. Did you see her with drugs in the room?"

Emma shook her head. "No. I had no idea."

She suddenly realized Grant had shown up. His face

was impassive. He placed an arm around her shoulder. "I'm sorry. She was your roommate, wasn't she?"

Emma nodded. Then noticed someone had placed a sheet over Tamara's body. She looked around. "Where are the police?"

Mack shook his head. "We have our own island security here." He looked down, then away. "Besides, this is an unfortunate accident. There's no need to call the police." He gave a nervous laugh. "They'll just shut us down."

"You're not going to continue filming, are you?" she asked incredulously.

Mack nodded and forced a smile. "The show must go on."

***

Emma answered a thousand questions, first from the producers, then from the island security police. Yes, she was the last one to see Tamara alive. No, she had no idea who may have taken the rose out of their room. Maybe Tamara had come back for it? Yes, she was sleeping in the bathtub and only woke up when she heard the screams. No, she didn't have an alibi, but she knew nothing about the drugs or Tamara's death.

Emma was prepared to pack up and leave the island, but Mack called everyone together and informed them he'd decided to continue production.

Emma turned in disgust. It felt disrespectful to go on with the show. A woman just died here. She wished she could call Laura and talk to her about everything that had happened.

Grant pulled her aside. "You must be in shock," he said, his voice low and soothing. "Why don't I walk you back to your room."

Emma let Grant lead her away. Only when they reached her door did the shock wear off, and she broke down in tears. Grant wrapped his arms around her and pulled her against his chest. "It'll be okay," he murmured.

She felt unreasonably safe in his arms. The horror of Tamara's death was already taking on a dreamlike quality. Only when Grant left and she locked the door behind him did she feel totally alone. Tamara's suitcase was gone, as well as the few belongings she'd unpacked. It felt cold, as if she'd never existed.

Emma looked over at the Polaroids she had taken. Something about the way they were arranged didn't feel right. She walked over and shuffled the pictures, counting then recounting. One was missing. Maybe it was the photo Tamara had been staring at? Did she take it with her? If so, why wasn't it found at the hot tub?

A knock on the door startled her. She turned, hoping Grant had returned. She'd felt comforted by his presence. But it was Sara. "I swear I heard Tamara talking to Mack. She told him she wanted to go home."

"When?"

"On her way to the hot tub."

So Emma hadn't been the last to see her roommate.

"But why?" Emma asked. "She seemed fine after getting the first rose."

"Something happened afterward, then. Something that made her want to leave."

Emma frowned. What could have happened between the time she left for the hot tub and the time she died?

"I just wanted to warn you. Something seems off." She turned to leave, then looked over her shoulder before opening the door. "Just be careful, okay?"

Emma nodded. Sara's words echoed in her mind long after the woman was gone. Maybe they were both being paranoid, but Emma made sure her door was locked before going to bed.

* * *

The next morning, Emma ran into Mack at the coffee station. "Someone told me Tamara asked you to let her go home."

Mack raised an eyebrow. "Who told you that?"

She poured herself a cup of coffee. "It's just something I heard."

Mack shrugged. "I've been doing this a long time. People get homesick. I have to remind them they're under contract."

"So you're saying we can't leave?"

"You did sign a contract."

"But a woman died here."

"Accidental overdose. There's no sense making more of it than it is."

Emma stared at the man. How could he be so cold and callous? Before she could say another word, they were interrupted by one of the production staff.

"A word," he said to Mack.

Mack walked away with the man, their heads bent together. What was that about? Emma lost her appetite. Sara's words kept ringing in her ears. *Be careful.* Of what? Or whom?

She left the dining room, taking her coffee to a lounge chair on the beach. The sound of the waves soothed her nerves. According to today's filming schedule, she didn't have to be on the set for another two hours. Normally, she'd pull out her phone and scroll through messages and emails. But now she couldn't even call her best friend for advice. She felt naked and cut off from the world.

She closed her eyes and took some deep, cleansing breaths. However, her meditation was cut short.

"Ms. Glade?"

Emma opened her eyes and squinted into the sun. She

made out the silhouette of a woman who pointed to the lounge chair beside her.

"May I?"

Emma nodded.

The woman held out her hand. "Fiona Drake," she said, taking a seat beside Emma. Then she flashed a badge.

"Detective?"

The woman shook her head. "No, private police. We take care of our own on the island."

Emma had a better look at the woman. Short dark hair, kind eyes, and a khaki shirt with the island police emblem on the sleeve.

Emma sat up straight. "I've already told everything I know about Tamara…"

The woman held up her hand. "No. This has nothing to do with Tamara. It's about Sara."

"Sara?"

"I understand she went to your room last night."

"Yes, she…oh my God, has something happened to her?"

The officer let out a slow breath. "Her room was ransacked this morning. You were the last person to talk to her."

Her shoulders dropped. At least Sara was safe. But this wasn't good. She was the last one to talk to Tamara and now the last one to talk to Sara. All eyes would be on her. "She told me that Tamara wanted to leave the island but was told she couldn't."

"By?"

"Mack," Emma said. "Sara said Mack told Tamara she couldn't leave. He said the same thing to me when I asked. Said we are under contract." She shook her head. "Poor Sara. I should go talk to her."

Fiona shook her head. "She's not here. She left the show. Moved into town."

"She did?"

Fiona nodded.

"Can I leave too?"

"No. We'd like everyone else to stay on-site while we investigate."

"Is that an order?" Emma asked.

The policewoman gave her a long, hard stare before answering. "It's a suggestion."

* * *

That afternoon, they filmed the next episode as if nothing had happened. The producers chose not to explain the absence of the two missing contestants but rather said that "due to unforeseen circumstances," there'd be no rose ceremony or elimination that evening. As soon as they finished filming, Emma changed from her glittery gown into a jogging suit and sensible shoes. Suggestion or no suggestion, she'd decided to go into town and talk to Sara. Since she wasn't sure exactly where the town was or how long it would take to get there, she asked Tony, one of the crew members, for a ride.

"I'm going into town anyway." He had a New York accident and a quick smile. "Where ya heading?"

Emily had no idea. "I, um, need to buy a new dress. I didn't pack enough."

"Sure thing," Tony said. "I know just the place."

When he dropped her off at an upscale boutique, Emily had a feeling she wasn't the first contestant looking to out-glam their competition. Once Tony left, she walked along the streets with no idea where she was heading. A tingle at the back of her neck made her turn, convinced someone was following her. She waited a few minutes, scanning the street, but didn't see anyone. Still, she felt vulnerable. After another block, she stepped inside a coffee shop, turning to see a shrouded figure come to a halt a few feet behind her. Someone was definitely following her.

A voice pulled her out of her trance. "What can I get you?"

Emma turned to the barista. "Um, nothing. I was just passing through."

The barista jerked her head to the side, gesturing toward the resort. "You from that show?"

"Yes. I was looking for a friend who's also on the show. Her name is Sara. Has she been here?"

The barista shrugged. "Get a lot of people in here. I don't check their license or anything."

Emma realized how foolish she'd been. She didn't even know Sara's last name. Did she just expect to run into her on the street or something? And even if she did, what would she say? *Any idea who trashed your room? Do you know more about Tamara's death than you let on?*

Maybe she'd had a family emergency. Or maybe she just wanted off the show. Emma sighed and ordered a cup of coffee, taking a seat at the counter. Tony had given her his card, but she forgot she didn't have a phone to call him for the ride back.

She sipped on her coffee. When the barista came over, she asked to borrow the shop phone. She called Tony and told him where to meet her.

When he arrived, she saw someone disappear around the side of the building. She went to look, but they were gone. Was it the same person she'd thought was following her earlier, or was she just being paranoid?

She got into Tony's car. "Did you see anyone suspicious on the street?"

Tony shook his head. "No, why?"

"I don't know. I just thought someone was following me earlier."

Tony looked up and down the street. "I don't see no one." Then he put the car in gear and pulled away from the curb.

* * *

Emma didn't realize she was hungry until the smell of dinner being served in the dining room hit her. She hadn't eaten since her aborted breakfast with Mack.

Someone called her name, and she looked over at a table where three women were sitting. Then she went and joined them.

"I heard they're postponing production," one of the women said. "Maybe even canceling the show."

Nicki exhaled a sigh. "That would be a shame. I was looking forward to having an island vacation and going on some romantic dates with Grant."

"Weren't we all," Maria said.

Another leaned forward and whispered. "I overheard one of the crew saying Grant was engaged right up until the day we started filming."

Emma frowned.

Was that true?

If it was, what else he might be hiding? She couldn't help but think of Carsen. Being engaged hadn't stopped him from flirting with other women despite his insistence that it was innocent.

A server came by and took their orders. Emma was too nervous to eat, so she simply ordered a small salad.

When their orders were placed, Nicki turned to Emma. "They said Sara went to your room last night."

All eyes turned to Emma, who nodded.

"Did she say anything? Like, who might have ransacked her room? Or why she planned to leave?"

"No," Emma said with a shake of her head. "Nothing like that."

Gloria, a petite blonde, spoke up, her voice trembling. "This has turned into a creep fest. I went for a walk on the beach this afternoon, and I swear someone was following me. You know how you get those goosebumps on the back of your neck? But when I turned, I didn't see anyone. Maybe it was just women's intuition, but I just knew someone was behind me, so I hightailed it back to the resort."

Emma felt a chill run down her spine. Could the shadowy figure who'd followed her in town be the same person who'd followed Gloria earlier? "The same happened to me."

"This is ridiculous," Gloria said. "The production company should be keeping us safe."

Emma cleared her throat. "If they are canceling the show and sending us home, I plan to be all packed and ready to go."She thought about Tamara's lifeless body. "The sooner the better."

Gloria reached out and placed her hand on Emma's wrist. "Do you really think we're in danger? Maybe Tamara's death wasn't an isolated incident."

"You mean someone didn't like her getting the first rose and decided to eliminate the competition?" Nicki said with a sneer.

Emma frowned. "Who would do that?"

They looked at each other around the table. They were all strangers. Who knew what one might be capable of?

Just then, their meals arrived, and they ate in silence as a fog of fear and mistrust settled around them.

* * *

After dinner, Emma left the group, setting off for the beach to think. How could someplace so beautiful and exotic be the scene of such ugliness? Maybe she should have insisted production call the actual police instead of leaving it to island security.

As she drew closer to the shore, she spotted a boat in the distance. The waves rocked it from side to side. She almost laughed. Maybe she should steal it and leave the island. A chill ran down her spine. Maybe someone had already tried that? Her feet sank into the wet sand. She should have turned back, but something compelled her to keep going. What she saw next came in vivid snapshots, one after another — a limp hand, wet hair, vacant eyes.

It was Sara.

Emm screamed.

Then she turned to run and crashed straight into a man's chest. Another scream erupted from her throat, then arms wrapped around her.

"Emma. Emma, it's all right. It's me."

Heart beating, Emma blinked in surprise. It had to be shock. First Tamara, then Sara. And now… "Carsen?"

"Yeah, it's me."

She trembled, pointing to the boat. "Sara. She's in the boat. She's dead."

Carsen released his grip on her. "Wait here. I'll check."

Emma wrapped her arms around herself, willing the trembling to stop. What was Carsen doing here? How did he even know she was on the island? Laura was the only one who knew she was here, and the last thing she would do was tell him.

Carsen came back, shaking his head. "There's nothing we can do for her. She's been dead for hours." He put his arm around Emma's shoulder. "Let's go back and inform the authorities."

"I was the last one to see her alive," Emma said. "They're going to want to question me. Again."

"We'll deal with that together."

She pulled away, looking up at him. "What are you doing here, Carsen?"

"We'll discuss that later," he said. "Let's get this taken care of first."

She hesitated but saw a crowd gathering outside the Villa. "It's Sara," she pointed toward the beach. "She's dead."

A flurry of motion surrounded her, women gasping, people running. Carsen gently led Emma away from the crowd and toward her room.

She slowed. "How did you know this was my room?"

"I'll explain everything once we're safely inside."

Safe. She felt anything but safe. Two women were dead. She was stuck on this island and didn't know who to trust. And now Carsen was here.

Once inside, Carsen locked the door behind them. He led Emma to a seat at the table and brought her a glass of water. "This wasn't supposed to be like this."

"Like what?" This was supposed to be a romantic adventure in a tropical paradise. Instead, she was thrown into the middle of a crime scene. And the biggest mystery of all was standing right in front of her. "So why are you here?"

Carsen took a deep breath and sighed. "It was Mack's idea. He contacted me and had me stay in town. Figured an ex-boyfriend showing up would add drama to the show."

Emma felt furious. It made sense in a twisted kind of way.

"I heard rumors in town about what was going on up here," Carsen continued. "I was worried about you. I got hold of an employee uniform and came up here to keep an eye on you. That's how I knew which room was yours. And why I was able to follow you to the beach."

"Were you the one following me in town?"

"In town? No. I was already here at the resort looking for you. Then, when I heard about the hurricane."

Emma's eyes widened. "Hurricane?"

"Yeah, there's a storm heading our way. All flights are grounded while we wait it out."

Emma closed her eyes. "We're trapped here? With a killer?"

"Just keep your door locked. Don't leave the room without me. And don't trust anyone."

Emma nodded, but a sneaky voice in her head warned her that was exactly what the killer would say. No. Stop it. She knew Carsen. He was a lot of things—unpredictable, flirtatious, and unable to commit, which is why they'd broken up in the first place. But he wasn't a killer.

Now, all those reasons seemed so unimportant compared to life-and-death scenarios. She lifted the glass to her lips and took a sip. "I think I'm going to call it a night."

"I'll stay if you want me to."

Emma shook her head. This wasn't the time or place for a reconciliation. "Not tonight."

He looked crestfallen, then straightened his shoulders. "I understand. But if you need anything, I'm here."

She walked him to the door of the suite. "Thank you. I appreciate it more than you know."

Before turning, Carsen leaned forward and pressed a gentle kiss to her forehead. "Sleep sweet."

* * *

When Carsen left, Emma turned on the television and watched the hurricane updates. The track had changed and was aiming right for the island. Was there someplace they could take shelter if the island took a direct hit?

Despite her promise to Carsen, Emma was determined to get out of there. Finding where their phones were locked away was the first step. She wasn't sure whether anyone had called the state police about Sara or not. That was the first thing she'd do once she found her phone. The second thing would be to find a way back home before she became the next victim. There had to be some flights that weren't grounded.

A knock on the door startled her. Thinking Carsen had forgotten something, she threw open the door, surprised to see Grant there.

"May I come in?"

Emma hesitated for a moment, "I, um…"

Grant nodded. "I understand. Look," he said. "I'm just as shaken up by these…" he cleared his throat. "These accidents. I was hoping we could put our heads together and see what we come up with." He glanced at the open door. "Maybe someplace more public," he added as if sensing her hesitancy.

Emma nodded. She closed the door behind her and followed him to the downstairs library. Despite the sincerity in his eyes, she still didn't trust him completely. Maybe he was simply a good actor.

Downstairs, Grant found a bottle of wine. "I figured you could use this after the day you've had."

She hesitated.

But then he opened it up, poured a glass of wine, and took a sip. "That make you feel better?"

She nodded.

And he poured another one, handing it over. "I heard you found Sara's body."

Emma nodded.

Grant shook his head. "That must have been terrible."

"It was—"

"— I was hoping to ask you a question," he said, cutting her off. "Now that the show is over, I can tell you that I had my eye on you right from the beginning. And I was hoping that even without the final rose, you'd be willing to go on a date when this is all over."

She stared at him. Two women had died. "I'm flattered. But with all that's happened, I can't make a commitment right now."

He tipped his wine glass in her direction and then handed her a key. "Well, if you change your mind, I'm in Room 209."

"Wait."

He stilled, looking hopeful.

"There's a rumor going around that you were engaged right up until the show started," Emma said.

Grant nodded. "That's half true. I *was* engaged, but my fiancé broke it off long before I signed up for the show." He reached for her hand. "I wouldn't have signed on if I was involved with someone else. You have to believe me."

* * *

Back in her room, Emma placed Grant's room key on the counter and focused on the television. The hurricane warnings were becoming more dire. Emma wasn't sure which was worse—getting caught in the eye of a hurricane or being trapped on an island with a murderer. She felt like a sitting duck in her room. Nervous energy thrummed through her entire body. There had to be something she could do.

She wished she could call Lauren. Maybe with all that was happening, Mack would let them have their phones back. It couldn't hurt to ask. Emma opened her door slowly and checked up and down the hallway. There was no one in sight. She slipped out and made her way to Mack's room.

When she arrived, she lifted her hand to knock on the door and was surprised when it slid open at her touch. "Mack? Are you in here?"

She heard a scurrying, then the sound of something breaking. She poked her head into the room, surprised to see it ransacked. "Mack?"

A shadow passed in the back of the room, and someone ran out the patio doors. *What the hell?* Emma rushed to the patio door, but the figure was already gone. Was it the same person who'd followed her in town? What were they looking for in Mack's room?

Before she could search for her phone, she heard footsteps and Mack's voice, obviously talking to someone on the other end of a call about having to cancel the show. "Do you have any idea how much money I've sunk into this project?" he yelled. "Yeah, I've told them we're stopping production, but I have a better idea."

She couldn't go back into the hall, so Emma escaped through the patio doors. Instead of following the same path as the intruder, she turned in the other direction, heading to the entrance of the Villa.

When she entered, Carsen spotted her and rushed to her side. "What are you doing out here?"

Should she tell him what happened? Maybe a half-truth. "I was hoping to find Mack and see if we could get our phones back now that production has been canceled. Have you seen him?"

Carsen shook his head. "No. But the important question is, why aren't you in your room? I can't protect you if I don't know where you are."

Emma ignored the frustration in his voice. "I don't need someone protecting me," she said with as much force as she could muster. "If there's a way to get off this island, I'm going to find it."

Carsen shook his head. "Because of the hurricane, all flights are canceled, and there are no boats on or off the island. The safest thing to do at this point is to shelter until the threat is over."

Just then, she saw Mack storming in. She pushed Carsen aside. "I have to talk to Mack about getting our phones back."

She rushed across the room, grateful that Carsen didn't follow. When she reached Mack, his face was pulled into a scowl.

"Mack," she said. "I was hoping we could get our phones back."

"Not tonight," he growled. "They're locked in the office, and I can't get in until tomorrow."

"But…"

He pushed her aside. "I have more important things to deal with right now. You'll get your phone tomorrow."

She grabbed his elbow. "Maybe I should talk to Grant."

If he wouldn't give her any information, perhaps Grant would.

Mack whipped around, pinning her with a scowl. "Grant's gone. He chartered a plane to get off the island before the storm hits." His eyes narrowed. "I know what you're up to." His breath, hot and foul, washed over her. She took a step back, instincts kicking in.

Just then, Carly came around the corner. "There you are," she said, eyeing Emma. "I need to do a quick voice-over if you have a minute."

Emma nodded, grateful to escape. She followed Carly, but when she glanced back, Mack's gaze seemed to hold a warning. What was it he thought she'd done? She spent the next half hour with Carly voicing over one of her diary segments. Once finished, she rushed back to her room and found the key Grant had left her.

It wasn't breaking in if she had a key.

She made her way to Room 209 and knocked on the door. When there was no answer, she unlocked the door and stepped inside. One look around was all she needed. If Grant had left the island, he'd left in a hurry, leaving all of his belongings behind. She glanced into the bathroom and noticed his toothbrush and pills were still on the sink. She didn't like the looks of that.

Moving to his desk, she noticed a dossier of all the contestants. Grant had scribbled personal notes in the margins, rating each of the contestants. Emma was disgusted by the notes he wrote about them, commenting on their bodies or negatively judging their personalities. Thank God she got a glimpse of his true personality. She picked up the files and left Grant's room, convinced that Mack had lied to her. If Grant had gone to the trouble to charter a plane, he'd have had plenty of time to pack up his personal items to take with him. She had a bad feeling something had happened to Grant. If that was the case, then Mack had blatantly lied to her.

Emma made her way back to her room. Maybe there were clues in the dossiers that would help her find the killer. Assuming she made it through the night.

* * *

The sound of banging on her door woke Emma the next morning. Rain pounded on the window and whipped branches on the trees. The storm was in full force. Her bedside clock flashed twelve, and Emma realized they'd lost power during the night. She'd been up late going over the individual files and was no closer to finding answers. Her sleep had been restless, interrupted by nightmare images of

Tamara floating in the hot tub and Sara's corpse being rocked in the beached boat.

The knocks came again, louder now, and she jumped out of bed. "Coming," she called. She opened the door a few inches and saw Nicki on the other side.

"The whole island is without power, and the storm is getting closer," Nicki said. "Everyone's gathering in the conference room to decide what we're doing next."

"Go ahead," Emma said. "I'll be right there."

She closed the door and listened to Nicki's footsteps rushing away, then changed into a pair of sweatpants and a T-shirt. She pulled a sweatshirt over her head in case they had to venture out into the storm. She spent a few minutes in the bathroom and was just about to brush her teeth when she heard a scream. Rushing out of the room, she found Nicki huddled in the hallway. Blood streamed from the wound at her side.

"Who did this?" Emma cried, kneeling alongside Nicki. She pulled the sweatshirt over her head and pressed it to Nicki's side, trying to stem the flow of blood.

Nicki's breath came in sharp gasps. "I didn't see," she moaned. "They came up behind me."

Emma glanced up and down the hallway, but there was no one in either direction. Surely, the assailant couldn't have gone far. But before she knew it, they were surrounded by people. Someone rushed in with a first aid kit, and once she was sure everything was under control, Emma stood and ran in the other direction, hoping to catch up to whoever had stabbed Nicki. Adrenaline crashed through her body, replacing any fear she'd felt the night before.

She rushed back in the direction of her room. Since Nicki had just left there, anyone coming up behind her had to come from this direction. She reached Mack's room, surprised to find Gloria inside.

"What are you doing here?"

Gloria looked up, startled. "I'm looking for Mack's satellite phone. I know he had one in here."

"HOW DO YOU KNOW THAT?"

"I saw it the other night when I was in here —" She stumbled over her words, a flush spreading across her cheeks. "I just know."

Emma narrowed her eyes. "Were you sleeping with Mack?"

Gloria turned away with a guilty expression.

"And did you find it?" Emma asked.

"No." Gloria shook her head. "And there's no sign of our phones either. I'm afraid we're trapped here."

"Trapped with a killer," Emma replied. "Someone stabbed Nicki in the hallway."

The shock on Gloria's face couldn't be faked. That, plus the fact that there was no sign of blood anywhere on her, convinced Emma that she hadn't found the assailant. By now, whoever had attacked Nicki was long gone.

That's when she noticed the photograph on Mack's desk. It was one of the Polaroids she'd taken. Why did Mack have it? She studied the picture. It seemed innocent enough, just a shot of the crew on the set. Then, she noticed a shadow in the background. Was that Mack? And who was that with him?

Backtracking, Emma returned to her own room. Her door was partially open. Had she left it that way in her haste to get to Nikki? She couldn't remember. She poked her head inside and saw a yellow envelope on her bed. She knew that hadn't been there before. The letter inside was written in big block letters:

Emma,

I know who killed Tamara. Trust me. You're in danger. You need to leave the resort immediately. Meet me in town. There's a vacant house at the corner of Main Street and Second Avenue. I'll be waiting there.

Carsen

EMMA DIDN'T STOP to think.

Maybe Carsen had found a way off the island. Or, at the very least, she wanted out of this Villa. It was easy to slip away since everyone was huddled around Nicki in the opposite hallway.

There wasn't time to find a ride, so Emma ran, feet pounding along the rain-slick road she'd taken to town ... was it just yesterday?

The wind howled, but at least the rain had let up slightly.

Emma brushed strands of wet hair from her face. The skin on the back of her neck prickled. She picked up speed. If someone was following her, she'd outrun them. She had trophies on her shelf back home from track tournaments in high school. Maybe that was a few years ago, but she was still in good shape.

A gust of wind nearly knocked her off her feet, only strengthening her determination to get to safety. When she reached Main Street, she was drenched but invigorated. The running had released endorphins that made her feel invincible. But she knew the rush wouldn't last long.

The streets were abandoned. Everyone seemed to be taking shelter from the storm. She wondered how close the hurricane was now. Would they even be able to fly out?

She reached the vacant house on the corner and pushed the door open, calling out Carsen's name. When there was no answer, she made her way into the dimly lit house.

Why hadn't she thought to bring a flashlight? Or a weapon of some kind? Her footsteps echoed through the silent house. She called out again. This time, she heard a sound coming from the basement.

She made her way down the stairs, stepping carefully into the darkness below. Her eyes adjusted to the dark as she crept deeper down the stairway. Muffled moans urged her forward until she was at the bottom of the stairs. A small window across the room let in enough light to see Grant, bound to a chair at the other side of the room. His mouth was covered with duct tape.

She rushed to his side. His eyes widened, and he shook his head from side to side. She realized too late that he was warning her away.

Then everything went black.

* * *

When she came to, her head was pounding, and her vision blurred. She was tied to a creaky wooden chair. The tight rope around her wrists made the nerves tingle in her hands and arms. She saw Grant rocking back and forth, trying to loosen his restraints.

She rocked forward and back in her chair and felt a nail give way. Not enough of the tip was exposed to cut through the rope, but with enough effort, she could saw away at it until the ropes fell free. If she had enough time.

Then, a masked man entered.

"Who are you?" she asked.

He raised a gun and aimed it at her. "You don't get to ask questions."

She recognized that voice.

"Mack," she cried out. He grunted, then turned the gun on Grant and shot him without any warning. The sound of the gunshot echoed in the room. Grant bellowed, then slumped in his chair, blood seeping from a wound in his side. When Emma turned back, she saw movement at the stairs, but the light was too dim to make out who it was.

"Oh dear," Mack said sarcastically. "Looks as if Grant is just one more of your victims, Emma. And this time, it will be ruled a murder/suicide. Case closed." He turned the gun in Emma's direction, but before he could shoot, Carsen bolted out of the stairwell and lunged at him.

Carsen and Mack struggled, grappling on the ground while throwing blows. At one point, the gun slid across the floor, nearly at Emma's feet. She could feel the rope between her wrists fraying as she frantically scraped it back and forth across the nail head. She could hear Grant moaning beside her and was grateful he was still alive, but for how long? If they didn't get help soon, Grant would become Mack's third victim.

Finally, the rope broke, setting Emma free. She dove for the gun but couldn't take a chance on hitting Carsen. Instead, she grabbed the chair, and when the men shifted, she used every ounce of strength she had to swing it like a baseball bat against Mack's skull. Wood splintered, and she heard a crack she hoped was Mack's skull. He let out an *oof* before collapsing to the floor.

Carsen got to his feet. "Nice shot, slugger."

Then he grabbed the gun, gesturing to the corner of the room. "Grab that rope over there and tie him up."

Emma found the extra rope and bound Mack's hands and feet. Then she rushed over to Grant. "He's still alive," she said. "We have to get help."

"The power's still out," Carsen said.

Emma glanced at Mack. "Gloria said he had a satellite phone. She was searching for it in his room."

Carsen knelt down and searched Mack's pockets. "Nothing," he said, shaking his head.

"Wait." Emma pointed to the corner where she'd found the rope. "I saw a backpack over there. It must be Mack's."

Emma scrambled to the corner while Carsen kept the gun aimed at Mack. She gave a yelp of victory when she found the SAT.

* * *

It wasn't long before the authorities and paramedics arrived. Mack was handcuffed and led away while Grant was ushered into an ambulance.

Emma turned to Carsen. "Why me?"

"I overheard Mack talking," Carsen told her. "He said someone was blackmailing him, and I think he suspected you."

The pieces began to fall into place. "Because of the pictures I took?"

Carsen shrugged. "I don't know for sure."

"And the letter?"

"Left by Mack. I saw him coming out of your room and followed him. You turned up not long after."

Carsen and Emma spent hours being interviewed by the authorities. The hurricane had taken a different course overnight, and power was restored to the island. After spending the morning checking on Grant in the hospital, they were visited by Fiona Drake. She told them that Mack had admitted he'd killed Tamara to keep her from telling the producers that he was having an affair with Gloria. When Sara discovered the truth, she threatened to go to the police, so Mack killed her as well.

"So, who was blackmailing him?"

"Grant. He figured he'd get rid of him using you."

Emma shook her head. "And he almost got away with it."

"He'll be in jail for a long, long time," Fiona said, leaving. "I'm just glad you weren't one of his victims as well."

When she was gone, Emma gave Carsen a look of gratitude. "Thank goodness you came when you did, or it may not have ended as well."

"I'll always be there for you," he said. Then he pulled out a rose he'd lifted from a vase on the table. "And I'm so sorry if I ever said or did anything to make you doubt that."

Emma eyed him. There was no doubting the sincerity in his voice or the love in his eyes. "Emma Glade," he said, holding out the bud. "Will you accept this final rose?"

Emma took a slow, deep breath. This wasn't the way she'd envisioned the reality show ending, but she knew it was the best ending possible. She reached for the rose. "Yes," she said. "Yes, I will.

And she couldn't wait to tell Lauren.

Alpha Incorporated

DAVID W. WRIGHT

Alpha Incorporated

DAVID W. WRIGHT

KYLE WAS BEING HUNTED. HE COULD FEEL IT IN HIS GUT even as he stared into the greenroom mirror, adjusting his tie and giving himself a once over. His hair was coiffed, and his 50K bespoke Merino suit from Saville Row fit like a glove on his shoulders and biceps. But something was off. The strange email that morning. The canceled security detail. A cold sweat formed at the nape of his neck. The way some of the attendees looked at him with something beyond admiration — something like hunger.

"You're going to fucking *kill* this," he told his reflection, forcing confidence in his voice to drown out the paranoia.

The point was, Kyle was amazing. Every man at the Alpha Incorporated Summit wanted to look like him, and their girlfriends all wanted to fuck him.

A sharp knock at the door made him flinch. He caught the momentary look of fear in his own eyes before masking it.

Little did they know how he truly felt about them and the movement his career had been built around. Everything started with the best of intentions — help lonely guys find the confidence and inner strength to do the hard work of being a man. But what started off as a noble mission quickly decayed into grown men arguing over who was the most Alpha and how women were the root of all their problems.

At first, Kyle tried to correct course, reminding his audience that being a man meant taking ownership of your problems, not blaming others. Success in this life is about finding the right solutions to your problems.

But these angry men weren't looking for the truth. They needed their egos coddled while they sought assurances that they were right: It was women who *were* the problem. Scapegoating was always easier than the work. Fail and you had someone else to blame.

But as Kyle's dad used to constantly say: "If you're not failing, you're not trying. Success is born from mistakes."

Lord knows, Kyle had more than his share. Each time he learned what he could, shed his old skin, then moved on to the next thing. Real estate, fitness coaching, private chef, and internet marketing. Each identity and vocation taught him something valuable. The biggest lesson was learning when to stay and when to surrender, something he still struggled with today.

Alpha Incorporated began with Kyle simply delivering the advice he wished someone had given to him as a young man. When he saw how his message was twisted by his fans, he nearly walked away.

Ariana had talked sense into him. "Sure, these guys are dickheads that don't really want to change, so why not exploit the opportunity?"

Of course, she was right, and had he not listened, Kyle would have left a previously unimaginable fortune on the table. Life required constant adaptation; it was one of Alpha Incorporated's primary doctrines.

Kyle had a rabid audience willing to spend money on spoon-fed justifications for their misery and prejudices. If he really leaned into their fears, Kyle could sell them "solutions" ranging from boner pills to questionable supplements, plus the granddaddy of them all: *an intimate Alpha Inc. experience where you can finally become the man you were born to be.*

Sometimes, he almost felt guilty for taking their money.

The truth was, when he started, Kyle believed about 80% of what he taught. The core principles of self-improvement, accountability, and strength were real. But as the money grew, his belief in his own teachings diminished. Each time he caught himself thinking like his followers — judging women harshly, feeling superior — he'd recognize the poison he was spreading. The cognitive dissonance was becoming unbearable, though the money made it easier to ignore. Because if it wasn't him, it would be someone else.

Kyle wasn't even close to the first big star of the media-described *manosphere.* That honor belonged to Cole Parsons. He was a former MMA fighter turned pickup artist and con man, spewing the sort of vile garbage that feminists had accused Kyle of peddling, including gems like, "There is no such thing as rape because all women secretly want to be owned." And, "A woman can't say no if her mouth is busted."

Parsons routinely attacked feminists and any man he deemed as lesser-than. The asshole had been charged with rape and accused of false imprisonment. The more trouble he got into, the more his star seemed to rise. Angry men loved him. And they made him rich.

Kyle probably wouldn't have found his personal pot of gold if not for Parsons getting busted for sex trafficking. He fled the country and started working out of Russia, where he was immune to extradition. But then social media and web hosting platforms made him invisible, making it easy for the snake to slither into the internet's darkest corners. Nature abhors a vacuum, and Kyle was in the right place at the right time, able to capitalize on a suddenly under-served audience.

Kyle would do it the right way, he told himself and Ariana. Sneak in through the back door of the language they understood while preaching self-improvement and responsibility. Fans were parroting his talking points in no time, all filtered through their hate and misogyny. It was hard to like his audience, but as Ariana liked to say, *What's better: for someone like Parsons to profit off of hate and misogyny or us, good people who mean well?*

Kyle looked at his watch. One minute to go.

He did a bump of coke to get in the right headspace. There were sheep to herd and one last payday to secure.

A knock at the door, two quick raps.

"Coming," he said.

Ariana opened the door and looked him up and down. Then she pointed at her nose. "You've got a little ..."

"Thanks." He wiped the residue from his nostrils, then leaned in for a peck on her cheek.

"You ready?" She asked.

Kyle bounced up and down a couple of times as the music got louder onstage.

"Hell, yeah." He sounded more pumped than he felt.

She handed him some index cards lined with the broad strokes of the opening day schedule. If the Summit was a performance, then he was the band, and Ariana — his wife — the maestro, conducting this elegant symphony. After majoring in marketing and working for one of the biggest agencies on Madison Avenue, she understood how to craft these events on a cellular level. Manipulating feelings and creating an environment of maximum engagement.

Ariana had written several of Kyle's most viral speeches, particularly the ones about loose women doing more to hurt the cause of feminism than all the misogynistic men put together. He had to admire her ability to make something she clearly didn't believe so damned persuasive. Most importantly, she knew how to get his fans to spend their money and thank Alpha Inc. for accepting it.

People frittered away irresponsible amounts of money to pursue an identity, belong to something bigger than themselves, or be included in any way.

Kyle had been doing this for three years. This was his largest event by far, but even so, he could do it with his eyes closed. The only difference this year — beyond the massive venue — was the one thing that had him slightly on edge. This was the first year his event would be under heavy scrutiny, following that bullshit in New Jersey last year.

Like it was his fault what that psychopath did.

He'd planned to cancel this year's event and lay low until the whole thing blew over. But Ariana noticed that engagement in Alpha Inc. was higher than ever following the tragedy. "If we cancel this year's event, we'll lose the money we spent booking the resort. But worse, we'll look weak, giving credence to the critics and opposition."

Kyle had been willing to take the hit. Alpha was becoming bigger than them, a beast they could no longer control. If they weren't careful, they would only invite more tragedies like Jersey. And he didn't want that on his soul.

Ariana made him a promise, knowing he loved a good

heist. "We do this last one, then we retire. One more big score."

So, in addition to the in-person event, they were doing a livestream to millions at $500 a pop. But Kyle couldn't shake the unease, the feeling that something was seriously wrong. An amplified feeling of guilt, the worst of all emotions.

Guilt was for the weak. A real man never felt shame because he always acted in his own best interests and, therefore, the best interests of those around him.

This was the right thing to do.

He did another quick bump before the unease killed his vibe.

AC/DC's Thunderstruck started playing.

Showtime.

*

Kyle watched from his spot backstage as lights circled the darkened theater to the opening riffs of his hype song.

The lights strobed two quick beats, light, then dark, as his fans chanted, "Thun-der."

He bounced up and down, the music swelling with his adrenaline until it went still, and the theater turned dark. Then Ozzy Osbourne's iconic Crazy Train intro and laugh echoed through the crowd.

Frenetic lights circled the crowd while Randy Rhoads's shredding further lathered the excitement. Curtains fell, and Kyle shot onto the stage, his fists pumping.

The music cut out, and Kyle closed his eyes, steeping in the standing ovation. Once the applause died down, he opened his eyes and roared, "WELCOOOOOME MEN!"

He played up to the camera crew, streaming his bellow to all the Alphas out there. He would miss these moments of adrenaline, of feeling like the world's eyes were on him. As a kid, Kyle had dreamed of being a rock star. But he'd never been good at singing or playing guitar. This was as close as he would ever come.

It felt even more phenomenal with all the cocaine flooding his system.

And then he started.

Fifteen minutes into his show, Kyle found his rhythm, kicking some serious ass as he framed the upcoming weekend, telling the men that they should expect to leave this place changed, ready to take what was theirs.

Kyle almost believed his own hype. The advice wasn't all bad. The core of his lessons had always been good advice for men in need of guidance. But it required liberal doses of sugar in the form of blaming women, the radical woke, and basically anybody else these guys were afraid of. Kyle then employed the old bait and switch, starting out with the usual platitudes and anger before working in some healthy advice.

It wasn't *his fault* if the men only ate the tasty appetizers then got up from the table before dinner was finished. He couldn't feed them, chew their food for them, *and* digest the meal. They had to take personal accountability before Kyle's lessons would work for them.

This was why he was so angry when the media unfairly came after him, blaming *him* for the actions of his worst fans. He had tried to reason with them, but it was a parade of hit pieces, one after the other. Media on all sides needed a villain to fit the narrative, drive the clicks, and sell ads. Reasonable conversations and meaningful debates could never compete with partisan rage and bubbles.

A half-hour in, and they were ready to bring their first guest to the stage, Lance Spalding, a controversial rising star in the manosphere who'd written three books on getting laid. Inviting the guy was a no-brainer. It excited his fan base and pissed off the people that hated Alpha Inc. So, basically, free advertising.

The 45-year-old Spalding had gotten canceled last year following an interview in which he suggested that the age of consent was a modern fabrication in need of examination.

It was Ariana's idea to make Spalding the keynote speaker at this year's summit because this was his first public appearance post-cancelation, and the Alpha crowd couldn't wait to hear the man tee off on their collective enemies.

As Kyle stood offstage with Ariana, Spalding didn't disappoint. He spent the first 45 minutes attacking his critics, then the next 20 doubling down on his most controversial takes.

The crowd was loving it.

Then Kyle spotted something odd: a group of men in the back row who weren't cheering with the others. They were watching him, not Spalding. One of them — a massive guy with shock-white hair — caught Kyle's eye and made a subtle slicing motion across his throat.

Kyle's blood ran cold. Was that a threat? He'd received plenty of death threats online, but never to his face. Maybe this wasn't paranoia after all.

Then Spalding started homing in on the message he and Ariana had been working on for weeks. The theme of the weekend: *Legacy*.

"What are you willing to do to ensure your legacy, to make your name matter?" Spalding asked though all of the weekend's speakers would deliver some twist on that theme. Then Spalding called Kathy Meadows, a fat cow who couldn't get laid with a bottle of Viagra and a gun on a desert island stocked with nothing but horny teenagers. Ariana laughed so loudly that Spalding heard. He turned and winked at her.

Ariana smiled back.

"Don't encourage him," Kyle said.

"What? It was funny."

"Meadows was right. You *are* an enemy to your kind," Kyle quoted a hit piece on Alpha in which the opinion host said that Ariana was even worse than the abhorrent, misogynistic men her husband pandered to.

"She's a humorless C-word."

He laughed. "Still can't say that word, eh?"

"Nope. It's vulgar."

"But you say 'C-word,' and it's the same as saying the actual word. It means the same damned thing."

"Nope." Ariana crossed her arms.

She loved pushing his buttons, and damn it if he didn't find it sexy.

He leaned in to kiss her neck, only to be interrupted by her assistant. Peter was looking down at his iPad, the one he took with him everywhere. It was infuriating the way he would hold his side of the conversation with his eyes fixed on the screen. His thorough lack of self-confidence would be comical if not so pathetic.

"So, um, the chef sends his apologies, but he's unable to accommodate your request. Said it was, and I quote, 'last minute and unreasonable.'"

"I told them two weeks ago," Kyle said.

"The chef sends his apologies," Peter shrugged and scrunched his face in a way that annoyed the shit out of Kyle.

Peter was so afraid to disappoint either of them that his actions almost felt phony. The way he always hedged criticisms or bad news with a stupid expression or soft-spoken mumble made Kyle want to throat-punch him. This kind of fear was born in his core. Kyle had told Ariana repeatedly. He was unfit for the job.

A good assistant wasn't just your mouthpiece and your right hand. They were your cudgel to get shit done.

Kyle's assistant, Serena, was twice the man Peter was. If he assigned her a task, it would be done without question. No excuses about why she couldn't get it handled or why someone said no. She would always find a way to get a yes.

Last month, walking around eight months pregnant and ready to burst, she still executed her job a hundred times more effectively than Peter.

It was a shame she was on maternity leave. Hell, she could probably come to work with her baby hanging from her tit and still run circles around Peter.

"Peter," Kyle said.

"Yes, sir?" He still didn't look at him.

"Eyes up here, son."

He finally looked.

"Do I make you nervous, Peter?"

"Kyle," Ariana said in protest.

"I asked you a question, Peter. Do I make you nervous?"

"No, sir."

"Do you … hate me?"

"No, of course not, sir."

"Then why don't you ever look at me?"

"I … don't know."

"You do know. You're not stupid, are you, Peter? I don't think my wife would hire an idiot as her right hand, would she?"

"No, sir." His eyes found the floor again.

Kyle snapped his fingers to draw the boy's attention back up. "So, tell me, Peter. Why can't you look at me?"

"I have a hard time looking people in the eyes."

"Good. We're getting somewhere. So why do you have trouble making eye contact?"

"I ... I don't know."

"Are you an Alpha, Peter?"

Ariana's hand found Kyle's elbow, a light tug, wanting him to end this.

He turned to his wife. "How can we teach men to be Alpha if we can't even help poor Petey here?"

Ariana's gray eyes stared through his, and he knew she was holding her words for when they were alone. Kyle had noticed something off about Peter from day one. The kid had a distant sadness in his eyes, like he'd seen something that permanently changed him. Kyle had assumed it was just the typical sob story — rejection, inadequacy, the usual. But there was something deeper there, something that made Kyle uncomfortable. It was as if Peter, by merely existing, was a mirror to all of Kyle's flaws.

Kyle pushed that thought away. The guy was just a beta, nothing more.

"Would you like to be Alpha, Petey?"

"Excuse me?"

"Did I stutter?" Kyle couldn't stop pushing him.

"No, sir."

"So, you heard the question?"

"Yes, sir."

"And yet, you said, 'Excuse me?' Weak language makes weak men. Do you have a girlfriend?"

Peter looked down, then back up. There was a pain in his eyes that *almost* made Kyle feel bad.

But he'd found the man's emotional wound. And no

work could be done on the self until you found your wounds and healed them through hard work.

"I've got an idea, Petey. I know this is your first event with us, but we do a thing each year where we bring someone on stage and help them to become the best version of themselves. Would you like that?"

"I ... I don't know."

"It's a yes or no question, Peter. There's no wrong answer. Do you want to change your life?"

"Yes, sir."

"Good." Kyle flashed his teeth and slapped Petey on the back. "Now, go and tell that chef that his answer is unacceptable. Make it happen. Can you do that?"

"Yes, sir." Petey nodded, maintaining eye contact before darting off.

Kyle turned his focus to the stage, watching Spalding as he called out one of the audience members' sorry attempts at having some game.

He could feel Ariana staring daggers at him, and he turned to her. "What?"

"You feel better about yourself?"

"It wasn't about me. I was helping him."

"You were bullying him, Kyle. And I'm not okay with that. You might act like an asshole for your fans, but I refuse to let you play an asshole with me or my assistant."

"He walks around here like a pussy. I don't even know why you hired him. I could throw a dart into the audience and hit someone more qualified."

"Maybe I hired him specifically because he's not like those men."

"No, he most certainly isn't. Please tell me it's not because you find him attractive." He laughed at the absurdity. Peter walked in a hunch. He was thinner than a beanpole.

"I hired him because he's nice. Because he reminds me of how you used to be before all this bullshit."

She turned and walked away, and he wanted to follow her, to argue that *he'd* wanted to shut down Alpha a long time ago, but she insisted that he stay the course and make bank on these assholes. But if Kyle wanted to take ownership of shit like he preached to his fans, then he needed to consider her point.

Was Ariana right? Did Peter remind Kyle of what he used to be, and that explained his gut reaction to the man?

But there was no time to ponder with Spalding wrapping up. Kyle bounded back out to join him on stage.

He turned to the audience of sheep. "That was amazing, eh?"

He looked up to one of the two giant screens on either side of the theater and saw the sweep of cameras over the enthusiastic faces of the thousands of young men. He felt the usual pang of sorrow, reminding him of how much he would miss this.

Was there a way to keep things going, but perhaps in a less toxic way?

A high-pitched screech ripped through the auditorium, causing Kyle and most of the audience to cringe.

He looked offstage at Ariana and Peter standing next to one another, looking perplexed as if to ask, *What the fuck was that?*

Then the screens changed from shots of the crowd to someone in a Guy Fawkes mask.

"Welcome, Alphas," said a distorted, robotic voice.

Who the fuck is that?

The screen cut to a photo of Kyle on one side and Ariana on the other. Text at the bottom of the screen read: *Actual phone call between Kyle and Ariana Baker.*

Ariana's voice came across the speakers. "And what about merch for the Summit?"

The taste of copper coated his tongue, and a cold chill slithered down his spine when Kyle realized what phone call was now being broadcast to a packed auditorium, plus the livestream. A conversation from a few months ago when Kyle had called her from the road, drunk and exhausted.

Ariana had been home, assembling the broad strokes for a PowerPoint to plot the event. Who recorded the call? How had they gotten it? And why were they broadcasting?

The last answer was the only obvious part — they were trying to call attention to Kyle, to embarrass and ruin him. As for the who, it could be any one of thousands of haters or media pundits with an agenda.

He turned toward Ariana and Peter standing offstage but didn't need to say anything. She was already leading Peter toward the control room stairs.

Kyle's smug laugh came over the speakers. "These rubes will buy anything."

Ariana spoke next. "How about a shirt with the Alpha wolf logo and text that reads, *I'm a strong, independent Alpha because Daddy Kyle told me I was.* And then the back of the shirt could be a sheep wearing a wolf head."

Their laughter silenced the crowd.

Kyle could feel the hateful gaze of thousands on him.

Spalding looked at him, nervously chuckling in denial, thinking that this had to be a joke. Kyle searched for something to turn the moment around and save everything from going totally to shit. But then he did something he'd not done in more than a decade.

He froze.

Meanwhile, their private conversation poured out of the speakers, each word more damning than the rest.

"We haven't heard back from Justin Kincaid yet," Ariana said.

"Fuck him," Kyle said. "So what if we sell a few less tickets to his nazi fanbase? Not like the trailer park trash has discretionary income after they blow it on meth."

More laughter from Ariana, made all the more damning because they did get Justin to agree. He was the next speaker. And now Spalding — one of Justin's regular podcast guests — was glaring at Kyle.

Kyle looked back and saw Justin standing with his arms crossed over his barrel chest. His dark eyes glared, his mouth a tight grimace beneath his bushy dark beard.

Kyle heard banging from backstage, presumably Ariana or Peter, trying to breach the control room and stop the recording.

He turned back again and caught sight of a dark blur moving towards him.

Only once the person was close did Kyle recognize the form as Justin Kincaid. A split second later, his fist came straight for Kyle's jaw.

*

Kyle woke sprawled on the stage. His and Ariana's voices were still going, damning conversations spilling out for all the world to hear.

But he couldn't see. Something was covering his head, smelling and itching like burlap. Both of his hands were bound behind his back.

He tried to sit and felt a crack to the back of his skull.

"Did I say you could sit up?" A man barked. His voice was familiar, deep and commanding, though Kyle couldn't place it. "Seems our guest of honor is awake."

Where have I heard that voice before?

"This man thinks he's better than you. But he's no Alpha. This man is a fraud, following his bitch wife's commands. Imposters playing pretend and exploiting your trust. Stealing from you. Today, we rip the masks off these false idols."

Hands beneath his armpits, hoisting him into a sitting position. Then, the burlap sack was torn away, and blinding light assaulted his eyes.

A silhouette moved in front of him, talking to the audience, wearing the Guy Fawkes mask, but the more he spoke, the more Kyle was certain he knew that voice.

"Today, we reveal who the true Alphas are."

He tore his mask off.

Cole Parsons. Beside him stood two men in black paramilitary gear with matching masks and assault rifles.

He looked down at the audience. "Who here feels most betrayed by this fraud? Who wants to be a true Alpha and take what's rightfully yours?"

Dozens of hands shot up. Parsons surveyed the crowd like a general inspecting troops.

"You," he pointed to the massive white-haired man. "What's your background?"

"Marine sniper. Two tours."

"Perfect. And you?" He pointed to another.

"Competitive hunter. Bowhunting champion three years running."

"Excellent. And you, the quiet one in the corner?"

"I just want to watch him suffer," said a skinny-looking incel with the unibrow.

Parsons grinned. "You'll do nicely."

He jerked his head, and within a minute, the three men had joined him on stage.

But Where was Ariana?

Kyle looked around, searching for his wife. He didn't

want to ask where she was and put her in jeopardy. He just hoped that she had found somewhere safe to hide.

Parsons circled him, and Kyle took in his surroundings, looking for the exits, scanning the crowd for anybody not staring daggers at him, searching for signs of danger beyond the gunmen.

What was Parsons' goal? Was he jealous that Kyle took his audience and wanted to embarrass him? But why the gunmen? Why the hood? What else was this asshole planning?

Kyle's mind filled with a horrible video he'd seen years ago of some man being slaughtered in the Middle East. His captors used a machete. His death was brutal and heartbreaking in a way that movies never truly captured.

It was always different, watching fiction. As much as you were into the story and the characters, once the credits started rolling, that reality began to fade. But an actual execution stayed with a person for years. Maybe forever. Kyle remembered thinking one thing above all else when he saw that video, that someone's life had been erased with no regard for all that they had been through or were yet to do. Erased from the lives of their friends and family. Erased like they never even mattered.

He remembered that bad feeling he'd felt earlier. Is this what he was sensing? Was he going to die today? Was Ariana?

Kyle had to do something. But what?

Parsons looked down at him. "What do you have to say for yourself, fraud?"

Then he put the mic in Kyle's face.

Kyle had never met Parsons before, so he didn't have much of a read on his body language. He did know that a man like Parsons would want him to grovel. But Kyle refused to give him what he wanted.

Kyle had never been afraid of death. Perhaps it came from seeing so much of it at an early age. Or from the depression he suffered throughout his twenties and that he still went to war with sometimes. Maybe it was the mindset Kyle had adopted long ago, that he would always find a way through whatever adversity life threw at him.

Go big or go home.

"It's all bullshit. Fake news."

The crowd booed.

Parsons pulled the mic back and laughed. "So, that wasn't you and your cunt wife making fun of these people?"

"I think you got one of those AI text-to-voice programs and are looking to become relevant again. Desperate people do desperate things."

"You don't even know the definition of desperate." Parson's dark eyes had a sick gleam. "But you will. Who here is tired of these elite pussies thinking they're better than us?"

The crowd cheered.

Parsons turned to Kyle. "Is that it? Do you think you're better than us?"

"No … just you."

Parsons backhanded Kyle across the right cheek with a THWACK! that reverberated through his teeth. Probably knocked a filling loose. Then he turned his attention back to the crowd. Kyle strained at the plastic cuffs binding his wrists. The closest gunman was eight feet away. The other was closer to the edge of the stage.

If Kyle could break free, he could wrestle for the nearest gunman's AR-15, fire at the second gunman, and then take out Parsons, who so far hadn't shown a gun. Though he did have a sheathed blade on his belt.

Kyle had done two years of mixed martial arts, but he'd let himself slack off the last six months because the increased touring schedule was brutal. But Kyle still figured he had a decent shot. Until the equation changed. A third gunman emerged, bringing with him Ariana and Peter.

Fuck.

"Here's the real brains behind Alpha Incorporated," Parsons said to stoke the anger in his now captive audience.

Another chorus of jeers.

But Ariana didn't cower. She held her head high, staring Parsons down.

Parsons stepped toward her.

Kyle leapt to his feet, ready to charge Parsons.

He barely made it a foot before Parsons spun and kicked Kyle's feet out from under him. Hands still bound, he crashed to the stage floor face-first.

Pain tore through his jaw, waves of dizziness washing over him. It was all he could do to look up and mutter, "Leave her alone."

Parsons grabbed Ariana by the jaw.

She could have swept his hand away. She'd undergone several self-defense courses. But she didn't move, either playing weak or not wanting to give him the pleasure of knowing she was scared.

Kyle tried to rise, but one of the gunmen was quick to stab a boot into his back, pressing him back to the floor. Seconds later, he felt the rifle pressed into his skull.

Parsons turned his attention to Ariana. "You think you're better than us?"

She didn't respond.

Kyle strained to look up at his wife, but the gunmen pressed the rifle harder against his head.

"And how about you, young man? Who are you in this little scheme?"

"P-Peter."

"Well, P-Peter, who are you?"

"I'm Mrs. Baker's PA."

"So you assist her?"

"Yes."

"Does it strike anyone else as odd that Ariana has a male assistant? You sure you're not assisting her in the bedroom, Peter?"

The audience, as well as the gunman with the rifle pressed into Kyle's head, laughed.

"No, I'm not." Petey sounded angry. Maybe he did have a bit of fight in him.

Parsons looked down at Kyle. "You let your wife have a male assistant?"

"Let? She's a grown woman. I don't make her decisions."

"Of course you don't." More laughter. "We all know she's the brains. Maybe even the balls. Lord knows you don't have any."

The audience guffawed.

"Surely you've wondered … right, Pete? How a fine piece of ass like Ariana might perform in the sack?"

Petey was probably too busy trying not to piss himself.

"What about you, Ariana? You ever look at Peter and wondered how big his little Peter is? Wondered if it's bigger than your pathetic husband's?"

Ariana remained silent.

"So, you're working with this fine-ass woman, and *somehow* you're not hitting it. How long have you been a beta cuck, Peter?"

"Don't disrespect her!" Peter cried out.

"*Ooooooh,*" went the crowd.

Seconds later, Kyle heard someone hit Peter and send him to the ground with a groan. He needed to do something before Peter said the wrong thing and got shot. Kyle might not like him, but he didn't want the kid dying because he was too dumb to navigate a psychopath.

"What do you want from us?" Kyle asked.

"I want ... *we* want ... to show the world what you really are. The good news for you is that if you're as Alpha as you claim, then maybe you, your wife, and her little 'assistant' might make it out of this weekend alive."

*

Kyle was freed from his restraints and back with Ariana and Peter. But that's where the good news ended. Because Parsons had just laid out the rules for a hunt in which Kyle, Ariana, and Peter were prey.

Parsons stood with three men he'd handpicked from the audience.

They were now at the edge of the woods, encompassing most of the private island.

Parsons' men placed two trunks on the ground between Kyle, Ariana, Peter, and the hunters.

"Kyle's team chooses weapons from the smaller trunk," Parsons said. "And the hunters will select from the larger one."

The man, with the shock of bright white hair, opened their box to reveal machetes, knives, swords, and a pair of wicked-looking crossbows.

"Team Kyle gets a head start. After five minutes, the hunters will start. If you manage to survive until morning, Kyle, Ariana, and Peter, you get to live. If not, it looks like we'll know who the real Alphas were."

"You can't be serious," Ariana said. "You're sanctioning murder. And streaming it."

"We cut the livestream," Parsons said. "And it's only

murder if you're killing another human. The rules for parasites are different."

"Come on," Kyle said. "You got what you wanted. You embarrassed me and exposed me as a fraud. Take Alpha Inc. It's all yours."

"And let you walk away without answering for your sins? Actions have consequences, Kyle. Isn't that one of your Alpha Rules?" Parson laughed, then turned to the hunters. "Whoever brings me their heads will receive one hundred and seventy grand."

"Please," Peter said. "Just let us go. I'm not going to kill anyone."

"Then you'd better be really good at hiding or running."

Parsons looked at his watch. "The clock starts in one minute. Choose your weapons, Team Alpha."

Kyle opened their trunk to some far inferior weapons. A knife, a rusty machete, and a metal pipe. He glanced at Ariana. "You first."

She grabbed the knife.

Kyle took the machete — he could probably do more damage with it than Peter. That left the pipe for Peter.

"Good," Parsons said. "You've got a five-minute head start. Now run."

The prey did as instructed.

* * *

The three of them headed deep into the woods. After about twenty minutes, Kyle leaned against a tree to catch his breath.

Ariana hunched over, hands on her knees.

"What do we do?" Petey asked, gasping for air. "Can any of you actually kill one of them?"

"I don't know," Ariana said.

330

"If it's kill or be killed, then yes, we need to strike," Kyle said.

Ariana sighed. "This is so fucked up. How did he even get those conversations? And why hunt us? Is he crazy?"

"We already knew he was crazy," Kyle replied.

"I think I know how he got the phone recordings," Petey said.

"How?" Kyle asked.

"I read a story about how you can hire people to hack any number or clone any cell phone. I'm not sure how easy it is, but I'm guessing he got one of your phones cloned and used it to spy on you."

Kyle thought about all the shit Parsons might have recorded and wondered what other things he'd talked about on the phone with Ariana. Sex, no doubt. It would be embarrassing, but that wasn't career-ending. However, they must have talked about tax fraud at least a half-dozen times.

That kind of info would fuck them. Not to mention the shit they said about their agent and publisher, plus all those digs at their fan base.

If even a fraction of that got out, they would be ruined.

Of course, none of that would matter if they didn't survive the hunt or escape the damned island.

"So, what do we do?" Petey asked. "Keep running or …"

Kyle said, "If we have a chance to ambush one of them, we take it. Otherwise, we keep going and stick together."

"Maybe you all can kill, but I can't," Peter said.

"Even if you're about to be killed?" Kyle asked.

"I … I don't have it in me to … murder someone." Peter looked like he might cry.

"It's not murder if someone is trying to kill you. It's

self-defense. There isn't a jury in the world that would convict us."

Peter still couldn't look at them, his eyes welling up.

Kyle had to do something to get the kid's head in the game, or he would be the first to fall. Not that Kyle really cared that much about him. But it was a numbers play. The fewer of them, the worse their odds. It was bad enough that they were going up against two men who looked like serious business and a weirdo who probably masturbated to fantasies of shooting sprees.

He thought of New Jersey and quickly shook it from his head. He had to get Petey on board.

"You'd better nut up, buttercup. If it's either them or us visiting the pearlies, and it'd damn well better be them. We've come too far and done too much good to have it ruined by this clown car of fuckery. Do you understand me?"

"Yes, sir," Petey said, staring at the ground.

"Say it like you mean it!"

"Yes, sir!" Petey's voice was sharp and impressively commanding.

"I might have to start calling you Peter now."

Peter laughed, smiling.

* * *

The group walked in silence for more than an hour, careful to avoid hunters, navigating the woods.

"*We need a plan beyond just running,*" Ariana whispered. "This island isn't that big. They'll find us eventually."

"The marina," Kyle said. "There were at least half a dozen yachts docked when we arrived."

"Can you drive a boat?" Peter asked.

"I spent summers on my uncle's fishing boat," Kyle replied. "I'm no expert, but I can handle a yacht well enough to get us to the mainland."

"What if they're guarding the marina?" Ariana asked.

"Then we improvise," Kyle said, adjusting their course toward the east side of the island where the marina was located. "But it's our best shot. We can call for help once we're off this island."

And then Kyle spotted the big beefy dude with a crossbow.

Kyle ducked into the underbrush, gesturing to Ariana and Peter to follow. But the hunter froze.

Shit.

They'd been seen.

Kyle gripped his machete, wondering if he could close the distance before the hunter's bolt found him. But he didn't like the odds.

Ariana looked at him, and she shook her head.

Footsteps behind them now.

"Any sign of them?" The incel asked, approaching.

Kyle's heart was a jackhammer. Beefy Crossbow scanned the underbrush, looking straight toward Kyle.

Incel was carrying a sword, much longer and sharper than Kyle's rusted machete.

"Not yet," said the big man.

And the incel changed direction.

Crossbow waited a few more seconds, checking the area. But eventually, he left. Kyle could finally breathe again. They hadn't been seen. Thank Christ for small miracles. Or big ones, in this case.

His heart was still pounding when the thunderclouds rolled in, darkening the skies. Fat drops of cold rain began to fall. They risked moving faster, knowing their sounds would be masked by the rain and their movements better concealed by darkness.

It took several hours to make their way to the edge of

the woods overlooking the marina, but now they were leaving tracks in the mud.

Disappointment was a brick wall when they saw Parsons and his gunmen sitting on the bow of a yacht with its owner, Billy Wachnell.

There were only two other boats. Everybody else had come in by ferry or water taxi, none of which were running again until Monday morning.

"So, now what?" Ariana kept her voice low.

Rain fell harder, and lightning flashed across the bruised violet sky.

"I saw a cave back there," Petey said. "Not too far."

"A cave?"

Peter nodded. "And it looked pretty well-hidden. Maybe they won't find it."

"And if they do?" Ariana asked. "Is there more than one way in and out?"

"Beats me." Peter looked from Ariana to Kyle.

All eyes were on him now, awaiting his direction.

If he chose wrong, they would all pay.

Kyle thought of another of his father's sayings.

Your first instinct is right nine times out of ten. Don't ignore it. Never let the chatter of self-doubt or What-if? lure you with their siren songs.

"Show us," Kyle said.

*

The cave was a welcome respite from the rain, but they were still cold and shivering.

They took shelter just far enough inside that some ambient light allowed them to see who might be approaching. Any thoughts of starting a fire for warmth were nixed because the flames might be spotted. Not to mention any smoke.

They passed the time making small talk. Normally, Kyle hated small talk. It was good for schmoozing and gathering intel, but beyond that, he found it dreadfully dull. Ariana didn't just have a gift for gab, but she seemed to — gasp — genuinely enjoy talking to people. So much of Kyle's participation in the cave was limited to answering Ariana's questions.

The rain outside came down even harder.

"You think the rain helps or hurts our odds of discovery?" Petey asked.

"That depends if they see the cave," Ariana said. "If they don't, maybe we're in the clear. If they do, they're far more likely to assume we came in to hide or escape the weather."

"Should we leave?"

Lightning crashed close enough to make them all jump.

"Maybe we wait a bit longer," Kyle said.

"Good idea, sir."

Kyle found himself craving nicotine for the first time in a decade. He'd kill for a pack of Marlboro Lights. Shit, he'd smoke menthols. He was about to ask Peter if he happened to have any smokes when he caught him staring back like he wanted to say something.

But, like usual, his gaze fell back to the ground.

"What is it?" Kyle asked.

"Nothing."

"Don't 'nothing' me, Petey. We're all being hunted. Speak now or forever hold your peace."

"Have you really been scamming these people?"

Kyle could feel Ariana's eyes on him. He considered letting her field this particular question — Petey was *her* assistant. She knew his temperament far better than Kyle. But Petey was in this mess because of him.

"Yes, it's true. We don't give a damn about these people."

Silence.

"You disappointed, Petey?"

"No. Not really."

More silence.

"Then what is it?"

"If you don't believe in the movement, then why do it? Just for the money?"

"We started off with good intentions," Ariana said. "Kyle wanted to help young men, especially since there were so many bad examples out there looking to fill Parsons' void."

"So, it was a market play?" he asked.

"No," Kyle replied. "Not at first, anyway."

"But later?"

"Our message changed to fit the audience. As much as Lynyrd-Skynyrd might want to play whatever shit they're churning out now, they can't say 'fuck Freebird.'"

"Didn't you ever worry about the effect of your words?"

Kyle stared back as the shadows gained weight, casting Peter in darkness. "You having regrets? You knew who you were coming to work for. You've been collecting a damn nice salary for six months, and *now* you're having a guilty conscience?"

"I ... I'd never seen the vitriol up close, how quickly these men turned on us. How quickly they're prepared to end our lives. And for what, *money*?"

"The world runs on money, and most of that money is tainted in blood in one way or another. I guess the only question is, can you lay your head down at night and feel like you did more good than harm?" Kyle asked.

"And have we?"

Silence, this time from Kyle.

And Ariana.

The quiet stretched for an infinity until Kyle finally had an answer.

But he was cut short by a stabbing pain in his left calf.

He looked down, confused to see a bolt sticking out of his leg, his pants now soaking with crimson.

"Got ya', traitor!"

Kyle looked up to see the big hunter in the mouth of the cave, lining up a second shot.

Peter dropped the pipe, grabbed a fistful of dirt, and, lunging, he threw it in the man's eyes. He bellowed and recoiled.

Ariana grabbed the fallen weapon and rushed forward, swinging the pipe into the man's kneecaps.

He buckled, but not before grabbing a handful of Ariana's hair. "You bitch!" He slammed her head into the dirt. Then he decked Peter.

He fell to the ground.

Panic choked his pain as Kyle grabbed his machete and darted toward the giant. Kyle swung the machete in a downward arc. WHUMP. The blade lodged in the back of the giant's skull embedded a half-inch into his flesh and bone.

Shit!

The man spun around so fast that the machete swiveled with his head, tearing it from Kyle's blood-slicked grip. He lurched toward Kyle, grabbing the bolt and driving it deeper into Kyle's leg, twisting it.

"FUCK!" Kyle screamed, the pain sending him to the ground. Moments later, the giant was on top of Kyle, hands around his throat and squeezing.

Kyle gasped as the man crushed his windpipes. He

tried to remember his martial arts lessons on how to escape this, but for the second time that day, he froze.

Ariana was suddenly above him.

She wrenched the machete from the man's skull.

He let go of Kyle's throat and spun around.

Ariana drove the blade straight through his gut, then wrenched it out before plunging it in again.

Hot blood splashed Kyle as the man's screams echoed off the cave walls.

Then he fell onto Kyle, blood gurgling from his mouth in thick bubbles, guts spilling out, soaking him in a sickly sweet stench.

Kyle heaved the carcass off of him.

Ariana stepped towards him. "Are you okay?"

"Check on Peter."

Ariana turned, then stopped.

The incel appeared, crossbow alternating between Kyle and Ariana. A smile spread across his face as he surveyed the scene.

The incel nodded at Peter. "Is he dead?"

Ariana nodded. "The big bastard got him."

"And who got the big bastard?"

"I did," Ariana said, holding the gore-coated machete. "I suggest you leave, or you're next."

"Put it down."

She laughed." You first."

Kyle crawled towards the fallen crossbow until the incel spotted him. "You touch it, she dies!"

"Come on, man," Ariana said. "You're not gonna kill both of us. Do you really wanna die for someone that doesn't give a damn about you?"

"Like *you two?*" He gave a sad, pathetic laugh. "You fuckers robbed me, robbed all of us."

"Bullshit!" Kyle snapped. "I was helping you. Think of

how far you've come since joining, and just think about how much farther you can go with our help. Get us out of here, and I'll reward your loyalty."

"Do you really think I've come far?" the man asked.

" Sure, man, you've made some incredible strides!"

"Yeah? How about you tell me one thing about me or the 'incredible' strides I've made, and I'll let you both live."

Kyle froze again. Of course, he didn't know the fucker's name. He stalled, trying to remember. Had he ever even spoken to this man before?

"I thought so." The incel aimed his weapon at Kyle.

"Your name is Richard Grant," Ariana said. "You broke up with Vicki two years ago, and when you first came to us, you were obsessed and wrecked."

His face softened. "What?"

"Do you want more?"

The man shook his head and lowered the crossbow, eyes welling up.

Just then, a pair of blades plunged into his neck from both sides, and his eyes went wide with shock. It was the John Wick Wannabe.

Kyle grabbed the crossbow and fired just as the incel fell to the ground.

The bolt slammed home between the attacker's eyes.

The man stood, and for two sickening moments, Kyle was afraid he'd not hit him in the right spot. Then the man toppled, face first, to the ground.

More footsteps approached.

Parsons entered the cave with an AR-15.

"And what happened here?" He looked down at the bodies, then at Kyle and Ariana. "I guess nobody wanted to win."

"So we're free," she said.

Parsons laughed. "No, I'm afraid it doesn't work that way."

"So, your word is bullshit?" Kyle asked. "You were never going to let us go?"

"Isn't that one of your pithy sayings? Never trust someone smarter than you to have your interests in mind."

"So what happens after I'm dead?" Kyle asked, collecting a handful of dirt "You think the police won't be looking for you?"

"I'm not the one going down for this."

Kyle noticed Peteyr's fingers twitching.

He was alive!

Kyle was surprised by his own sense of inner joy. "You say *I'm* the hypocrite, but you don't give a shit about these men. And you care even less for the women that they terrorize."

"Why would I care about a bunch of parasitical whores?" Parsons asked.

Kyle was careful not to look, but he could sense Peter trying to get up. He had to keep Parsons distracted.

"They can't *all* be whores. That's bullshit," Ariana replied. "And you perpetuate that bullshit, peddling the lie to vulnerable, hurting young men, twisting them and fucking them up even further to ensure that nobody will want to be with them, making it a self-fulfilling prophecy. They're rude to women, and, surprise, more women find them disgusting. Big shocker there, pal."

"You did the same damned thing." Parsons scoffed. "At least I'm not delusional, thinking I'm on the side of women or SJWs — didn't they find your books and podcasts in the house of that Jersey shooter?"

"And yours. You radicalized him first."

Parsons laughed. "Keep telling yourself that you're

different, but we both know you're not. Neither one of us give a fuck about those women."

"Wrong," Kyle said. "I lost plenty of nights of sleep! There's not a day that goes by I don't wish I could trade all my wealth for even one of those six women's lives to be spared."

"Well, there we are different. Because I would gladly give my fortune away for a *higher* kill count. Dumb cunts don't deserve to—"

Peter grabbed the pipe from the ground and lunged. Bringing it down on Parson's head. He went down in a blink. But Peter kept bashing and bashing at the man until Parsons was coated in blood, brain matter, and flecks of bone.

"She was my fiancée, you fuck! My fiancée!"

Parsons barely resembled a human now. Peter was shaking, holding the pipe, tears streaming down his cheeks, his eyes in vacant shock.

Ariana and Kyle traded a look.

"Fiancée?" Ariana asked.

Peter looked at them and dropped the pipe.

Then he reached down and picked up the AR-15. Then he looked Kyle in the eyes.

"Marley Jackson. She just wanted to lose a couple pounds before our wedding. I don't know why. I often wonder if it's something I said to make her think I didn't love every bit of her exactly as she was. Marley was there when that piece of shit walked in. I couldn't protect her. I had to watch her die. I couldn't stop one man with a gun from destroying her future, from destroying her family. Then I saw you in that interview, both of you, so fucking smug, insisting that it wasn't your fault. I knew in that moment that I wanted you to feel what I felt, for you to suffer like we suffered. I took this job to make you feel this pain."

Kyle's mind raced. "You were working with Parsons."

"Not exactly." Peter's laugh was hollow. "I hacked your phones months ago. Recorded everything. I sent the recordings to Parsons anonymously. I knew he'd use them — he hated you for taking his audience. I didn't care what happened to me as long as you both paid for what you did."

"But why kill him and not us?" Ariana asked, gesturing to Parsons' body.

"Because he was worse. He celebrated what happened to Marley. Said the shooter should have killed more." Peter's hands trembled. "I wanted you to suffer, but him … him I wanted dead."

He raised the rifle and aimed it at Ariana.

Ariana said nothing.

Kyle leaped in front of her, ignoring the agony from the bolt embedded in his leg.

"Please, don't make her pay for my sins," Kyle said. "I'm so, so sorry. There's nothing I can do to bring her back, but I swear I'm so damned—"

"Bring who back?" Peter asked.

"Your fiancée."

"What was her name?" Peter steadied his aim at Ariana. "What was her fucking name? Or weren't you paying attention? So busy trying to figure out how to stop me you didn't hear a word I said."

"*Marley*. Her name was Marley Jackson. And I swear if I could take her place, I would in a heartbeat."

Peter stared at Kyle, then he turned to Ariana, tears still soaking his cheeks.

"I'm sorry," Ariana said, her voice cracking. "I knew what we were doing was wrong. I was the one who pushed

Kyle to keep going when he wanted to stop. I crafted those speeches you heard, the ones that painted women as enemies. I did it for the money, for the power. I convinced myself it was just entertainment, that we weren't responsible for how people interpreted it."

Then she looked at Peter directly. "I was worse than Kyle. He at least started with good intentions. I just saw dollar signs." Tears streamed down her face. "The New Jersey shooting ... when I heard about it, I threw up. I knew it was on us. But instead of stopping, I doubled down. I buried my guilt in more work, more manipulation. More money."

She drew a shaky breath. "I can't ask for your forgiveness. What I can do is promise that whether we survive tonight or not, Alpha Incorporated dies here. Whatever platform I have left, I'll use it to undo the damage we've caused."

Kyle stepped closer, taking the barrel in his hands and clasping it tight so if Peter shot, there was nobody else he could kill. "I'm sorry, Peter. If it helps ease your soul, take the shot. I promise I won't blame you in the slightest."

Peter met his eyes again, then let go of the rifle and fell to his knees.

Kyle placed the rifle on the dirt and sat down next to him.

Ariana dropped next to Peter and hugged him as he cried into her shoulder.

Outside, the sounds of sirens filled the air. Someone must have come to their senses and called the cops. Maybe not everybody here was a murderous bastard.

And maybe Kyle shouldn't give up on trying to spread a better message to them.

He looked at the blood on his hands — both literal and figurative. Six women had died because of the poison he'd helped spread. He couldn't bring them back, but he could change. Not just his words or his public image, but deep inside where it mattered.

"When we get out of here," Kyle said, voice breaking, "I'm turning myself in. The fraud, the tax evasion, all of it. And I'll testify against everyone in this movement who's breaking the law."

"Kyle ..." Ariana's eyes widened.

"No. This is it. The whole empire coming down. I'll use whatever platform I have left to publicly denounce everything we've built — properly this time. And then I'll disappear." He looked at Peter, whose tears had finally begun to slow. "I can't bring Marley back. But I can make sure I never cause another death like hers."

Outside, the sirens grew louder. But Kyle knew this reckoning was only the beginning.

A Good Day To Die

JAY TINSIANO

A Good Day To Die

JAY TINSIANO

THAT SONOFABITCH WAS AIMING HIS REVOLVER RIGHT AT Clyde Patton, and then he pulled the trigger. Clyde sensed the noise from the standard issue Glock 17 only at the fringes of his consciousness, but boy, did he feel it rip into his chest, blowing his lungs and bone to shreds.

Clyde could only grunt at the impact on his body as his butt hit the concrete road. Something cracked, his pelvis maybe, then blood began to soak through his shirt like Niagara Falls. Clyde clutched his wound in a pathetic attempt to stem the flow, but it just kept coming, pooling onto the road. The jaunty jingle from one of the ice cream trucks, jack-knifed by a cop car and now burning on the highway, danced around his head in an insanity-inducing loop, mocking Clyde for his failure to stop the bleeding.

He saw the cop who had stalked his every turn for years — the man who had taken his once-fledgling criminal empire and not only burned it to dust but ground it down with the sole of his boot — slowly walking towards him, pistol aimed high. The figure looming over him was blurred as Clyde's vision ebbed away, his senses all whisked together like some fucking tepid pancake mix, but he couldn't mistake that smirk on the craggy face of Sheriff Emmitt Shaw.

"You never stop, d'ya Clyde. Ya jus' can't help yourself."

"F...fuck," Clyde spluttered, but his intended venomous swipe at the cop died in his throat before it even began. His last thoughts, wilting on the vine. How the hell had Shaw shadowed his every move for so long? Did Aisha know? Had she betrayed him?

This was it. He had lost the battle and the war.

"Hey, fuckface." It was the leering cop, standing over him, still smirking, his chin doubled over his tight, short collar.

"You know something?" Shaw asked, looking around at the scene of carnage. "All you bad guys think you're so goddamn smart. But you ain't. You will never win, none of you. Not in this lifetime, not in any goddamn lifetime!"

"Fuuuck you!" Clyde's venom was back; he reached up with both hands with renewed vigor and attempted to grab Shaw's gun as if he actually had a rat flea's chance of avoiding the inevitable.

Then, suddenly, he was awake. Eyes open. Sweat-soaked sheets wrapped around his naked body, the words of venom still coming out of his mouth.

His hands were clutching his chest, but there was no wound, no blood.

"Oh fuck," he gasped. "Oh fucking, yes." Clyde chuckled quietly with absolute relief as he lay in the darkened room.

"...a goddamn dream, Jesus, it was a dream..."

Clyde looked at the digital clock on the side that read 4:09 a.m. Through the parted drapes, the lights of Las

Vegas glinted seductively. There was the familiar Picasso print on the wall, his clothes sprawled all over the chair. Yes, this was the hotel room he was holed up in, under one of his numerous identities to keep that bitch cop guessing as to his whereabouts.

It was still the day of the heist, and he wasn't dead. Not even close. He could still beat Shaw, grab the seized gold, and give the sheriff the finger from his Caribbean hideaway.

Twenty-three hours earlier, give or take, his ex-lover and crime rival, Aisha, had dropped him one of their secret messages, a single white rose by special delivery, a signal to meet at their usual place, a car garage out in the suburbs. She appeared from nowhere and slipped into the passenger seat of his car.

"Fucking Shaw. I nearly got caught on a job," she said, almost spitting over his dashboard. She looked stunningly beautiful as always: jet black hair tied in a bunch and body-hugging jogging gear. But Clyde knew that road was a treacherous one, leading to all manner of unexpected traps. She was dangerous, especially when cornered, and although they had shared a bed at one time, Clyde would have to bite down hard on any wanton desires. This was not the time. She was his criminal rival now, albeit a beautiful one.

"You and me both," Clyde growled. "You know full well he's cleaned me out. Destroyed my life and forced me to hunker down in the dark, jerking off and crying, taking shit jobs for gambling hustlers and lousy house break-ins." He inhaled, then added, "So, what do you want, Aisha?"

"I need to hunker down for a while. I need your basement in Tule Springs until I figure out how to get my gold back from Shaw."

"Gold?"

Aisha grimaced and said nothing.

"You said 'gold.' How much gold, exactly?"

"None of your beeswax, and don't take that tone with me. Are you going to hand over the keys to your hideout or not?"

Clyde aggressively adjusted his body weight in the car seat. If there was one thing he had learned from his extensive life of crime, it's that everyone will betray you, which is why he always betrayed them first.

He shook his head.

"No way."

"Fuck you, then." Aisha opened the door of the SUV and got out.

"Hey, don't—" he began.

Aisha slammed the door so hard Clyde could feel his teeth rattle.

"—slam the fucking door," he finished quietly.

He sighed before taking out his burner phone.

Hours of planning and scheming later, and with a renewed sense of purpose, Clyde untangled himself from the bedsheet, put on the coffee maker, and showered, pushing the bad dream to the back of his mind, at least for now. Emmitt Shaw always loomed in his dreams, nightmares, and waking thoughts like a pissed albatross, but now was his chance to bat that bird back into the sea. He had found out the gold was to be transported from the safe at police headquarters to the city bank, and today, he was gonna swoop in and take it all, like a badass criminal albatross, toting some massive guns.

Yet, as he sipped his inky black coffee, that dream with the bullet ripping through his heart had felt so real, so ominous. He'd wear body armor today. Just to be sure. He'd make this go right, double-check every detail, and stick it to Shaw between the eyes.

Clyde headed to the old warehouse on the outskirts of town. He walked in, glad to see Melvin and Stan, his trusted associates from many years of criminal enterprise, already in their white uniforms, complete with dickie-bows, checking over the last-minute details. Three ice cream trucks had been stripped of all unnecessary weight and stood ready with brand-new 800 hp fuel-injected engines installed.

"Morning," Clyde chirped.

Melvin mumbled in reply, looking a bit sheepish.

"What?" Clyde barked.

Then Aisha stepped out from behind one of the trucks, her face flushed with anger.

"Oh Jeez..." Clyde suddenly felt very deflated. The spring in his step was well and truly popped.

"What the hell do you think you're doing, Clyde?" Aisha marched up to him, her boots clicking on the concrete floor.

"Working ... a job." It was Clyde's turn to be sheepish.

"A 'gold job' perchance?"

"I never talk about my work," he muttered.

"You're going to steal back my stolen gold, are you not, Clyde Patton? Are you using Melvin and Stan too? I originally introduced you to these guys. I should get first dibs."

Clyde glanced at the two henchmen, who seemed to have spuriously stepped backward away from them both, looking increasingly embarrassed.

Aisha swung around to face the two men.

"Who do you prefer working for? Me or him?"

"Err..."

"Um."

"Aisha! Stop all this. I know I can ace this job," Clyde said, annoyance rising. "Let me have a crack, fuck over Shaw. It's what we both want."

She turned back to him, hands on hips.

"We toss a coin for it. But your job better not interfere with my job plans."

Clyde tossed a coin, and it landed in his favor.

He gave Aisha a broad grin.

"Gonna wish me luck?"

"Fuck you," she replied and stomped away to the exit.

Clyde checked his watch. "Right. Let's do this."

He took out the body armor from the box on a table, strapped on the chest protection, checked his weapons, and got into the first ice cream truck as his henchmen did the same and got into their trucks. They traveled north in a convoy before turning off onto a long road leading out of town into the desert. After a few miles, they arrived at a crossroads, populated by an abandoned gas station and a dormant housing development, and took positions off the road.

Clyde checked the police scanner, picked up the radio traffic he was looking for, and listened to the garbled voices for a moment. Satisfied with the information, he grabbed his walkie-talkie.

"This is Alpha Red. We have incoming. ETA five minutes."

"Roger that," came both replies.

Clyde put on his Ricky Gervais mask and readied his assault rifle. He glanced over and saw Melvin and Stan do the same.

Further up the road, the security trucks approached, led by a police vehicle. Just as they slowed and approached the crossroads, Clyde put the truck into gear and drove straight out in front of the security convoy. He stopped in the road, hopped out, and tossed a smoke grenade just as Melvin's truck sped out from its hidden spot in the abandoned garage and jack-knifed the first police car.

Then, all hell broke loose with a relentless barrage of bullets flying in every direction. The M16 assault rifles and handguns made a deafening, banging noise. Stan lumbered toward the side of the armored vehicle, laser cutter in hand.

Clyde held up his pump action at the armored car windshield and fired. It would never penetrate the bullet-proof glass, but the idea was to terrorize. The blast had barely reverberated when Clyde was thrown to the ground by a force from behind — a loud explosion.

A shower of burning embers covered him and the road, and he rolled onto his side to see that his truck had been hit by something and was blazing into a crisp.

He struggled to his feet just as Emmitt Shaw came through the rising smoke, tossing a discharged grenade launcher to the ground while simultaneously pulling out his Glock 22 pistol with the other hand.

As Shaw lifted his weapon, that malevolent, broad smile spread across his leering face as he aimed at Clyde's head and pulled the trigger.

CLYDE SHOT upright in his bed.

"Fuck!"

He glanced at the clock: 04.09 a.m. Then he looked at the framed Picasso print on his hotel room wall, the parted drapes, and the city lights beyond.

He rolled out of bed and thumped to the floor on his knees, the sweat-soaked bedsheet still wrapped around his torso.

"Fuck!"

Two hours later, he had his foot hard on the gas pedal of his ice cream truck, heading to the crossroads, armed with extra grenades, a metal hockey mask, and full body armor.

When the convoy came, Melvin tossed live grenades into its path. Stan took out the rear vehicle with a grenade launcher as Clyde tossed three smokes and headed into the maelstrom.

Stan moved to the armored vehicle and fired up the bulky laser cutter while Melvin took care of the rear vehicle with a barrage of fire from his Heckler & Koch MP5 submachine gun, one of the specials from his collection.

Then, through the smokey haze, Shaw came, like a Samurai in riot gear, wielding a grenade launcher aimed right at Clyde's torso.

"OH FUCK!"

4:09 a.m. The day of the heist. Again.

He was in a loop. Reality and dreams had blurred. What was real, and what wasn't? But there lay the opportunity. To get it right and learn from mistakes.

Clyde made some calls. He'd have Sean "Mucho Guns" McGarth on his team this time to cover his back. There would be no mistakes.

Into the trucks. The crossroads. And as the familiar smoke rose and the barrage of gunfire erupted, Clyde took a different route, away from where Shaw usually jack-knifed his truck in his dreams or in the loop. He wasn't sure anymore. He headed through the smoke in his bullet-proof onesie with bullet belts over his shoulder, taking refuge on the far side of the armored vehicle. Just as Stan gave the go-ahead through their earpieces, saying that he was inside and the gold was there, stacked and ready, the gunfire receded.

"Make sure the area is secure," Clyde ordered, bringing his gun barrel up as he cautiously crept out of his position.

"All secure, boss. Everyone's dead. We can load and…" Stan's voice cut off in his ear.

"Alpha Blue, you there?"

No response.

The gunfire had ceased, and it was eerily quiet. Clyde moved around the truck to the far side, eyes darting left to right, alert to any danger. He came around to the side of the truck that Stan had lasered a great big hole into. Melvin was already loading gold bars into his truck across the road on the abandoned garage forecourt.

"Stan?"

Clyde got to the hole and saw Stan lying on the floor amongst a pile of gold bars — a bullet between his eyes.

"Fuck, no! Stan!"

He jumped inside and went over to the body, checking for a pulse. Stan was gone.

There was a noise that made him turn.

"Peekaboo." It was Shaw, the same smile but happier like he was thoroughly enjoying himself this time.

Keep him talking, thought Clyde.

"Alright. Your bullets can't hurt me, Sheriff." Clyde tapped his armor with one hand and quietly felt around for his compact SIG Sauer P365.

But Shaw lifted some kind of the nozzle, and Clyde realized it was a flamethrower.

"Oh fu…"

4:09 A.M. THE day of the heist. Again.

Clyde caught his breath.

"Burnin' me alive … the fucker," he muttered.

He lay in the dark for a while. This loop was getting to him. Shaw always won. Clyde needed a different approach. He reached for this burner phone.

Aisha stood, hands on hips, looking at Clyde with a wry smile as he explained how they might work together. He had a deal.

"You want me to cut you in? On what planet do you think I will give you any of the gold that's rightfully mine."

"You stole it first, then the police recovered it. It's not yours."

Aisha sighed and shook her head. "You know what I mean. When it comes to the world of crime, it's mine."

Clyde grimaced. "Look, Aisha, who do you hate more? Me or Shaw?"

"Oooh, tough one."

"Don't be ridiculous."

"Alright. I don't hate you, Clyde. We were good together." She gave him a look he hadn't seen for a while. A look of suggestive intrigue. A flash of passion.

"Well, we'd better saddle up. I have a plan," she said, turning away from him.

Forty-five minutes later, they were airborne in an aged UH-60 Black Hawk helicopter, head to toe in combats, while below on the road, the convoy of ice cream trucks sped along the highway, kicking up plumes of dust in their wake.

The helicopter moved ahead of them, and through his goggles, Clyde could see the crossroads beyond and the approaching gold truck with accompanying police cars as he pulled on his gloves and rechecked his rappelling gear and carabiners that secured his harness to the rope line. As the gold convoy slowed, the ice cream trucks headed at full speed until they were right up at them. Smoke grenades flew into the convoy, and grenade launchers hit the frontal and rear police vehicles simultaneously. One ice cream truck veered off the road into the abandoned garage. Clyde could hear a symphony of gunfire through the loud helicopter engine.

"Good to go," came the pilot's voice through his earpiece.

Clyde moved to the open side door and looked back at Aisha, who was crouched on her haunches, a handheld radio held to her mouth. She gave him a nod and whispered, "Good luck" before he jumped, zipping down the fast rope toward the roof of the armored vehicle below. Stan, his laser tool strapped to his back, quickly followed. They landed on the roof of the armored truck, and Stan immediately got to work, directing the blue laser beam in an arc as Clyde crouched, swooping his rifle toward any potential threats from the rising smoke. Where was that fucker?

The ground crew appeared to have neutralized the police. Melvin had caught one officer and had him face down on the road concrete to zip-tie his hands behind his back.

Crates were being hauled up to the hovering chopper overhead.

Then, when all had been reclaimed, Clyde zipped up and was hauled back up to the helicopter while Stan made his getaway with the ground team in the trucks, leaving behind a scene of carnage — burning trucks and police cars all covered with drifting smoke.

Clyde unclasped his attachments to the zip line and removed his goggles. He exhaled slowly as the adrenaline pulsed through his body. He looked up to see Aisha checking the crates.

"Did we do it?"

She looked up at him and smiled.

"We did it. We got the gold."

Clyde punched the air. "Yes!"

He had beaten Shaw. Finally.

Then, Aisha's smile disappeared, and she whipped out a Heckler & Koch VP9 with an attached suppressor.

"I'm sorry, Clyde. I'm sure you would have done the same. In fact, I knew you were going to. I work for Shaw; no choice in the matter, but there you have it."

Clyde felt his heart sink and his bowels move. It was true. He had planned to screw her over, take it all, but working for Shaw?

"You work for that prick?" Clyde could only rasp out the words.

She steadied herself as the chopper wavered from a gust of strong turbulence.

"I'm afraid he's got shit on me, shit that'll stick, and he wants you out of the way. I'm sorry, Clyde, but it's just cleaner all around if you're out of the way."

As Clyde opened his mouth to argue, a distant thud barely registered in his consciousness, followed by a void of darkness snuffing out his brief moment of victory and life.

4:09 a.m.

Clyde opened his eyes, glanced at the clock, and sighed. Sure enough, it was the day of the heist. He rolled over and let the sweat marinate on his skin for a while. Today, he would message the guys and cancel the heist. Best to stick to the small jobs. Maybe that grandma he had been tracking would leave her house today, and he'd get in and take those pearls he knew she had stashed somewhere. Or take the day off. He liked the idea of playing cards downtown, eating hot dogs, whatever.

He showered, swigged down a coffee, left his hotel

room, jumped into his old beat-up Ford, and wound down the window. It was another hot day. He drove along the boulevard towards the Golden Nugget and stopped at a red light. He mindlessly flicked the radio channels, glanced at his side mirror, and saw a hobo approach his car from behind.

"Not today, dude, not..."

Then he saw the hobo was Shaw with his waspish, malevolent smile, too late. The gun barrel was right at the back of his head, and the distant popping sound echoed through his brain like a familiar shitty hangover.

4:09 a.m.

Clyde opened his eyes, teeth gritted. He was never going to beat Shaw. If it wasn't the cop shooting up Clyde's shit, it was fucking Aisha. He sat up on the bed.

Maybe he didn't have to beat Shaw.

He picked up his phone and sent a text to Aisha.

They collaborated again. This time, he went through the motions, let her take charge, didn't even argue on the minor points, and the heist went off without a hitch.

As the chopper headed across the desert and Clyde unclasped his harness, he looked up at Aisha, just at the moment he knew she was planning to whip out that fucking weapon of hers.

"Aisha! I know about your 'Shaw deal,' and you're about to blow me out of the proverbial airlock, but hear me out, okay?"

Aisha looked at him in surprise.

"Okay?" he repeated, shouting over the helicopter engine, holding up both hands in a surrendering gesture.

Aisha didn't say anything but wasn't reaching for the gun either.

"I'll give myself up to Shaw," he said with conviction. "You get what you need out of the deal, whatever the fuck it is; Shaw gets me, which is what he wants. I'll walk into the station downtown; he won't get away with killing me there. In theory, anyway."

Aisha adjusted her body weight as a gust of turbulence shifted the chopper, then frowned at him. "Bullshit. Why would you go along with the job if you planned to give yourself up?"

"I can't do this anymore, Aisha! You won't understand, but I am in some fucked up time loop thing." Her blank look told him she did not, indeed, know what the fuck he was talking about.

"I can't just be a lone wolf," Clyde continued, "betraying everyone around me, playing these games. I was going to betray you today, Aisha. Yes, yes, I was, and I understand why you might. Kinda. But I can't do this shit any longer." He dropped his head. "I'm done."

Aisha was closer to him now, and she leaned down. He looked up, half expecting to face the barrel of her VP9, but she was holding up her hand and caressing his cheek with a mock, sad face.

"I have to take a different path, but first, I'll make it right with Shaw," he continued. "I'll do my time, and then, after that, well, that's tomorrow's problem."

"Alright, Clyde. I'll drop you off."

Clyde walked into the police station and announced himself to the duty officer. He was immediately arrested, fingerprinted, and photographed before being slung into a cell. It was cold, and he lay on the hard bed with a gray blanket draped over his shivering body.

What was the right thing to do? He wasn't sure anymore. He would wake up in his hotel anyway. Then what? Do the same thing. Head straight to the airport and get the first flight out of the States. Yeah, that's what he'd do. He drifted off to sleep, a myriad of possibilities swirling around his brain, most of which involved him just surviving in some mud hut in a third-world country because, with no big cash stash or gold, that's all he'd be able to do.

A loud clanking of a metal door woke him up. He slowly opened his eyes and squinted, confused, at the leering police officer looking through the cell window.

"Time for breakfast, shit heel."

There was another clang, and he bolted upright.

Where the hell was his hotel room? Was he still here? He jumped off the bed, ran to the cell door, and shouted through the food tray slot.

"Hey, sir. What day is it, what date?"

The deputy had started to walk away, but Clyde could hear him reply: "It's the day you go down for multiple crimes, Clyde Patton."

"What day? I need to know. Please."

The cop stopped and turned his head.

"It's Tuesday the 15th. A date I'll always remember." Then he took off.

It was true. The loop had been broken. It was the day after the gold was to be transported and the consequent heist.

Clyde paced the cell.

Jesus, what had he done? He had given himself up. How many years was he going to get? Fuck!

He collapsed onto the bed and held his head in his hands, quietly sobbing. It was over. His life was over.

WHILE HE LANGUISHED in the cell every day, Clyde went over what he could have done differently. Whether he

361

could have brought in more backup, more equipment, more helicopters. The days drifted by, and there was still no word on his charges or removal. As he had no access to cash and there had been no word from Aisha, who clearly had taken the gold and ran, he couldn't even post bail.

The door rattled, and the deputy called through the door: "This is Deputy Jonas. Face the wall and keep your hands visible. You're going to be taken to the interview room. Clear?"

"Clear," Clyde replied as he followed the routine. More questions, he guessed. They had been trying to break him down, but Clyde was seasoned enough in his now-defunct criminal career to withstand any games they played to coax the truth.

The deputy came in and cuffed Clyde before leading him out of the cell to another empty interview room, where he was left alone to stew.

After twenty minutes, the door opened, and Shaw walked in carrying a clip pad and slowly took a seat opposite. Clyde noticed there was no leering grin or smugness about Shaw today. Instead, he looked serious, forlorn even.

"I'll keep this short, Patton. This pains me no end, boy, but I've had to do a dirty deal with Aisha Patel. The authorities that be are breathing heavy fire upon my ass. Ms. Patel has agreed she will return the stolen gold, two tons, in full, in return for your release and hers. No further charges will be brought. However, the conditions are extensive, including that you leave the United States immediately." Shaw glared at Clyde before continuing. "You show even a sweaty hair on your grizzled ass, I shoot you down, and you'd better believe that, boy. Do you understand me? Now, it's this, or I guarantee I'll make sure you serve every single day for the rest of your life inside the worst prison we can get you in. I know all the judges in the courts, so you'd better believe that."

"Do I get a lawyer? Maybe?" Clyde asked hesitantly.

The glare he received in return was a firm "no."

Three hours later, Clyde had been escorted to the city airport with only the clothes on his back. His passport had been handed to him, and he was allowed to take back his wallet with the bare minimum of funds. He scanned the outgoing flights, booked one to Panama City, and headed through security, carefully watched by a couple of Shaw's deputies. Clyde headed to the bar and ordered a beer before slipping into a booth.

Seconds later, Aisha appeared opposite him and clinked his bottle with hers.

"Happy Freedom Day," she said with a triumphant grin.

"What the fuck, Aisha? What're you doing here? What did you do?"

"I had to do another deal with Shaw. The gold for our freedom."

He shook his head. "We've got no money, nothing. Shaw won. He won!"

"That's the thanks I get? Fuck you, Clyde."

Clyde held up the palm of his hand. "No, I mean, don't get me wrong, I'm fucking glad to be out of that cell, thank you, but, jeez, all that gold! You gave it back? Why? You could've retired. I don't get it."

Aisha rolled her eyes.

"I think some part of me would prefer to be in the cell, knowing you had beaten Shaw and got away with the gold," he muttered.

"Look, we were always a great team, Clyde. You said it yourself on the chopper. You're sick of this betrayal shit. Well, so am I. I have some money, enough so we won't starve, and we'll pick up a few jobs. Where are we going, Panama City? Hmmm, well, not for too long. But it'll do for now."

She took a swig of beer while Clyde eyed her suspiciously.

"I still don't get it," he said.

She gave him an exaggerated, knowing grin again while Clyde struggled to hide a grimace.

"I gotta make a call or two. Sunny Panama, here we come." She stood.

TWELVE HOURS LATER, Clyde and Aisha had landed, headed straight to a motel in the Obarrio district, and freshened up before heading out to eat in one of the local restaurants. Everywhere was busy and noisy, surrounded by endless concrete car parks and towering white blocks. They ate in silence and headed to a bar to finish off with drinks.

"Tomorrow, we go over to the Caribbean coast," Aisha said out of nowhere.

Clyde shrugged. "Sure. I've got old friends in Colombia and Brazil, but I won't object to some Caribbean sun while I figure out what the hell I'm doing with my life."

"And you'll be sleeping on the spare bunk tonight, by the way. In case you wondered."

Clyde smiled and lifted a beer to his lips. "I did wonder."

They hired a car the following day and drove out of the city, heading north along the Autopista Alberto Motta highway. After an hour, the road hit the coast, and the Caribbean Sea came into view.

"Looks like a good place for a splash," Clyde said.

Aisha veered off the road onto a sandy track that led

them down to a marina with lines of boats, yachts, and a boatyard.

"You got a boat?" Clyde asked with a rising degree of excitement.

Aisha said nothing but was smiling as they pulled over by a sizeable single-story building that stood by the marina.

Some locals milled around, and a group of locals played cards on an upturned plastic crate, smoking. Aisha led Clyde down to the pier, then they walked along the dock, the boats gently rocking on either side of them on their moorings.

Then, Clyde saw a familiar face on one of the 70-foot yachts. It was Stan, milling around the deck, shades on.

"Who let you reprobates into the country?" Clyde shouted.

"Could ask you the very same, Mr. Patton," Stan replied with a broad grin.

Clyde turned to Aisha. "But really. What are we all doing here?"

"Let me show you."

They stepped down into the haul, and Stan lifted a hatch below a crate filled with gleaming gold bars — stacks of 12.5-kilo bars, each worth a cool $850K.

"What the—" Clyde gasped at the sight. He gaped at Aisha. "You done another job or something?

"No, this is the same gold."

"Then what the hell did you give Shaw?"

"Some gold, but not the real thing," she said, a wry smile spreading across her lips.

"What exactly?"

"Gold-plated tungsten. It's vastly cheaper than gold and has the same density and similar weight. Of course, we had to trash your warehouse and turn it into a fucking foundry getting it all done. We brought in a big-ass furnace. It wasn't easy matching the color, chemical, and surface hardness of gold perfectly. But we did. And there were costs, but…" Aisha looked down at the gold bars like a mother cat purring over her kittens. "It's going to be a nice return on investment for this little batch."

On the deck, drinking a bottle of champagne to celebrate, Clyde was still stunned.

"Shaw will be spitting blood when he finds out. I guess they will find out?" Clyde managed to say.

"Eventually, someone will drill into one of the bars, or they'll use X-ray fluorescence to scan it. Whether the surface layer of pure gold is enough to stop the X-rays from reaching the tungsten is anyone's guess. But I was assured it would buy enough time."

"Time for?" Clyde asked.

"Time to turn these bars into cash, crypto, or whatever we decide."

"And who will take this hot, stolen gold off our hands?" Clyde asked.

"We'll sail to Colombia. Melvin is there setting up a deal. There's a guy…" Stan interjected.

"Yeah, I'll bet there is," Clyde said cynically.

"Hey, it's all good, okay? We beat the fucker," Aisha reassured Clyde, raising her champagne glass.

Clyde nodded, and they clinked glasses. He felt elated yet hesitant to enjoy the moment fully.

Early the following morning, they set sail and headed out into the endless ocean. Stan talked Clyde through the proverbial "ropes" after he admitted he wasn't the seafaring type. As Stan explained the steering and maneuvering in the yacht's cockpit and pointed out the basics of steering the boat, they both heard the distant whooping of a helicopter.

A second later, Aisha burst in through the helm side door.

"We've got incoming!"

"Shit. The authorities?"

"Don't think so!"

"We got any weapons on board?"

"A few."

"Everyone grab a walkie-talkie. We'll need comms. Stan, get this mother at full speed."

Stan nodded, turned to the cockpit dashboard, and began flicking switches frantically before pushing the throttle forward to get the fuel pumping through.

Aisha led Clyde down into the equipment store. Aisha handed Clyde a Barrett M82 rifle and ammo, which he checked and loaded.

"You think it's him?" he asked, his voice low and grave.

"I know it's him."

"Fuck. How?"

"Did he give you anything that might make you trackable?"

Clyde thought for a moment.

"Just gave me back my clothes, wallet, and watch at the police station, so yeah, I'm probably bristling with surveillance bugs."

"Great." Aisha pushed past Clyde, her rifle locked and loaded.

On deck, Aisha checked the pursuing helicopter through her field glasses.

"Is it armed?" Clyde asked, coming up behind her.

"Yeah, it's a fucking AH-64 Apache."

"Oh, Jesus. Those things fire rockets and shit. Maybe he just wants to arrest us again."

"He's in the wrong country for that. He's gone rogue. No, he wants us dead, and maybe he wants the gold now."

"We'd better get into position behind the cockpit."

"Yeah, stay low."

The symphony of rotating blades from their pursuer was clear now, and the detail of the chopper could be seen clearly as it moved in their slipstream, catching up fast. It veered off to the right side of the boat, then looped around and came back at them from their starboard side, moving lower as it did.

"Oh shit!" Clyde realized this was an attack move and aimed his rifle at the oncoming threat. He fired a couple of rounds but then saw a pop of smoke from underneath and a rocket whooshed toward their yacht.

"Incoming!" he yelled as loud as he could before scrambling away to the far side of the boat. Within a second, a crumpling explosion rocked the entire vessel and threw Clyde to the deck on the port side. He hit some railings and nearly went overboard but managed to grab onto them as the boat rocked back and forth. Billowing smoke rose overhead as the helicopter buzzed low overhead. Clyde swore he heard Shaw laughing from above. More shots were fired, but this time, it came from the front deck. The bird began banking around again.

"Aisha!"

"I'm good," she replied from somewhere near the front deck.

Clyde's walkie-talkie crackled into life. It was Stan.

"Hull's hit. It's bad news. I don't think we're gonna make it."

Clyde groaned out loud before shouting to no one in particular, "We're gonna lose all that gold?"

The boat had slowed to a crawl, then the engine died.

The helicopter had already maneuvered itself and was heading back.

With gritted teeth, Clyde aimed with his rifle carefully,

found his spot on the airborne pursuer, and fired once, twice, three times. A pop and smoke instantly bellowed out from the helicopter's fuel tank. It erratically veered off course and turned away from them before heading back across the sea towards the coast.

Their own situation was equally perilous. Rising smoke continued to billow from the hull, and Stan appeared carrying a load of life jackets.

"Put this on. We're screwed," he shouted and tossed a life jacket over to Clyde before heading to the front where Aisha was situated.

As the yacht began to sink slowly, Clyde shouted, "I'm abandoning ship! What the hell are you guys doing?"

There was no response as Clyde jumped from the deck and hit the water.

"Hey?" he shouted. "Aisha!"

The hull had disappeared from view, and only the cockpit section of the yacht was visible now.

Was she still in the boat? Shit!

Clyde frantically swam along the length to the front of the boat, but there was no sign of her.

"Aisha! Stan! Where the fuck are you?"

He frantically wheeled his arms, moving around the front to the other side, but all he could see were their floating life jackets.

Empty.

He shook his head in despair. Suddenly, he regretted every little nugget of mistrust between them.

Then, a head bobbed up from under a wave, and Aisha appeared with slicked-back, wet black hair, which, to Clyde at that moment, was a beautiful sight. She coughed and breathed in air as he swam towards her.

"Thank god you're okay," he said as he kissed her lips and wrapped his arms around her.

Aisha smiled brightly and kissed him back.

"Wow. I never knew you cared."

"Get your life jacket on. Where's Stan? Stan!"

Another head bobbed up, and Stan appeared right on cue.

"Can you guys get a room?" he spat.

"Goddamn room's below water now," Clyde said, watching the yacht completely disappear beneath the bubbling water, and then it was gone as if it had never been there. They all wore their life jackets, floating aimlessly in the bobbing sea.

"Goodbye, gold."

"Yeah, goodbye, fucking gold," Clyde added despondently.

Clyde looked around. "Is there a way of knowing where we are so that we can get back? Do a salvage op?"

"We need to survive first," Aisha replied.

"Hey, Shaw ditched!" Stan shouted. "Look!"

On the horizon, they could make out smoke from the shape of the helicopter that had hit the ocean.

"You think Shaw's alive?" Clyde asked.

"I fucking know he is," Aisha replied.

They floated in the water, watching the smoke slowly thin out before it disappeared and drifted silently, each deep in their own thoughts. Clyde shut his eyes, and his body felt colder by the second. His breathing slowed, energy sapping away like a slow tire puncture.

"Hey, you okay, Clyde?" Aisha whispered. He managed to smile through chattering teeth and shortening breaths.

"All g-g-good."

"Anyone seen *Titanic*?" Clyde heard Stan ask. His voice sounded far, far away.

Clyde opened his eyes but couldn't see either of them, just a dense mist rising from the water.

"Aisha?" he could only croak her name. He was drifting, losing himself. "We did good, right?"

"Yeah, we did good." He wasn't sure if the reply was Aisha, Stan, or if he'd said it himself, but it didn't matter anymore.

He let his body float and his spirit rise.

4:09 a.m.

Motherfucker!

Special Delivery

SAWYER BLACK

Special Delivery

SAWYER BLACK

2:17 PM

Mary strained against the thick tape around her wrists. Sweat had worked in to soak the adhesive. It was no longer tearing at her skin, but it seemed to be holding her just as tight as when Dan had first bound her up.

Hands behind her back. Ankles taped to the metal legs of the folding chair.

She held her breath, straining to hear the hushed conversation up front. But all she heard was silence in the dark stockroom at the rear of the Strides shoe store. Fresh tears filled her eyes. The flying reindeer and smiling snowmen decorations turned into smears of color.

She had discovered their plan – just doing her job – and now she was going to die alongside everybody else in the South Coral Mall.

Because, according to Dan, the bomb was set to explode in less than thirty minutes.

EIGHT HOURS EARLIER

Mary climbed the stairs to her apartment on shaky legs. The humidity was always a sticky mess, but the extreme heat – unusual so close to Christmas, even for South Florida – made it nearly impossible to run outside.

She hadn't been the only one giving it a go, though. She passed several other joggers on the path alongside the green water of the swampy pond next to the apartment parking lot. Gasping nods and half-hearted waves. Shrugs that almost looked apologetic.

Mary shouldered through her front door with a groan of pleasure as the cold, dry air from the conditioner hit her exposed skin. She closed the door behind her and leaned back for a deep breath. "Thought this was supposed to be locked."

Melissa popped up over the back of the couch. She was the kind of kid that thought thirteen years was already a lifetime. Thin, no matter how much she ate. Messy hair from bed, but still looking like she could grace a magazine cover. Her grin was closer to a smirk. "It *was* supposed to be."

The Christmas tree lights flickered off. Mary had been chasing down a bad bulb for days.

She pushed off the door toward the open kitchen. "Then why wasn't it?"

Melissa shrugged before turning back to the TV. "A mystery that will probably remain unsolved."

"Cuz you didn't lock it behind you, Mommy?" Meagan said. She jumped out from behind the counter with a box of Mega Puffs held to her chest. Seven years old, she looked like a fairy, albeit one with no wings. Red hair fluffed around her head, burning bright from the sunlight that shone through the window behind her.

Mary pointed at the cereal. "You using milk this time?"

Meagan frowned like she had heard a sour note in her

favorite song. "Of course not." She reached in and pulled out a single pink puff. Then held it up like a jeweler examining a diamond. "It would ruin the crunch."

Mary reached in to grab a puff of her own. "I told you girls to lock it when I left."

"I *did*," Melissa shouted.

"Then why is it not locked now?"

Melissa sighed. "Because Mr. Terrance dropped off a flier. Something about decoration restrictions."

"So you didn't lock it behind *him*?"

"Right."

"Next time," Mary said, eating the sickly sweet morsel of cereal on her way to the coffee pot. "Lock it."

"Uh huh," Melissa said.

Mary filled her mug to the brim, then walked to the dining table. "I need to stop sweating a little before I take my shower."

"Why do you do that to yourself?" Melissa asked.

Mary dropped into her chair, pulling her wet shirt away from her chest. It made a sucking sound, rebounding with a SPLAT when she let it go. "Cuz it makes me feel good."

"Does it, though?"

Mary laughed. "Someday, maybe."

Meagan climbed into the opposite chair. "Mrs. Tilton says it makes you healthy."

Mary smiled over the rim of her coffee cup. "Then listen to your teacher. She's right. It does."

"Then keep doing it. You have to live to be a hundred."

"Why?"

"So you'll still be around when I'm grown up."

Melissa walked in for a handful of cereal. Meagan's brow furrowed in anger, but she let her sister dig into the

377

box without complaint. Melissa tossed a couple puffs into her mouth. "We'll all be dead in a hundred years, dummy."

"I'm not a dummy!" Meagan said. "And we will not!"

Mary drew in a breath, preparing to end the argument before it started, but the front door flew open. And Madeline rushed inside like she was trying to beat the flies in.

Small and lean, she looked twenty years younger than she was. More like Mary's sister than her mother.

She kicked the door shut, plastic grocery bags crinkling along her forearms. Then she leaned back against the closed door. "Why wasn't this locked?"

"Exactly what I was about to say," Melissa said.

Meagan shoved another puff into her mouth. "It's a mystery."

Mary hid her snort of laughter behind another drink of coffee.

Madeline walked into the kitchen, depositing her grocery bags. "You girls ready?"

Melissa headed back to the couch but stopped to give her grandma a hug. "Ready for what?"

"For Santa."

Meagan stood up in her chair. "SANTA!"

Melissa rolled her eyes before disappearing back into the living room. "That's not until like two-thirty."

Madeline emptied the groceries onto the counter. "It's never too early to be ready for Santa. We can get there early and do a little shopping."

Mary stood to put her empty cup in the sink. "Not too much shopping. It's almost Christmas."

Her mother had a habit of spending money on the girls like it would guarantee their love.

Madeline aimed a sheepish smile over her shoulder. "Of course not. Just a *little* bit."

Mary knew it was an argument she would lose. Micheal had been dead for five years. And his family were – to quote her mother – a bunch of assholes.

Mary had thrown herself into her job in a fierce bid to prove she could survive on her own. And even though a mail carrier's salary was enough for that survival, there never seemed to be enough for the rest.

Great insurance and plenty of days off aside, living with just the necessities grew tiring without a little bit of fun every once in a while.

"Not too much shopping," she said again. "I'll switch up my drop-offs to be at the mall right when Santa gets there so I can stand in line with you. Deal?"

Meagan stuck her hand out for a shake. "Deal."

Mary shook her hand with a single pump and a theatrical nod. Then she pulled her daughter into a crushing embrace. She couldn't imagine ever letting go.

"Eww! You're sweaty!"

Mary opened her arms and released her.

Madeline dropped her hand on Mary's arm. "You go get ready. I'll make you a sammie for breakfast."

Four independent gals helping each other get by. Mary left the room, knowing they were going to be okay.

1:15 PM

Mary pulled into the delivery lane outside the food court entry and shut the LV down. A white truck with rounded corners, worn shocks, and no air conditioning. The small fan mounted next to the sun visor slowed to a stop with a rattling wheeze.

This close to Christmas, every mail truck was stuffed with packages. Often, she would empty one vehicle while delivering to the mall shops. And the station would send another driver out to replace her empty LV with a full one, along with a new scanner for Big Brother to keep watching.

But today, this was her only truck. It was a lighter day than usual. Nothing close to a full load. She figured she could deliver everything well before Santa showed up. Then, take an extra long lunch while Meagan had her turn in line, and finish quickly enough to avoid any overtime hours showing up on her timesheet.

Bing Crosby blared from the outdoor mall speakers. But there was nothing white about the Christmas around her except for the blinding glare of the sun.

The interior of the mall seemed like a tomb compared to the parking lot. Mary dragged out the wheeled cart from its stand next to the wheelchair-accessible doors. Johnson Marris in Security kept it there for her. A nice guy with a handsome, weathered face. Lately, she had even thought about responding to his constant flirting.

It had been a long time since she had been on a date. Not since Michael …

Mary banished that train of thought by joining in with Bing on the last chorus. Her voice was a little too loud, and she looked over her shoulder to see if anybody had noticed. Nope.

Loading and scanning packages focused her attention away from the bad memories. Just do the job and get past it. That's what Madeline always said.

Strides had more packages than normal. Many of which were heavier than a pair of shoes, but the contents could have been *anything*. Staplers or copy paper. She barely paid attention until she got to the last one.

A package the size of two shoeboxes. Every square inch wrapped with packing tape. It was strapped to a small plastic pallet just a few inches bigger than the box itself.

"The hell is this?"

She would have to separate the two if it were going to fit on the cart with the rest of the mail.

She reached into her pocket for the tiny knife she used to cut the plastic shipping straps back at the station. It was attached to her office key, dangling from a retractable chain hooked to her waistband. Right next to the canvas pouch that held her pepper spray.

She snatched the little blade out and sliced through the front strap. It snapped back, and the box swelled.

Mary leaned over it with a weary groan. Garner loaded her truck. He was an ox, usually unaware of his own strength. Sometimes, she got a package that was well over her weight limit, even though she knew he had tossed it in with barely a thought as to how heavy it might be for somebody else.

"Great," she sighed.

Mary cut the rear strap and rocked the box up from the pallet to test its weight. She heard the sound of sloshing liquid, and she almost dropped it. The bottom glistened like condensation.

An odor rose from the box, and she wrinkled her nose. It smelled like cat pee. A small puddle had formed under the lower rack below the pallet. She looked down at her hands with disgust that spiraled into panic when she saw moisture on her left palm. A faint brown tint.

She wiped her hand on the leg of her shorts. When she looked at it again, she expected to see a burn on her skin. But three was just a faint redness from rubbing it against the rough fabric of her uniform.

"Shit," she said. "Now I have to call it in."

While she waited for the station to answer her HAZMAT call, she realized they would have to come out and retrieve her LV. They would replace it with a fresh one and transfer the remaining packages for her. She could take all the time she wanted with Meagan, and overtime was now guaranteed. Nobody would give her grief about it either because this wasn't her fault.

Just doing her job.

1:35 PM

Mary scrubbed up in the bathroom, then began her deliveries.

She always started at the top and worked her way back to the door. Sears used to be first, but since closing, that space had become an arcade bar. Play all the classic games for free as long as you're drinking.

Sometimes, she and her mother would share a bottle of wine while the girls played Frogger and Burger Time.

First up was Strides. One of three shoe stores. In her opinion, the worst one. The old owner was Charles Scott, pale with freckles all the way up into his thin white hair. "Nothing but shoes," he used to say. "No shirts or ball caps or any of that bullshit. Just shoes."

A nice man who always seemed genuinely concerned about her and her girls. He always slipped her a hundred-dollar bill at Christmas. Better than the six-pack of Steel Reserve the Michael's family left her after New Year's.

But then Charles Scott died and left Strides to his sons Dan and Johnny. The store seemed to suffer from the loss, but it did stay open. The inventory never seemed to turn over, but Mary was always bringing more shoes in, so something must have been going right. Besides, last year, they had continued the hundred-dollar tradition.

The hints that the brothers might be politically extreme stayed hidden behind the business, and Mary was a *to each his own* kind of girl. Keep it professional and move on.

Before turning into the back hall, she looked out over

the railing at the winter village down in the food court. Everything sparkled with glitter and fake snow. Kids were already lined up for Santa, their voices echoing off all the metal and glass.

Just before she got to the red Ford F150 pickup parked on the mezzanine, she steered away from the public space into the service corridor leading to the rear of all the stores. There was never as much polish and shine back there, but it always made her feel more comfortable being away from all the shoppers. She could do her work in private.

She pushed the cart down the back hall toward the Strides stockroom entrance, hoping Dan was there instead of Johnny. Dan was polite and quiet, whereas Johnny was a loud topper. He had done everything everybody else had done. Only twice ... and three times as well.

Mary pushed through the door and pulled the cart in behind her. She looked up with a relieved smile when Dan entered to meet her. His camouflage pants and combat boots at Christmas time made her pause, but she dismissed it as one of Melissa's mysteries before transferring packages to the receiving counter. "Merry Christmas, Dan."

"Hey."

She finished up and headed back out.

He held up his hand, walking towards her. "Wait."

She stopped.

"Where's the box?"

"What box?"

"THE box."

Did he mean the box Hazmat was collecting?

Mary pulled back half a step, her hands fluttering up to grab the front of her shirt. A nervous habit she had acquired while in the hospital watching over Michael.

Every time a doctor or nurse walked in with news. She'd tried to stop, but it continued to spring up.

"There was another box," Her voice was a squeak. She cleared her throat. "It was leaking, and I had to call it in."

"Johnny!" Dan pushed past her, dropping into a squat to survey the rest of the packages on the cart.

Mary backed into the corner where the counter met the wall. She didn't like that Dan was now between her and the door. She smoothed her shirt, then forced her hands back to her sides.

Johnny trotted in. "Hey, Mary. What's going on?"

"The box isn't here," Dan said.

Johnny looked confused. Or was that angry? "They said it was on the way." He dug his phone out of his pocket. "They said it was on the fucking truck."

Dan stood, pointing at Mary. "She stole it."

Mary held her hands up. "I didn't steal anything. It tore open and leaked all over my vehicle. I had to call HAZMAT –"

Johnny stared at her. "You called HAZMAT? The fuck for?"

Mary flinched. "Procedure! I'm following procedure. I can show you the paperwork and–"

"I don't give a fuck about paperwork, you dumb bitch. I give a fuck about my box."

"This was your fault," Johnny said. "We didn't need another one."

Dan turned to point at his brother's face. "You shut the fuck up! The bomb wasn't big enough."

Bomb?

Mary felt like a freezing blanket had been thrown over her shoulders. "I need to go."

Forget her cart.

She tried to shimmy towards the door. But Dan spun

around and grabbed her by the throat, driving her head back against the wall. "What did you tell them?"

Mary grabbed his fingers, trying to pull them free. Blinking the white spots away from her eyes. "Who?"

Dan shook her. Her teeth clacked together.

"Whoever you called. HAZMAT."

She pulled in a difficult breath. "It's not really … more like a fucking janitor."

Dan let her go. "And what are they gonna do?"

Mary grabbed her throat, trying to massage away the pain. "Swap out the LV and take the box back to the station to containment."

"And who will they call?"

"What?"

Johnny closed the distance between them until their noses almost touched. "He's asking if they will report it."

Mary pressed her back into the wall. "Yeah, but probably not 'til tomorrow morning. Ron's not really a self-starter. More of a drunk, really."

She wished she could think of more to say. Maybe talking would give her time.

"Who the fuck is Ron?" Johnny asked.

"The station manager."

Dan stepped back and narrowed his eyes. "Do they know where you are?"

"Well, yeah. It's my route."

"Like, tracking you?"

She shook her head. No. She was about to tell them her scanner was in the LV, and if it sat too long, they'd send someone to check on her.

"I don't believe you," Johnny said. "Government knows where everybody is all the fucking time."

Mary took a deep breath. "Not Ron would. He once locked up after the shift with Janine still inside the building.

He doesn't notice really anything that's not marked with a proof label."

Dan looked over at Johnny with a smile. "Doesn't notice, huh?"

Mary forced herself to smile. "Janine was afraid of setting off the alarms, so she stayed in the break room all night."

"Okay, then." Dan grabbed her arm, pulling her along to the opposite wall.

Mary felt panic. "What are you doing?"

Dan spun her around and pushed her down into a folding metal chair. Johnny tossed him duct tape. Then Dan grabbed her arms, pulling them around her back. Her left shoulder popped. Pain shot up into her neck.

"Please."

A few loops of tape went around her wrists, and when Dan crouched to tape her ankles, she tried to kick him in the face. But Johnny grabbed her feet.

She drew in a deep breath for a scream.

Johnny straightened and punched her in the chest just below her throat.

It wasn't a knockout shot, but it was enough to drive the breath out of her lungs. She cried out, but the sound caught in her throat. And then Dan pressed a strip of tape over her mouth.

Mary groaned through her nose. A ribbon of snot dripped into her lap.

"The fuck we gonna do with her?" Johnny asked.

"She can stay here. You need to put the last box in the F150. Soon, this place is gonna become the fire of redemption."

Mary stared at their faces in confusion. They had mentioned a bomb earlier. And now...

The *truck*.

The F-150 wasn't new, but South Coral Ford was known for their "gently used" trucks. Painted all leather and fire-engine red in honor of Santa's visit.

That's where the bomb was going to be.

Mary tried not to cry.

Dan looked over at her with a smile. "You've been delivering our bomb to us for months now. One shoebox at a time. The U.S. Post Office. Best mules in America."

2:17 PM

The brothers had gone. Leaving her alone in the stockroom.

Mary reviewed all the packages she had delivered to Strides in the past year. Counting every one that seemed a little too heavy for shoes. Or the ones that looked like a six-year-old had gotten to use *all* the tape.

Every offhand comment the brothers had made about commies and revolutions. The quick bitterness in a snarled complaint about *what's wrong with the world today*.

This was how it happened. Nobody saw it coming because nobody paid attention. Head down with blinders on. Going about their business.

Just doing their job.

Like her.

While on walks near the beach, Meagan would sometimes start to ask a question about someone. "Mommy, why is that man –"

And Mary would always cut her off. "People are the way people are. We just mind our business."

Meagan.

Was she out there in the line for Santa right now? Asking questions. Saying *hi* to strangers. Being the center of everyone's world who came into contact with her?

Mary squeezed her eyes shut, but all she could see were the faces of her girls. She couldn't die here. *They* couldn't die here. She had to do something.

The helplessness reminded her of Michael. How it felt to just watch him fade away. How she never prayed for *something* to happen but how she prayed for God to let *her* do something.

She couldn't breathe.

She had to calm down.

Despair became anger. And then anger deepened into rage.

She opened her mouth as far as it would go, pulling her lips back in a broad sneer. The tape pulled at the skin, tearing and burning. She poked her tongue against it and threw her head back.

The tape tore free from the right side of her mouth, and she worked her tongue into the opening. She took deep breaths through the widening gap.

And then she forced her hands toward her right pocket. Her shoulder screamed. But she needed to reach the chain looped between her waistband and pocket.

She kept her eyes on the door to the store.

And she didn't want to look away in case the brothers returned. She clenched her teeth and pushed. Her right pinky finger hooked a link of the chain, and she froze, risking a glance down at her hip.

The edge of her station key poked above the seam of her pocket. The tiny knife sat right behind it. Mary looked back to the door, her fingers working to pull the chain free.

The knife and key popped free with a loud jangle as the chain rubbed along the metal seat, and she hissed. She knew Dan and Johnny were still in the store. She could hear their muted voices. She hoisted the chain link by link to keep it quiet.

When the small knife slid between her fingers, she sagged with a sob.

Doing everything by feel — with sweat-slick fingers — kept her pace at a crawl. She started sawing at the tape, jabbing her wrists and fingers. Blood joined the sweat, and the knife almost slipped from her grasp.

She clamped her teeth against the cry of frustration, tightening her grip, and finally cut through the last half inch of tape.

She leaned forward with a gasp of relief, her hands dropping into her lap. The knife and key clattered against the chair when the chain retracted back into the fob at her hip.

It took three tries with her right hand to get the knife back out. She pulled the flap of tape off her mouth, bent forward, and sliced at the tape holding her right ankle.

She felt the change in the air before she saw him.

Looked up.

Johnny was staring at her, surprised.

And then he charged at her with both hands. The knife wasn't going to be enough. She jumped up and kicked Johnny in the balls mid-stride.

He collapsed with a bellow, crashing into her and driving her back into the chair. He landed on top of her, driving the air from her lungs. And then Mary stabbed Johnny in the face.

Again and again.

And then the chair gave way. They crashed to the floor, and Mary's head bounced off the carpeted concrete. The tape holding her left leg tore free, and the chair clanged flat beneath her.

Johnny writhed on top of her, rolling to a seated position between her knees, one hand cupping his balls, the other covering the gash in his cheek. For a moment, they looked like mother and son about to go down a slide together.

Mary grabbed for the fob and hooked her legs around his waist.

Johnny grabbed her ankles, trying to release himself. And that exposed his throat.

Mary threw the loop of the chain around Johnny's neck, then tucked in her chin and pulled as hard as she could.

His hips bucked, and his heels pounded off the floor. Mary saw Meagan and Melissa in the center of a ball of orange light. Their hair burned as the skin on their faces melted. She pulled harder.

And then Dan appeared in the doorway, blinking down at them.

"What the fuck?"

Mary froze, and Johnny's body flopped to the side.

Dan charged and grabbed her right wrist, and with a wrenching heave, he jerked her out from under his brother. She tumbled to the side, crashing into the counter. It cracked. All the boxes she had unloaded from the cart fell to the floor around her.

Dan squatted down to look into Johnny's darkening face.

Then looked at Mary, grabbing her, hoisting her.

And then she kicked loose and ran, flying like a wobbly arrow through the doorway into the front of the store, past the sales counter, and through a haze of rubber and leather footwear.

She stumbled, plowing headfirst into the clearance rack.

Pain exploded behind her eyes and in her shoulder. The rack crashed over, and shoes tumbled around her like the froth on the crest of an ocean wave.

She rolled over to look up at the ceiling. A lot of water spots on the tiles. Cobwebs in the corner.

And then Dan's sputtering face filled her view, and he hauled her up from the floor. His fingers twisted in her hair. She grabbed for her pepper spray. And then she jammed the nozzle in Dan's face, closed her own eyes, and squeezed, filling his eyes with a burning jet of OC.

It caught her as well.

But Dan dropped her with a scream and stumbled back. Mary hit the pile of scattered shoes, looking up through squinted eyelids, making sure to keep the spray aimed at his face. The red smearing through his fingers looked like whipped blood.

Mary scampered back, trying not to breathe. Dan spun around to stagger toward the front of the store.

She rolled to her hands and knees and used another rack to pull herself to her feet. Blood dripped down her scalp. She patted the top of her head and hissed. She'd definitely cut her head open.

Dan stopped at the wide window next to the door and punched the glass with a whine of pain. The window shuddered from the impact. He scrubbed at his eyes with the other fist. But he was only making it worse for himself.

Mary ran. In less than four steps, she was at Dan's back, and she spread herself out like a star.

She hit him straight on, driving him into the window. It shattered from the force of her tackle, and they fell out onto the mezzanine in a wave of glass that sparkled like emeralds.

Mary rolled away with a groan, cradling her left arm to her chest. Blood spread across the front of her shirt from a gash that ran the length of her forearm.

Dan pushed to his knees in a panic, slapping his hand over a slice in his neck. Blood pumped between his fingers, and he sat back on his ass. The glass crunched beneath him. "You fucking bitch." His teeth were edged in red.

Mary crabbed walk away until the back of her head hit something solid. She jerked around with a squeak of fright, but it was just the red Ford. She sagged back against the tire. Blood dribbling into her eyes.

She had killed one of the owners – the other looked like he was going to die soon – and she didn't even know why they had done it.

No, that was wrong.

She *did* know. And she probably wasn't getting that hundred-dollar tip *this* year.

2:45 PM

Shouts from below filtered up to the mezzanine. Then, she was surrounded by people with shocked expressions. Phone cameras pointed at the mayhem. All the people gathering for the truck raffle.

"There's a bomb," she said. It came out as a choked whisper. Mary swallowed and tried again. "There's a bomb in the truck."

She looked over at Dan. He stared back at her, his eyes large and black against his pale face. Blood streamed into his lap.

Mary turned and reached up to grab the side mirror of the truck, dragging herself to her feet to look inside the cab. The keys were in the ignition, but no bomb was on the seat. It must be cargo instead. Hand over hand, she stumbled to the back of the vehicle, her blood leaving a shiny trail on the red paint.

"Hold it right there!"

Mary looked back over her shoulder. Johnson Marris

stood there, his legs spread for stability. The gun he pointed at Mary shook with tension.

She smiled at him, waving her bloody hand. "It's me, Johnson."

He lowered the gun, turning it towards Dan. "What the fuck is going on?"

Another guard skidded around the corner. Cam Wallace. Mary thought he was skeevy, always staring at her breasts when he talked to her, even though the uniform was less than flattering.

Onlookers started to crowd around.

Cam looked at Johnson. "You call it in yet?"

"No, I just got here. You make it." Johnson looked back at Mary.

She dropped the tailgate. Felt the impact of it hitting the bumper through the floor. Jesus. The bed was full of Strides boxes. "They put a bomb in the truck."

She reached an arm in and swept a bunch of boxes out.

"What?" Johnson said.

Mary reached in again, her fist hitting metal. She ducked down for a better look. Steel framing around canisters of liquid. Batteries and wires. Blinking lights.

Mary stepped back from the tailgate and pointed into the bed. "Come see for yourself."

"Oh, *shit*," a voice hissed from the crowd behind her.

Before Johnson could take a step, Cam spread his hands and screamed. "Everybody out there's a BOMB!" Then, he fired his pistol at the ceiling three times.

The crowd panicked.

Shoppers would no doubt bottleneck the exits. Get trampled and stuck. Dead before the bomb exploded.

Mary lunged towards the escalator. "My daughters! Meagan and Melissa are down there!"

And then there was another shot.

She turned around.

Johnson was staring down at his chest. Blood blossomed across it.

"Johnson?"

He fell back against the glass railing overlooking the food court.

"Down," he said, reaching for his weapon.

Mary lunged behind the truck, craning her head around to look under the truck's suspension. What had happened?

Cam walked over to Johnson and pointed his pistol at Johnson's head. Two more flashes. Mary jerked away.

Cam.

He was in on it.

Sparks erupted at her feet. Hot blisters of impact on her cheeks. The *thunk* of bullets in metal. She scrambled alongside the truck.

"Where ya at, Mary?"

Mary rose up to peek over the bottom edge of the passenger window. Cam held his pistol up so the magazine slid out.

She ran, jerking the door open, and climbed inside. Then she lunged across the center console and turned the keys. The engine roared to life in a smooth rumble. She looked out the window, wedging herself into the driver's seat.

Then she dropped the lever into DRIVE and slid down into the footwell to stomp on the gas.

The rear tires squealed on the slick floor and fishtailed, smashing the hanging tailgate into the glass railing. The entire section shattered, and without the glass holding his body, Johnson tumbled over the side.

And then the truck got traction and launched forward.

Cam fired into the windshield. But he was too late. The front bumper hit him above the knees.

The windshield became an instant spiderweb. Cam folded up and onto the hood, and his pistol bounced out of his hand to skitter away. Then she braked. He slid off. She hit the gas again. The truck climbed over his body with ease. Mary clenched the wheel and stayed on the gas.

She could barely see through the cracks and blood. Her left hand wouldn't close all the way. The noise of the engine couldn't hide the whining moan rising from her chest.

Just get the truck outside. Just do your job.

Somehow, she got her seatbelt on.

The wide stairs leading to the food court were topped by a sunglasses kiosk and a booth that sold fake tattoos. They exploded into tinder when the Ford hit them. A jolt sent another bolt of pain up her neck, and then her stomach rose into her throat when the truck zipped over the edge of the top step.

She tipped down and slammed into the first landing. Her head smacked off the ceiling of the truck. Her spine compressed with a pop. Then, the truck tipped down the rest of the stairs with a grinding of metal on stone tile.

Santa's Village stood right next to the Hill of Beans coffee shop, and elves and kids scattered when the truck tore toward the entrance doors. The crowd trying to leave was packed against the glass, so Mary drifted into a turn that would take the truck down through the maintenance hall, where shipping and receiving were located. Wide bay doors for truck trailers. An empty parking lot. And no shoppers.

No kids.

Mary hung her head out the window like a dog on a

summer joy ride. It made it harder to keep pressure on the accelerator, but at least she could see.

Another corner past the restroom, and Mary put the truck into a skid that brought it into the warehouse. Metal shelves and forklifts. Two workers in yellow vests watched her drive past with expressions of equal parts mild surprise and boredom.

How soon was the bomb going to go off? Five minutes? Ten seconds?

Mary slowed to survey her options. Every loading door was occupied except for one that was two doors to the left of where she was facing. The door to the left of *it* held an empty trailer. The sun shining through the tinted polycarbonate roof made it look like it glowed.

Like an invitation.

Mary adjusted her course and hit the gas. Smoke from the rear tires filled the cab. The rubber bit and the truck shot forward.

The truck wasn't winning any drag races, but it was powerful and fast. She didn't have time for a plan. She couldn't count or calculate. She just opened her door and fell out.

She hit the slick concrete next to the metal loading plate. The truck door slammed shut with a screech of metal, and the truck flew through the open bay door. Sparks flashed in her periphery.

Her shoulder crunched, and her temple bounced. She rolled in a darkening spiral into the empty trailer to land against the side in a crumpled ball.

The sound of the Ford's engine became a faint hum that pulsed in time with her heartbeat. The flash of light behind her eyelids looked like the halo of fire the sun had lit around Meagan's head this morning.

Then the light went out.

The two workers in yellow vests jogged up to the door to watch the truck sail into the rear parking lot. Its weight drove the undercarriage into the asphalt. A rooster tail of sparks exploded from under the rear bumper.

The Ford bounced a few more times, continuing toward the edge of the parking lot, through two dumpsters, and into the overflow lot of delivery vehicles. It rolled along at idle straight down the center lane toward the field at the lot's edge. A Sloppy's was going up in the spring, but there was nothing there but the restaurant's shell.

The truck continued into the field like it was going to make an order at the drive-thru. It cleared the other side of the construction to nose over a berm of dirt. Then, it disappeared into the hollow on the other side of the hill to stop with a puff of dust and exhaust smoke.

Before the cloud settled, the bomb exploded.

Fire erupted out in an expanding ball just behind a rippling shockwave. The Sloppy's was swept aside like a kid kicking over a sandcastle at the beach. Delivery trucks overturned. Thunder preceded the hot wind that rocked the trailers in the dock. Dark smoke expanded to fill the sky, turning the afternoon into a stormy night.

Mary only saw the dark spiral into her own unconsciousness.

EIGHT HOURS LATER

Mary opened her eyes to see they were still there with her. Her girls. Her mother. Meagan curled up in the space between her legs. Melissa swiping furiously on her phone. Madeline pacing in front of the hospital window.

Broken left shoulder. Right wrist. Bruised spleen. Cracked ribs. Whiplash and concussion. A total of seventy-two stitches. Staples in her scalp.

Four dead men. Three of whom *she* had killed.

But she had saved thousands. Including children. Two that were *hers*.

Just doing her job.

"I always knew you were a badass," Melissa had said the first time she'd woken. "But I never *really* knew it."

Meagan had just put her head against her hip and cried.

"Why are you crying?" Mary asked.

"Because you're hurt."

"Yeah, but I'll be okay. I have to live to be a hundred, remember?"

Meagan looked up with a wondering smile. "Yeah."

Mary wanted to reach down and ruffle her fuzzy head, but the thought of moving anything made her want to vomit. She would just lie there and feel the warmth.

The love.

Four independent gals helping each other get by. Mary closed her eyes, knowing they were going to be okay.

Field Trip

CJ LYONS

Field Trip

CJ LYONS

PITTSBURGH POLICE SERGEANT MADDY McKEE STRODE across the precinct lobby to where her second-in-command, Corporal Ames, anxiously hugged an overlarge stuffed giraffe.

"You're never going to make it," Ames said, falling into step beside her.

She ignored him. "Did Yancey say to take the tunnel or bridge?"

"Tunnel." He stepped forward to open the door for her. They continued outside to where her SUV waited at the curb. "Doesn't matter, there's no time."

"I'll make it." Maddy climbed into the driver's seat. She started the engine, rolled down the window, and reached a palm out.

Ames reluctantly handed over the giraffe he'd been clinging to. Maddy tossed the stuffed animal into the passenger seat and sped away from the curb, somehow finding an opening in the rush hour traffic streaming past. Ames watched her weave through the crush of cars, shielding his eyes from the setting sun, watching until she was out of sight.

"Never gonna make it in time," he mumbled morosely before returning inside the precinct.

* * *

Focusing on the traffic around her, Maddy turned up her music—Halestorm's I Like It Heavy—and turned down the police radio with its constant squawking. She was off duty, so no lights and sirens, but that didn't rule out an occasional judicious tap of the horn while she made her way over to the Liberty Tubes. Both the tunnels and bridge were snarled; construction had them down to one lane— typical illogical timing of PennDOT—but Maddy edged out of traffic into the construction workers' lane, where a man in an orange vest waited for her.

"You literally saved my life, and this is the favor you ask in return?" Yancey's hearty voice carried over the noise of traffic with practiced ease.

Maddy reached for the giraffe and thrust it out the window. "Seriously, you're saving my life this time. The twins will kill me if I'm late."

Yancey cradled the giraffe in his calloused hand. "The baby will love it. Thanks, Maddy."

"Hugs to her and Maria!"

He waved her onto the rutted lane awaiting paving. The SUV bounced over the patched Macadam and gravel, Maddy goosing the accelerator, one eye on the clock: 5:54. After exiting the tunnel and racing through a maze of back streets and cobblestone alleys, she turned onto Forbes Avenue. As her car passed the life-sized Dippy the Diplosaurus guarding the entrance to the Carnegie Natural History Museum, her phone's alarm rang out with the theme from *Jurassic Park*. Right on time.

She parked and grabbed her gym bag from the rear of

the SUV. As she made her way up to the entrance, two ten-year-old girls came running out of the museum: Emma, her chatterbox extrovert fashionista, and Ella, her nerdy DandD-loving Whovian. Should've named them Night and Day, her ex had marveled when they brought them home from the hospital, their personalities already shining through. Ten years later, he was in Tokyo, managing partner of an intellectual property law firm and starting a brand new family while she'd sacrificed her career as a detective for a desk job that allowed her to raise their girls on her own.

But she wouldn't trade any of it, not for the world or all the riches in it. Ella was in the lead, but with a glance over her shoulder, she stuttered a step that allowed Emma to "win" and envelop Maddy in a hug that turned into a twirly dance. Emma loved winning, and Ella never minded. After her sister celebrated, she came in for a bear hug and nuzzle that lasted twice as long.

"You made it, you made it!" Emma said. She waved to their teacher at the entrance, who was not so patiently waiting alongside the other fourth graders and chaperones. "Mrs. Chao, she's here. She made it!"

"Hang on a sec, girls." Maddy detached the twins and removed her uniform belt, depositing it along with her service weapon into the SUV's lockbox. Then she removed her backup weapon in its paddle holster and closed the hatch. Only to meet Emma's disapproving glance at her uniform.

"Mom, you're not wearing that! Can't you be a normal mom for once?"

Maddy tossed her gym bag to Emma. "Brought civvies. See if you approve."

Together, the three walked toward the museum entrance, Emma scrutinizing Maddy's clothing selection while Ella held Maddy's left hand—the girls had learned at an early age that their mom always, always needed her right hand free. There were other various rules as well, like letting Maddy enter any room first, always knowing where exits were, and never forgetting the family code word: rutabaga.

"You know," Maddy said, "you used to love it when I came to school in my uniform."

"But not the gun." Ella, her budding pacifist, said. "Even though I know you've never used it."

"I liked it better when you wore nice clothes," Emma added. "Detectives are cool. I think I'm going to be one. But with better shoes than you wore."

"Right." Maddy tousled her hair—Emma hated that. "Along with a marine biologist and an astronaut and a fashion designer—"

"And a lawyer like Dad and then President," Emma finished for her. "I'm gonna do it all!"

As they neared, Maddy thought the sprawling century-old museum looked like a cross between Buckingham Palace and Alcatraz with its imposing stone facade. But she also remembered her own enthusiasm every time she came here as a kid. Hell, she was still a bit excited tonight. Dinosaurs? All to themselves, with the museum closed for the day? Who wouldn't be thrilled?

Mrs. Chao was waiting for them inside the museum lobby. She frowned at Maddy's uniform. "Sergeant, I very much appreciate you volunteering to help, but I'm afraid some of the children might be distracted by—"

Maddy smiled and took her gym bag from Emma. "Just need a second to change."

Mrs. Chao nodded in relief. "Emma, Ella, we'll join your classmates. Nessa, can you—"

A tall twenty-something woman clutching a clipboard came rushing over. Nessa,

"This is Nessa," Mrs Chao said. "She'll be one of our guides today. Show Mrs. McKee Where she can change?"

Nessa nodded. "Right this way."

"She's not a Missus," Emma piped up. "Not anymore."

"Come along girls." Mrs. Chao took their hands and led them down a side corridor.

Nessa led Maddy across the massive reception foyer. Marble glistened on every surface: the floor, the columns that it'd take three adults to encircle, and the walls. But the focal point of the immense five-story atrium was the massive marble staircase that seemed to almost float in the air.

A man in his late thirties leaned over the reception desk, deep in conversation with a security guard. His hair was long enough to fall in his face as he spoke—some new trend or past due for a trim, Maddy wasn't sure. Although his clothing, jeans and a neatly tucked-in Oxford shirt, was appropriate for a dad wrangled into class volunteer duty, his body language was off, small herky-jerky gestures that screamed tightly coiled tension.

Maddy paused, her instincts alerted. "He belong with the group?"

"Let me see," Nessa said, consulting the clipboard. "In the meantime, that's the ladies' room is to the right." She pointed past the Grand Staircase that commanded the atrium's center stage.

Maddy watched as Nessa approached the desk. The man seemed to relax as Nessa introduced herself. Maybe the poor guy was as anxious as Maddy was to make sure his kids had a fantastic time. Even though she'd given up her career as a detective so she could spend more time with the girls, somehow, it never seemed to be enough. Especially not now that Paul was able to provide them with every luxury. No way Maddy's day trips to Kennywood could compete with first-class jaunts to Tokyo, Paris, and London.

With a sigh, Maddy opened the door to the restroom.

* * *

Nessa checked her list one more time. "I'm sorry, Mr. Conway. Adam's name isn't on my list of students. What school does he go to? Maybe they're scheduled for a different date?"

Adam's father—Caleb, he'd introduced himself as— pushed both hands through his hair, tugging in frustration. She understood why he might be angry, but there wasn't much she could do about him getting the date of his son's field trip wrong. "Or maybe he's listed under another name? His mother's?"

Instead of helping the man, her question only seemed to agitate him more. His hands flew away from his head so abruptly that Kevin, the guard standing beside him, flinched. But Mr. Conway kept them stiffly at his sides, turning around in a circle, scanning the atrium, his movements stiff and jerky. Nessa wondered if he was maybe on the spectrum. She'd been diagnosed with Autism at an early age, and with Pittsburgh attracting so many tech companies and academics, many of her classmates and their parents were diagnosed. She took a deep breath and tried to think of ways to help calm him before he spiraled into a meltdown.

"Maybe try calling—" she began.

"No, no, no." He turned back to her, eyes wide. "I can't. Not his mother—she's, she's—" He broke off, blinking rapidly. "No." His voice was firmer this time. "Adam's here. I saw him. He was right here and then—"

His tone rose. Kevin edged closer. "Then he was gone. He's here. He has to be."

"Do you have a photo?" Nessa asked.

Mr. Conway fumbled for his phone, thumb trembling as he unlocked it. The screen filled with a photo of a woman and boy—obviously his wife and son. Equally obvious was the love and joy that filled their faces. Kevin leaned in to examine it. "Nope, he hasn't been in today."

"How can you be so sure?" Mr. Conway said, re-pocketing the phone as if it was a treasure.

"It's my job. I pay attention to the kids. Never know when one's gonna get lost or hide; try to pull a *Night at the Museum* stunt. Plus, we checked at closing time. The only kids here are the ones on the field trip."

Mr. Conway shook his head vehemently. "The dinosaurs are upstairs, right? I'll just go—" He turned and jogged toward the Grand Staircase.

"Sir!" Kevin raced after him, grabbing his arm. Mr. Conway whirled and lunged so fast Nessa almost couldn't process what happened because the man now had Kevin's gun and was pointing it at her, and Kevin lay on the ground, stunned, his head bleeding from where he had hit it against the bottom marble step.

Nessa froze, unable to make a sound; the breath shocked out of her. The clipboard slipped from her grasp, spinning to the floor in slow motion. She didn't even hear it hit the ground.

Mr. Conway stepped forward, grabbing her by the waist, the gun to her head. "You and I are going to find my son."

* * *

Maddy changed quickly into cargo pants and a baggy tee that covered her backup weapon, which was holstered at the small of her back. She shoved her uniform into her bag and headed out the door, tugging her barrette off to free her hair.

When she strode toward the lobby, she was surprised no one was at the reception desk—it was after hours, but why would the guard leave? Change of shift? Then she spotted him sprawled in front of the Grand Staircase.

She ran over to him, dropping her back. "Don't move, I'll call an ambulance." She dialed with one hand and checked his pulse with the other. Fast, but strong. "What happened?"

He raised a hand to his head and frowned when it came away covered in blood. "He—I—" His hand went to his empty holster. "My gun—"

"Where's Nessa?"

"Took her." His color turned grey. "I'm gonna be—"

She ducked in time to miss the worst of his vomiting. Then, the dispatcher came on the line. "This is Sergeant Madeline McKee. I'm at the Carnegie Museum on a school field trip. We have an injured guard and an armed hostage taker. There are children—" her voice caught as Emma and Ella's faces filled her vision. She cleared her throat and fought to keep her tone professional. "The HT appears to be in emotional distress. The lobby is clear for entry, but don't proceed further until I assess the situation. I'll keep the line open."

She secured her phone in the side pocket of her pants, drew her weapon, and sidled down the hall to the classroom the kids were in, angling for a view via the door's window.

The far wall was lined by bookcases. Tables and chairs filled the middle of the room, and there was no other exit. Mrs. Chao had her back to Maddy. The kids were gathered around an elevated box near the door, digging for bones as a grad student demonstrated tools and techniques of anthropology. Nessa and the HT stood beyond the worktables in the rear, the man holding the gun behind him as he scanned each child's face, shaking his head.

While Maddy appreciated how Nessa had kept the gunman calm and hadn't alarmed the others, she wished the grad student had an ounce of tactical awareness—by taking the man to the rear of the room, she'd placed the kids in the crossfire. There was no way Maddy could get the kids out of the room if the gunman began shooting.

She got out her phone and videoed the man, plus the children.

Then she backed away, whispering a sit-rep to the dispatcher, before sending her those few seconds of video. After which, she returned to her position, her focus torn between watching the gunman and trying to catch the eye of one of her girls. If she could at least get them safe…

Suddenly, Nessa left the man's side and approached the door. What was she playing at? Maddy scooted into another classroom, staying out of sight as Nessa left the room, closing the door behind her. Then she turned toward the lobby, walking past Maddy.

She scrambled to catch up with her. "What the hell is going on, Nessa?"

She started. "He doesn't want to hurt anyone. He's looking for his son. He said if I help him, he'll leave."

"Help how?"

They reached the lobby, where the guard was seated on the steps. His color had improved. Nessa ignored Maddy. "Kevin, I need your key. I promised Mr. Conway I'd go through the cameras and make certain Adam isn't here."

The guard — Kevin — handed over his ID badge without a word. But Maddy blocked her path. "You're not going anywhere. Who is this man?"

Nessa stood her ground, her gaze focused beyond

Maddy. "He says his name is Caleb Conway. He's terrified. His son, Adam, was here for the field trip but vanished."

Maddy frowned. "I don't remember any Adam in the girls' class."

"He's not on the list I was given," Nessa said. "But Mr. Conway insists he's here. He didn't mean to hurt anyone— Kevin grabbed him, and when Mr. Conway pulled away, Kevin slipped and hit his head."

Maddy didn't give a shit if Kevin's injury was a result of an accident—nothing changed the fact that Conway was holding a gun, was obviously emotionally unbalanced, and was in a room with Maddy's girls. She didn't understand how Nessa could be so calm, so ... clinical. "Stay here with Kevin. Help should be along in a few minutes."

"No. I promised Mr. Conway I'd look for Adam. He said if I did, he'd leave."

"I'm not letting—"

"I promised." She tried to move past Maddy, but she blocked her, one hand held up in the universal "stop" position.

Hell. Maddy could use eyes on the cameras and someone to research Conway. Let SWAT deal with Nessa when they got here. At least she'd be safe in the security office. "Give me your phone."

Nessa obeyed. Maddy dialed her second in command. "Ames, I need you to find everything you've got on a Caleb Conway and coordinate with SWAT. There'll be a civilian in the security office when they arrive; she's monitoring the cameras. Tell them to keep things soft until I say otherwise."

"Got it," he said. "ETA's three minutes. But you should know, Hamlin's acting commander."

"Hamlin? They let that trigger-happy asshole—"

"Trevasion's out. Hernia surgery."

"Whatever. Nessa will be your eyes. Here she is."

She handed the phone back to Nessa. "Go to the security room and stay there, got it?"

"Yes."

"Kevin?" The security guard nodded. "Stay with Nessa and keep her there. You stray outside when SWAT arrives, and you're both liable to get shot."

Kevin paled. "Got it."

Maddy retraced her steps, returning to assess the classroom. She peered through the glass window in the door. Nothing had changed except Conway appeared more agitated, kept rubbing his head and tugging at his hair as if he was fighting to stay in control.

Maddy holstered her pistol. Then she stepped inside, smiling, and joined the group at the mini-excavation.

"Mom!" Emma called. "Look what we dug up!" She raised a fossil, some kind of dino-bone, Maddy supposed. She didn't actually give a damn. Instead, she put her arms around both girls, squeezing their arms to get their attention.

"Wow!" Her voice sounded false even to her. "That's as big as a rutabaga!"

Ella snapped to attention. Emma was still engrossed in the digging process, and it took a few seconds for her to stop.

"I have to go to the bathroom," Emma said. "Don't you, Ella?"

Good girl.

"The ladies' room is just off the lobby," Maddy said, pulling them away from the table. Ella grabbed Emma's hand, and the two headed for the door.

Maddy glanced over at Mrs Chao. "Why don't we all take a ten-minute washroom break before we go upstairs, Mrs Chao?"

Mrs. Chao glanced up, met Maddy's eyes, and frowned in confusion.

Maddy smiled and gestured with her hand. "Shall we?"

The girls were almost to the door, Maddy slowing her gait so she was between the children and Conway.

Then Conway stopped pacing and realized what was happening. Maddy drew her weapon and stepped forward, hoping to cement his attention. "Mr. Conway, I know you have a gun. I need you to keep your hands—"

Too late. Conway pulled out the weapon. Maddy almost shot him, but he wasn't aiming it at her or the kids. He seemed confused, as if he'd forgotten he even had it. "Don't leave," he said. "Don't anyone leave. Please." His voice was taut with something that sounded like fear. "Please. Just tell me where Adam is. I need to find Adam."

Maddy waved her free hand behind her, gesturing for the kids to get out. "That's why I'm here, Mr. Conway. To help. To help you find Adam." She gave her tone a bit of an uptick that matched his own. Dared to take a step closer to him, drawing his attention away from the children. "Let's find Adam. Together."

His head bobbed with every word, but his eyes were narrow with suspicion. "Together?"

"Together." She nodded, mirroring his own movements. "All I need is for you to put your gun on the floor. Then we'll find Adam. That's what you want, isn't it? To find your son?"

Behind her, she heard the kids' footsteps. She was desperate to look to see if the girls were safe but kept her focus on Conway. He stared at her gun, then at her. She stretched her free hand out and down, mimicking placing the weapon down. He began to follow her movement, slowly, so damn slowly, like he had no idea what was happening. Or maybe it was just time moving like molasses

—how long did she have before SWAT arrived? Hamlin would take Conway out in a heartbeat; he'd love to add him to his "success" rate.

Then Conway stopped, the gun dangling from his hand, less than an inch from the ground. "Do you know where Adam is?"

Tears slipped down his cheeks, but he didn't notice. Maddy knew this man didn't want to hurt anyone. He was just a dad as worried about his kid as she was about hers. Choosing to trust her gut more than her training, Maddy stepped closer, crouching to his level and meeting his gaze.

"Tell me about Adam," she said. "What's he like?"

Conway instantly relaxed, seemingly forgetting about the weapon. "Adam? He's the best kid. So smart. And funny. He loved—" He paused between each word, his brow furrowed as if he was fighting to find words. "He loved—" He gestured with his free hand.

"Dinosaurs? So do my girls." She edged closer, closer. If she could just secure his weapon, this would all be over. "Which one is Adam's favorite?"

That stumped him, his mouth trying to form words. More than emotional distress, it was clear he was suffering from some kind of cognitive impairment as well. "All of them," he finally said. "Terri, his mom, she gave him a-a book." He was crying now. "He took it with him everywhere. Loved that book. Knew all the dinosaurs by heart."

The gun finally slipped from his grasp. Maddy stretched out, grabbed the weapon, and slid it away. "Help me, please. Help me find my boy." The agitation had returned, and he stood abruptly, fast, too fast.

A laser sight glowed red against his neck, creeping up his face for a kill shot. Maddy didn't think, simply reacted. She lunged forward and tackled him right before the first shot exploded through the window.

Then she heard Ella's screams.

* * *

Nessa recognized her body was responding to the situation with age-old reflexes: her stomach heaved, her pulse quivered like hummingbird wings thrumming in her chest, and everything was too loud, too bright, too... much. But she was a scientist, she dealt in facts. Fact: adrenalin and cortisol were natural side effects of fear. She was afraid, that was it. Fact: a boy was missing, his father was afraid but not in control. Fact: one of her responsibilities was to care for museum visitors. Fact: science was a promise to find the truth, and she always kept her promises.

Which meant her fear was secondary. Her job was to find Adam and keep her promise.

By the time she'd processed this, she was seated in the security office with Kevin. As she focused on her search for Adam, her breathing calmed, her pulse settled, and the rushing in her ear faded, allowing her to hear the man's voice coming from her phone.

"Corporal Ames, I'm in the security office," she said.

"Good. Pull up the room where the hostage taker—"

"Mr. Conway. He's not here to take hostages. He's looking for his son."

Ames' curse was unwarranted. "Pull up that screen and send me a livestream. Can you do that? Or do you need me to walk you thr—"

"I'm perfectly capable of utilizing my phone, Corporal." Within seconds, she had their conversation switched to video and the phone propped up to provide the best view of the classroom. "The children are leaving." She glanced at the lobby view. "Emma is leading the children to the sculpture garden fire exit—it's the closest to the classroom."

"Yep, Maddy trained them right."

"But her sister isn't with them. She's still in the classroom."

"What? Where?"

Nessa rolled her eyes. She thought police officers dealt in facts just like she did, but clearly, all he focused on was Mr. Conway and Sergeant McKee. She pointed to the monitor. "There. She's in the bookcase under the window."

"Ella, what the hell—" He swore again. "McKee's got the subject calmed. He's about to surrender his weapon." He was clearly speaking to someone other than Nessa, so she focused on searching for Adam.

"We've got visual now, Ames," another man's voice, clipped with an undercurrent of excitement, came through. "Time to end this."

"Didn't you hear me?" Ames shouted. Nessa glanced at the classroom screen. Mr. Conway was in tears—and she had promised to help him. Then she noticed something she'd missed before. Ella was holding something. Oh no. Oh no, no, no.

"Greenlight," the new man said.

"No! Abort!" Ames shouted.

"I found Adam," Nessa whispered.

The classroom window exploded.

* * *

Two shots, then silence. Maddy rolled back, dragging Conway with her until they were under the cover of a table. As she pivoted to where she'd heard Ella's scream, she grabbed her phone—the line with dispatch was still open.

"Hamlin, stand down," she yelled above the ringing in her ears. "Stand down, you shit! Do you hear me?"

"Standing down," came a recalcitrant mutter.

"I mean it. Everyone stay clear until I give the word." Silence from the phone. "Acknowledge, damn it!"

"Acknowledged. But it's against regs, and any consequences are on you, McKee."

She didn't have time for Hamlin's bullshit. Where was Ella? She reached the bookcases below the shattered window. Blood dotted the splinters of glass. "I'm standing up," she said. "Don't shoot me."

She heard a grumbled response from Hamlin.

"Ella? Where are you? Are you hurt?"

"Here, Mama." Her voice came from behind the sandbox. Maddy ran over to her. Her hair sparkled with broken glass, and she had a few small cuts on the back of her neck.

"Baby, baby." Maddy gathered her into her arms, thumbing tears from her daughter's eyes. "What were you thinking?"

"I'm okay, Mom." Ella's voice was strong and steady—steadier than Maddy felt.

"Wait here," she ordered Ella, setting her aside. She retrieved Conway's weapon then went to check on him. He was sitting, dazed, not even noticing the ribbon of blood streaming from his scalp. He didn't even resist as she checked the source—a graze, no signs of penetration. He'd gotten lucky. They both had. She crouched down to meet his eyes. "Caleb, are you hurt anywhere else?"

He blinked slowly, still not looking at her. "I don't know. What happened?" He touched his head and stared at the blood on his hand, frowning. "Adam! Is Adam okay? Terri, Terri—where's Adam?"

Maddy rested her palms on his shoulders. "You're in shock, Caleb. Your wife, Terri, she's not here—"

Ella came up behind her and yanked on her sleeve. "I know where they are, Mom. Mrs. Conway and Adam."

That penetrated Conway's confusion. The weight of his gaze fell on Ella as if she was the center of the universe. "Adam? You found Adam?"

Ella nodded. She handed a framed photo to Maddy.

Maddy glanced at the photo.

"I saw it and knew you'd need it to help Mr. Conway. That's why I stayed," Ella said.

"Oh, sweetie." Maddy pulled her into a hug. "My brave, brave girl."

* * *

Maddy waited as the medics arrived and stabilized Conway—Ella insisted on staying as well while Nessa and Emma somehow talked their way through the crowd and back into the classroom. Another strike against Hamlin. Although Maddy was sure he'd find some way to try to blame her.

"I should have known," Nessa told Conway, not actually touching the man but her hand hovering over his as if she wanted to. "It's my first day. I saw the memorial plaque while I was setting up, but it had nothing to do with paleontology, so I didn't pay it much mind, still... I am so sorry, Mr. Conway. I could have stopped all of this."

Maddy handed the photo Ella found to Conway. "I think you might want to keep this." She glanced at the medics who were standing by. "You were right, Caleb. Adam did have a field trip here. Months earlier. You and his mom were driving him here."

Conway hugged the photo of his wife and son, Adam, clutching a well-worn dinosaur encyclopedia. "Adam was so excited. Talked about it for days." The tears returned. "But then—"

"You were on your way here when you got in a car crash," Maddy continued. "Dispatch told me. You were in a coma for months, only just left rehab a few weeks ago."

Conway didn't seem to hear—or if he did, he didn't understand... or didn't want to. "Today. Today's dinosaur day."

"That's right, Caleb. A year ago today was Adam's field trip."

He glanced up at her, beaming. "Today's dinosaur day, the field trip. Adam will be so happy."

Maddy spied the clock from the corner of her eye: 6:48. But for Caleb Conway, time had stopped a year ago with the death of his wife and son.

Caleb looked to the medics. "We're going to get Adam, right? And my wife? She'll be waiting for me. She hates it when I'm late."

The medic shrugged. "Let's get going. All right, Mr. Conway?"

Caleb nodded, smiling. "Can't be late for Adam's field trip."

Maddy stepped back and watched him leave with the medics. And then she went and joined her daughters.

Divine Intervention

SEAN PLATT

Divine Intervention

SEAN PLATT

KAT GRUNTED.

Then, she pushed the barbell loaded with plates up and over her chest, arms straining, sweat beading on her forehead. Clinking metal and harsh breaths echoed off the concrete walls, her headphones pulsing with Metallica's "One,"blocking out everything but the burn in her muscles and the rhythm of her reps.

Her left leg buckled on the last press, and she cursed. The barbell teetered, but she gritted her teeth and managed to re-rack it with a resounding clang that made her wince.

Kat sat, wiping her face with the towel she had laid on the floor next to the bench. She glared at the sleek metal-and-plastic prosthetic jutting out from beneath her running shorts. Two tours in Iraq had taken her entire left leg, most of her unit, and all of her faith. But sometimes, when she really got in the zone, especially during a workout, she could still feel her shin and toes, even flex phantom muscles. All in a limb that was no longer there.

The doctors had told her about that.

But it was still surreal to experience it.

A knock sounded over the music. Kat tugged out her earbuds. The side door swung open to reveal her mother's pursed and disapproving face. At sixty-two, Margaret Collier still had the air of a math teacher, exaggerated by her iron-gray bob.

"Katherine, we will be leaving in an hour, and I don't want to be late." Her gaze flicked to Kat's sweat-soaked tank top and the gleaming barbell. "And put that away before you hurt yourself." She shook her head, then added: "*Honestly*."

Kat swallowed a much more sarcastic reply and forced a smile onto her face. "Got it, Mom."

She waited until Margaret had shut the door before sighing and running a hand through her damp, auburn hair. Then she took a swig from her water bottle, unhitched her prosthetic, and slid into the wheelchair beside the bench.

The familiar routine of wiping down the equipment and re-racking the weights helped ease the apprehension constricting her chest. She wanted to cancel this whole goddamn church concert thing, but she had promised Margaret. After all, for the sake of peace, surely Kat could tolerate one night of biting her tongue while people called her a "hero"and whispered pitying prayers on her behalf.

Or so Kat kept telling herself.

A hot shower helped to loosen the knots in her shoulders while rinsing away the buckets of sweat. She took her time toweling off, then strapped on her "dressy leg" — the one without scuff marks and dents.

Margaret had laid out a floral dress on her bed, but Kat opted for jeans and a plain black T-shirt instead. She agreed to church but drew the line at playing dress up.

A delicious aroma of rosemary chicken and potatoes

greeted her when she entered the kitchen. Margaret had set the table with the good china and an impressive display of lit candles flickered shadows on the wall. Part of Kat softened at the obvious effort the meal had taken, even as she bristled at the implied bribe.

"You're wearing that?" Margaret sighed, looking over her outfit. "This is an important night, Katherine. People want to honor your service and sacrifice."

"I'm not some prop for them to fawn over." She rolled up to the table and, ignoring Margaret's folded hands awaiting Grace, stabbed a piece of chicken much harder than necessary. "I did my job. End of story."

"Sweetheart, I know your ... experiences have made you cynical. But Pastor Rick is different. He understands what veterans go through. His Power of Faith program has helped so many soldiers. He talks about it all the time."

"Sorry if I have a hard time believing that prayer can heal my PTSD."

Margaret exhaled slowly and set down her fork with a clink. "I'm not asking you to be a true believer overnight. Just ... keep an open mind. After everything you've endured, is it so hard to consider that a higher power might have spared you for a reason?"

Kat snorted. "Pretty crappy higher power for taking my unit but only one of my legs. Let alone Scalpel."

Her mother's forehead creased. "Scalpel?"

"Charlie Miller, my medic. He's the only reason I made it. Patched me up after the IED, even with shrapnel in his own gut." Kat took a long swallow of water, but it failed to dislodge the sudden lump in her throat. "Fat lot of good his miracle hands did when a sniper's bullet found him two weeks later, though, huh?"

Margaret reached across the table to clasp her hand. "I'm so sorry, honey. I ..."

"He had a kid on the way." Kat squeezed her eyes shut. "What kind of God rips a good man away from his family but keeps me alive?"

And now she was crying, damn it. So much for getting through this night like a stoic.

"Oh, Katherine …" Margaret got up and stepped around the table to envelop her in a hug, rocking Kat slightly as she stroked her hair like she was six years old again and waking from a nightmare. "I'm grateful you're alive."

Kat grimaced but allowed herself to be held, counting the seconds by focusing on the familiar scent of her gardenia perfume.

Then, she gently extricated herself while wiping her eyes. "Sorry. I shouldn't have unloaded on you like that."

"You have nothing to apologize for." Margaret dabbed at her own glistening eyes. "I'm your mother. I'm always here to listen. I wish you would tell me more about what you went through."

Yeah. No way in hell was that happening. First off, Margaret wouldn't be able to handle it. And second, and most importantly, Kat didn't want to relive it.

They finished the meal in an awkward silence. Kat knew Margaret was just trying to help in the only way she knew how by dragging Kat to some idiotic megachurch praise-a-thon.

At least she didn't seem too offended when Kat declined the offer to touch up her mascara. This wasn't a fancy photoshoot, and it wasn't like the jagged scars on her cheek could be hidden with any kind of makeup (Lord knows, she'd tried). But then Kat had come to the conclusion that she preferred that people saw her as she was: a broken Marine, in both body and soul.

"Phone," Margaret said. Her own sat on the hall table.

"Pastor Rick doesn't allow them in service. They're a distraction from God."

Kat stared at her. "You've got to be shi-kidding me."

"Katherine."

Kat growled, then chucked her phone on the table. No shit, it was a distraction. That's how she was planning on getting through the service, by being distracted.

Now, she was going to be forced to listen to whatever drivel Pastor Rick let fall from his lips. But she still rolled herself out to the car and got in.

Margaret loaded the wheelchair in the trunk and then got into the driver's seat.

"Remember our deal, Mom — if I'm still a godless heathen at the end of this service, no more come-to-Jesus ambushes, right?"

"Yes, dear." Margaret sighed, starting the ignition. "But don't write off the experience before you've even had it. You used to love church as a girl. Just see how it feels to be part of a community again."

Kat managed a half-hearted salute, then pulled on her seatbelt. Kat had zero interest in being "healed." All she wanted was to sit in the back, grit her teeth through all the hallelujahs, and figure out how to have a private chat with Pastor Rick Moore.

Because Margaret had pledged $25,000 to the church for the privilege of this little ambush, and it was salt in her wound. Kat wanted the money back. Her mother's pension only stretched so far, and there was no way in hell she was letting some snake oil Bible thumper take it away from her.

Margaret's Corolla merged onto the highway, heading toward the twinkling Dallas sprawl. Kat closed her eyes and prayed for strength. Not to any meddling deity, but to herself. One way or another, she'd figure out how to get through the night.

And then, miracle of miracles, maybe Margaret would finally accept Kat for who she was.

Someone holding onto life by the fingertips.

* * *

The sprawling parking lot of the Lamb of Salvation glittered with what seemed like acres of polished SUVs and luxury sedans. Kat raised an eyebrow while Margaret circled twice before wedging her humble Toyota between an obnoxiously red Porsche and a gleaming Lexus.

The demographic for this church apparently skewed more Country Club than blue collar.

Kat eyed the glass-and-steel structure before them. Ringed by soaring palm trees and gleaming spotlights, the monolith looked more like a Hollywood soundstage than any place of worship. A massive digital billboard flashed photos of a beaming Pastor Rick and his glamorous wife Esther alongside plugs for the Salvation Fitness Center and Divine Brew Smoothie Cafe.

Kat gripped the door handle, suddenly wishing she had fought harder to get out of this. No way was there any kind of peace or redemption hiding in that building.

But it was too late.

Margaret was already retrieving her wheelchair.

"Well, this looks … expensive," Kat said, opening her car door.

"Don't start, Katherine." A chiding look while Margaret manhandled the chair into place. "The church does a lot of good with its money. In fact, they're the top private donor to the VA hospital."

Kat shrugged. "I'm sure those vets would rather have better healthcare than shinier pews, but then again, what do I know?"

426

Within seconds, she hoisted herself into the chair, and Margaret was wheeling her toward the gleaming glass doors. She'd prefer to wheel herself; she hated when anyone touched her chair. But now wasn't the time to litigate a debate about tithing versus tangible aid, let alone who was responsible for her chair.

Besides, with Margaret pushing, it took them longer.

A blonde teenager in a powder blue dress greeted them at the entrance. She might possibly have the widest smile Kat had ever seen.

"Welcome, I'm Grace. We're so happy you can join us tonight." She handed Margaret a glossy concert program. "You must be Katherine — Mrs. Collier has told us so much about you. And Pastor Rick is very much looking forward to meeting you."

Great. Exactly how much had Margaret told these people about her? Although the pitying glance Grace gave her missing leg answered that question reasonably well.

"Thanks," Kat said.

"Before you go."

Kat looked back at Grace. She pointed to the free-standing poster next to her on the step. *God's Call is the Only One You Need — No Phones in The Lamb of Salvation.*

"I got the message," Kat said.

Grace beamed like she'd just announced she was reborn.

The church was like a luxury mega-mall inside, with smartly dressed ushers guiding attendees through an atrium with a soaring glass ceiling. Flatscreen TVs flickered with nature montages and Bible verses rendered in script. Music and laughter spilled out from the smoothie bar. A gym — all gleaming chrome — displayed motivational posters about *honoring your temple.*

Now Margaret was moving much too fast.

Kat rested her palm on one of the wheels. "I've got it."

Margaret started, looking disappointed. But then she fixed a smile on her face and followed after her. Kat wheeled into the cavernous, stadium-style auditorium. Murmuring pockets of parishioners sat on plush crimson seats while a pulsing contemporary hymn piped through a state-of-the-art sound system.

It took every ounce of Kat's discipline not to pivot and roll herself right back out to the car.

"Margaret!"

Her mother smiled and waved. Seconds later, Kat found herself surrounded by a throng of well-coiffed women in Chanel suits fawning over Margaret's "hero Marine daughter."

"We prayed for you every day, dear. Your strength is such an inspiration."

"I can't imagine how difficult it must be. But you're in the right place — Pastor Rick will help you heal and find purpose again."

"God never gives us more than we can handle. You're a living testament to that, sweetie."

Kat aimed for a gracious nod, but her fingers were white-knuckled on the armrests. Margaret had said people might want to "honor her service," but this was beyond the pale. She hadn't even done anything that heroic — her squad had been on a routine patrol when they got hit. It wasn't like she lost her leg trying to rescue anyone.

That's what happened to Mikey. He'd gone to help their radio operator when he hit a mine. The coffin he'd been sent home in wasn't even a quarter full.

Survivor's guilt was a bitch under normal circumstances. Having it reframed as some agent of divine intervention? *Fucking obscene.*

Margaret must have sensed her discomfort because she

gestured to the aisle. "We've got wheelchair seating down in front."

Kat blew out a long breath and followed her mom. Of course, the *handicapped seating*, as the sign said, would be down in front. Jesus. She was practically gonna be eye to eye with the ol' Pastor.

This thing couldn't start soon enough. Because she wanted to go home. She slid into the open area and locked her wheels, hoping to release some of the tightness in her chest. Getting through the next two hours without snapping was gonna require an Olympian's strength.

Margaret squeezed her shoulder and in the row of chairs behind her as the auditorium began to fill. She glanced at her watch. Two minutes until go-time.

And they started right on schedule. The lights dimmed, conversations ended, and Esther glided onto the stage. She was a statuesque brunette with a gleaming white smile. In her tailored scarlet sheath dress, she looked more like a news anchor than a pastor's wife.

"Good evening, everyone, and praise Jesus!"

The audience echoed Esther's greeting. It was followed by a scattering of hallelujahs.

Kat settled in her chair, staring down at her lap, tracing the embossed dove on her program. There was a long moment of silence. A few murmurs in the crowd. Kat looked up.

Esther's smile seemed brittle at the edges. She clasped her hands. "Now, I know you're all eager for the concert to start, but unfortunately, Pastor Rick is running just a few minutes behind — you know how it is with that Dallas traffic!" She gave a strained little laugh, but no one joined her.

Margaret leaned forward, a crease in her brow, and

whispered in Kat's ear. *"Rick is never late to a service. I hope everything is all right."*

Kat perked up.

He was never late? But tonight, he was? Maybe the traffic would keep him from arriving. Maybe they could all go home. Which meant Kat's prayers were being answered and she might have to rethink her stance on there being no divinity.

Esther gestured to the band and then left the stage. A moment later, the guitarist struck up another jangly praise tune. Soon, the drummer and saxophonist joined in as well. But the anticipatory mood had evaporated. Ushers paced at the rear doors, looking worried and engaged in hushed conversations. The air felt thick with some sort of unspoken yet collective anxiety. The cheerful worship music now rang hollow in the tense stillness.

Several agonizing minutes limped by.

Kat turned to Margaret. "Maybe we should go?"

Her mother frowned, only to smile a second later. Esther had returned to the podium. But even all her professionally applied blush couldn't quite hide the sickly pallor of her skin.

"Saints, I must ask for your continued patience and prayers. We seem to be experiencing …some technical difficulties—"

The rest of her appeal was severed by a loud burst of static. Then, the giant screen behind the altar flickered to life, showing the image of a man slumped in a metal folding chair, his wrists duct-taped to the armrests, and a gag in his mouth.

Okay, this was a weird way to start a church service.

She glanced at her mother.

Margaret was staring at the screen, pale, her mouth parted. Kat knew that look. Her mother was frightened.

Margaret had given her the same one she'd arrived home missing a leg.

Pastor Rick? Margaret mouthed the words, but no sound left her lips.

Kat turned back to the screen.

The camera pulled back to reveal a man in a black ski mask. He held an AR15 under the pastor's chin. The Pastor's eyes were wide and glassy with fear above the duct tape, his breathing rapid and shallow.

"Greetings, sheep of the Lamb of Salvation." The masked man's voice reverberated through the speakers, digitally distorted into a flat and grating buzz. "Your shepherd has unfortunately found himself in dire need of saving. If you wish to prevent his untimely ascension to Heaven, I suggest you open your hearts — and, more importantly, *your wallets*."

Gasps and cries arose from the congregation. A young woman on Kat's right began sobbing. The masked man dug the muzzle into Pastor Rick's neck, forcing his head back at an awkwardly garish angle.

"You have until dawn to transfer ten million dollars to the account number on this screen. Fail to do so, and your precious man of God will pay the ultimate price for your selfishness."

Text scrolled across the bottom of the screen: it was a Swiss bank account and routing number.

Pastor Rick's eyes bulged, and he shook his head.

"And in case this isn't convincing enough …" The masked man raised his gun toward the camera and pulled the trigger.

Screams.

Even Margaret recoiled.

It was an effective show of force. But then the camera

panned around. A man lay on the floor in a puddle of blood and brain matter.

Screams erupted throughout the auditorium. Panic swept through the crowd. And then came the rush. Parishioners filled the aisles, clawing over each other in a blind attempt to flee. Kat reached back and grabbed Margaret's hand. "Don't. You'll get crushed."

Margaret nodded, gripping Kat's hand tight.

And then more shots rang out.

Silence filled the room.

Kat turned to see armed men in tactical gear had positioned themselves at the doors, weapons trained on the panicking crowd.

"Wallets in the collection plates," said the masked man onscreen. "And if anyone tries to signal for help, you'll be joining Pastor Rick's security guard."

Slowly, people began to filter back down the aisle to their seats.

The time to move was now. She was the only wheelchair in the auditorium. She had a clear shot to the exit.

She pulled her hand away from Margaret's. "What are you doing, Kat?"

"Saving your life. Stay here."

She swung her chair around and rolled to the exit, passing the heavy red curtain that blocked the door.

The masked man's voice crackled through speakers behind her. "I want to see those donations rolling in, people."

Margaret had no idea how to make an online payment. She still went into the bank to pay her cable bill. Expecting her to pony up money fast was a sure recipe for disappointment.

If no one here had a phone, Kat needed to find one.

She didn't believe these assholes were just gonna let

them all go at the end of the night. So she needed to find a phone and call for help.

Kat rolled through the door and into the hallway beyond. The lights were out, and it was dark. At least something was in her favor. She stayed close to the wall, heart pounding. But this was nothing. She once belly-crawled two endless seeming miles to avoid an insurgent patrol in Fallujah.

And what had her Sergeant said?

One step at a time.

Only in this case, one wheel at a time.

* * *

The hallway in which she'd found herself dead-ended in the gleaming industrial kitchen of the Divine Brew Cafe. Surely there was a phone in there?

She rolled past stainless steel counters and racks of coffee mugs emblazoned with Bible verses. The rest of the church may have been plunged into chaos, but this room was eerily untouched — blenders sat idle beside pyramids of organic fruit. An espresso machine sat placidly blinking, waiting for someone to press a button.

A TV was mounted on one wall. She rolled over, finding the remote on the counter. Flicked it on. It showed an overhead shot of the auditorium. A masked man dragged Esther toward the center of the stage.

"The Lord's work don't come cheap, friends!" The man shoved Esther onto her knees and rested the muzzle of a P226 Scorpion on her temple. Tears ran through her foundation, leaving stripes on her cheeks. "Care to set an example, honey?"

A man in a business suit brought over a laptop and a camera. A second later, Esther's trembling fingers tapped out a banking password, and a six-digit sum vanished from the church accounts.

Kat curled her lip, muting the screen. She couldn't get distracted. She surveyed the kitchen. And there it was.

A wall phone. She rolled over, her pulse jumping at the sight of nine illuminated buttons. She grabbed it, cradling the receiver between chin and shoulder, punching 9-1-1. She got nothing. She hung up.

Silence.

The bastards had cut the landlines. Of course, they had. What had she been thinking?

Goddamn Pastor Rick and his stupid no-phones-in-church rule.

Time for Plan B.

Kat wheeled herself over to a computer terminal at a desk. Probably used by staff to order supplies. Maybe it wouldn't have a password. She could shoot an email to the Dallas PD tip line. But as soon as it was booted up, the login screen blinked expectantly in the password field.

She tried a few: *Pastorrick, salvation, faithful.* And finally: *godsucks.*

None of them worked.

She spun around, surveying the kitchen yet again, searching for anything that could possibly connect her to the outside world. But there wasn't anything.

But what it did have was weapons. She rolled to a drawer. It was locked. So was the next one. Great. Was Pastor John that worried about losing forks and spoons?

She rolled to the door.

And caught the sound of boots. Heavy ones. And they were headed this way. Fuck.

A photo collage on the wall caught her attention — shots of Grace and other youth volunteers in powder blue choir robes and matching visors while they served smoothies and proselytized. A banner above them read, *Salvation Summer Soul Fest 2024.*

She rolled over to a supply closet and found a stack of plastic-wrapped uniforms. She pulled on a navy Divine Brew polo and visor. Then she shrugged out of her shirt and pulled the polo on over her tank top.

A second later, the kitchen door opened. She rolled over to the fridge and opened it, letting the cool air drift over her. There were cartons of milk and juice inside. Packaged smoothie drinks (so they weren't made fresh every morning, after all). And heavy crockery plates of meats and vegetables. She pulled one out.

"Hey!" A gruff voice called out behind her. "What are you doing back here?"

Kat turned slowly, setting the meat plate on her lap. A masked man held a Glock on her. She rolled back, hoping she looked scared. "I was supposed to start getting ready for coffee hour."

"Well, there ain't no coffee hour happening tonight." He gestured with the gun. "Come on, let's get back to the others."

She nodded, rolling toward him.

"You look a little jacked for a barista," he said.

Kat grabbed the plate, slamming it against the stainless steel stove. Charcuterie went flying. The ceramic shattered. Leaving her with a sharp piece in her hand.

Not as big as a Ka-bar, but it would do.

She jackknifed forward, burying the blade deep in her captor's thigh.

For a moment, he didn't move, almost as though he was surprised by her speed and actions. Then he bellowed, his leg buckling.

From then on, it was easy.

He wasn't the kind of guy that was used to pain. Kat grappled the gun from his hand and slammed the butt across his jaw, breaking several teeth. He cried out again, blood spattering.

The kitchen door burst open. A second masked man entered.

Kat squeezed off two quick shots, double tap. He dropped to the floor dead.

"Sorry about that," Kat said, breathing hard. "But the kitchen's closed."

She looked down at the guard sprawled before her. He curled into a ball, clutching his leg.

There was a handful of zip-ties in this back pocket. She yanked them out and pinned him to the stove. He wasn't going anywhere. If he was lucky, he wouldn't bleed out before help arrived. She checked his pockets. No phone.

She pulled off his mask but didn't recognize him. Not that she would. Then she retrieved his spare clip before rolling over to the other man. She took his gun and clip as well, stowing them down the side of her wheelchair.

The asshole didn't have a phone either. Then she rolled over to a door and shouldered it open. But it wasn't an exit.

It was a storage room. And someone was huddling in the shadows.

Kat pointed the Glock. "Show yourself."

A moment later, Grace stumbled out, her face stained with tears.

"Jesus, Grace. You scared the fuck out of me."

"I'm sorry. I ran when I saw the masked men come in."

"Smart."

Kat rolled backward out of the doorway, and Grace followed. Her eyes widened at the blood-streaked floor, and then her voice climbed octaves. "Y-you killed them!"

"That one, yes," Kat said, glancing at the one in the doorway. "I think the other one is clinging to life."

A groan supported her words.

Grace grabbed her shoulder, pointing to the nearest man. "That's Brother Davis! He's head of church security."

"He is?" Kat said.

Grace nodded.

"You got a phone on you?"

Grace shook her head. Of course not.

"Is there an office with a working phone?"

But Grace was rocking back and forth on her heels, hugging herself. "I don't ... what did you say?"

Kat reached out, squeezing the girl gently on her arm. "You're safe now, okay? But I need to get help. So I need a landline or a computer."

Grace bit her lip, glancing at the muted TV. "Pastor Rick's office. It has cameras, phones, everything. He sometimes runs online services from in there."

Kat tapped her fingers on her armrest.

"What is it?"

"Just wondering if I should cut the power instead. Fill one of these sinks and toss in the coffee machine. Short the whole damn place out."

"What does that do?"

"Lots of things. First off, it gives us an advantage. They'll be fighting in darkness. Easier for the congregation to panic. Get the upper hand, maybe. Second, it stops all their bank transfers, making the hostage-taking redundant. Only thing is, if we do get to a phone, we won't be able to use it."

"So what do you wanna do?"

Kat looked at the girl's face, clearly terrified.

"Phones."

Grace uttered a cry and pointed to the screen. The masked men were approaching Margaret's row.

437

"Now," Kat said.

* * *

Grace knew her way through the megachurch hallways. Thank God Kat had found her because the place was a maze. They'd almost gotten caught twice, but Grace knew just where to hide.

"*Almost there*," Grace said, pointing to an ornate door at the end of the administrative wing. "That's Pastor Rick's—"

A burst of radio chatter cut her off.

Kat yanked Grace behind a large podium with a Bible on it right before two men came around the corner.

"… found Davis and Grady in the kitchen," one was saying.

"*Shit.*"

"Somebody's picking us off."

The taller of the two thumbed his radio. "Hayes, you got that hostage headcount for me yet?"

The radio squelched back. "Still working on it."

"Work harder."

Kat's blood ran cold. If they started asking who was missing, it wouldn't take long for someone to mention the wheelchair user. Kat kind of stuck out like a sore thumb. Then Margaret would be in even more danger than she already was.

Kat looked over at Grace, meeting her wide and terrified eyes. She glanced around the corner. The two men were already gone.

"You ready?" Kat asked.

Grace nodded.

"Let's move." Kat was already rolling down the hall toward the door. Grace pulled a keycard from around her neck and swiped it through the scanner. The office door unlocked with a *hiss*.

Kat shouldered through, gun ready.

Then froze.

Pastor Rick sat back behind a mahogany desk as chill as a CEO at a board meeting. Untied and unbloodied, sipping a glass of amber liquid while watching himself sob on the CCTV feed.

He wore a headset. "Transfers are looking good." His southern drawl was devoid of the trembling fear he displayed onscreen. "At this rate, we'll hit eight figures before the 11 o'clock news."

Three masked men sat with him. Not captors, collaborators.

Terrorists never breached the church — this was an inside job from the start. Kat cursed. She should have known that. The men in the church had never asked for phones. Because they already knew the parishioners wouldn't have them.

Rick's bushy brows climbed his forehead when he registered Kat and Grace in the doorway. "What in the—"

"Go," Kat said.

And Grace did, running out.

"Stop her!" Rick said, gesturing.

One of the three men darted after her.

Kat rolled backward. He tumbled into her. Then cursed as he shoved her, strong enough to topple her chair.

She fell to the floor hard, losing her grip on the Glock.

A heavy boot landed on her hand, pressing her fingers to the floor. A few seconds later, the masked man returned. Alone.

Rick got up from his desk. "Where is she?"

"Gone."

He gritted his teeth. "Find her. And deal with her."

"You got it, boss."

"And you," he looked at the other two men. "Take care of this one."

One of them grabbed Kat by the shirt and hauled her up while the other righted the chair.

Kat flattened her palms against the seat, sliding her fingertips to the right. Feeling the reassurance of cold steel. The gun was still there.

The tall asshole jerked her chair toward the hallway. Then they were out of the office, and he was pushing her towards an exit at the other end.

"How'd you lose your leg?" the smaller one asked.

"Kind of like this." Kat pulled the Glock. Shot him first. Then fired over her shoulder. They both fell.

She dropped the Glock into her lap and hit her wheels.

God, she hoped she remembered where she was going.

Kat passed a screen and saw her mom, fragile and frightened. A door opened behind her, and she heard Rick bellow.

She kept going, needing to reach the kitchen so she could kill the lights.

Maybe even find some cleaning chemicals and engineer a few strategic IEDs. Maybe then they'd have a better-than-decent shot at escaping this place. But only if Kat had the time to MacGyver some ordnance without getting ventilated by Pastor Rick's rapidly dwindling crew.

But when she rounded the corner, someone was waiting for her.

Hayes, most likely.

She reached for the gun in her lap.

He pulled the trigger.

A bullet ripped through her side. "Next one hits something vital."

She froze. Blood wetting her shirt and jeans. It hurt, though not nearly as much as losing a leg. She met his eyes.

"Time for something vital," he said.

Kat flinched.

A loud SNAP. The lights went out.

For a moment, Kat didn't move. What the fuck— Grace had killed the lights.

Kat rolled to the side.

Hayes fired twice. Both bullets missed her. But the flash let her know exactly where he was.

She fired twice. Heard him grunt, then fall.

She rolled toward him, bumping around him with her chair.

Kat didn't care about finding a phone anymore.

She was getting her mother and leaving. If she had to kill every security guard to do so, she would.

Margaret was the gentlest, most selfless person she knew. A lifetime spent as a small-town teacher, diligently clipping coupons and volunteering at the local food bank. She didn't have an ounce of guile or cynicism — which is exactly what made her such an easy mark for a parasite like Pastor Rick.

Kat had already lost one parent to a war someone else started. She couldn't stand the thought of losing her mother to a two-bit huckster playing soldier of God.

She passed an open door and caught the unmistakable smell of C4. She stopped, rolling into the room.

Light filtered in from the parking lot.

Apparently, the pastor had more than just smoke and mirrors up his apostolic sleeves. He was planning on blowing up the joint after. Probably get a hell of a payout. Easy to blame it on the terrorists.

Kat needed to move fast.

She was running out of time.

She turned left, right into a wheel. *Fuck.* She'd lost track of the route. Kat reviewed the way in her mind, recalibrated, and realized she needed to go straight. Then left.

And found herself in the main hallway.

Screams bled from the auditorium.

Seconds later, one of the doors erupted, vomiting parishioners, all of them running to the main doors. Emergency battery-powered lights had gone on inside the hall. Kat caught sight of one of the masked men.

He had been trampled by Rick's escaping sheep.

She maneuvered around the horde, making her way down the aisle. Hopefully, her mother had remained seated.

But she wasn't there.

A flicker of movement on the stage caught her attention. Esther and Margaret were being dragged toward the rear employee-only door. Fuck Rick. No way was she gonna let him take her mother hostage.

Kat headed back out the door, her tires crunching over broken glass and busted tiles. There had to be a rear exit. No way would they be going out the front.

She retraced her route. Going back towards Rick's office.

Only instead of turning left, she turned right. A dark figure collided with her. "Kat, it's me!"

"Grace."

"Did I do okay with the lights?"

"You did fucking amazing. Back door?"

"Uh, left, then right, then—"

"Just push me," Kat said.

Grace did.

And while she ran, Kat checked her clip.

They arrived at the back door, and Kat edged it open.

Hearing the distinct thud of rotors. Helicopter. So that's how Rick was getting out of here.

She kicked the door open and gestured for Grace to push her out. Above, a sleek silver helicopter crested the church roof.

Then it banked sharply, pinning Kat in the stabbing beam of its searchlights.

Grace yanked her back, charging behind a corner of the building.

Esther was no longer being dragged but walking free, helping with Margaret.

A hail of bullets tore up the ground in front of Kat and Grace.

Kat aimed but couldn't get a clean shot with her mother in the way.

Rick got on board, then Esther, along with the guard. Who shoved Margaret away.

The chopper rose. The guard aimed his Glock at Margaret.

Kat knew what was gonna happen next. She fired a trio of shots into the tail rotor.

"MOM!"

Margaret rolled to the side.

Sparks erupted from the rotor housing, smoke belching. The craft lurched wildly to one side.

Kat rolled toward the chopper. But her tires sank in the grass.

Grace grabbed the handles and pushed. If it landed on Margaret, she was gonna rip the pilot's fucking spine out of his back with her bare hands, choke him with his own intestines—

The chopper lifted, then spun, its nose tipping toward the dense tree line bordering the property. The chopper careened left into high-tension wires.

The explosion lit up the sky like the Fourth of July.

Grace cowered. Flaming shrapnel rained down around them while a plume of greasy smoke mushroomed over the tree line.

Kat stared, uncomprehending.

The wail of approaching sirens filled her ringing ears.

"Kat! Oh, thank God!"

A soot-streaked figure in a tattered blue blouse stumbled across the field, one shoe missing and pearls askew, gray bun undone with hair spilling down her shoulders.

"Mom?" Kat croaked, sure she was hallucinating. But no, those were Margaret's strong arms crushing her close. Chanel perfume tickled her nose.

They huddled together. Then Margaret pulled back, looking down at her hand. "You're bleeding."

Kat touched her side. "I've had worse."

Margaret shrugged out of her cardigan, wadded it into a bundle, and pressed it against Kat's side.

Grace stood, staring over at the burning wreckage.

"Is he … are they …"

"Yeah," Kat said.

"I suppose we should wait for the police." Margaret sat on the grass next to her.

Grace walked toward the flaming chopper.

"Don't get too close," Kat warned her.

But she kept going, then leaned down and picked something up. A moment later, she was back, holding a slightly singed laptop. "Hopefully everyone can get their money back."

"Yeah," Kat said as the three of them sat watching the flames. "How do you feel about church now?"

Margaret smiled, then leaned forward and kissed her leg. "You're the only miracle I need."

About The Authors

Wade Peterson crafts award-winning stories that linger in your mind long after you've finished them. He's poured his heart and soul into these worlds, drawing inspiration from his love for tabletop gaming, '80s and '90s hair metal, electrical engineering mishaps, and his collection of dog-eared paperback novels.

When he's not forging tales, you can find Wade unraveling the arcane mysteries of Texas barbecue in his backyard, deciphering the passive-aggressive demands of two cats, or nodding in agreement with whatever wine his wife chooses to accompany their evening feast.

Sean Platt has always been an entrepreneur, but knew he'd rather tell stories. When his wife bought him a laptop for his birthday in 2007 he dropped everything to start writing fiction.

Since making the leap, Sean has written hundreds of novels (including the international best-sellers Yesterday's Gone and Invasion), penned dozens of scripts, and founded the IP Incubator Sterling & Stone where more than thirty storytellers work together to create world changing IP. Sterling & Stone's stable of writers come to Sean for ideas, mentorship, and "better words."

Emme Jackson is a lover of books, coffee and treasure hunts. When she's not writing, she's usually off on an adventure dragging her beleaguered children behind her. She resides in Southern Indiana with her husband, three children and countless fur babies. If Josh Gates wants to know where the South Carolina box is, tell him to give me a ring.

~

Kim M. Watt Originally from New Zealand, Kim (she/her) now inhabits a slightly different world, crafting funny fantasies and off-beat cosy (or cozy) mysteries in which tea-drinking dragons collude with resourceful ladies of a certain age, baking-obsessed reapers run petting cafes for baby ghouls, and cats always bring the snark.

Kim's stories blend myth and reality in small and spectacular ways, where the Apocalypse comes on a Vespa, and the healing magic of tea and a really good lemon drizzle cake is unquestioned. But most of all, her tales are about friendship, loyalty, and people of all species looking out for one another. Because these, above all things, are magic.

~

Cameron Stone has been telling stories since he was four, always looking for ways to capture the world as he saw it. When his mom politely reminded him in a scathing yet honest review of his first book that bats aren't birds, the four-year-old Cameron doubled down and wrote another book. This time with rainbows and flying snakes.

Cameron writes thrillers and the supernatural for the "weird" and "queer" kids, with the hope that they will see themselves in stories he never had when he sashayed out of the closet. He lives in Southern Arizona with his husband.

~

Kathryn Cottam spent over ten years writing screenplays before turning to novels, penning multiple books with her co-writer sister. In 2022, her dream of joining Sterling & Stone came true and she has been able to expand her creativity by exploring more genres and ideas than she ever thought possible. Kathryn currently lives with her two cats in a one-traffic light town on Vancouver Island, Canada. Home is tucked between a mountain, the lake, and the ocean. Which is exactly how she likes it.

~

Linda Bleser began her writing career publishing short fiction for women's magazines. Since then, she's published several award-winning novels in multiple genres, from rib-tickling comedy to bone-chilling suspense. Reviewers have hailed her work as unique, original, and impossible to put down.

Writing as both Linda Bleser and L.B. Milano, she has over a dozen books, short stories, and novellas in print. Linda is the proud recipient of the EPPIE Award, the Dream Realm Award, the Dorothy Parker Reviewers Choice Award, the Royal Palm Literary Award, and several readers' choice awards. She also received a top ten placement in the Preditors and Editors poll.

A transplanted New Yorker, Linda, and her husband have retired to sunny Florida, where she continues to dream up new stories on the beach.

~

David W. Wright is the co-author of edge-of-your seat thrillers including the best-selling post-apocalyptic series *Yesterday's Gone*, the paranoid sci-fi *WhiteSpace* series, and the vigilante series, *No Justice*, as well as standalone thrillers *12*, and *Crash* which was recently optioned for a movie.

David is an accomplished, though intermittent, cartoonist who lives in [LOCATION REDACTED] with his wife and son [NAMES REDACTED.]

He is not at all paranoid.

He is "the grumpy one" on the *The Story Studio Podcast* with fellow Sterling and Stone founders, Sean Platt and Johnny B. Truant.

David writes about books, TV shows, movies, and video games he enjoys; his struggles with anxiety and OCD; writing; and posts the occasional drawing at his personal blog at davidwwright.com

You can email him at david@sterlingandstone.net

We swear, he almost never bites. Unless you feed him after midnight.

~

Jay Tinsiano is a USA Today bestselling author obsessed with international, fast-paced conspiracy thrillers, espionage narratives and broken post-apocalyptic worlds, whether he's reading, watching, or writing them.

Jay draws inspiration for his international action thrillers from his travels—from the sweltering humidity of Southeast Asia to Escobar's prison in the hills above Medellín, Colombia.

Jay currently lives in Bristol, UK, usually in the dark

corners of local cafes (facing the door), sipping endless Americanos, taking notes, watching and waiting.

Start the mission at jaytinsiano.com

~

Sawyer Black writes dark and violent fiction for people who secretly love puppies and rainbows. In addition to being a U.S. Army veteran, he's also a beardsman. In fact, that's where all his ideas come from. The beard. Speculative stories about struggle and triumph and brutal emotion, written mostly for his ideal reader, his wife of nearly twenty-five years. He's an independent woman who likes cigars and margaritas, and he holds the deep belief that the earth is round.

~

CJ Lyons *New York Times* and *USA Today* bestselling author of over forty novels, former pediatric ER doctor CJ Lyons has lived the life she writes about in her cutting-edge Thrillers with Heart.

CJ has been called a "master within the genre" (Pittsburgh Magazine) and her work has been praised as "breathtakingly fast-paced" and "riveting" (Publishers Weekly) with "characters with beating hearts and three dimensions" (Newsday).

She has assisted police and prosecutors with cases involving child abuse, rape, homicide and Munchausen by Proxy; and has worked in numerous trauma centers; as a crisis counselor; victim's advocate; as well as a flight physician for Life Flight. CJ credits her patients and their families for teaching her the art of medicine and giving her the courage to pursue her dream of becoming a novelist.

Her novels have twice won the International Thriller Writers' prestigious Thriller Award, the RT Reviewers' Choice Award, the Readers' Choice Award, the RT Seal of Excellence, and the Daphne du Maurier Award for Excellence in Mystery and Suspense. Also, CJ's short stories have appeared in anthologies edited by Lee Child and Margaret Atwood.

Over 3 million books sold worldwide.

Learn more about CJ's Thrillers with Heart at www.CJLyons.net